Adrian Deans

Adrian Deans is a lawyer, journalist and novelist. He is the author of three richly praised previous novels: *Straight Jacket*, *Mr Cleansheets* and *THEM*, and a sporting biography *Political Football: Lawrie McKinna's Dangerous Truth*. He lives at Avoca Beach with his wife, Karen.

Praise for *The Fighting Man*

'*The Fighting Man* is a rollicking read, a non-stop action-packed adventure full of romance, battle and humour. I read it on the train, walking down the street, well after my usual bed time and when I was supposed to be working. Even though I knew exactly where the story was headed, I was compelled to know what happened next.'
— Jane Rawson, *From the Wreck*

'Historical novels that feel truly authentic are one of life's great joys. Not since reading Sharpe have I felt such a sense of *being* in the story. Outstanding.'
— Stuart Quin, Full Circle Films

1066

THE FIGHTING MAN

Adrian Deans

High Horse

Published by Adrian Deans/High Horse 2017
www.adriandeans.com

Cover design: Lucy Barker, *www.lucybarker.com.au*

ISBN: 978-0-9876129-2-2

A catalogue record for this title is available from
the National Library of Australia

For my Mother

And for Bernard Cornwell, in gratitude

PART ONE

Chapter 1

The Mind of God

It was the Year of Endings and Beginnings, when the wild men came to sweep away my old life like chaff in a sudden gale. Hard men with iron swords and huge hungers – they had not been seen on our coast for many years but we heard rumours from the north and east. Always from the sea they came and to the sea returned, and on a gentle bend of a small obscure river we thought ourselves safe from their fire and death.

It had been a quiet year in the village of Stybbor in East Anglia where my father was reeve and thegn, but less quiet in other places. The old king Edward was yet to produce an heir and, as he continued to age, the various candidates were jostling for position in the Year of Our Lord 1060. Those weighty matters were of small moment to the folk of Stybbor. The land enjoyed a period of prosperity it was said, although being a lad of only fourteen winters at the time, I had never known any different. A fruitful summer followed a vibrant spring and my interest grew like a spreading vine – tendrils of my vigour and curiosity seemed to encompass the village and its trade and, while I knew my father was proud of me, alas, I was not the older son. The older son learned the family business, the younger was given to the church.

But on the morning of my brother's wedding, not even my conjugations with Brother Waldo and the imminent prospect of entering the seminary could curb my spirit.

'Portendere, portendo, portendis, portendatis,' droned my tutor, his back to the bright sunshine which bathed the usually dim room.

'Brother Waldo,' I interrupted.

'Yes Brand?' he enquired, opening his eyes. He usually kept them closed when conjugating, as though reading the words off a tablet in his head.

'Tell me about the seminary.'

'The seminary?' he repeated. 'You've been there … spoken to Abbot Oldred … walked past it many times.'

'Of course,' I replied, 'but what of its daily life? What of the men who live within those walls … most of whom I've never seen?'

'Never seen?' he echoed. 'And rightly so … the brothers are hidden … cloistered so their commune with God cannot be sullied by intercourse with the world.'

'They truly speak with God?' I asked, trying to quell the unworthy feelings that always seemed to bubble up from my core when people spoke of God as something real and present in our lives.

'All the time,' replied Waldo, as though such were beyond question.

'I have tried to speak with God,' I said. ' … really tried, but he never answers.'

'Aah,' said Waldo, 'that's why you must go to the seminary … to learn how to listen when God speaks. It's not the same as the manner of our speaking now.'

That seemed to speak truth to me, and I had the glimmer of a vision – like sitting at the mouth of a cave and hearing the vaguest murmurs from its depths – terrifying in its way but also frustrating. Brother Waldo resumed his conjugations but I felt an itch in my soul that needed scratching.

'Does God speak with you, Brother?'

'Eh?'

'God … does he speak to you?'

'Of course he does … what sort of question is that?'

'What does he say?'

Brother Waldo's eyes glinted at me from under thick, white brows, which meant his patience was sorely tried. In normal circumstances I would immediately have backed down and returned to study, but that day I felt a strange sense of urgency – as though this was something I needed to understand before I could go any further. I repeated my question, trying to show him I was asking politely and respectfully.

Waldo sighed and said, 'The Word of God can only be perceived through study of the scriptures and much prayer … but the mind and thought of God is personal to each of us and beyond expression. He doesn't gossip like women in the market place.'

I laughed but quickly stilled myself, sensing Brother Waldo was entering one of his rare muses.

'The mind and thought of God is in all things ... wind in the trees ... birdsong ... thunder and lightning. His mood changes constantly but our capacity to understand Him is so weak ... so lacking in the necessary tools ... that all we can do is devote our lives to serving Him, and from time to time we are rewarded with a flash of inspiration ... a moment gleaming like a precious jewel when a ray of the thought of God strikes you in the eye to leave you breathless. For one shining moment you see clearly and understand the full majesty of His creation but, as we are human and imperfect, the moment passes and all we are left with is a hazy memory of joy ... the inspiration fades like a puddle in high summer.'

As he spoke, Waldo's face became red with the depth of his conviction – revealing his mystery, and I felt happy for him.

But for some reason, the itch in my soul was worse than ever.

'Do all the brothers receive such inspirations?'

And Waldo's mood changed as suddenly as the whim of the God he served.

'All?' he snapped. 'All? I should say not. For every pious man of God there are ten intriguers and twenty sodomites!'

For the first time he had put my fears into words (or at least one of them) and I felt emboldened to reveal the doubts I had dutifully kept to myself.

'If that is so, then why does my father send me to such a place?'

Waldo shook his head impatiently and waved my fears away.

'You would never be touched, Brand. For a start, you are a big lad ... not too far in years from the fullness of your strength. More importantly, you are a member of the nobilis ... and therefore likely to become Abbot in time. No-one would risk such a future enemy. Your arse is safe, boy.'

With that he returned to his conjugations and, partly reassured, I resumed my study.

∞ ∞ ∞

5

Five miles downriver from the town of Stybbor, a long boat with forty shields hung over the side was pulled onto a bar at a bend of the Arwan. Two horses were tethered together, and munched the thick grass as a sentry patted their flanks and muttered unfamiliar but soothing words, while their owners were led up a plank to meet the chieftain.

The leader of the two men was tall and slim, with a neat black beard which didn't quite hide a scar on his left cheek. He was dressed in fine clothes as if for a mass, and if he was afraid to be among the savage Danes, he didn't show it. His companion was shorter and broader, dressed in a shirt of rings and carrying a large war hammer which he surrendered with a menacing grunt at the top of the plank.

'I see you Malgard.'

The words were spoken by a handsome young man with the iron collar of a thrall, but it was clear that he did not speak for himself.

'I see you Ulrik Dragontooth,' replied the tall man, ignoring the thrall but speaking directly to the hulking redbeard beside him dressed in wool and heavy leather. His words were translated almost as he spoke and Malgard marvelled at the thrall's skill which enabled an almost seamless conversation between men of different tongues.

'I expected you a week ago,' said Malgard, determined to assert himself despite his need to escape the stink of sweat, fish guts and rotting meat that all such longboats carried.

Ulrik grinned, showing off the reason for the name by which men knew him. His mouth had lost all of the front teeth, upper and lower, in one of his first battles. The remaining teeth, unnaturally long where the adjoining teeth were gone, looked indeed like the mouth of a serpent.

'There was good hunting, to the north,' he replied, his toothless sibilance untranslated. 'We are not here solely at your bidding, but do you grudge your brother an extra week of life?'

'I grudge him this!' said Malgard and, before the Danes could move, pulled a dagger from his sleeve and drove it deep into the gunwale next to Ulrik's hand. One or two stepped toward Malgard in anger but Ulrik, pleased he hadn't flinched, waved them back with a laugh.

'This is what he gave me in compensation for my home,' hissed

Malgard. 'A knife! A stinking, fucking knife! When you kill Holgar, I want him to see that knife before you stick it in his heart.'

Such was the malice of the man that all, including Ulrik, made the sign to ward off the evil eye.

'Malgard is a not a man to have for your enemy,' said Ulrik, pulling the dagger free and examining it closely – a beautiful piece with a silver handle carved in the shape of a coiled dragon.

'Remember that,' said Malgard, 'when you do your work and come to seek your payment.'

Ulrik was tiring of Malgard's arrogance in front of his men.

'If you don't keep a polite tongue in your head,' he muttered, 'I might say fuck your work and fuck you … and take my payment now.'

A huge man with dirty blond hair and blinded in one eye laughed loudly and the thrall hesitated before translating. Ulrik growled and the thrall complied, but in a softer tone than Ulrik wanted. He responded with a clout over the back of the slave's head and a guttural snarl which Malgard could not understand. Then the white faced thrall repeated the threat in a louder, if unconvincing shout.

'I heard the first time,' sneered Malgard, but he pulled a pouch from his belt and tossed it at Ulrik, who caught and weighed it without looking inside.

'This is only half,' he said.

'There will be more when I have access to Holgar's treasury,' replied Malgard. 'Most of that I will need for rebuilding after you and your men wreak ruin, but I will surely be able to spare a little. Of course, in the raid you will also take lambs, and there is much food and drink prepared for the feast.'

'So the wedding is today,' mused Ulrik, summoning a slave with a platter of meat. 'We were here in time after all?'

'Only because the wedding was delayed to allow the guests to assemble,' said Malgard, waving the platter away. 'The summer storms have made the roads and fords difficult. If the wedding had been before now the family would have dispersed and there would be competing claims on Holgar's legacy.'

'How will I know Holgar,' asked Ulrik.

'Holgar you will know by his position, and his chain of silver and gold,' said Malgard, glancing anxiously at the sun approaching noon.

'Gram the son is the groom, and there is a younger son, Brand. Kill them all.'

'What of the women?' asked Ulrik, gnawing at a pig's trotter.

'Do what you like with the women,' replied Malgard. 'Fyllba the bride is very beautiful.'

Ulrik shrugged, as he continued to give the pig's trotter most of his attention.

'No-one is beautiful after being used by twenty men,' he said. 'It's almost a kindness to let them go over the side … their lungs full of water, their holes full of seed.'

'Holes,' echoed the one-eyed giant, whose name was Olaf Pighammer, and the men listening grinned. Olaf was known as much for his strange tastes as his huge strength and violence.

'You are indeed merciful,' sneered Malgard. 'Now, as for the rest, I will be at my brother's side, helping to protect him. Obviously, I am not to be harmed, but I will be fighting. Send one of your slaves against me, so I might blood my sword. I must be seen to fight so none can question my allegiance to my brother and my right to take over … when you have gone.'

Ulrik spat a knuckle over the side and considered.

'There will be wine at the wedding feast?'

'Of course,' replied Malgard.

'Perhaps we will allow the guests a last celebration,' said Ulrik. 'Drunken men are less able to defend themselves, and I cannot afford to lose anyone.'

Malgard glanced again at the sun and prepared to leave.

'Very well … but wait not overlong, and do not let me down Ulrik. There is more at stake than you have wit to understand.'

Ulrik laughed, as he spat the last of the bones into the river.

'Fear not Malgard. You will be prince of your shithole town by sundown.'

For the first time, Malgard indicated his companion.

'This is Angdred. He is loyal to me and will lead you to the village via hidden paths so your presence will not be known until it is too late for the rats to escape the trap.'

Ulrik and Angdred half nodded at each other with the wary mistrust of warriors recognising each other's prowess.

And with that, Malgard disappeared back down the ramp and climbed onto his horse.

'Farewell Ulrik,' he called. 'I go to celebrate my nephew's wedding … to which you are uncordially invited.'

∞ ∞ ∞

I had always hated the smell of shit.

Most men seemed not to notice it, going about their lives as though thousands of turds, both of animals and men, were not heaped in the street or piled in the tanner's yard. But they were, and I was constantly aware of them. Only on cold winter's nights did I get relief from the creeping miasma that seemed to permeate all of God's creation.

At least my father's house was a half mile from the town and the worst of the stench, but the wedding feast was to be held in a pavilion on the green outside the church. And while fresh latrines had been dug for the occasion, they were never deep enough. I knew from experience that vast quantities of rich food and heady ale would soon have the pits overflowing with shit, piss and vomit, and as it promised to be a hot afternoon, my head was swimming in advance with the noisome prospect.

As if to somehow magically emphasise my foresight, a horse in front of me lifted its tail and shat copiously, the coincidence reminding me of Brother Waldo's words that God spoke in mysterious ways and I found myself wondering if this was His idea of a joke. Then the hair rose on the back of my neck with the awesome realisation that God was indeed aware of me and was privy to all my thoughts.

The horse shat again.

'Brother Waldo?'

Waldo and I were at the very back of the procession, making its way slowly towards the little town for the mass and midday wedding, accompanied by players with pipes and tambors.

'Yes Brand?'

'Are men animals?'

'Animals?' he asked aghast. 'Of course we're not animals … we're men! Created in God's image.'

9

'But we're made of flesh and do all the same things as animals.'

'Do all the same … ' he began angrily. 'Do animals pray? Do animals know grammar or geometry?'

'Perhaps not,' I allowed, 'but they eat, root and shit, the same as we do.'

'Animals eat, root and shit wherever they please,' whispered Waldo furiously, anxious not to disturb the procession with our profanity. 'Men have rules about such things … rules ordained by God himself, to signify that we are His chosen ones … made in His image.'

'So that we might eat, root and shit in His image?' I asked, strangely wilful, and laughed despite the look of thunder that crossed Waldo's face.

'Take a care not to utter such blasphemies in the presence of the Abbot, young Brand. There are rules … those of the blessed Benedict, and yet others. And there are punishments that will teach you piety and humility if the Abbot deems those qualities lacking.'

I had the sense not to press the argument further and, as we passed under the high stone walls of the monastery on the edge of town, I felt the cold shadow and shivered.

∞ ∞ ∞

The church at Stybbor was a cool, stone building with a window on the west through which the first slanting rays of the afternoon entered in a flash of red and green through candle smoke. Saint Ybbor, after whom the town was named, had been dismembered hundreds of years previously by earlier occupants of East Anglia who had known not the scriptures and resented Ybbor's efforts to illuminate their vacant souls. The window on the west was supposed to show the various body parts of the martyred Ybbor lying on a field of green, but to me it just looked like a red and green pattern, which no more resembled severed limbs than the stars in the sky resembled a scorpion, or a lion, or a set of scales.

But I did like the window and the way the green and red beams played over the congregation as the sun moved westwards. It seemed to me once again, like the shitting horse, that I was on the brink of understanding something of the mood of God and His way of sending messages to the faithful. Dutifully, I listened to Father Maynard singing the Latin and it seemed that I understood him better than before, as though I had made it to a new level of understanding. That thought should have made me eager for the seminary, as mastery of learning was within my grasp, but strangely I felt more anxious than ever about leaving behind the familiar pleasures of my home for the solemn house of God, even if there was less need to worry about my arse.

I found myself staring at my brother, Gram – four years older than me and already a man with a reputation. He had twice killed Danes as a member of the fyrd which had been assembled by King Edward to stem the raids on Lundene and the Temes Valley. Indeed, he was only home for his wedding to Fyllba and would shortly return with my father and uncles to the king's army encamped near the mouth of the Temes. And suddenly I knew what I wanted. A red beam of light struck me full in the face as I knew with sudden certainty that I did not want the seminary with its learning and its prayer. I wanted the battlefield and the company of men.

The first part of the mass droned to its conclusion and then the marriage ceremony commenced. It was harder to understand the words that were less familiar to me, but I understood that marriage was a kind of sacrament – less lofty perhaps than holy orders but still an honoured place in the sight of God and the proper place for a warrior. For the first time, I found myself jealous of Gram – tall, strong – about to be married to the golden-haired Fyllba and then return with my father to the fyrd, while I must stay close to the shit stink and learn prayer and abstinence and celibacy.

In that moment I found myself in the grip of terror and it was all I could do not to cry aloud at the prospect of my entire life, the possibilities of which I was only beginning to appreciate, being utterly wasted in God's house. Surely there were others more worthy, whose tastes and aptitude were more fitted to that role than I. Perhaps I could go to my father before it was too late and have him agree to me becoming a page, or even just a foot soldier in the fyrd. Anything was better than—

'Brand!' hissed Waldo, and I realised to my embarrassment that I was still standing when the rest of the congregation had knelt for the benediction. I fell to my knees, whacking my kneecap against a part of the stone floor unsoftened by rushes as Waldo glared and Father Maynard stared bleakly, and I found myself wondering whether they were as aware of my thoughts as God seemed to be.

∞ ∞ ∞

Holgar was proud of his son.

Gram had grown into his strength and would soon be producing sons to continue Holgar's line, which he reckoned back into the mists of time. His own father's father had not known how long the family had owned the lands around Stybbor, but it was sung that the family were immigrants from Saxony who occupied land abandoned by the Romans and offered protection to the benighted weaklings left in their wake, bereft of leaders. Holgar's family had offered that leadership and protection in return for work and fealty and the occasional need for the stronger lads to join the fyrd for summer campaigning against the Danes (not that the Danes had ever ventured so far upstream as Stybbor).

Gram had fought well in battles on the Temes and closer to home at Gipeswic, and was now accounted a man of prowess. He could fight single-handed or in the shield wall and had even had the honour of standing to Holgar's left – trusted to spear Holgar's foes when Holgar's own rightward thrusts left him vulnerable to the man directly in front. Gram had fought with the urgent terror of a man who fears his father's death more than his own, and truly Holgar knew his son loved and honoured him and would carry on the family line as well or better than he had done himself. What man could ask for more?

Therefore, it was with impossible pride that he raised the loving cup at the wedding feast and the guests drank, as they had done all afternoon, with the exception of Malgard, and Holgar felt an irritation that his younger brother was not entering properly into the spirit of the occasion.

'Why don't you drink Malgard?'

Malgard, in response, took a delicate sip of mead and Holgar could have choked him.

'You drink like a woman!' he scorned, slamming down his own cup to be refilled with the expensive wine from Burgundy he'd imported specially for the wedding.

Even as he spoke, Holgar realised he was being unfair. Malgard had been steward of the hill farm for nearly ten years and, even if it had always been understood that he held it in trust for Gram, he appreciated that Malgard would feel the loss. The hill farm was Gram's wedding gift.

'My apologies brother,' said Holgar. 'And let me apologise also for the loss of the farm. You should have some something of your own, and I will give thought to it ere long.'

Malgard acknowledged Holgar's generosity with a courteous nod and stood to propose his own toast.

'My honoured brother ... allow me to wish you the joy of many grandsons, and a long enough life to see them join us in the shield wall ... if the Danes come again.'

Holgar grunted with a wine-fuelled contempt.

'Danes,' he sneered. 'Danes won't come to Stybbor. We beat them at Gipeswic, and again at Margate. The Danes are finished ... or near enough.'

There was a roar of acclamation led by Gram and others of Holgar's retainers deep in their cups.

'Nevertheless,' continued Malgard, 'all here are in your debt, Holgar. And we pray that you will continue to lead us and keep us safe until young Gram has the years and wisdom to take over.'

There were more shouts of approval, this time from the younger men who had grown up with Gram or joined Holgar's household more recently and looked to Gram as their natural leader. Holgar frowned with small disapproval as he noted that Brand was shouting with the rest and it seemed to him unfitting that a boy destined for the church should be carousing with warriors. He would say something about it later though, as Malgard was still giving his toast.

'To Holgar!' cried Malgard raising his cup. 'To Gram ... and to the continuation of Holgar's line for many sons ... into the years uncountable!'

Malgard drained his cup and all cheered his fine words and drank deeply as the sun began to sink behind the green, western hills, while the serving girls brought platters of sweetmeats to follow the beef, mutton, pork, fish and fowl that had already been consumed in vast quantities with breads, broths and greens, and ever more ale and wine.

Holgar found himself relaxing – understanding that the various arms of his family were falling into their rightful places. Malgard had spoken well and Holgar resolved to reward his younger brother with a stretch of forest and fen to the south that would need draining but would doubtless prove very fertile, and there was game aplenty in the woods. It would require hard work but a man needed work to be happy and the end of the Viking raids would afford him time to grow into his proper place in the family – a lesser place now Gram was grown into his manhood – but an honoured place nonetheless.

Yes, Malgard deserved a reward, he thought, clapping a huge arm about his brother's shoulder.

∞ ∞ ∞

I was not accustomed to drinking ale. At least, I had never drunk so much of it in my almost fifteen years, but with my life about to change so profoundly, I wanted to know what it was like to be drunk. I matched the warriors cup for cup, hanging on the edge of their conversations and laughing at their jests. It was wonderful and I felt even sadder at the prospect of the monastery. Monks spend little time jesting about raping women and vomiting beer, or so I had thought.

And before long, I had my wish. What started as an ecstatic feeling of power and destiny soon became a thick and heavy sickness. I had been staring at the muddy ground as the men joked, and suddenly my head was whirling, and I was staring up from the mud at the early evening sky, fringed with a ring of laughing faces. And then vomit burst from my guts to cover my face and the fine linen blouse my mother had imported from Bruxels for the wedding.

Then the laughter ceased and the cold voice of my father reached me through the fog of my sickness.

'Fine behaviour for a man of God,' he growled. 'Get up!'

I was raised to my feet by Guthred, the youngest of my father's retainers and, with his help, made it to the latrines where (naturally) the overwhelming shit stink caused me to start retching. Desperate not to vomit again in front of my father, I lurched past the heavy canvas flap and was quickly bent over the logs above the pit, from which arose the sulphurous breath of Satan. Immediately a great gush of vomit erupted from my very core and it seemed the stench grew even worse, as though the vomit was stirring the piles of turd and gallons of piss to release more of their noxious vapour – all of it funnelled up into my face. And just the thought of that seemed to make me vomit again. Guthred pissed into the pit just next to me, and so my afternoon continued.

It's possible that I slept but after some time, I became dimly aware of shouting and the clinking of fine, glass goblets, and so I thought that more toasts were being made to the bride and groom. Somehow the clinking of glass became the clash of metal blades and, with my face still full in the blast of stench, I idly wondered whether some entertainment featuring sword play had been arranged.

Then another wave of nausea ripped through me but there was nothing left to spew and I simply lay along the log with my guts clenching and spitting the foul taste of bile and beer into the pit. It occurred to me that this might be a good time to approach my father to ask his permission to join the fyrd instead of the monastery. Clearly my behaviour did not merit the intimate acquaintance of God (even if He did seem to be paying close attention to my thoughts and sending messages). I found myself giggling as I remembered the shitting horse and wondering what Waldo would have to say about God's arcane responses to my thoughts and desires. Then in the church I had wished to become a warrior and—

Suddenly the shouting and the clash of swords was close and an unfamiliar voice bellowed in a strange language – a hoarse guttural shout full of violence, reality and imminent death and I felt rather than heard heavy footsteps coming to the latrine. Without further thought, I tumbled face first into the pit – too terrified even to notice the thick, stinking slop in which I lay, half submerged.

I heard the canvas snatched back and the sound of swords and screaming was loud. My mind was strangely cleared of its ale fog and I moved not an inch, but the pit was not deep. If they were looking for fugitives I would surely be found.

Suddenly, my world darkened and, to my profound disgust, I

realised what was about to happen.

Even warriors in the midst of battle need to shit.

∞ ∞ ∞

Victory was always sweet reflected Ulrik Dragontooth. Even victories won cheaply by sudden ambush over drunken warriors were a matter for celebration and song. It was a victory of cunning and strategy, which although more pleasing to Loki than to Thor, would still be accounted to his credit in Valhalla. He would drink there, perhaps, with Holgar who had been a mighty warrior until the day of his doom when he had been confused at the sudden appearance of Danes among the wedding party, then infuriated, then terrified as he realised that his weaponless men, drunk and helpless were being methodically cut down by the invaders.

Holgar had died badly. Armed only with a ceremonial sword – jewelled, light and useless – he'd stood shoulder to shoulder with Gram and Malgard until Malgard jumped out of the line to pursue the lightly armed and terrified Irish slave prodded into his path. Then Holgar was surrounded by Ulrik's men and cut down with his son, confronted at the last with Malgard's silver dagger. But doubtless Holgar would laugh about it with Ulrik when they met in Valhalla.

Ulrik shifted his buttocks on the uncomfortable log. His guts were churning and he suspected the pig meat he'd eaten in the morning had not been properly cooked. The fight had lasted only minutes and already the men were slaking their various thirsts and hungers while he had raced for the nearest latrine. The women, mostly, had survived. The bride, as Malgard had promised, was indeed beautiful in her terror and on the day of her wedding would have some twenty husbands, lucky girl.

Finally the turd erupted from Ulrik's arse and he grunted with satisfaction, immediately feeling a lot better. He squeezed out another couple of gushers of brown water but failed to notice the muffled exclamation of disgust that came from the pit below him.

'Ulrik!'

The voice was Malgard's.

'Leave me in peace you treacherous Saxon turd!' he shouted,

knowing that Malgard would not understand him, but would recognise his voice. Seconds later, the canvas flap was torn back and Malgard entered with Carl Two-tongues.

'It is over,' said Malgard. 'All the men are dead, save a few scattered townsfolk, whom I will need for rebuilding. I have ordered an end to the killing.'

Ulrik laughed in response to Carl's simultaneous translation.

'And my men … they took heed of your order?'

'Of course,' said Malgard.

'I rather doubt it,' replied Ulrik, straining to squeeze the last of the poisonous turd from his guts. 'My men all know I would rip the balls from anyone who obeyed another man's order. I'm guessing your order simply coincided with the end of the warriors and the beginning of the women. Am I right?'

'It is of no importance,' said Malgard, irritated and impatient. 'What is important is that one of the sons is missing.'

'So?' sneered Ulrik, climbing to his feet and fastening the two layers of heavy woollen breeches. 'Is not the victory complete? My men are already celebrating and I make it a rule not to stand between Vikings and plunder … especially of the female kind. I advise you to follow that same rule.'

'The only rule that matters,' said Malgard, 'is the rule of inheritance. Brand is the thegn's son. His claim is greater than mine if he lives to stand before Edward. He must be hiding and he must be found before he gets away.'

'That's your problem Malgard,' said Ulrik, stumping down the slippery log stairs. 'It is time for play.'

'I will pay extra!' shouted Malgard in his wake.

'What did I tell you?' laughed Ulrik, waving a hand in dismissal as he walked into the midst of his celebrating men. 'Never get between a Viking and his plunder. I am a Viking.'

∞ ∞ ∞

It was dark and getting cold.

There was a constant stream of men using the pit, which had perceptibly filled, since my descent, but I hardly noticed the stench any more.

I am not ashamed to say that I was confused and utterly terrified. I hadn't understood all that I'd heard but it was clear my uncle Malgard was allied with the Danes and had arranged a surprise attack on the town. My family were dead or despoiled and I was being hunted so that Malgard could take the posts of reeve and thegn, which had been my father's and would have been Gram's. So fixed in my mind was that certainty that I had never even idly entertained the possibility that the titles could be mine. Now my heart flared with a cold fury at the treachery of Malgard and my own impotence. I was now the rightful thegn – the king's representative charged with keeping his peace and doing his justice – but instead of marching into the Viking camp and seizing Malgard, I was cowering in a shit hole, accepting all the turd, piss and vomit like a king collecting tribute.

But the one thing I knew I wanted was revenge. And to get revenge, I had to stay alive. That meant getting out of the pit before dawn because I would surely be discovered when light came and men were face down vomiting.

The Danish celebrations went on for some time, but eventually the laughing and singing and occasional screaming of women subsided to a murmur and then silence. It had been a while since I was last shat, pissed or spewed upon and the common sounds of a summer's night – insects, frogs and owls – caused me to conclude that all were asleep.

Except the sentries.

I knew for certainty there would be sentries. Even drunken, pillaging Vikings remember to set sentries in an enemy's land, but there was a greater threat.

Malgard.

Malgard would be sober and would certainly be hunting me. And while the loss of my family was like a dull ache in my heart, my terror at the prospect of capture meant I had no time for the luxury of grief. I waited, scarcely breathing, for the sound of another soul.

I counted two hundred seconds.

Then another two hundred – the counting warding off the need for action. But at last I stood, the shit stench foul around me as my painful unfolding from the cess pit disturbed the turds and set them stinking again.

My fine clothes I simply abandoned. It was better by far to emerge naked from the hole and would be easier to clean myself. New clothes could be found later. I kept only my shoes as I clambered dripping from the pit – a thing of slime – and peered out from behind the canvas into the moonlit nightmare. Bodies lay upon the ground in poses that could only mean death. Perhaps thirty yards away still glowed the embers of a bonfire but no shadows passed in front of it. I needed to skirt the green and get through the town to the stream that fed into the Arwan.

The moon was high and two days from full. Its light was enough to present a danger if the sentries were alert, but it passed behind cloud and I took the opportunity to creep across the green through a field of cold and clammy corpses – ever ready to assume a similar pose. Then I heard a low growl and might have vomited as I realised that dogs of the village were feasting on their former masters. But there was nothing in my stomach to throw up and no tears either for these fellow folk and kin who lay in ruin while the dogs and Danes fed. I couldn't even force the dogs away for to do so would risk alerting the sentries. But no sooner did I have that thought than a large cur trotted towards me growling – then two more yelped at me and a man I hadn't seen shouted in a strange tongue. Despite the terror that begged me to bolt, I believed he was shouting at the dogs and forced myself to lie still among the corpses and was utterly revolted when one of the dogs nuzzled at my ear and then started licking the side of my face. Then all three of the dogs were rubbing and rolling against me. The sentry shouted again, his voice suddenly much closer, but then he made some exclamation of obvious disgust and backed away choking, and the dogs – well fed and perfumed – resumed their peregrinations about the conquered town.

At that moment the moon came out from behind a cloud and I all but cried aloud as I recognised Holgar – my father – lying close by. His body was rent by many wounds but his face was unspoilt and he seemed to stare straight through me as though I was the ghost and he the man with unfinished business. Now there were tears. The enormity of the disaster was plain and real and I groped for his hand – hoping to find it warm still with life, but snatched my own away as I felt his flesh like cold mutton. Somehow I found the courage to touch his hand again and was surprised to discover that he still wore his ring – a thick ring of copper and gold given to his father's father's father by the king – that bore the seal of his office which he would press into ink or soft wax to make his official mark on letters of credence.

A sudden flame of ambitious hope, coupled with vengeance, grew in my heart as I realised that if I could bring the ring to King Edward and tell my story then maybe the king would appoint me his reeve and thegn, despite my tender years, and empower me to take my family's revenge on Malgard. It took some time, but I managed to twist the ring off my dead father's finger without needing to cut it off. I also, with some effort, relieved him of his fine leather belt, to which was attached his favourite dagger, that he'd mainly used for eating.

The night got worse. Next to my father's body was my elder brother's – although his face was so disfigured by axe and sword cuts, I recognised him by his cloak – a beautifully embroidered, fine spun garment of pale green with the boar's head and two towers of the family badge in white and gold. I was equally surprised that such a fine cloak had not yet been plundered, but as I removed it from Gram's corpse, the reason was possibly explained by the many rents which I tore further in taking it from him.

After rolling carefully on the grass to remove the worst of the turd-slime, I made it to the copse on the western outskirt and considered my next move. There was no point heading for home. It would certainly have been occupied by Malgard and I had no wish to see him without a sword in my hand (and the skill to use it).

No, I had to find the king before Malgard did; or if not the king then someone I could trust to hide me until I could get to the king and seek justice for my kin. But the king was in Lundene, or nearby, and I had no idea of how to get there or even in which direction it lay. Many times the size of Stybbor Lundene was said to be – bigger even than Gipeswic – and I felt excited at the prospect of seeing the great city when I should have been feeling only grief. I wondered if God was aware of my excitement and, presuming yes, hoped that He would also be aware of my penitent shame. Then I realised that such a hope was impiously self-serving and that God would be aware of that, causing me to hope that self-knowledge and regret for my self-serving penitence might somehow be worthy of …

I gave it up and concentrated on getting through the copse and then the tanner's yard with the ring overlarge on my finger, the cloak rolled up in the belt and the dagger clutched in my trembling fist. It was suddenly silent – the night noises strangely still and I crouched at the tanner's gate – hardly breathing, sending tendrils of my intellect and instinct into the night to locate potential dangers. There was someone close.

My scalp seemed to tighten with cold and my empty gut was sour with dread. There was a presence, lying in wait, and I became slowly aware of a low rumbling sound – an unworldly portent of evil – and I felt my limbs frozen into immobility as the sound grew louder. And just as I realised what was making the sound, the dog that had been stalking me erupted with furious barking and lunged at my throat – moonlight glinting off snapping fangs, but instinctively I thrust the dagger up to ward off the beast and the night was rent with piteous howls. There was a shout to my right and without a further thought I bolted into the darkness towards the river and lay on the low-tide mud, looking up over the bank to where the dog whined its pain and a torch came sparking through the night, revealing a broad, squat warrior, who examined the dog as he held the torch high, casting about for whomever had caused its injury. It was Angdred – Malgard's man – whom I knew to be a dangerous fighter. Beside the torch he held also a naked sword and, if he found me, the implications were clear.

He was only twenty yards away and if he ran straight towards the river bank I'd be trapped for certain, but he glanced first into the tanner's yard, giving me a few precious moments to scuttle backwards into the water like a crab, and by the time he did come running over to investigate the bank I was lying face down in knee-deep water, holding my breath and still clutching my bundle and dagger and fearing that my white, naked body would be easily revealed in the moon and torch light.

At this point, I was resolved to fight. My body was tense as an iron rod, ready to explode into action at the first hint of an approach, but after some time, the need to breathe cooled my desire to take the initiative and, with infinite caution, I raised my head out of the water and opened my eyes.

The breath was sweet but sweeter still was the fact that I had not yet been discovered. Angdred was side-on to me, only five strides away, examining the mud on which I had lain and would soon work out where I must have gone. In the small light of the torch, my arm looked strangely dark and I realised that the muck from the pit had dried on my skin, possibly helping me to blend with the river's mud and obscure me from Angdred's vision. The current was tugging gently at my legs so inch by inch I pushed myself backwards into the deeper water and began to drift away from danger. Twenty feet … twenty-five … then Angdred finally realised where I must have gone and charged into the water holding the torch aloft and muttering angrily, standing in the spot in which I had lain only seconds before. The deeper the water, the stronger the current – I drifted further from Angdred but he was still close. He picked his way out of the stream and strode along the bank in the direction of flow, peering out over the dark water and occasionally splashing into the shallows to investigate a lump or eddy. At one point he came within six feet of me but I held myself inert like a submerged log and he saw me not. Soon I was twenty, forty, sixty feet away and lost sight of him as the river bent south and I felt my fear start to ease.

The river held no terrors for me. I was not much of a swimmer but I'd grown up playing around the shallow stream and knew it to be fordable for most of its length until it joined with the Greater Arwan some miles further south and east near the town of Gipeswic. I allowed myself to drift for a few more minutes, my heels occasionally scraping against silt and stones. The moon was sailing in an open patch of sky and the night seemed unusually bright. There were trees on either bank, so I had passed into the wood south-east of the town. I kicked over to the opposite bank and hauled my sodden burden onto the dry mud. Then I returned to the cold water and scrubbed at my hair and skin until it gleamed white in the moonlight and I could no longer smell turd.

As the immediate danger subsided, the grief became sharp again and I lay for some time on the bank surrendering to tears. Then, reflecting on the events of the afternoon and evening, I was overcome with a terrible guilt. I had known that God was privy to my thoughts and seemed disposed towards answering my prayers, and yet I had wished for the chance to become a warrior. Almost immediately God had responded by sending Danes, to the ruin of my family. It was my fault that my father and brother were dead and that slavery and worse had befallen my mother and sisters. It did occur to me that Malgard's arrangement with the Danes must have preceded my prayer in the church, but God must have been aware of my desire before I had even admitted it to myself. Malgard was simply an instrument of His design. The disaster was not Malgard's doing – it was mine.

I must have slept, because I woke shivering and hungry in a grey half-light. For a few blissful moments, I recalled not the events of the previous day, but then it all came back and I realised I was lying in full view of the far bank and was still only a few hundred yards from the town. I picked up the still-wet bundle of Gram's cloak and crept another fifty paces into the wood, where I found a small hollow with a comfortable log.

The ground was damp from the heavy rains that had only settled the day before the wedding so the rising sun found me in a heavy mist which shimmered and sparkled silver and green as stray bolts of dawn sun pierced the forest. Birds began nervously to announce the day and I relaxed, knowing I was safe from searching men while the birds continued to sing.

I spread Gram's cloak on the ground and tears once again pricked at my eyes as I noted the pink stains around the many rents. But I needed warmth (and to cover my nakedness) so, using Holgar's dagger, I cut a wide strip from the bottom of the cloak and was about to wrap my groin and butt when I realised I was not alone in the hollow.

I half cried out in panic but it was a young woman – a woman I'd never seen before. She had long, black hair and was dressed in a tunic of animal skins with hide boots held in place with leather thongs. She was very thin, and more or less my age – certainly no older. I scrabbled for the knife and held it up as though to defend myself.

'Always the knives,' she said, in a tired voice, and I felt faintly ridiculous despite the perils of the last twelve hours.

I lowered the knife and took further stock of her. There was blood on her hands, and at her feet was curled a dog of medium size with shaggy, red-brown hair.

'This is the dog you wounded last night,' she said. 'His former master was killed by the Danes, so he is now your responsibility. That is justice.'

I was so amazed at this turn of events that, for some moments, I was unable to speak. Then at last I said, 'I don't have time for dogs. I must get to King Edward to warn him of the raid … and get revenge for my family.'

'Your family are dead,' she said, 'but the dog can be saved. I have wrapped a poultice over the wounds in his chest and foreleg, which you must change in three days. If the wounds are clean and sweet smelling, the dog will live and will simply need a cloth bandage for another three days … perhaps the cloth you are holding.'

To my shame I realised that I was still completely naked and had been standing there for a minute or so holding a conversation with the girl without concealing my manhood, which then started responding to her presence. Hastily, I turned away and, with some discomfort, managed to wrap myself in the hem of Gram's cloak.

When I turned back, the dog lay whimpering on the ground, but the girl was gone.

Chapter 2

A Small Prick

Malgard stared at the corpse of Holgar, feeling the fury rise within him. He had forgotten the ring, and now Holgar's outstretched hand seemed to point directly at Ulrik who yawned and belched at Malgard's side.

'Holgar's ring has been taken … the ring of his office given by the king. Your men are welcome to any other treasure from the field of battle but I must insist on the ring's return.'

Ulrik shrugged and farted carefully – his stomach still tender from yesterday's bad meat and the night's debauch.

'I know nothing of rings, Malgard,' he said, scratching at his dags through his woollen breeches. 'And what does it matter? If a king gives one ring, he can give another. You will still be thegn, so start acting like one. Take command of your shithole town.'

'His belt also is taken,' said Angdred, standing close by, ' … and the dagger in his chest.'

Malgard examined his brother's body more closely. It was clear that someone had partly stripped him and taken the ring with some effort. It was then that he noticed that Gram, lying close to his father, had also been stripped.

'His cloak,' said Malgard. 'His cloak has been taken … the green cloak with the boar's head.'

'Aah, so this was the groom?' laughed Ulrik. 'It's not just his cloak we took. His bitch of a wife required some persuasion, but now she knows her place.'

Malgard winced. As head of the family now, the rape of Fyllba was not something he wished to hear about, but Ulrik was in a loquacious mood.

'She was unwilling at first … the fine ladies usually are. The best way to break them is to fuck them in front of the other women. Once the other women have seen them enjoying Danish cock they can no longer hide their dignity behind a wall of pretended shame. Of course, you have only a Saxon cock, Malgard … but it might work.'

'Saxon cock!' laughed Olaf Pighammer, spitting food and even his blind eye glinting merrily. 'You'd send a mouse to do the work of a stallion?'

'He could at least try,' said Ulrik. 'The size is less important than the public fucking. Even Saxon cock should work with nobles and nuns.'

'I'm sure you know best, Ulrik,' responded Malgard, refusing to be goaded and pondering the missing ring and cloak. It might just be random pillage, but taken together, they were two items of evidence to enhance Brand's claim if in his possession.

'Where is Brand?' he wondered aloud, and Angdred cleared his throat nervously.

'In the night, Lord,' he said, ' … I cannot be certain, but I chased a shadow. Into the river it went.'

Malgard turned fiercely on him.

'Why did you not report this?' he demanded, and Angdred shrank from his angry gaze.

'I never actually saw him, Lord. For all I know, it was nothing.'

'Nothing … and yet you chased?'

Angdred shrugged.

'I was patrolling as you bade me. A dog yelped, so I ran to investigate and he seemed to have suffered an injury. Then I examined the river's edge and saw fresh marks in the mud that seemed to lead into the river. I hunted along the bank, but—'

'But nothing,' Malgard finished with contempt, and then considered – putting himself in Brand's shoes. If Brand lived, then the chances were that he knew that Malgard was allied with the Danes. He would also know that his father and brother were dead and that he, therefore, had the greatest claim on his father's title. Or at least, he would realise that before long. In which case, he would try to get to the king.

Suddenly, Malgard knew fear – a small prick of it only, but his satisfaction at the success of the raid was soured by the realisation that Brand could ruin him, if he reached the king.

'Find him!' he snarled at Angdred, and then appealed once more to Ulrik Dragontooth. 'I need men, Ulrik … to find the boy who slipped our net.'

Ulrik shrugged again as he headed to the fire for warmth, and something solid to shore up his jittery guts.

'I shall rest here two nights. If any of my men are finished with fucking your women and prepared to accept your coin, you may use them, until I'm ready to leave.'

Malgard gritted his teeth but nodded his acceptance and turned back to Angdred.

'He has gone into the forest, I am sure of it. Scour the woods with Ulrik's men, but I shall ride east in case he has gone that way to Lundene. Meet me there when the deed is done.'

'The deed?' enquired Angdred.

Malgard just stared at him, his eyes black, and Angdred cowered as though he had been struck.

'Brand is not to reach Lundene,' growled Malgard. 'If he does, then your own life is forfeit … need I make myself any clearer?'

∞ ∞ ∞

My first problem was food. I'd hardly eaten at the wedding feast, and what little I had was lost when I'd vomited the ale.

My second problem was that I had no idea in which direction Lundene lay. Judging by the sun, I must have travelled north, but I hadn't gone far because of my third problem.

The dog.

Having wrapped the rag about my waist and groin, I pulled the remains of Gram's cloak around my shoulders and tied it in place with my father's belt. Then, thanking God it was summer, I set off through the wood away from Stybbor. My intention was simply to abandon the dog, but when I reached the edge of the hollow, the dog started growling. And as I stepped into the forest he barked until I ran back in panic to make him quiet.

The dog lay on the ground, his tail wagging happily as I stood over him, trying to soothe him into silence with soft words, but as soon as I tried to leave he started barking, and again I had to race back to make him still. I was not that far from Stybbor and, if the Danes were patrolling, they may already have heard the dog and even now be rushing to investigate.

I considered the knife, and even pulled it part way out of the sheath ...

My fourth problem was that I could not kill the dog. Accordingly, I had to take him with me, which meant carrying him. He wasn't overly large, but he was cumbersome and heavier than he looked. I made slow progress – hauling him through the undergrowth, tripping on tree roots as he alternated between angry growls and licking my face.

It did occur to me to kill and eat the dog – it was at least a justification for carrying him when I had such pressing problems – but another part of me knew that I could never do that. I was simply carrying the dog far enough to abandon him in a place where the Danes wouldn't hear his protest.

The sun climbed higher and my labour became intense. Sweat was pouring down my face and re-drenching the cloak, and the hunger in my gut became a torment. It was time to turn west, I decided. There were villages to the west of Stybbor where, no doubt, I could get food and directions. But despite my perils and hardships and recurrent stabs of grief, the thought that most absorbed me was the girl. Who was she, and why had I never seen her before? She must have been local because she spoke my tongue with little or no accent. At the summer fairs I had met folk who lived only valleys away who were all but foreigners in their speech, and even my mother's people required patience to understand.

I slipped on a patch of moss and the dog yelped as I almost dropped him.

'Be careful with him!'

Once again the girl had appeared out of nowhere, like a sorceress, and I felt a cool thrill of danger. But I took the opportunity to lower the dog to the ground and stretched my aching back.

The girl ran a few paces back in the direction I had come and peered into the forest. For the first time I noticed she had a small quiver of arrows on her back and gripped a bow small enough to be a child's toy. And yet, such was her air of assured competence, I doubted not she could use the bow to lethal effect.

'Who are—' I began, but without glancing back, she raised a hand to silence me. She seemed to be listening, then abruptly she turned and paced towards me.

'They are coming,' she said.

'Danes?'

'Men,' she shrugged. 'What difference does it make where they come from?'

She seemed to cast around in all directions, as though looking for something, and finally decided on the east.

'This way, quickly! Bring the dog.'

Once again I took up my burden, which seemed even heavier than before, and followed the girl into dark green, trackless bracken under tall elms, ash and larch. Perhaps a hundred paces off the path she told me to wait with the dog within a thicket.

'Where are you—'

'Quiet!' she hissed, ' … if you wish to live.'

With that she was gone, vanishing swiftly into the trees and I settled onto a comfortable root, watching back towards the path. It was a beautiful day around the end of July – warm – the air filled with birdsong and the scent of wild herbs. My stomach was growling and bubbling with need and the dog also alternated between soft growls and whimpers of pain. All around me was growing what looked like a form of wild parsley, so I plucked it and found it pleasant enough of taste. The dog whimpered anew, watching my hand go to my mouth and wagging his tail, but when I held out the parsley he didn't even sniff at it – just continued to whine. I ate a few hands full, but it didn't make a dent on my hunger.

I realised the forest had gone silent. The whips and twills of birdsong had stilled and a brooding sense of anticipation seemed to descend. I peered intently back towards the path and then heard the sound that has terrified fugitives forever.

Dogs.

Or at least, a dog. The noise was still some distance away, but it was the unmistakeable excited yapping of a hound intent on a trail and struggling to be let off the leash. Why were they hunting me, I wondered, and immediately knew the answer. Vikings couldn't have cared less about one boy who'd escaped the carnage – this was Malgard's doing. He'd realised my corpse was not lying with the rest of the family and so he was hunting me – to finish what he had begun. And in that moment I all but despaired. How could I escape Malgard and Angdred, allied with Danes. My life surely was over and tears dripped anew as the hideous scene of slaughter returned to me once again, but now my imagination placed my own rent and twisted body beside my father and brother.

Voices.

I could hear Danes laughing and calling in their weird, oafish tongue as the yapping took on a new excited frenzy. I couldn't see them but I could picture the men encouraging the dog as it raced back and forth across our spoor – probably in the place I had dropped the dog to the ground when the girl reappeared. It would not be long before they started pushing off the path towards me and I prepared to flee.

At that moment there was a loud howl of bestial pain, and then silence – followed by angry shouting and I saw men charging into the forest in the opposite direction to where I lay. The shouting subsided, and a minute later, the girl reappeared beside me.

'This way, quickly … bring the dog.'

She took off to the east and I jumped up to follow, the whimpering dog once more in my arms and licking my face. The rest had done me good, and combined with my urgent need to escape, seemed to give me greater strength to bear him.

For some time we passed through forest, sparse with trees but thick with bracken and bramble and I took the opportunity to eat some barely ripe blackberries, still hard and a little tart. The girl walked in front of me, ten paces or so, and turned angrily on me whenever I spoke. Her skin, where it showed through her cloak of pelts, was brown as though used to the sun and she seemed very certain in her movements – almost like a warrior. Once again I found myself speculating about her and where she might have sprung from – and why she was so different from every other maid or lady I had encountered in my life.

Before I knew it I was uncomfortably aware that my manhood was straining against the rag which wrapped it, but before I could rearrange myself, the girl halted and said, 'We shall rest a moment. Put the dog down.'

The cloak had been drawn back over my shoulders and the rag was slipping. Suddenly, the dog was the only thing between me and the girl and there was no way I could lower him to the ground without being profoundly shamed.

'Put the dog down,' she repeated, but I stood there dumbly as the dog started whimpering again. The girl stared piercingly for a moment, then her eyes hardened and she turned away.

Quickly, I placed the dog on the ground then turned away myself to retie my rag and pull the cloak tight. I wasn't sure whether she was aware of my condition which, if anything, was getting worse.

'Why are men such animals?' she asked.

'We're not animals,' I responded. 'Do animals know grammar and geometry?'

'Men know rape,' she replied. 'Grammar, geometry and rape.'

With that she padded back the way we had come and listened once again, but the birdsong was undisturbed. After a few seconds she appeared satisfied, then leaned against a tree and pulled a waterskin from a satchel. She poured water into her hand and held it for the dog to lick. Then she drank herself, and at last she tossed the almost empty skin to me.

Finally, my condition had subsided enough for polite conversation and I asked the question that had plagued me since we escaped the Vikings on the path.

'Did you kill the hunting dog?'

'Of course,' she replied, as though I were a simpleton. 'I shot him from the far side of the path, let them see me, then ran into the forest. Then I doubled back … the oldest of fox tricks.'

'But why kill that dog when you're so intent on keeping this one alive?' I asked, genuinely puzzled by her.

'Are you really such a fool?' she asked. 'Or are you simply one of those men who cannot bear silence and must endlessly fill it with empty braying?'

I have to say, I was not accustomed to being spoken to in that manner – not by women at least – and a flush of anger washed over me. I had a mind to threaten her – to remind her that I could overpower her, if I wished, but I held my temper and mustered all my dignity.

'I am Brand, son of Holgar ... reeve and thegn of Stybbor. Have a care how you address me, else you earn my wrath.'

And to my annoyed surprise, she laughed.

'Reeve and thegn,' she sneered. 'Why don't you explain that to the Danes? Maybe they'll apologise for killing your family and chasing you.'

With that she took off to the east again and, not sure as to whether I was still welcome to follow – or whether I wanted to follow – I picked up the dog and waited uncertainly until she turned and beckoned. And as no alternatives presented themselves ...

We went east for another hour or so and eventually I realised we were following a narrow path, like a game trail, which picked its way around rocks, in and out of glades until the ground began to rise and a small spring splashed out of a wall of stone.

There was a feeling of peace and remoteness about the place and, without discussing it, we fell onto the grass and drank deeply from the natural stone basin, from which cold water trickled away into a fen.

'The Arwan broads are not far from here,' said the girl. Then, doubtless responding to the look on my face, continued, 'Fear not. The Vikings cannot come ... there is nothing but fen and marshes between here and the sea for many miles. They will not carry their dragon boats across the mud, so I am safe here.'

'You live here?'

'Here ... and other places.'

On the southern side of the hill was a small cave which had been extended with a frame of branches covered with turves to make a small chamber, out of the weather. At the entrance was a screen woven of dried reeds and a pit of ashes surrounded by a ring of blackened stones. All around us was a field of bluebells that filled the air with a sweet and pleasant smell.

I laid the dog near the fire pit and stretched my aching back.

'I shall catch something for us to eat,' said the girl, reaching into the chamber and pulling out a small iron cauldron. 'Fill this with water and gather firewood. Also herbs ... they grow wild.'

'Wait!' I said, and she turned impatiently.

'I don't know your name.'

She considered me a moment, as though weighing the consequences of a hard decision.

'I don't know your name,' she said. 'Neither do I wish to know.'

With that she was gone, leaving me humiliated and angry. Who was this girl to treat me like the meanest villein when I was, by right of my lineage, the chief official and lord of the entire district. And in fact she did know my name. I'd told her only an hour before. To claim otherwise was a grave insult and I felt my anger rising once again.

'Fetch your own water,' I said aloud, but the sound of my voice in that remote place was small and shrill and I knew that, for all her breathtaking arrogance, I was completely dependent on the girl.

I fetched the water.

I also found herbs proliferating and even some rampion that looked as though it may once have been planted and was now gone wild. I ate a few hands full of parsley and sage while still feeling painfully hungry. But every time I started to feel pain or fear or insult I was reminded of the fate of my family and my uncle's treachery and the ongoing peril.

Suddenly I laughed aloud as it occurred to me that things could have been much worse.

I could have gone into the church.

Chapter 3

The Ring of Office

'My name is Valla,' she said, and I felt my skin tingle.

The sun had already set beyond the low western hills but the summer light would linger for an hour or so. We sat on a couple of rocks near the fire where the cauldron bubbled, filled with jointed hare and herbs. The hare's guts were wrapped in the skin and roasting under the coals. The ears and tail had already been devoured by the dog, whose appetite suggested he might yet make a full recovery from the wound I had dealt him. (I didn't like the dog and had started calling him Malgard.)

'Valla?' I repeated.

'You have heard the name,' she said, and of course I had, but ...

'I am two hundred and forty-two years old,' she continued, as though that somehow explained matters, and I didn't know whether to feel terror or scorn. But pride decreed I should assert myself.

'I am Brand, son of Holgar, as I told you before. I am lord of this land ... I am your lord.'

She actually laughed at me as she stirred the cauldron and tasted the broth.

'Lord of the land,' she scoffed. 'Can you make it do your bidding? Can you force the land to grow mountains or split apart to form rivers and seas?'

'Of course I can,' I replied, 'given men and time.'

She shook her head, then leaned forward to stir the cauldron again.

'Men and time will be the bane of this world I deem,' she said, passing me a ladle of broth. 'But you can't control it ... no more than you control the Danes.'

The broth tasted magnificent after my long fast and the smell coming from the cauldron and the coals was intoxicating. Using a forked stick with blackened tines, Valla pulled the charred skin from the coals and unwrapped the roasted hare's guts, which were gone in seconds (despite burning my mouth).

With a morsel of hot food inside me, my confidence began to return.

'Once I reach the king I will have his support ... and with his aid I'll control the Danes ... and you.'

Even as the words left my lips I would have recalled them if I could, but once they were out, pride required that I stand by them, however ungracious or unwise.

In less than a heartbeat, Valla whipped a knife from under her skins and thrust it within an inch of my eye.

'Want to control me do you?' she asked, and I slipped backwards in a delayed reaction, lying across the stone like a sacrificial offering. Quick as a snake, her free hand went under my rag and seized my manhood while the point of the blade pressed against my throat.

'I asked ... do you want to control me?'

'Yes!' I gasped. 'I am your lord! Unhand me!'

Then to my further confusion and embarrassment, I realised that I had become hard in her hand, and she released me as though stung.

'Get out!' she snarled. 'Leave this place and never return, else I tear your balls from your body and feed them to the dog.'

Speaking of which, the dog was now whimpering anew, wagging his tail and looking from one to the other as though imploring us to be friends.

'I have nowhere to go,' I said, rewrapping my rag and drawing the cloak about me once again.

'It is no concern of mine,' she replied. 'I bring you safe from the Vikings and you repay me with arrogance and the threat of rape! Get you gone and learn your proper place in the world.'

'Rape?' I exclaimed, in some confusion. 'I haven't threatened to rape you!'

'You've thought of little else!' she said. 'Ever since we met in the wood you've wanted me. Even now you are rampant ... your bestial urges kept in check only by the threat of my blade!'

'That's not true!' I insisted, despite the evidence that would not allow itself to be properly covered by the rag. 'But even if it were ... what of it? I claim lordship of this land, which means I have rights concerning its people.'

'Lordship,' she sneered, once again raising the knife. 'If you have to claim it then it can't be so ... lordship is natural and self-evident. Your claim is ridiculous.'

'You think I make ridiculous claims?' I exclaimed hotly. 'I'm not the one claiming to be two hundred and forty-two years old!'

But at that moment the dog growled and Valla looked up sharply, scanning the encroaching woods.

'Aid a fool and share his doom,' she spat, and I stared into the forest, noting the evensong of the birds, so noisy a minute before, was ominously still.

'This way, quickly,' she hissed, and took off around the east face of the hill. Immediately, there was a cry from the woods – something like a barn owl, or something trying to sound like a barn owl.

With a last longing glance at the cauldron, I ran after Valla, leaving the dog to guard the fire. There was maybe an hour of twilight left but, for the moment, we would be easy to spot unless we could get into the forest.

But Valla was running away from the forest and down into the fen, where she soon disappeared down a lane of reeds. For a moment I hesitated – all children have heard tales of the unwary who sink down into the sucking, grasping mud, never to be seen again, but then I heard more barn owl cries, and chose the reeds.

It stank.

Not as bad as the turd pit, but every step disturbed noxious vapours that erupted from the ground and pursued me like a foetid fog. Worse than the stench was the clinging mud itself that slowed my movements and stalled my flight. The reeds seemed to be criss-crossed with little paths and trails and I soon lost all sense of direction.

And I'd lost Valla.

I'd not seen her tracks in the mud and it occurred to me that I would probably make an excellent decoy for the Danes to aid her own escape – and of course, it was me the Danes were chasing in the first place. She would be safe once I was captured.

'Hssst!'

I spun around and saw Valla, concealed within a thick screen of reeds, pointing back behind me to another large thicket.

'Leave no trace,' she whispered.

But rather than go to the other clump of reeds, I pushed through to where she was lying low in the mud, and glaring at me.

'Fool!' she hissed. 'Now if one is caught both are caught and the one cannot aid the other!'

There was wisdom in her words but it was too late to argue. I huddled down beside her – hardly breathing – straining to hear whether we'd been followed – and realised for the first time that I had snatched up a weapon in my flight.

Not much of a weapon – a stick of firewood about two feet long and only an inch thick, but it was heavy, hard and hefted well and was far better than nothing.

We lay for some time as the twilight faded, and after a while I breathed into her ear, 'We never actually saw anyone ... could it be that we are hiding from no-one?'

'Do owls hunt in daylight?' she whispered. 'Be quiet!'

The light, such as it was, was going and I started to feel cold. My legs were cramping from staying in the same position so long but the slightest movement caused the sucking mud to gurgle and squelch – and at that moment, we heard the sound we'd feared. A squelch. Just the one, which indicated stealth and I felt Valla's body go rigid.

If God was privy to my thoughts and desires, then He must have known, even before I did, that I was fascinated by Valla and wanted to be worthy of her approval, yet everything I did or said seemed to inspire her scorn. Despite the cold and discomfort – despite even the terror of pursuit – I was almost painfully conscious of her body against mine and remembered with a weird pleasure the feeling of her fierce hold on my manhood as she'd held the knife at my throat.

As impossible as it seems, I realised to my dismay that I had become aroused again, and the urge to make some noble gesture became overpowering. They obviously knew we were close – if I could lead them away from the reeds then Valla might escape and think better of me.

I knew such a thought was a suicidal impulse but, possibly due to the desperate need to stretch my legs, I made my decision. I pulled the ring of office from my finger and placed it in Valla's hand.

'Keep this for me,' I whispered then, before she could object, I stood and bolted.

I crashed out of the reeds and was immediately aware of a figure right in front of me. Without thinking, I struck with my wooden club and felt a satisfying crack, but my victim screamed and I heard the hue and cry begin.

Somehow I knew the ground would be firmer at the base of the reeds and ran swiftly down the right of the lane.

A hoarse shout in a tongue I didn't know sounded from behind, and in that moment I saw two more emerge from the reeds to my left – both Danes by the look of their long hair and beards – young and fit and much stronger looking than I.

But not as quick to realise that the mud was thickest and deepest away from the roots of the reeds and I slipped their grasps, even as both clutched at me from the middle of the reed lane and fell over each other into the mud.

I reached the firmer ground and saw three men, two of whom immediately pursued me, while the third – Malgard's man Angdred – pointed and shouted.

Then I knew terror. If Malgard had sent men to hunt me then he knew I had escaped the butchery of my brother's wedding and was going to extreme lengths to ensure my father's line was completely destroyed. Fear gave me wings and I all but flew along the edge of the mire, heading for the woods on the northern side of the hill. I had about twenty yards on my pursuers, but knew I could not outlast them. I had to find a place to hide.

My brother's wedding cloak, with the beautiful green web and embossed with our family badge in white and gold, was sodden with mud and I gathered it into a ball as I ran, to prevent it from slowing my escape. Then, as I crashed into the trees, I tore the cloak from around my neck and flung it to my right, even as I swerved left and bounded over a giant log, simultaneously flinging my stick weapon high into the trees back in the direction of the cloak.

I hit the ground and watched under the log as two men ran into the darkening forest, just ten yards away, then my stick crashed to the ground off to the right, and they immediately took off in that direction. Losing no time, and wearing only my muddy shoes and a rag about my groin, I scuttled in the opposite direction until I could no longer see the men, then I leapt to my feet and ran like the wind for about ten paces, when a huge man stepped from behind a tree and swung a fist that knocked me off my feet and caused an explosion of lights and stars in my head.

∞ ∞ ∞

When I awoke, I found myself stretched face down over the giant log – hands tied together, feet splayed uncomfortably apart – and my head feeling like it had been used as an anvil. One eye was swollen and closed, and my cheek rasped against the rough bark of the long dead log. I could taste blood and felt weak with sickness and fear.

'Throwing a stave one way and running another,' said a voice behind me – a sneering voice I'd mainly ignored in the past, as he had no place in my father's household.

'The oldest of fox tricks,' laughed Angdred. 'But a man will always outwit a fox … or a vixen … once he knows it's foxes he's dealing with.'

We were in a small clearing and it was now quite dark. Torches of rag and pitch were held aloft by two of the younger Danes and a fire crackled behind me – throwing strange shadows against the wall of trees in front and warming my arse.

It was then that I realised I was naked – my loin cloth stripped away and my splayed feet tied to pegs – and horror crept over me as I realised what they intended.

'If we'd caught your friend we might have had some fun with her,' said Angdred, as though reading my mind. 'You'll have to take her place young Brand.'

'I am the king's representative,' I slurred through parched and swollen lips. 'Release me at once or know his vengeance.'

Angdred roared with laughter.

'King's representative? Are you saying that Olaf *Pighammer* is about to fuck the king? That's treason boy!'

'What? What are you—'

I could not bring myself to mention, or even put into coherent thought, the thing that I feared most in the world – more even than death – had resisted the monastery to avoid. But in case there was any doubt, Angdred put me out of my misery.

'Normally I would not approve of sodomites and their filthy practices,' he said, coming closer, 'but in this case I will make an exception so you learn the full extent of your fall, my lord. Your husband to be is called Olaf the Pighammer, but he is a mere instrument. As he tears your ring apart with his mighty hammer, know that in truth it is Lord Malgard that mounts you and takes your place as head of the family.'

As he spoke, his face came even closer until he was all but whispering in my ear like a lover, and without thinking I snapped my head back and felt it connect hard with something.

Angdred cursed, and then I shrieked with pain as he kicked me between the legs, where my unprotected nuts hung.

The two young Danes in front of me laughed so hard they all but dropped their torches and then Angdred kicked me again.

There was no way I could protect myself and tears of pain blurred my vision – distracting me from Angdred's vengeance.

'Thank you Brand,' he said at last, still behind me. 'Thank you for giving me a reason to hate you. Before, I admit, I felt some sympathy for your position … you did not ask to be born between Malgard and the thegn's seat, and so it was to be a clean death for you unless Olaf wanted you for his concubine. But now we shall take our time … flaying your skin inch by inch and finishing with the blood eagle. You know of the blood eagle don't you?'

I didn't respond – just struggled vainly against the ropes that tore into my flesh – causing the torch-Danes to laugh even harder.

'The blood eagle,' explained Angdred, 'is the pinnacle of Danish cruelty. First we shall smash your ribs with hammers. Then, we will carve you open and pull your broken ribs apart … and you will still be alive Brand, I promise.'

There was a hoarse muttering from behind me, and Angdred laughed.

'Olaf is impatient for his bride, I deem … not long now Olaf.'

Once again, Angdred's sneering voice was close behind me (although not quite as close as before).

'Finally, your lungs will be pulled out and arranged over your shoulders like an eagle's wings. Although you won't have long to enjoy them … by that point, death will be close … close enough perhaps for you to see your father and brother watching your rape and murder from limbo.'

'Help!' I screamed, on the brink of madness. 'Help!'

Once again the torch-Danes doubled over with purple-faced laughter and the shadows on the trees seemed to dance wildly, then were snuffed out by a vast shadow that could only mean someone very large was between me and the fire behind.

Two huge hands took me by the hips, and a loud voice grunted in Danish.

'Erm … my name is Carl Two-tongues,' said a different voice – a kind-sounding voice, if that was possible. 'Olaf has asked me to translate … I am sorry you have to suffer—'

'Just translate!' snarled Angdred.

'Very well. You are my sweet piglet,' began Carl – his voice becoming harsh as the hands on my hips gripped harder and stinking breath like rotting fish warmed the back of my neck. Then a sound like a butcher's mallet thunked behind me and the hands fell away. Olaf made a small mewing noise, and the Danes suddenly shouted with fury – immediately turning and holding their torches up – peering into the forest in front of me. Then one of them staggered backwards and dropped his torch – gurgling and groaning horribly, with an arrow in his throat.

'The bitch!' shouted Angdred. 'Find her!'

But the Danes ignored Angdred, who shouted at Carl to translate his orders. The torch-Dane who only moments before was purple with laughter was now pale with dread – forcing his dying comrade's fingers to close around the hilt of his sword.

Angdred leapt over the log and kicked the sword away – pointing angrily into the trees and shouting with rage. To my amazement, the unwounded Dane simply stood and drove a dagger into Angdred's throat, then retrieved the sword and, with tears in his eyes, tried to hold his comrade's fingers around the hilt. But the wounded Dane

41

had died, and the Dane who had knifed Angdred now stood over him as he lay on the ground, clutching his throat as gouts of blood splashed between his fingers.

Without a word, the Dane stamped down onto Angdred's head, then hacked with his comrade's sword until the body stopped moving. Then he continued to chop, two handed, until the head came away completely – and I might have thrown up except there was too little in my still-groaning stomach.

Two other Danes stood and watched, as the first finished the job. Then they all turned to me.

Then the kind voice spoke again from behind me, but it spoke in Danish. Carl Two-tongues he had called himself, and as he spoke, I saw fear come into the eyes of the Danes. They muttered quickly in their ridiculous tongue, sounding like pigs grunting in swill, then they swept up the two torches lying on the ground and ran.

Leaving me in darkness.

Not quite darkness. There was still a faint red glow before me from the dying fire behind – I could no longer feel its warmth on my naked flesh and, despite it being summer, I began to shiver.

'So,' said a voice, ' … the Lord of the Land?'

'Valla,' I said, in relief, submitting to her sarcasm. 'I knew it was you who shot the Danes … thank you.'

There was a silence, and the red light seemed to be dying further. Then I flinched as a dagger traced my spine.

'I was tempted to let the big Dane have his way with you,' she said, the tip of her dagger moving slowly between my buttocks and then pausing at my nuts and pressing a touch harder, 'to teach you the horror of rape.'

'Thank you,' I repeated, desperately trying to squirm aside, but I was staked so tightly I couldn't move an inch.

'Do you promise never to rape?' she asked me.

'Of course,' I replied.

'I want a promise that comes from the heart,' she said. 'Not just desperate words under threat of a gelding knife.'

'You'll have to take the knife away then,' I replied, and to my small amazement, she laughed.

Chapter 4

The Chain of Valla

It seemed an age, yet it had only been an hour or so since we'd sat in front of her cave with its turf and wicker extension. The coals of the fire were still smouldering deep and the dog thumped its tail at our return. The ordinary night noises of the forest told us the Danes were gone, so we felt safe enough to rebuild the fire and think once again of the food that Valla had been preparing.

The broth had boiled down a little too thick but still tasted magnificent, despite the absence of salt – fasting and fear had given me a noble hunger. We ate in silence straight from the small cauldron and shared a wooden mug of spring water.

After a while, I asked her, 'Where did you learn such skill with the bow?'

'From my mother.'

'Your mother?'

Valla said nothing further, and I remembered her uncanny claim – of being two hundred and forty-two years old. Then again, I had grown up hearing about the witch of the wood, whose name was indeed Valla, but she was supposed to be an old crone. I found it impossible to believe this young woman could be the same – and yet, she had a manner and an effortless skill that was as far beyond mine as my father's, or Brother Waldo's. The hair rose on my neck as I recalled stories of shape shifters and other mysterious creatures and I crossed myself.

'What did you do that for?' demanded Valla.

' ... Do what?'

'Make that stupid gesture with your hand. You're not a Christian are you?'

'All men are Christian these days,' I replied. 'Long has it been so, in these parts.'

'No Christian god walks among these trees,' replied Valla, who had collected some bluebells and was twisting their stems into a chain. 'The old gods are still strong here, ruling rock, brook and tree. They suffer not the eastern invader.'

Until very recently, I would have had only an academic interest in such a conversation, but my own communications with God had given me, I believed, a far deeper appreciation of His reality in my life.

'I have spoken with God,' I said softly, remembering, staring into the fire.

'You?' she sneered, as she completed her chain of bluebells and placed it around her head like a floral crown. 'And what did he tell you? That you were born to rule ... that you were entitled to rape?'

Despite my gratitude to Valla, I was beginning to find her obsession a little tedious.

'Why are you so concerned with rape?' I demanded. 'It can't be that bad ... not for a woman.'

She stared at me for a thunderstruck moment and then her eyes flashed with anger – but in that second the dog started growling and we both glanced up at a man standing on the edge of the firelight, holding a sword.

'Forgive me father,' said the man, dressed in the woollen breeches and skins of the Danes, but wearing a thrall's collar and speaking our tongue in a strange manner.

Valla and I leapt to our feet, but the stranger made no move to attack.

'I have sinned,' he continued, speaking to himself it seemed. Then he tossed the sword onto the ground and held up his hands in token of parley.

'I am Carl Two-tongues,' he said. 'May I share your fire?'

∞ ∞ ∞

Carl was a monk he told us, who had been raised near Gyrwu – somewhere far to the north – and kidnapped by the Danes on one of their summer raids.

'They slew many of my brothers, but spared me,' he said, drinking some of the thick broth, 'and as I quickly learned their tongue, they found me useful.'

'You were a slave?' I asked.

'A thrall, yes,' said Carl, touching his iron collar. 'And worse.'

Valla and I glanced at each other, both understanding him but knowing not how to respond.

'I was raped many times in the last three years,' Carl continued. ' … by Olaf, and I assure you Brand that rape is a terrible thing … for man and for woman.'

I was fairly certain he was wrong, but it might have seemed ungracious to argue with his greater experience.

'But more terrible still,' he said, 'was my own sin … of joy at Olaf's death.'

I stared at him, uncomprehending.

'Thou shalt not kill,' quoted Carl, in genuine distress. 'I should have turned the other cheek.'

'Where are the Danes?' I asked, wanting to change the subject. 'Those that still lived … will they return?'

'I doubt it,' he said, crossing himself. 'They are a superstitious people. I told them they had stumbled into the domain of a mighty witch. They had seen a dog and three of their comrades slain … it was simple enough to inspire their panic, and then slip away as they fled.'

Valla grinned, pleased with Carl's description.

'I am a mighty witch indeed … and I'll thank you not to call on the Christian god in my domain.'

'It is His domain,' said Carl, mildly, ' … as are all places.'

'The Christian god is a pillager,' Valla spat, ' … like the men who brought him here, burning, thieving and raping the old gods who have dwelt in the wood since the beginning.'

'Rape again,' I muttered, glancing at Carl.

'Call me obsessed,' sneered Valla, 'but men are beasts and think of little else than pleasing the serpent coiled between their thighs.'

'That is why they need God,' said Carl, 'to teach them love and forbearance. But, as Brand implies, you do seem unusually sensitive to the idea. Have you been raped, my child?'

'I am not your child,' snarled Valla, once more whipping her blade from under her skins. 'And no man has ever touched me. Nor will they … until it is time.'

Once again, I found myself strangely aroused and hunched closer to the fire to better conceal the uncoiling serpent.

'Time?' I enquired.

Valla's eyes narrowed, as though she sensed my discomfort once again. I didn't expect her to answer, but after a few moments she said, 'Know this Christians … Valla is a witch, passing from mother to mother in a chain unbroken for two hundred and forty-two years.'

My cheek muscle was twitching in disbelief, but at the same time the hair was rising on the back of my neck.

'That is why I fear rape. Once I am unmaidened, the power will pass from me to the daughter in my womb … I will no longer be Valla.'

With that she rose, pulled her skins close around her shoulders and disappeared into the darkness of her cave.

Chapter 5

My Errant Shafts

It was a cold night. I wasn't sure of my welcome in the deepest and warmest part of the cave, where Valla slept with the dog. Carl and I spoke in low voices for a while and I swore with vengeful fury when he gave me full details of the arrangement between Malgard and his former master, Ulrik Dragontooth. Then, as the fire died, we found places in the wicker and turf extension which kept out most of the wind and some of the cold. It occurred to me that Angdred and the two dead Danes had clothes they wouldn't be needing any longer, but I wasn't going to go stumbling through the forest to search corpses in the dark – alone.

The next morning, while Valla stirred the fire, Carl and I went back to the site of the battle – a clearing just inside the forest on the marsh side of the hill. The ground was red with blood where the young Dane and Angdred had been slaughtered, and Olaf lay staring on his back with an arrow in his throat and his breeches around his ankles. Even in death, it was clear he had been a man of mighty endowment and I shuddered at what I had been spared. I expected Carl to kick the body or make some kind of vengeful gesture, but if anything he looked a little sad and muttered a prayer.

We stripped the bodies and examined the small hoard of clothing, goods and weapons. As well as the sword carried in by Carl the previous evening, there was a large battle-axe born by Olaf, two bows with quivers full of arrows, several knives, an excellent pair of boots, Angdred's shirt of rings, three good belts, a couple of whetstones, some salt and some coins.

I dressed myself in thick woollen hose and a leather jerkin, from which I scraped the worst of the blood. The shirt of rings was overlarge, but like the axe it was valuable. I took all the weapons and wrapped them in my brother's cloak, with the exception of the sword, which I strapped at my waste and one of the knives which slipped neatly into my new boot.

'How long have you known Valla?' asked Carl, as we covered the bodies with the remnants of their clothing.

'A day,' I answered, well pleased with my new gear. 'I met her near Stybbor, about this time yesterday.'

'The Lord can throw us some challenges,' said Carl, looking back towards the cave. 'In all my days as a thrall, I never looked to be delivered by a pagan witch.'

It was the first time I had seen Carl in daylight – he seemed younger than I'd first thought – early twenties perhaps. And he didn't look like a monk, having lived with the Danes for three years. His brown hair was long and untonsured and his beard dark and thick. His arms, accustomed to pulling the oars of Ulrik's dragonboat bulged with muscle. He looked more like a warrior than a monk – more like a warrior than I did.

'How is that a challenge?'

'A sorceress succeeds where the church and armies failed? I'd call that a challenge. His mind is mysterious and His whims inconceivable … but He does nothing if not to test us.'

'You have spoken with God?' I asked.

'No man can truly claim to have done so,' he replied. 'But sometimes we can be fairly sure we know what He wants of us.'

'It is perilous to speak with God,' I said, with some feeling. 'I have experience of this … it cost me my family.'

Carl stared at me for a few moments.

'It would surely be perilous to act as though authorised by God … only the Holy Father in Rome may do that.'

'Nevertheless … I have so acted. I wished to be a warrior and God responded by sending Danes to attack the village.'

Once again, my eyes filled with tears – it was only a day and a half since my world had been destroyed. I pulled the heavy sword from its leather scabbard, lined with greasy fleece.

Carl stepped back as I took a couple of clumsy swipes at the air.

'What do you mean to do?' he asked.

'I have to get to the king,' I said, 'to let him know of the treachery of Malgard and claim my father's thegnship.'

'Then you had best hurry young Brand. I know Malgard left for Lundene yesterday. He sent his man to hunt you … wishing to take no chances with the succession.'

I looked down once again at the corpse of Angdred – lying in two pieces – and without thinking, struck at his thigh with the sword. The blade cut about two inches into the jelly-like flesh with a dull thunk, and I shuddered as I pulled it free of the cold, sucking meat.

'It takes time to learn sword craft,' observed Carl, and I grimaced as I realised how inexpert my swings must have appeared.

'What do you know of fighting?' I demanded, resenting his bearing witness to my lack of skill.

'I can teach you the little I have learned … watching and listening to the Danes, who are all great warriors … and the first thing is this: keep the sword clean and sharp. Get to know it like you know your own right hand. The Danes say the sword must become part of you … before it can become part of someone else.'

He seemed to speak with authority and I found myself submitting to his instruction.

'You and the sword must become one … a single engine. The sharp point is the killing device that starts with your head, reaches down your arm through your hand and into the blade. But before you practice slashes and lunges, you must acquire sword-strength … as the Danes call it.'

'Sword-strength?'

'Men fall to the swords of other men less by lack of skill and more by lack of wind. He that can hold his sword up the longest has the better hope of victory. Practice by holding the sword out at shoulder height until you can keep it up for an hour.'

That made sense to me and I resolved to start practising immediately, but Carl gathered up the hoard and started back towards Valla's fire.

'Come Brand … there is much to discuss.'

∞ ∞ ∞

Valla was typically moody and aloof when we returned, but she examined the gear and chose for herself a quiver of arrows (she had her own bow), the lightest of the belts, a whetstone and a long, pale knife decorated with runes and a dragon coiling about the hilt. It looked familiar and I felt a moment's regret that I hadn't claimed that for myself, but Valla was more than entitled to her share of the plunder.

She stirred more herbs and water into the remains of the broth, and to my disgust fed the last of the boiled hare to the dog who wolfed it down in seconds.

'Malgard is healing,' she said with satisfaction, causing Carl to stare at her in confusion – as though she was divining.

'I've named the dog Malgard,' I explained, and Carl laughed grimly.

'You have a dangerous sense of humour young Brand ... no wonder God takes an interest in you.'

Valla had heard my story concerning commune with God and snorted with amusement.

'Takes an interest,' she laughed. 'Give me a sign Lord, cried Brand ... and lo, the horse shat!'

She was at least sounding less unfriendly, and once again I found myself keenly aware of her strange attraction. She was not at all like the ladies of my father's household – or the village – not that I had known that many. She was wiry and thin, festooned with furs and short breeches that looked to be made of harts hide. Her hair, as I've said, was long and black – tied into two thick braids and crowned with bluebells. And her face was brown with full, pink lips and green-black eyes blazing fiercely at me once again.

'What are you staring at?'

'Nothing,' I stammered, beginning to suspect she was as privy to my thoughts as God seemed to be.

'Good ... so when are you leaving?'

'Erm ... well ... today I suppose. I have to get to Lundene.'

'If you will ... I'll come with you,' said Carl. 'I would see Lundene ... and you'll need a witness when you accuse Malgard before the king.'

As he spoke, I was aware of how daunting was my task. Malgard was a man, who had fought with my father in the king's fyrd and had doubtless many friends and supporters. No-one knew me, and even if I did manage to come before the king, there would be plenty prepared to side with Malgard – a man they knew and with whom they'd stood in the shield wall.

'Thank you Carl,' I nodded. 'I look forward to your company ... only, do you know in which direction Lundene lies?'

'Alas, my home is in the north,' said Carl. 'All I know is that Lundene is a great city in the south ... on the Temes.'

'You must go to Gipeswic,' said Valla. 'It is not far from here, down the Arwan. From there you can take a ship ... there are many fleece barges which ply between Gipeswic and Lundene.'

'He cannot go to Gipeswic,' said Carl. 'At least ... not with me. My former Danish masters sailed up the Arwan, past Gipeswic, and must return that way. In all likelihood, they'll stop for trade and to visit the inns and stews around the docks. I have no desire to be recaptured.'

Valla considered for a few moments, then she said, 'I can put you on the western road to Lundene ... but have no desire to leave my own domain. I will take you to my border and no further.'

Inwardly I bridled at her reference to her domain – this land was all my domain, now that my father was dead – but if I wanted her help ...

'There is a condition,' she continued, 'if you want my assistance.'

'Name it.'

'If your claim is recognised by the king, you must grant to me this forest ... forever.'

I was shocked – not so much by her ambition, as by the realisation that I had left the world of childish fair play behind and that life from now on would be a constant wary struggle – not only against warriors and assassins, but also against sharp merchants and courtiers who would steal my property if they could.

'That seems a high price for a guide.'

'Nevertheless ... it is my price.'

'I might consider giving you the run of the forest ... with rights to harvest timber, game and fruits.'

'Enjoy your trip to Lundene then ... give my regards to the king, if he still lives when you find him.'

I stared at her for a moment, suddenly feeling the need for urgency.

'Alright ... I'll grant you a portion of the forest ... from here to the place you killed the Danish dog.'

It was a generous offer – if made under duress – but she wasn't satisfied. After some further consideration, I realised I was loath to part with Valla – for all her strangeness and moods – and it was liable to spoil my judgment.

'Alright, I will grant you the entire forest ... but there are two conditions.'

Valla cocked an eyebrow, as though amused at my effrontery in daring to haggle with her.

'First ... you must teach me your method of using the bow ... '

'If you are capable of learning it in the time we take to reach the edge of the forest,' she said.

'And second ... you must come with us, all the way to Lundene.'

Once again her eyes flashed with anger, but I raised my hand to forestall another outburst.

'You are an expert archer,' I explained. 'I desire your ... protection.'

I suspected that such a statement would appeal to her pride. As for the forest, which had been in my family since time immemorial, it occurred to me that, in all likelihood, my own claim would never be made. I could therefore afford to offer her anything.

∞ ∞ ∞

'Don't aim at the target ... just pull back the shaft, picture the arrow buried in the target, and release. It's uncanny how well it seems to work.'

'Like magic?'

'If you like, but it is warriors' magic ... not the deep magic of the forest.'

We had walked for some hours, heading due north to skirt Stybbor and find the western road. We were moving slowly as Valla had insisted on bringing Malgard – who seemed to be healing well and was able to limp along by himself. He was also fascinated by every passing scent and had to be pulled away from every second tree. Progress was slow.

We had paused for a morsel in the mid afternoon, and then Valla had taken me hunting – to learn the bow and find some meat for the evening meal.

'Shouldn't I start by shooting at a tree?' I asked.

'A tree?' she sneered. 'Will rabbits, deer or soldiers stand like a tree and wait for you to shoot?'

I nodded, as her words made sense, and wondered about the countless hours I had spent in my childhood, shooting at butts.

'The way I was taught,' she said, 'if you can't practice with a moving target, you have to move yourself.'

With that she started walking to her right and almost casually shot into the centre of a tree some thirty paces away. Then she walked back to her left and placed her second shaft no more than a handsbreadth from the first.

I gaped at her effortless skill and said, 'Olaf didn't stand a chance.'

'It's a bit harder to judge … shooting out of the dark into light … the different light seems to play tricks on the eyes. But at least you are hard to see if you are in the dark and the target is in the light. I was only twenty paces from Olaf when I shot him.'

There was no mistaking the pride in her voice, and I envied her prowess. I took two arrows from the quiver, as she had done, and started walking to my right. I stared hard at Valla's arrows, pictured my own nestled alongside, and released …

And saw a flicker past the tree and heard a distant thunk as the arrow struck an object deeper in the forest.

'You're thinking too much about the bow,' said Valla. 'You have to just think the target dead, so the bow is an unconscious medium of death … between your brain and the target.'

I wasn't entirely sure that I understood what she meant, and although I had asked her to teach me the bow, I couldn't help but resent her talent. Without further word I nocked the second arrow and started moving back to my left – which seemed even harder – and sure enough, the arrow flashed away, missing by a greater distance than the first.

'Come on,' she said. 'We can't afford to lose those.'

We paused at the tree to pull her arrows and then began the search for my errant shafts. I went left as she went right and after a few seconds heard her call, 'Found it.'

I hadn't heard the second arrow strike anything so it could be anywhere. I pulled another arrow from my quiver and nocked it as I moved silently forward – desperate to prove my worth.

As I rounded a large tree, I was confronted with a hare caught in a snare and, after snatching a quick glance over my shoulder, shot the already dead hare from two feet away, then swiftly released it.

∞ ∞ ∞

'That was a mighty shot,' said Carl yet again as Valla skinned and boned the hare to prepare a similar meal to that we'd eaten the previous night. She was smiling.

'Tell us again how it was done.'

I had already told the story twice and was getting a little embarrassed in the face of Carl's admiration and Valla's silent mirth. I suspected that somehow she was aware of my subterfuge.

'I heard a scrabbling ahead,' I said. 'I raised the bow as the hare suddenly leapt from cover and … without even thinking … loosed the arrow and saw the hare bowled over.'

'Amazing,' repeated Carl.

'Yes … amazing,' said Valla. 'One minute he can't hit a tree, then moments later he takes a hare on the fly with an arrow through the throat. Incredible.'

'You are a fine teacher Valla,' I said, hoping to change the subject.

'That may be,' she said, amused, 'but not so fine as to teach you to shoot into yesterday.'

Carl looked up at her, confused, as I burned with embarrassment.

'Shoot into yesterday?' he queried.

'The hare's been dead for at least a day,' she explained, tossing some of the skin and scraps to Malgard, 'so if it was killed by Brand, that can only mean he is able to shoot backwards into time past.'

Valla burst into laughter as Carl continued to look confused.

'Let's just hope that the owner of the hare doesn't miss it yet,' said Valla. 'And doesn't have too many friends.'

∞ ∞ ∞

We roasted the hare over a small fire and washed it down with spring water and some more early blackberries. We had no cave or other shelter, and despite it being summer we were all conscious of the chill as darkness fell.

I had collected plenty of dried wood while there was still light, so was able to tend the fire, but the chill grew worse and we huddled closer – our faces hot and our backs cold.

'What do you know of the king and his politics?' asked Carl.

I wasn't sure I understood the question and shrugged.

'How do you think you will be received?'

'Aah … I have heard my father say that King Edward is just in his dealings. I can only trust that he will hear me … I do have this.'

I held up the ring of office which I wore precariously on the thickest finger of my right hand.

'Malgard was deeply distressed when he realised that was gone,' said Carl. 'But he thought it more likely one of the Danes had taken it than you. It is a delicate alliance he has with Ulrik Dragontooth.'

'The Danes that escaped will go back to Ulrik and report that no ring was found on Brand when he was captured,' said Valla.

'That news will take a while to get to Malgard,' said Carl, 'unless Ulrik sails to Lundene to trade. But when it does, he will be angered and fearful to know that Brand lives. He will send out more assassins.'

The chill crept over me – both future threat and present cold – and I shivered. More wood went onto the fire and I found myself drawn into its black and red depths like watching a vision of life in a great city. It would be strange and searing in such a place, but at least I'd be safe from the cold – and Malgard.

'It is time for sleep,' said Carl, disturbing my reverie and bringing me back to present danger. 'We should lie together for warmth.'

I glanced at Valla and her eyes narrowed.

'I don't trust Brand,' she said.

I was indignant, but Carl said, 'Lie back to back with Brand … and I also shall turn my back to you, but you will still be warmed by two backs.'

After some muttering and difficulty, we arranged ourselves – with Malgard the hound also curled between my and Valla's knees. It was warm enough, but as I knew it would, the feel of Valla's body and her soft breath against my neck caused the serpent to uncoil and I lay restively as the breathing of the others became slow and regular.

The serpent saved our lives.

As I huddled against Valla resenting both her mistrust and rejection of my lordly rights, I became aware that the night noises had stilled. That usually meant a new presence, and I remembered my sword was lying in its scabbard on the far side of the dying fire.

I lay without breathing, trying to pick out the sounds of stealth that would confirm my fears, then I pressed my leg down on Malgard to gently wake him.

Almost immediately he began to growl softly and I felt a horror – there was something, or someone, very close.

Without further thought, I leapt up from the ground and ran for my sword just visible in the red glow of the embers, and no sooner had I done so I heard a thump and then a curse.

'Valla!' I shouted, pulling the sword from the scabbard and peering vainly into the darkness. There were black shapes moving and I leapt towards them, swinging the sword and feeling it catch against something – then the shapes were backing away and more red light bathed the clearing as Valla and Carl threw kindling onto the fire.

'Who was that?' I exclaimed, but Valla shrugged.

'The owners of the hare. Get out of the firelight … unless you want to be a target.'

We all shrank away from the deadly warmth and light, but not before I noticed a large rock part-buried in the ground, where my head had been.

'Some of your magic might be useful?' I muttered at Valla.

'Still!' she hissed, and crouched low with an arrow nocked, searching the immediate trees for targets. Suddenly a wild laughter rang out of the darkness – taken up by several voices – all around us.

'We mean you no harm,' cried Carl, and the shrieking laughter got louder.

'We mean you harm,' replied a voice, high pitched and mad with mirth.

'They fear our weapons,' said Valla. 'They have none of their own, save rocks and sharpened staves … but they have some skill with those.'

At that moment I realised that the tip of my sword was dripping blood. I must have caught one of them swinging in the dark – and couldn't help but feel a little pride. They had no weapons? They weren't so tough.

'I am Brand,' I shouted, planting the sword at my feet. 'Son of Holgar ... thegn and reeve. I am lord of this wood. Who wishes to taste my sword?'

If anything, the laughter got louder and more deranged. One voice began shrieking, 'Lord of the Wood! Lord of the Wood!'

I estimated that there were at least five or six voices contributing to the laughter, and took a couple of paces in the direction they seemed thickest, when suddenly the small clearing flared brightly with a greenish light and I spun around to see Valla standing over the fire with her hands raised above her head. The fire burned green with a great intensity that faded quickly, and left the air stinking like a cess pit.

'Behold! I am Valla! Leave this place or I will boil the blood in your veins, wither your children and bring terror to your dreams.'

The laughter ceased.

Valla held her pose, still as a clay figure, until the green flames turned red again and her arms drooped to her sides.

'They will return,' she said, softly. 'Only one of us can sleep, the others must watch and keep the fire alive.'

As for that, we had only collected so much fuel, so I strode to the edge of the light and, always with an eye on the forest, began collecting bark, twigs, cones and anything else that might burn and keep us alive.

'How did you do that?' I asked, dragging a good-sized log while still brandishing my sword and keeping my eyes to the forest.

'You said my magic would be useful,' said Valla. 'I agreed. It was time to unveil my power ... but the Rockers will return.'

It was all a bit much, and I wasn't sure which of the two lines of questions I most wanted to pursue.

'The green flames?' I faltered, once again feeling the hair rise on the back of my neck. 'What sort of spell ... '

'Sulphate of copper,' said Carl, '...blended with pitch to keep it burning bright for a few moments.'

I turned to glance at him, peering calmly into the trees, holding only a stave.

'So you know the ingredients,' shrugged Valla. 'It doesn't reduce the effect of the magic.'

'There is no magic save the Lord's,' replied Carl. 'Yours is just the application of basic alchemy.'

'Magic or alchemy … does it matter? I brought the preparation for such a happening … and now the Rockers have withdrawn.'

'Who are the Rockers?' I asked.

'Outlaws … dispossessed … poor folk without clan. They live deep in the forest and keep to themselves … until they are invaded and robbed.'

'I didn't know it was their hare!' I said hotly, raising my voice slightly in case the Rockers were within earshot.

'You knew it was someone's,' said Valla.

'You ate it too.'

'Can I suggest we remain silent?' asked Carl.

The noises of the forest slowly returned, meaning either that we were alone, or that the night creatures had accepted the new presence of the Rockers.

'So, they kill with rocks?' I whispered, examining once again the rock lying exactly where my head had been.

'That is their way,' whispered Valla, 'and rarely do they fail at it. You were lucky.'

'We were all lucky,' said Carl. 'If Brand hadn't woken us, there would certainly have been more rocks in the dark … although, perhaps not for you.'

I couldn't see Valla's face, but I laughed softly, despite the continuing threat from the darkness.

'Aren't you going to tell us again that all men are beasts?' I said, and to my vague dismay, Valla said, 'Yes, all men are beasts … but know this Brand. I would gladly rut with the foulest peasant before I lay with you. So keep that in mind next time you picture me naked and lying beneath you. It will never happen.'

I had no idea how to respond to that, but it left me feeling sad. And of course, the serpent again began to uncoil.

Chapter 6

A Strange Device

We took it in turns to snatch a little rest, with always two watching, but sleep had not come easily with the constant threat and also the knowledge that you would be woken as soon as you shut your eyes.

And yet, we did shut our eyes. Carl and I had been watching, as Valla slept, and the next I knew I was waking with a start – in cold, grey mist which hung about us but swirled with every breath or movement like gossamer pricked with tiny crystals. Beyond the clearing, the trees were dark shadows, like brooding chessmen from an unfinished game.

Carl and Valla were asleep, and the forest was quiet. I sensed the Rockers were not close, but climbed to my feet and stretched, pulling my sword from its scabbard and examining the half-dried blood on the tip. I knew that I ought to be cleaning and sharpening the sword after blooding it, but felt a strange unwillingness. The blood marked my first effort as a warrior and I was loath to lose it.

We were in a small clearing, only twenty paces across, but so thick was the mist it was almost impossible to see from one edge to the other. I strained ears and eyes but caught no warning, so began collecting more fuel and added kindling to the fire which had all but died. I dug into the coals, found some still faintly pink and blew, crumbling dried bark onto the embers as they glowed. Soon the fire was crackling once again and Carl stirred. So I decided to leave the clearing discreetly.

As I've said before, there are some stinks I cannot bear – one in particular. Some might suggest that my experience of lying all night in a latrine might have inured me to the stench of turd, but if anything it had made me even more squeamish. There were certain conventions about shitting near camp sites. At least thirty paces into the woods was regarded as good manners, but that was never enough for me so, sword in hand, I crept through the misty bracken, twisting and turning past rocks and huge trees, until I found a place sufficiently remote for my taste.

After completing my ablutions I began to retrace my steps, and soon realised I'd lost the trail.

I stopped – the loudest sound being my own breathing – and turned slowly in a complete circle, trying to recognise a landmark leading back to the clearing. Nothing seemed familiar, so I chose the most obvious path – and found myself back at the place of my ablutions.

The faintest stirrings of panic began to grip me, but I took a deep breath and reminded myself that I was only fifty or so paces from the clearing. Dare I risk a shout? Or a whistle perhaps?

My low, tuneless whistle sounded dead against the ever-swirling mist, so I tried a little louder. There was no response, and I began to feel terribly alone. Again, I shook my head and breathed deeply to clear the beginnings of panic. I felt the urge to start running and shouting but quelled it, knowing that panic would only lead me astray, and shouting could bring the Rockers.

Picking a direction slightly to the west of the first I had tried, I determined to go as straight as possible for fifty paces and then if necessary, return and try again – gradually radiating until I found my companions.

Halfway through my third attempt, I heard Carl shout, but it sounded far behind me and I immediately turned and headed in the direction of the shout. Then he shouted again, and Valla screamed, and I started running, pulling the sword from its scabbard as I leapt over logs and crashed through bracken.

Then I heard strange voices and rough laughter and raced toward the new danger. I could see shapes moving in the mist up ahead and smell the smoke of the fire. Then there was the sound of a blow and a cry, so I cast all caution aside and leapt into the clearing.

Which was filled with men dressed in fine clothes and heavily armed, and immediately I assumed that another of Malgard's assassin troops had found me and swung my sword at the nearest – who ducked effortlessly and kicked my legs from beneath me.

'No Brand!' screamed Valla, but I heeded her not, jumping back to my feet and brandishing the sword – threatening all six of the strangely clad men.

Who all started laughing.

∞ ∞ ∞

Such was my surprise, and so friendly did they seem despite being large, fierce-looking and arrayed for war, that I lowered my sword.

'A fighting man with a blooded sword,' boomed the largest of them – a tall man with blondish hair and a fine moustache. 'And offering battle to all six of us. Who've you been killing lad? One of these?'

He had an unusually loud voice, like an actor playing a role, but exuded a natural authority, to which I submitted without question. Lying on the ground and groaning was a filthy looking creature dressed in skins and rags not unlike Valla, although not as clean and fair.

'The Rockers,' I stammered, ' ... the people of the wood.'

'Indeed ... so you're on our side,' he said. 'But there is a strange tale here ... three travellers ... two dressed as Danes but speaking our tongue ... the third dressed as one of the forest folk whom we have sworn to scour from these woods.'

'Scour from the woods?' I repeated in sudden doubt. 'These are my woods. Why would you wish to do me such a service?'

Once again the men roared with laughter.

'Your woods?' asked the blonde leader, smiling. 'By what authority do you claim the woods?'

'By this authority,' I said, holding up my fist with the ring of office outermost. 'I am Brand, son of Holgar ... thegn and reeve of Stybbor.'

In the distance a horn blew and the men all turned in that direction.

'The hunt is on!' cried another man, younger and shorter than the leader, but not unlike him of face. Like the leader, he was heavily muscled and dressed more richly than the others – all of whom wore moustaches in the style of the leader.

'I would hear your tale Brand Holgarsson,' said the leader, 'but we have work to do for the present … to finish the fight you started.'

He nodded once again at my sword, grinning, then lifted a hunting horn that hung on a baldric at his side and blew a great double blast. Then all but one of them took off into the mist, which was now thinning enough to let a few stray beams of sunlight into the clearing.

The soldier that remained pointed at the ground where Valla sat with Carl, and I squatted – not knowing whether to feel fear or great excitement.

Carl was white-faced and Valla simmered with her usual rage.

'Why were you not watching?' she demanded.

'Peace!' insisted the soldier, and we fell silent. The mist still swirled and the forest was quiet, but a brooding sense of anticipation was strong in the air and I simply couldn't sit still. I stood, but the soldier ignored me as he leant on a spear and peered into the mist. A horn rang out again to the right, answered by another to the left, and then someone was running towards us. Almost unconsciously, I drew once again my sword to face whatever was coming.

Then there was a pounding through the bracken and a wild man flew out of the mist, swerved away from the soldier and straight onto my sword. He managed to avoid the point but was forced to stop and the butt of the spear took him in the back of the head. Then there was a scream as he crumpled to the ground and a woman ran to his body, glaring at the soldier and snarling at me.

She looked remarkably like Valla, or at least was dressed in a similar panoply of skins and rags. But Valla was clean, whereas this woman was covered in dirt and her hair hung like filthy tangled cords. Her man also was filthy – very thin, with lank, red hair and snaggled teeth. He had a red rag tied around his upper arm, wet with fresh blood, and I knew immediately that his wound had been caused in the night by my sword. In all likelihood, this was the Rocker who had tried to kill me in my sleep.

The horns blew again much closer, and there was shouting and laughter. More shapes emerged from the thinning mist but moving slowly – defeated. There were six more of the Rockers – four men and two women – herded by the soldiers into the clearing and forced down onto their knees – snarling, spitting and swearing at their captors, until the man who looked like the brother of the leader kicked one of them in the face, and they fell silent – awaiting their doom.

The leader now swung back a cloak to reveal a strange device – a grinning warrior with a raised sword, legs bent into an angular position for the sake of a pattern, which had a Viking look to it.

'You have been warned,' he declaimed. 'You have been told to leave my domain or know my justice.'

The man with the red rag suddenly groaned and his face twisted with pain. The woman stroked his brow with such tenderness that I actually felt a flash of envy – remembering suddenly the loss of my own family.

'Now you have a final chance,' continued the man, who seemed to be claiming my woods for himself. 'Will you serve or die?'

He seemed to be offering them serfdom or death, and one of the men stood and spat at the ground at the leader's feet. Without another word, the leader's brother swept the man's head half off his shoulders and all in the clearing were sprayed with hot blood which continued to pump like a stuck boar in a shambles as the women screamed and the men stared.

'Will you serve?' repeated the leader, uncaring of the horror at his feet, and all the rest hung their heads in submission, save the wounded snaggle-tooth who lay still on the ground – and his woman staring at Valla. She muttered something to the others and they all glanced up in fear, and a couple crossed themselves while others made the sign against the evil eye.

The leader of the armed men looked at Valla with sudden interest.

∞ ∞ ∞

'Call me Harold,' said the leader. 'And this lout is my brother, Tostig.'

The three of us walked at the back of the procession towards a town with the name Theodford. The Rockers were all bound together at the neck, save the snaggle-tooth who was carried on a rough stretcher of boughs and rags.

I told Harold and Tostig my story, at which they swore and exclaimed with anger at all the appropriate points and I found myself warming to them (despite being yet wary of their violence).

'I knew Holgar,' said Harold. 'Not well … but I've not spent much time at home in East Anglia since the king saw fit to promote me to Wessex.'

'East Anglia?' I echoed in confusion, and Tostig laughed.

'You're in the presence of your lord, fool!'

'My lord?'

Harold slapped me over the shoulder and laughed himself.

'Our brother Gyrth is your lord … but Gyrth is with the king. Tostig is Earl of Northumbria. And I, by the grace of King Edward, am Earl of Wessex, but I own many hides yet in East Anglia … which I suppose makes you my tenant and vassal Brand Holgarsson … thegn of Stybbor.'

Such was the confidence I felt in this stranger – and such was the sudden overwhelming sense of acceptance and welcome – that I fell to my knees and blinked at him through tears of relief and adoration.

'My Lord! Please accept—'

'Get up you idiot!' roared Tostig, and all in the procession turned to stare at us. Even the serfs seemed to be laughing.

'Nay,' smiled Harold, 'offers of love and fealty are solemn matters and not to be taken lightly. Do you offer your fealty Brand?'

'I do Lord … gladly.'

'Then rise … and my first command is that you tell me about the woman in your party.'

'Valla?'

I was surprised, and strangely disturbed by the question, but before I could answer, Valla ten paces ahead of us turned and said, 'I am Brand's wife, Lord.'

If I was surprised by Harold's question, I was stunned by Valla's response – Valla who had scorned and insulted me at every turn.

'So,' said Harold, giving me a queer look. 'You are young to be married. Is she a Christian wife or Danish?'

'Wife *more danico*,' said Carl, also turning to join the conversation.

'Your bride dresses strangely for the wife of a thegn,' remarked Tostig.

'He has only recently become thegn,' reminded Valla, 'in unexpected and desperate circumstances.'

'There is that,' agreed Harold.

'And there was no opportunity to dress properly when we took flight … was there husband.'

Valla stared at me most pointedly and, in my confusion, I just nodded – aware that she must have some powerful reason for the lie.

'Well, married then,' said Harold, cheerfully. 'Good thing you told us before Tostig swept her off to his own bed.'

∞ ∞ ∞

I was still more than a little bewildered, some time later, when I managed to fall in step with my 'wife' out of earshot from the others.

'Well, well … it looks as though my visions of you lying naked beneath me are coming true after all.'

'I believe you owe me your life,' hissed Valla. 'Not to mention your ring … of office.'

'Why did you tell Harold we're married?'

'Isn't it obvious?' she replied. 'We're surrounded by men of war … men accustomed to taking without asking. I must preserve my maidenhood, and the only way to do that among such men is to be already married to one of them.'

As she spoke, I knew it to be true, but I had a few questions of my own.

'But … as your husband, I'll be expected to go to your chamber at night … '

'And so you shall while we're in their company … but you'll not be sleeping in my bed.'

'What?' I demanded. 'You suggest the thegn of Stybbor should sleep on the floor like a dog?'

'The thegn of Stybbor can please himself, as long as he plays the part I require of him.'

'And if I refuse?'

'You can't refuse. You've already confirmed the arrangement to Harold and his brother, which according to Carl makes it official. Danish marriage … *more danico* … is simple to arrange.'

'You mean we really *are* married?'

'In all senses but one … there will be no consummation.'

Strangely enough, I found myself grinning. Valla might have

said that she would never lie naked beneath me but, now I was her husband, I considered my chances had rather improved.

Chapter 7

A Profoundly Arousing Pleasure

We could smell Theodford long before we could see it.

There must have been nothing but tanners and butchers because the place smelled like rotting meat, turd and piss – all mixed together with vomit and fermenting into a stench so strong and foul I thought I would never scour it from my nose and throat. And that was from half a mile away!

When it finally came into view, I was amazed not so much by its size as by the concentration of so many dwellings in one place. There had to be hundreds of shacks and hovels all clustered together around a church and a strange-looking conical hill, which looked like a good site for a fort – and sure enough, as we approached, I could see men watching from the summit. Harold raised a great standard – *The Fighting Man* he called it – with the strangely angular warrior brandishing his sword on a white field with a red and gold border, and the banner was answered by those on the hilltop who dipped their own flag twice in acknowledgment of Harold's return.

A shallow stream flowed through the town, which we forded – the water rising no higher than our knees and the stench increasing with every step. In area, the town was not much bigger than the village of Stybbor, but Stybbor had only twenty or so small buildings between the church and the monastery, whereas Theodford must have had hundreds all crammed and clustered together with wattle walls, thatch and wooden roofs, and in between them tiny, twisting lanes like the game trails of the forest. And although it hadn't rained for some days, the lanes were all thick with mud. As we passed, women threw scraps and slops onto the ground outside their doors and grimy children pissed against their own wattle walls. There were butchers hanging joints and carcases which dripped onto the ground and tables of eels and fish next to a vast tannery with its vats of piss and pig shit for the curing of leather. Smoke seemed to pour from every roof and fires burned in forges and open kitchens.

The main street of the town headed more or less straight towards the church. People – hundreds of people – far more than I had ever seen in one place – thronged from their houses and lined the street to catch a glimpse of Harold and his party. Harold was cheered but the serfs were jostled and jeered and pelted with garbage. Slops and buckets were thrown over them and the stink of turd was stronger than ever.

Valla looked terrified and, dressed in similar fashion to the serf women, she was soon mistaken for one of them and attacked by the hags of the town. A woman, snarling with delighted venom, threw a bucket of piss at Valla, splashing me also. But before I could react, Tostig bellowed in anger and clubbed the woman with a mailed fist, so that she collapsed into the mud with blood streaming from her broken nose and mouth.

'Can't you protect your own wife, Brand?' laughed Tostig, as I stared at the woman groaning and bleeding in the filth until she was trampled and obscured by the crowd that followed hard behind us, calling for Harold to resolve arguments or give favours.

As we approached the church, I could see yet another large building standing well away from the cluttered mass of shacks and hovels, raised above the ground on stone foundations but with sturdy wooden walls and a wooden roof. It was surrounded by a six foot fence of thorn and sharpened stakes, with a large courtyard and even a stable. I had seen few horses in my short life.

'Welcome to my house,' said Harold. 'I stay here rarely, but for tonight we will linger.'

The new serfs were led over to the stable where a huge man with a black beard was tending a forge, and the women began to wail.

'What will become of them Lord?' asked Valla, and Harold glanced over with little interest.

'Do you have no bonded servants of your own?' asked Tostig, strangely amused I thought.

'We have servants,' I replied.

'Then your wife should know that these scum will be marked with Harold's device so that should they ever stray they can be reclaimed and corrected.'

As he spoke, the first of the men – the snaggle-toothed red head – was branded on the arm where he'd been cut by my sword, thus marking and sealing his wound in one action, causing him to erupt yelping from his stupor, and causing Tostig and the other soldiers to laugh – Tostig almost doubled over with mirth.

The rest of the serfs were pushed into line for marking but Harold was beckoning me up his stairs and shouting for servants.

'Rooms!' he shouted to a fat and flustered chamberlain, who glanced at me askance from his deep bowing.

'I need two extra guest rooms,' boomed Harold. 'One fit for a man of God ... and one for a thegn and his lady.'

Harold's house was large and open, and despite our proximity to the stinking town, smelt clean and sweet, not unlike my home in Stybbor. Carl, Valla and I were ushered down a passageway by a couple of servants as Harold cried after us, 'Come to me in an hour Brand. We have much to talk about.'

∞ ∞ ∞

'Tostig wonders,' said Valla, sitting at a low table, brushing the tangles out of her long, black hair.

'In that case,' I said, 'you should act in a way to allay his suspicions.'

Valla was dressed in a pale green samite gown with a black girdle. It had been delivered by one of the servants with the message that Harold wanted to see Valla restored to garb befitting her station. Valla had ordered me to turn my back as she changed out of her skins and rags but I had managed to sneak a glimpse of her and felt heady with desire – to be in a rich bedchamber with my naked 'wife' was a profoundly arousing pleasure.

'He stares at me,' shuddered Valla.

'I do not!'

'*Tostig* fool ... what sort of husband misses the carnal stares of other men?'

'Maybe if I had the rights of a husband, I'd be more attentive to the duties … '

'Your right, husband, is to continue living … in gratitude to she who slew Olaf the Pighammer, and could slay thee in thy turn.'

I laughed, amused by what (I was fairly sure) must be a novel situation in the strange lives of men and women.

'I'm not going to argue with you on our wedding night,' I said, and for the first time, Valla seemed to relax a little in my presence. She might even have smiled at my jest.

'How long do we need to maintain the pretence,' I asked, enjoying watching her comb. 'I'm going to Lundene, but now we're out of the woods and in the company of Harold, I suppose I could release you from your contract to come with me all the way.'

Valla paused in her combing.

'And you will honour your promise? To give me the forest?'

I gulped, but nodded. The promise so easily given when it had little chance of being fulfilled, now seemed absurdly generous. With the support of Harold, who could choose between Malgard and me as our liege lord, it seemed that my victory was already complete.

'I have no desire to go to Lundene,' said Valla, resuming her combing, 'but we made a contract and I feel honour-bound to fulfil my part of it. I shall continue.'

'Perhaps that's just as well,' I said, greatly pleased that she was staying. 'It would be difficult to explain your return to Stybbor … where surely you lived as my wife in blissful content, until the Danes came.'

'The man I truly marry,' she said, putting her comb down. 'Must be worthy of me.'

'Worthy!' I exclaimed. 'In case it's escaped your attention, your husband is thegn of Stybbor. Most people would say that, for a cave-dwelling bog-witch, you've rather come up in the world.'

Valla stared at me – her eyes freezing with contempt.

'Simpleton,' she hissed. 'Fool! Is that how you account worth? The peculiar manner of your birth?'

'It is God's way,' I said, remembering Waldo's teaching. 'God has appointed his church and the king to make order for other men. But who are you to talk about peculiar births … oh Valla of the two hundred and forty-two years?'

'If you were truly worthy,' she said, ignoring my deft revelation of her hypocrisy, ' ... truly worthy of taking my maidenhead and sending Valla on to a new birth ... you would demonstrate that, like Valla, you are above or beyond the petty rules and orderings of other men ... thegn or no.'

'How do I do that?' I asked, genuinely perplexed.

'That's for you to work out ... husband.'

∞ ∞ ∞

Carl looked very different.

Gone were his Viking breeches and smock, and Harold's smiths had removed the iron collar. He now wore a long linen shirt, tied at the waste with a light silver chain, white stockings and a brown cloak and cowl, thrown back off his shoulders. His beard was shaved, his long hair had been cut, as though shaped with a bowl, and a tonsure had been shaved in his crown.

'It is three years since my capture,' he said, constantly running his hand around his neck which was heavily scarred from the collar. 'I have much time to make up ... to resume God's work.'

'Did you achieve no evangelism among the Danes?' asked Harold, standing in front of a crackling fire in the largest hearth I had ever seen. Harold also was washed and shaved and dressed in a dark blue tunic, richly made of fine spun wool, and matching blue stockings. Around his shoulders was hung a heavy chain of bronze with a gold pendant like enough to the shape of *The Fighting Man*.

'Perhaps,' said Carl. 'Conversion to the one true God can happen suddenly in the heart of a man who has spent years in the company of Christians ... and didn't know he was becoming a Christian until the moment it happened.'

'What about Ulrik?' asked Harold. 'Could he ever be Christian?'

Carl shuddered.

'I will pray for him,' he said.

'I will also pray,' I added, 'although I freely concede my prayers for Ulrik have little to do with salvation.'

That got a laugh from the warriors listening and more ale was poured into wooden cups. I tried to take it slowly, remembering my last bout with ale at my brother's wedding, but Tostig kept jogging my arm and encouraging me to drink cup after cup.

'Drink Brand!' he cried. 'We are warriors, you and I. We must take our pleasures as they come for do we not risk all in the service of our lords? It is meet that your lord lavishes now food and drink upon you so waste not the opportunity to gorge!'

I found myself very much liking Tostig, but I was starting to notice the looks he gave Valla. She stood close to me – close enough for a wife, but not close enough for me to take advantage of the situation and hold her with husbandly affection.

Harold had me repeat my story for the benefit of his favoured retainers and for his Minister Olwin.

'Olwin was Minister to my father Godwin,' said Harold, 'and a wiser man never drew breath in all Inglalond.'

Olwin, a tall, elderly and rather dignified looking man with still some black in the edges of his moustache and beard bowed deeply in response to his master's compliment.

'If I have any wisdom sire, then it can only have been gotten at the feet of your honoured father.'

'To Godwin,' shouted Tostig, raising his cup. 'The true power behind the throne of Inglalond. His victory is at hand!'

'To Godwin!' roared the room, and I raised my cup in turn and drained it as they did.

Somehow, in the last few seconds, the mood had changed. Suddenly, the men all seemed ready to fight and Harold glared at me, and then at Carl.

'Know ye that we serve the king, Brand?' he asked.

'Yes Lord,' I said, confused by the question and a little befuddled by ale.

'The office of the king we hold in the highest esteem,' said Harold, insistently, as though speaking before the witan.

'The office of the king,' agreed Olwin, ' ... but not always the man!'

If I was confused by the question I was frightened by the elaboration and the glares of defiance. Then Valla said, 'You hold not Edward in esteem Lord?'

Harold considered her for a moment and said, 'Your wife is political Brand?'

I didn't know what to say or think. Part of me was confused utterly by the conversation and I was wary of insulting my lord and host through ignorant response. Another part of me was embarrassed that my 'wife' was taking part in the speech of men – a part I should have been playing myself.

'I'm not sure I know what you mean by political,' I replied, dragging my ale-sodden wits together, 'but she speaks her mind Lord, and 'tis perilous to stop her.'

It was the right answer. Harold boomed with laughter, and Valla gave me a genuine smile – the first time ever, and I felt a warmth.

'The Lord protect us from wise women,' laughed Harold. 'The Lady Valla reminds me of my own Lady Swanneshals, who will join us at table.'

'The Lady Valla,' I whispered, smiling at her, but her own smile faded and she said to Harold, 'Are you political Lord?'

'What man is not?' asked Tostig, answering for his brother. 'But I know what I would do with a political woman young Brand … give her something else to think about. Some sons perhaps?'

Most of the men laughed, and I found myself saying, 'Valla hopes for a daughter.'

'A daughter, Lady Valla?' asked Harold.

'Yes Lord,' she replied, and at that moment, the room temperature changed again as all marked a new presence in the doorway – a woman – tall and comely, with long blond hair and dressed in white samite with a silver bodice.

'Eadgifu!' announced Harold. 'My Lady Swanneshals … come meet our guests and neighbours, from Stybbor.'

And so I first beheld the beautiful Swanneshals – daughter of Danes and married to Harold *more danico* – a union regarded as honourable among men but unbinding by the church, which is why Carl had suggested it to Valla as useful for her predicament.

'You were discussing motherhood?' enquired Swanneshals, gliding towards us but with eyes only for Valla – the only other woman in the room. 'But surely this wife is yet young to bear children.'

Valla blushed, embarrassed by the attention, as Swanneshals examined her and continued, 'For a young woman, motherhood is akin to heaven. We all want to get there … but not yet.'

The men all laughed, admiring her wit.

'As I was just saying, my Lady Swanneshals,' said Harold, 'the Lord protect us from wise women.'

'We are perilous,' agreed Swanneshals, 'but more tragic yet it is to go through life without a partner of whom one is worthy.'

There were some tight smiles but also frowns as her words were digested. She seemed to be staring at me, as though her words had special meaning for me personally and I felt an awe, as though she had been an invisible presence during my conversation with Valla on the same subject. The ale seemed to be surging again in my head and I resolved to speak as little as possible in order to retain the dignity I knew I was in danger of losing – although it was hard to seem undignified in the company of Tostig, who threw his arm around my shoulders and shouted to the room, 'Six men he would take on, when we met him! Six! And two of them Godwinsons! Not yet fifteen but this Brand is already a warrior after my own heart and together we shall slay thousands!'

I was in my element among the warriors (despite never having slain anyone), and held myself tall as my bones and sinews would allow. Despite my youth, I was already taller than some of the retainers and seemed to understand for the first time that I might grow to be a large man. Certainly my dead brother Gram had been tall, and Holgar also had been large and well muscled. I joined eagerly into the drinking and the boisterous conversation but was aware of Swanneshals leading Valla by the hand to an alcove with divans either side of a window made of many glass panels, which flickered red in the light of the hearth. There were rushes on the stone floor and many candles about the room giving a strange but cheerful glow to proceedings. The other men, retainers and warriors for the most part, were already quite drunk and boasting of their various exploits. The petty skirmish of the day was soon forgotten as they passed on to more honourable and close-fought battles against Danes and others of whom I'd never heard.

'The Danes are few and scattered these days,' said Harold, 'which is one of the things that makes Brand's tale so curious. We are entertained more regularly by the Welsh.'

'The Welsh?' I echoed thickly. 'Who are the Welsh?'

'Sheepfuckers!' shouted Tostig. 'The Welsh are a race of sheepfuckers who live in the west ... and Gruffydd ap Llewelyn is their king. King Sheepfucker!'

'All hail King Sheepfucker!' roared Hereborn, one of Tostig's men and somehow it seemed like the funniest thing I'd ever heard. My head whirled with delirious mirth and I felt my lungs and guts would explode trying to get all the laughter out. Tostig also was purple-faced once again, with tears rolling down his cheeks. Only Harold seemed to be unaffected by either ale or laughter, but he smiled at the mood of the men.

'Fond of sheep they may be,' he said, 'but they fight well, and 'tis perilous to go into their marches unprepared. They will not show themselves in numbers but raid camps in the night, ambush stragglers and shoot shafts from thickets to take brave men in the van. So tell me Brand ... how do you fight an enemy that will not openly fight?'

'Make them fight,' I said, without thinking. 'Go where they have no choice and burn their homes ... as the Danes do.'

Carl glared at me, tight-lipped with disapproval, but most of the men growled their agreement.

'That must be the final resort,' agreed Olwin, 'but if you are to rule these people Lord, I would have them love you ... not hate you and swear revenge.'

'Rule?' I echoed drunkenly, as a servant refilled my cup, and once again I sensed the hidden violence in the room. 'Doesn't the king rule?'

But at that moment a bell rang at the end of the hall, and the fat chamberlain bowed to Harold, announcing that meat was now set on the boards.

∞ ∞ ∞

We were seated at three large tables, and I was honoured to sit with Harold and Tostig, but disappointed that Valla and the Lady Swanneshals were seated separately with Carl.

The food was like a wedding feast – rich and varied – with hot, fragrant loaves, thick cuts of pork and beef, game pies, eels and duck. There was salt, for those who desired it, and herbs steeped in broths of pease, grain and chicken bones. Then there were honey cakes and a sharp, pleasant cheese.

And ale. Ale was poured constantly into the wooden cup by my right hand, although some of the men were now drinking a wine like blood from goblets fashioned of dark metal. It was incredible that I could be so full, accepted and content just days after the slaughter of my family, then the flight and famine and somehow I understood that it was the acceptance more than the ale that was responsible for my happy mood. With Harold's support, my revenge on Malgard seemed a formality.

But through my drunken haze I was slightly troubled by Olwin's words. 'Doesn't the king rule?' I had asked, stupidly speaking my thoughts aloud. And Harold had agreed, 'Yes Brand … the king rules.'

Amid all the laughter and tumult, I found myself staring at him – a tall, strong and handsome man. Kingly he seemed, yet not the king.

'Lord Harold,' I asked, aware that I was possibly trespassing on delicate ground, but heedless under the influence of ale. 'How does one become king when not the son of the king?'

There were some surprised glances about the table, and suddenly the room was silent.

'One must have the favour of the witan,' said Olwin. 'Even the son of a king cannot rule without the witan.'

I dimly knew from listening to my father and brother talking politics that the witan was a council of lords that met twice a year to discuss matters of importance to the realm, but Olwin seemed to accord them power concerning the king.

'Lord Harold already has such favour,' claimed Tostig, but Harold shook his head.

'I have the favour of the witan as Subregulus … no more. Edward may select his successor, and I have little hope it could be a son of Godwin.'

'The witan will not accept his choice unless it be you Lord,' insisted Olwin, but Harold seemed to withdraw into silence, and a mood came over the hall. I found myself staring once more at Valla – my 'wife' – and admiring her beauty, which seemed so more pronounced with combed hair and dressed in a fine gown.

A skald who had been plucking on a harp for some time now

raised his voice to sing sweetly in a strange tongue. The words I knew not but the music seemed to paint pictures in my drunken head of mountains and mist-filled valleys in a far land untouched by men. Valla came from such a land – from the empty marshes on the far edges of my forest – and I pondered her words again: that the man she truly married must be worthy of her. Well, if being a thegn wasn't worthy of her, what chance did I have? A vague resentment grew in me but also a bubbling lust. Until I'd been promised to the church and encouraged to chastity, the drabs and wenches of my father's hall had been mine to use as I took the fancy, so why not Valla? And she was my 'wife' after all.

The skald's song had moved on and was now louder and more urgent. He was singing in our normal tongue of Harold and his deeds and the men became loud again – cheering the exploits of their Lord, until Harold – seemingly embarrassed by the praise – bid the skald peace and the conversation returned to its former raucous din.

Not only did I feel taller, the ale made me feel older and wiser amid the councils of the great and I turned to Tostig to ask a man's question, 'You mentioned before that your father was the true power behind the throne?'

Tostig eyed me keenly for a moment, then shook his head.

'Our father, the Earl Godwin, has been dead these seven summers … but his time is at hand.'

'His time,' I echoed, feeling drunk and stupid once again.

Tostig glanced quickly over his shoulder to check who was listening to our conversation and spoke in a lower voice, 'You have sworn your vengeance on Malgard, have you not?'

'Yes Lord.'

'I too have sworn revenge … although Harold will not. He prefers peace to his own advancement. But I would have weregeld for our father, our exiled brothers … and our sister. The kingdom.'

'You've sworn vengeance on Edward?'

Tostig stared at me and I felt a tremor of what it would be like to have him as an enemy – almost certainly fatal.

'Edward banished our father Godwin,' he snarled, revealing somewhat of the angry passion he normally kept in reserve. ' … sent us from Inglalond. But we returned … stronger than ever …

and made Edward take back our sister whom he had married but abandoned to a convent.'

Tostig poured more ale, for himself and for me, and continued, getting angrier and louder, 'Long has he abandoned her. He comes not in her chamber and she is childless … thus is his revenge on the house of Godwin. There is no heir.'

'But now Edward grows old,' said Olwin, alerted to the conversation by Tostig's anger. 'All Inglalond looks to Harold for the safety of the realm. Edward must name him.'

'All Inglalond perhaps,' said Tostig, 'but there are others beyond this island who have their own designs. The aetheling Edgar for one … Hardrada for another … and even the Bastard of Normandy has been heard to claim that Edward promised him the succession.'

'The Bastard of Normandy?' I asked.

'Duke William,' said Olwin. 'He rules the western duchy of the Franks.'

'But he is far away,' sneered Tostig, 'and has no friends here, save the king.'

'He has another friend,' said Harold, also joining the conversation. 'Duke William is a good man … a strong man. I admire him … from an ignoble beginning he has grown wise and strong in war.'

'Beginnings,' muttered Tostig. 'No family begins noble. It is endings that fill the pages of history books.'

'To happy endings!' I slurred, raising my cup, and Harold smiled.

'I trust we will all make good ends and be remembered,' he said, 'but speaking of endings, I must leave this feast and bid you all good evening. It was good to meet you Brand … you mean to go to Lundene?'

'Yes Lord. I must see the king before Malgard learns I yet live, ere he do further evil.'

'Then travel with us … for to Lundene we go ourselves, in the morning.'

He rose, as yet another drunken wave coursed through me – somehow making me feel strong and invincible. Valla had left some time earlier – affecting the manners of the Lady Swanneshals she had curtseyed to Harold (and to me, to my great amusement) – and now I was filled with the hot burning lust of youth as I drunkenly contemplated my 'wife' waiting in my chamber.

We all staggered to our feet as Harold left the room, and I resolved immediately to test Valla's resistance to my husbandly affection. 'Give her one from me!' shouted Tostig as I followed the chamberlain's candle, my shoulders bouncing off the walls of the corridor behind his rounded shadow. He paused at a door and stepped back to allow me access.

Taking a candle from the chamberlain, I strode into the room feeling ten feet tall and very confident that my wife must do as I bade her – bog-witch or no.

The green gown lay discarded on the floor and my pulse quickened at the sight of it, but as I raised the candle I perceived the bed was empty.

'Valla,' I whispered hoarsely, my mind filling with lustful images. 'Where are you?'

The silence of the room finally convinced me that I was alone, and I moved towards the shuttered windows which were wide open, allowing a cool breeze despite the time of year. Then I noted that a stool had been placed beneath the window. Surely she hadn't gone outside.

I placed the candle in an embrasure by the bed and peered out the window, the breeze in my face inspiring a fresh wave of drunkenness as I peered into the moonlit courtyard.

'Valla!' I called in a loud whisper, but there was no response. The yards were silent except for the noises coming faintly from the town beyond the gate and the night-speech of crickets and other small and nameless creatures.

The lust I had felt so strongly only moments before had completely passed. I was very drunk, very tired and tempted by the large bed, but I was horrified at the prospect of having to explain an absent wife in the morning, so I clambered out the window and resolved to find her.

I dropped to the ground, landing on my slippered feet but toppling forward into dry mud which caked the knees of my fine stockings.

'Fuck!' I shout/whispered, brushing at my knees in anger – getting mud on my hands. Looking along the wing of the large house, only my shutters were open, so it would be simple enough to find the room again – but in my drunken state it would be an awkward climb back to the window, about six feet from the ground.

Which way could Valla have gone? To my right was the gate – some thirty yards away – where two sentries stood with their backs to me, facing the town. To my left was darkness – the back of the house and the smaller buildings housing animals and servants.

I went left, stepping carefully in the pale moonlight. The crickets seemed to get louder and two dogs started barking in the distance. The largest of the unattached buildings loomed in front of me – the stable I believed – and immediately stepped in a pile of dung to confirm it. Again I swore in anger and disgust and found the edge of an open door to scrape my soft leather slipper. There was a rich smell of hay and horses coming from the stable and I wondered whether the door was usually left open. Perhaps Valla had come this way?

I stepped into the deeper darkness of the stable and heard the nervous movement of beasts detecting my presence. I remained still, just inside the door – straining my ears for any sound.

A thud – like the sound of iron on wood – did not seem the kind of noise an animal would make, so I turned in that direction and crept through the darkness. Presuming it was Valla, what on earth was she up to? Not stealing a horse, surely! I could think of no other reason for her being here and felt both anger and fear – anger at her ingratitude to our host and fear of my humiliation were she to succeed.

And fear of losing Valla.

If she was stealing a horse then clearly she was leaving, despite her agreement to go all the way to Lundene. I didn't want to lose her so soon. In fact, I didn't want to lose her at all, and was amazed at the depth of my feelings in such a short time. Despite her insults – despite her distance and warnings – despite even her occasional threats to geld me I was drawn to her helpless as a silk-bound fly in the web of a spider.

Another thud, and further restive shuffling from the animals.

'Valla!' I called, in a louder whisper, and continued moving towards the sounds, stubbing my toes against some heavy object. I groped on the ground and found a long-handled tool – possibly a rake left by a farrier or groom or such – and decided it might be useful. Clutching it like a weapon, I moved forward.

Another thud, and one of the horses snorted irritably. Then a louder clang as something of metal was broken. Then muttering voices in the darkness.

I froze, suddenly perceiving what was happening.

The animals whimpered as I groped my way back towards the door, limned with moonlight, but in my haste I kicked something in the darkness which clattered loudly to the ground.

There was a muffled shriek, and a sibilant curse, and then I heard them moving swiftly towards me – escaping serfs – Rockers skilled at killing in darkness.

I made it to the doorway, holding my weapon before me, when suddenly they came from all sides – rushing past me.

'Stop!' I shouted and swung my weapon, connecting only with the side of the barn, but the shout and the whack of my weapon on wood inspired an answering shout from the sentries and I knew help was coming.

Then someone barged into me, throwing me heavily to the ground, but I held onto my weapon and from my knees swung it again in the darkness, this time connecting hard against flesh and bone.

There was a cry, and further scattering of shadows as sentries came running with a flaming torch.

'Serfs escaping!' I shouted, as a hand wrapped around my mouth, but I bit hard on a finger and heard a female squeal.

More soldiers came running from the house and more torches shed light on the confusion.

I was on my knees, pissed in the mud, blinking at the men holding torches and shouting angrily. One large fellow – a sergeant in a shirt of rings, like Angdred's, was barking orders and men ran about the yard and behind the stable searching. Stretched out in front of me was a body – the red haired snaggle-tooth, bleeding from an ugly wound on his right temple.

'What the fuck is this?' demanded the sergeant, standing over the body.

'Escaping serf,' I slurred stupidly, brandishing my rake.

Yet more torches came, from the house, and Tostig was suddenly striding about in our midst, barking orders and clearly enjoying himself, apparently unaffected by all the ale and wine he'd drunk.

'Sconed the fucker?' he asked me, kicking the red-haired snaggle-tooth in the guts, causing him to stir and groan.

'Where are the rest?' shouted the sergeant. 'Find 'em … quickly!'

No more serfs were found but a hole in the thorn fence was discovered, behind the stable. Then another soldier showed Tostig the broken lock from the room where the serfs had been held.

Tostig swore and kicked the snaggle-tooth until he was curled into a ball, vainly warding the blows.

'Someone helped you!' he shouted, between kicks. 'Who the fuck let you out?'

'Leave him!'

A woman's voice, cold as wind off snow, cut through the shouting and violence, and all turned to see the Lady Swanneshals, standing on the edge of the torchlight.

'Put him back in the stable,' she said. 'He has suffered enough.'

'For now,' agreed Tostig, and allowed the snaggle-tooth to be carried away.

'Well done Brand,' said Tostig, fury turning instantly to glee as he remembered my part in the battle. 'Can't keep you out of a fight, can we lad?'

The rest of the men crowded about me, praising my vigilance and resourcefulness.

But Swanneshals just stared at me for a moment and returned to the house. Tostig and I followed.

'Fucking inside help,' muttered Tostig. 'Someone has made a hole in the fence and then broken the lock on the serfs' prison. The rats knew where to run when they got out.'

'Except one.'

'Except one,' he agreed, laughing. 'That ginger bugger's had a good day hasn't he? First he gets cut by your blade last night … then he gets thumped by Hereborn this morning … branded, locked up, clouted by your rake and now he's getting the shit kicked out of him by the lads. Happy fucking Tuesday!'

I laughed, but inside I was in a turmoil. Valla had clearly been the one to set the serfs free and now she was gone. This would certainly be established in the morning when she was revealed as missing, and maybe even the snaggle-toothed red head would identify her as his temporary liberator. I would be humiliated, and it even occurred to me to go back to his cell and find an excuse to kill him before he could tell that damning truth to his interrogators.

But, warrior though I wished to be, murdering defenceless serfs (however inconvenient) was not the honourable path. It would have been an act worthy of Malgard, no doubt, but not Brand Holgarsson.

As the tumult died down, I found my way back down the passage and re-entered my chamber. It was dark and I muttered angrily about the candle having gone out, but a little light came in the open window.

Enough light to show that someone slept in the bed.

'Valla?'

'Be quiet,' she said, sleepily. 'You may sleep in the bed, but leave your clothes on and keep your back to me.'

Relief washed over me as I sat on the bed to remove my muddy slippers.

'Why did you set them free?' I asked.

But Valla's breathing had become slow and even.

I just sat for a moment, listening to her breathing and imagining how it would be to have her in my bed forever. Then, I reached under the blanket and felt her feet.

I'd expected to find them muddy but they were quite clean, and she murmured, 'I'm sorry ... sorry ... ' but whether to me or in a dream, I was never to know.

And despite her warning to keep my clothes on, I shrugged them all onto the rushes and slipped into the bed, to lie in chaste nakedness against the sleeping body of the beautiful girl I had married *more danico*. The girl who had become to me the profound quintessence of womanhood.

Chapter 8

His Greatness and Subtlety

I woke to the smell of turd, and found Valla shitting into a pot.

She had her back to me, but turned and saw me watching her.

'May I not have some privacy?' she demanded and I closed my eyes, but in my mind I could still see her shapely back and the side-glimpse of her small breasts.

'Why did you do it?' I asked, ignoring the smell.

'Do what?'

'Release the serfs.'

I snuck my eyes open a fraction and saw her reach for a handful of rags – then I rolled over.

'The serfs have escaped?' she asked.

'All but one.'

Valla affected nonchalance, but I could tell she was concerned.

'Which of the serfs failed to escape?' she asked.

'Who knows?' I lied. 'They all look the same to me.'

Then I said, 'Do you have any idea how humiliated I would have been if you'd run away?'

'I didn't go anywhere,' defended Valla. 'I went to see the Lady Swanneshals.'

'You went naked did you? Your dress was on the floor when I came back to the room.'

Valla didn't deign to answer. She pushed the pot under the bed and dragged her cloak of skins and rags over her shoulders.

'You can't wear that to Lundene,' I said. 'You're the wife of a thegn, remember?'

She continued to ignore me and I started to feel anger.

'I won't have you keeping secrets from me!' I said, raising my voice as I might have with one of the servants of my father's household.

'Is that how you would talk to your wife?' snapped Valla.

'My wife, if she were a proper wife, wouldn't sneak about in the night releasing prisoners.'

'But I'm not a proper wife, Brand ... you know that. I saved you from Olaf and now you are returning the favour.'

It was all getting too confusing – like we were having three different conversations at once.

'But you did release the serfs.'

It wasn't a question and Valla didn't answer.

'Harold and Tostig will be furious,' I said. 'There will be an investigation and if you are identified it will ruin my relationship with Harold ... who has agreed to help me defeat Mal—'

I was stunned into silence as Valla suddenly cast off her skins and rags and stood naked before me.

I felt my jaw gaping like a fool and tried to marshal my wits into some sort of order. Valla's body was staggering – lithe and strong – lightly browned from the sun, with breasts like small hard fruits and a downy shadow between her legs that seemed so refined in contrast with the thick bushes of the servants of my father's hall.

Suddenly embarrassed to be staring, I tore my eyes from her body and looked her in the face.

'What was I saying?'

'You were lecturing me, husband.'

'... I was?'

She turned her back and picked up the green dress, pulling it over her head – every movement an enticement and it was all I could do not to throw myself upon her.

'I did not leave this room last night, did I husband?'

'Erm ... '

'If the Lord Brand swears his wife did not leave her chamber, then who shall dare suggest otherwise?'

'Well ... no-one I suppose.'

'You suppose correctly,' said Valla, straightening the dress, and if it were possible, looked even more desirable clad than unclad.

'It's time you started thinking like a lord, Brand. If you will something then it shall be so.'

'Truly?' I asked, beginning to grin.

But her lip curled in a fine scorn, and she said, 'Except, of course, where I am concerned.'

∞ ∞ ∞

After a late and leisurely breakfast, the household was assembled in the yard. There were about a dozen warriors led by Harold, another four led by Tostig, and myself. Most of the warriors had a page or other servant to help with their baggage and weapons. There was also a wagon pulled by a horse with victuals for the journey and other gear, including a large canvas tent and the spare weapons I had collected from the Danes. There was also Carl Two-tongues, looking very fine in his new brown robes, and Valla – the only woman in the party. And already I was jealously aware of the sly looks the other warriors turned in her direction.

There was also the red-haired snaggle-tooth, who was dragged out of the barn and thrown to the ground before Harold. He looked half dead after his ordeals, which had clearly included rough handling during the night. There was dried blood on his ear and around his nose. His lip was split and there was a new gap in his teeth. A black bruise coloured his right temple and he clutched his ribs as he breathed in shallow gasps, in obvious pain.

'What is your name, serf?' demanded Harold.

'Elric,' he lisped thickly through his broken mouth.

'Elric,' repeated Harold. 'I will give you a choice Elric … death, or service of the Lord Brand.'

If it was possible in his beaten state, Elric managed to look faintly amused.

'The Lord of the Wood?' he asked.

He actually seemed to be considering which might be worse, but eventually bowed before me.

'Kneel,' commanded Harold, and Elric sank into the mud of the yard.

'Place your hand on his head Brand,' said Harold, then in a loud voice he proclaimed, 'Let all here witness the bond of fealty between Brand Holgarsson, lord of Stybbor and the serf Elric. In return for the lord's protection, let Elric serve faithfully and well. And should he break this sworn promise, let vengeance or other doom take him swift and hard. Do you swear Elric?'

'There was a barely audible muttering from Elric, until Tostig half-pulled his sword from its scabbard, and Elric spoke up, 'I swear!'

My hand was shrinking from contact against the lank, greasy hair, crawling with lice, and I foresaw that my own gear would soon be lousy if he came into contact with it – but there was no option other than to swear before Harold, Tostig and their men that I would honour Elric's fealty with protection. Then I snatched my hand away and wiped it against my breeches – an action witnessed by Elric, and I was embarrassed by his challenging stare.

Harold had bid me cast off my Viking gear and had clad me in fine garments of similar look and weave to those worn by his warriors, although I kept the long boots, which fit me very well. Harold had also had my brother's cloak repaired during the night, and I was delighted to see my family's ill-fortune being restored, but saddened to be reminded of my brother's untimely and treacherous death.

Suddenly I was overcome with the urgent desire to get to Lundene where my vengeance might be had. The company drew itself together for departure as the Lady Swanneshals came out to the top of the stairs to wave us off. Harold ran back up and knelt before her, took her hand and kissed it – and I noticed the hand was bandaged. In that moment I remembered biting a finger during the escape of the serfs, and a woman's scream.

I stared at the bandage then looked up and saw her regarding me – knew that she was aware of my recognition – but then she smiled, and I suddenly felt like laughing, as though all treachery was just harmless jest.

∞ ∞ ∞

Malgard was furious.

News of the Viking attack on Stybbor had reached Lundene quickly via the fleece barges that plied from Gipeswic on the Arwan – only a day's journey down the Temes – it would take three or four days to march.

87

The drunken barge captain, with whom he sat in one of the rat-infested inns that clustered about the cess-stinking wharf-side, had told him of the massacre, and also that further Danes had hunted fugitives in the wood and returned defeated – beaten by a witch according to the terrified raving of those that returned to the Danish camp at Stybbor.

Now the captain slumped forward with his head on the table as Malgard racked his brains. That Brand was alive was almost certain, he thought – so let's say he is alive. Let's also say that he knows of my part in the massacre. Malgard's eyes turned black as he realised his peril should Brand bring word to Edward. And he will bring word to Edward, so let's assume he is already coming.

Retracing in his mind his own journey by horse to Lundene along the ancient way, he recalled the large inn at the crossroads at the town of Breahinga. Anyone coming from Stybbor on their way to Lundene was all but certain to stop there – or at least be seen passing by.

Malgard drained his cup and rose from the table. It was time to visit an old friend.

Sleppa would know how to solve the problem.

∞ ∞ ∞

The going was easy for some time.

We marched through the town again, Harold and Tostig at the head of a column of warriors looking grim and purposeful, and there was none of the importuning of the day before, as if the townsfolk knew not to approach their lord in such a mood.

I marched behind Harold and Tostig with Valla and Carl, and behind us came the warriors in two lines, armed with axe, spear and sword. Several of them wore shirts of rings despite the expense, and I understood that these were elite troops – members of the household guard of the two greatest lords of the realm, after the king. Behind them straggled the servants and last of all creaked the wagon, loaded to the brim with food and war gear. Elric, due to his battered condition, was allowed to ride on the wagon, but I suspected it was also a measure to prevent his escape, should such occur to him.

Little did I realise, at the time, how much of the next few years would be spent in that way – marching with warriors, going to or from a battle. It had its horrors and its hardships, but also its joys, and if I am honest I am rarely so happy as when marching.

Certainly, on that blue morn, as we left behind the smoke and stench of Theodford Harold's mood lifted and, as though sensing his lightness of heart, the men started singing as we marched through the winding lanes of East Anglia.

'We should be riding!' said Tostig.

'Not this again,' laughed Harold, and I understood they were continuing a long debate.

'It is not just a means of transport,' insisted Tostig. 'The Frank lords go heavily armoured on horseback and fight above the heads of the fyrd.'

'I will not command men to fight unless I stand with them,' replied Harold. 'And I will not imperil a beast in war because men choose to fight.'

'A commander should know how the whole battle fares,' said Tostig. 'In the shield wall, we see only the foes before us but, from horseback, you can see where the shield wall is holding and where reserves are needed.'

'I have trusted men ... wise in battle along the line. Would you have me usurp their trust by calling all orders myself?'

'All I'm saying,' replied Tostig, 'is that there are new ways of doing warfare. The Franks ... and especially the Normans ... use horses and 'tis said the shield wall cannot stand against them.'

'Maybe not a Frankish shield wall,' sneered Harold. 'But in any case, we have no quarrel with the Normans, and if we did, they could hardly bring their war horses to Inglalond, could they?'

Tostig fell silent and Harold laughed.

'And how would you use your sword atop a horse, brother? One swing of your blade and you'd have its head off! Horses are expensive!'

The sun grew warmer and we all began to sweat. Valla, struggling along in her green dress suddenly vanished into the forest.

'Halt,' called Tostig, raising his arm.

'I'll catch up,' called Valla. 'Don't wait.'

'I'll wait for her,' I said, and the brothers marched on with the column. As the wagon creaked past, I nodded at Elric who nodded in turn but his eyes passed over me to stare at Valla vanishing through the trees. Then he glanced back at me with a look of such insolent triumph I immediately knew something was wrong.

I turned and ran into the woods.

'Valla!' I shouted once, then knew further shouting would be pointless if she chose not to answer.

I ran some fifty yards into the forest but then stopped – stared about at the encircling trees and knew she was the better woodsman. If she wanted to leave, she could leave at any time. With heavy heart, I headed back to the road before I lost myself.

'Why did you shout?'

I looked up and Valla stood on the deeply rutted path, dressed in her cloak of skins – the green dress stuffed into the top of the leather satchel she always carried.

What's more, the dog Malgard was with her – I'd all but forgotten him.

'I smelled the poison of the town,' said Valla. 'It would have been bad for his wound, so I bade him wait for me here. He is a good dog and obeyed, but now he is hungry.'

The meaning behind her words was obvious.

'If he obeys you, then he's your responsibility,' I said. 'And why are you wearing that hideous cloak when Harold gave you such a fine dress? He'll be insulted.'

'The green dress is fit for halls and feasts but 'tis heavy work for marching. And Harold has more to occupy his mind than the garb of women.'

She started walking in the wake of the wagon – a couple of hundred paces ahead – and Malgard romped after her, no longer troubled by the knife wound I had dealt him only four nights ago. I remarked on his recovery and Valla laughed.

'I have some skill with healing,' she said. 'The poultice I made for him contained much of my power. It has drawn out the hurt and repaired the rent … but it was only ever a small wound … oh slayer of yesterday's hares.'

She smiled and I knew she was mocking me, but it was too nice a day to be angry with her. I suddenly felt free and full of purpose. My ambition had cost me my family, due to the manner of God's testing me, but now my mission of revenge had the support of the lords Harold and Tostig, and I was marching to Lundene to see the king in company with Valla, my wife – who seemed to be thawing towards me. She was striding ahead and watching her brown shapely legs was a torment. The cloak of skins seemed to offer glimpses of what it concealed, like a gauzy veil blurring my vision and my wits.

There were things she wasn't telling me – that much was clear. I was all but certain that Valla, in league with the Lady Swanneshals, had freed the serfs the night before. But why? Why would the wife of Harold defy him in such a manner?

I could never think about Valla for long without growing uncomfortably aroused, which did not make for easy marching and I tried to think about something else. Revenge upon Malgard – that soon had me distracted and I began to imagine my audience with Edward, with Harold and Carl at my side to vouch for me – then Malgard in chains, pleading for mercy before his treacherous head was struck from his shoulders and stuck on a spike on Lundene Bridge where the crows and ravens would flense the flesh from his skull while his body was cut to shreds and left in the gutter to be devoured by rats and curs as low as he.

It occurred to me that God would be aware of my vengeance fantasy and would therefore do aught to aid or hinder me as suited His purpose. It then occurred to me that God must be aware of my desire for Valla and that in all likelihood He would devise another test for me.

'I have made a decision,' said Valla, wrenching me out of my reverie.

'What sort of decision?'

'I have decided, husband, that there is some good in you. Therefore, when the time comes … you *may* be the one to take my maidenhead.'

I couldn't have been more shocked if the skies had suddenly opened and God Himself appeared before an army of angels to make the same announcement. I fell to my knees between the ruts of the lane and raised my eyes to heaven – awed and humbled by His greatness and subtlety. I felt tears trickle down my cheeks as Valla approached smiling.

As she did, I felt myself overwhelmed with a love for her so powerful it hurt. I could hardly speak, so overcome with emotion as I was, and it seemed that all of His creation was glowing with blessed perfection like a glimpse of Eden as she stood before me.

'There is a condition,' said Valla, and immediately, I was alert – the love hurt slightly less. 'You must prove yourself worthy … you must swear an oath that you will touch no other woman in this life but me.'

'Willingly,' I cried. 'Only … this time you speak of. When will the time come?'

'That is not yet clear to me,' she smiled. 'It could be days … or it could be years.'

'Years? You ask much of me Valla.'

She stood over me smiling and placed her hands on my shoulders, looking young and beautiful and full of secret promise.

'Am I not worth it?'

Chapter 9

The Equal of a Serf

The two travellers came to Breahinga in the mid afternoon and took ale in the famous inn that had stood at the crossroads since time immemorial. One of them was a large man with a scarred face and nose smashed flat by old arguments. The other was smaller and fine of feature, with quick eyes that reflected a constant weighing of threats and opportunities. Though they hardly spoke to each other, anyone watching the pair would soon be convinced that the smaller man was the leader. He had the air of command, and in fact had led men in battle on many occasions.

Not anymore.

Now he worked for Sleppa. The life was easy and the pay was good for a slayer such as he. His name was Gorik and it did not take long for him to pick out one of the idle locals, begging for ale.

'Sit friend,' said Gorik, to the nervous young man who accepted the invitation, but then looked like he might have regretted doing so as he perceived the malice of his new companions.

Gorik poured him half a cup of ale from their large jug and began to settle his fears with the usual comments about the weather and the coming harvest. There was no talk of politics. Life was quiet in East Anglia – in all of Inglalond – in stark and blessed contrast to all the reigns since Cnut. Edward had no rival for the throne, and since Earl Godwin had died Inglalond had been untroubled. There was no heir, but all expected that Edward's right-hand Harold would be persuaded by the witan to accept the succession. It was so obvious a future than none bothered to remark upon it.

Gorik introduced himself and his companion, Hasted, who appeared to take no interest in the young local, nor Gorik's conversation.

'Rude bastard, ain't he?' laughed Gorik. 'Comes from too much war … when you've seen as many battles as us, you don't bother getting friendly with people. They probably won't be alive for long.'

The young man, whose name was Fassbekka, grinned uncertainly and sipped his ale – accidentally downing all of it in his nervousness.

'How often do you get travellers through Breahinga,' asked Gorik.

'All the time,' said the young man, eyeing the jug. 'Travellers along Stanes and the Way all rest in Breahinga … and the pot merchants of course.'

Gorik picked up the jug and examined it.

'Very fine work,' he remarked, 'but a soldier's more interested in what a pot contains than the manner of its making.'

He poured another half cup for Fassbekka, then topped up his own and Hasted's cups.

'I'm interested in one particular traveller,' said Gorik, lowering his voice. 'Only fourteen years, but a biggish lad … sandy-blond hair … goes by the name of Brand Holgarsson. He might be wearing a green cloak … and he'll probably come down the north-east road.'

'Haven't seen him,' said Fassbekka, once more eyeing the jug.

'Priest,' growled Gorik's large companion.

'Thanks for reminding me Hasted,' said Gorik, then turned back to Fassbekka. 'It's possible that young Brand will be travelling with a monk, by the name of Carl … long brown hair, although he could have shaved it by now.'

'Brand and Carl,' muttered Fassbekka, as Gorik poured him another half cup.

'They're friends of ours,' explained Gorik, 'but we want to surprise 'em … don't we Hasted.'

The hulking Hasted glared back at him and grunted.

'So, if you happen to see Brand … ' said Gorik. His words trailed away but he opened his palm upon which rested a silver coin, at which Fassbekka's eyes widened.

'Few pots of ale there, Fassbekka?'

Fassbekka nodded eagerly as Gorik's hand closed over the coin, but he filled the young man's cup.

Towards the end of the second day of our march, I was walking with Carl – enjoying the unfolding scenes of forest and field as the road wound its way through primrose, anemone and early blackberries towards Lundene. Whole fields of bluebells also grew along the road and Valla would sometimes lie among them, eyes closed and simply breathing until I pulled her smiling to her feet. We saw few people abroad, but many folk were preparing for the harvest which must commence over the next few weeks. Apples and pears were in abundance and barley filled the fields innumerable. It would be a good year if the rains held off.

Elric had been told to walk, so limped along behind me. I wasn't sure what to make of him – obviously I'd known servants all my life, but none had ever seemed so untame as did Elric, with his disturbing glances and knowing smiles. Valla had cleaned up his wounds and bound a poultice over his scarred and branded arm – much to the amusement of Tostig.

'You have a kind-hearted wife, Brand,' he laughed. 'Does she minister so to all beasts?'

I wasn't sure how to respond. I enjoyed Tostig's company, but there was something about him that unnerved me, like a string wound too tight and liable to snap with the wrong pressure. He was too subtle for me, and I suspected that he understood more about my condition than he let on. If I am honest, he scared me – but he also excited me, and made me laugh.

'And what about you Elric?' continued Tostig. 'Did you enjoy having your fetlock repaired by such a fine young lady?'

Elric stared at him, with none of the humility a serf ought to employ in the presence of such a lord.

'I do believe your servant would like to kill me Brand,' laughed Tostig. 'You'd better keep an eye on that one. Didn't he once try to crush your head as you slept?'

With that he strode away grinning, like a boy who had farted in church.

As we walked, I was practicing weaponry – wearing the shirt of rings despite it being overlarge and heavy, and holding the sword at arm's length – trying to build the strength of arm and body I would need to stay alive in a battle.

'Is that the sword that cut me?' asked Elric.

'It is,' I replied, feeling vaguely uncomfortable.

'Shame it didn't take my head off,' he said and fell silent. But not for long enough.

'I hear as you receive messages from God,' said Elric, and I determined in that moment to put him in his place.

'You will speak when spoken to Elric … and not otherwise.'

'Don't be so rude!' exclaimed Valla, and I stared at her in confusion.

'Rude? To a serf? Next you'll be telling me not to be rude to the cat.'

'All people deserve politeness,' insisted Valla.

I glanced at Carl for some sort of support, but he was grinning. Elric looked expressionless, but I sensed his amusement.

'He tried to crush my head with a rock, Valla. That doesn't seem like politeness to me. Just letting him stay alive after that is all the politeness Elric needs.'

'If you want to seem worthy,' said Valla, her eyes like flint, 'you will treat Elric with honour and thanks.'

'Honour and thanks? Forget it!'

Then the word 'worthy' registered, and a good deal of the wind dropped out of my argument.

'This worthiness will become a burden,' I sighed, but Valla smiled and at once I forgot my indignation.

'Very well. Elric, you may speak as you wish … as long as you are polite yourself and show due respect.'

'Due respect?' mused Elric. 'There's plenty of folk don't warrant respect so no respect is what they're due.'

'You are not to be the judge of other men,' I insisted at once. 'If I show respect to any man then you also show respect.'

'But that would rob him of his right to choose,' protested Valla, and I felt like I needed to shake my head to clear it of the nonsense I was hearing.

'No man has the right to choose,' I said, 'save the king. And even he is subject to the choices of God.'

'Is that one of the things you heard from God?' asked Elric.

'Yes,' I said, getting annoyed and impatient with what I suspected was insolence. 'God has ordained Himself the ordering of man's society and it is the lot of serfs to be ruled. Wives also,' I added as Valla began to argue again on Elric's behalf.

'I shall never be ruled, husband,' she hissed, and I could see all the progress we'd made collapsing back into enmity – for what? The rights of a man with no rights?

'It is true that God has ordered the society of men,' interrupted Carl, 'but He has put the clergy at the top of that order, so you must accept my judgment on this.'

Valla sneered, but I nodded tentatively.

'Good,' said Carl, smiling. 'Now ... there is no doubt that Brand, as thegn and reeve of Stybbor, is senior in rank to Valla and Elric, but!' He raised his hand to quell the objection of Valla. 'Out on the road, the conventions are more relaxed ... can we not just be friends and fellow travellers until we come again to the halls of men?'

'Suits me,' said Elric.

'Of course it suits you,' I complained, 'you go from serf to the equal of a thegn ... yet I am asked to be the equal of a serf!'

'It would be a worthy thing,' smiled Valla, and I stared at her.

'Worthy tonight ... or worthy in ten years?'

'Who knows,' she said, suddenly melting my wits once again with her beauty and desirability.

'If I could be worthy tonight,' I said, 'then Elric can be king for all I care.'

∞ ∞ ∞

We came to Breahinga in the late afternoon. A major town at the old crossroads with an inn that Tostig declared to be one of the best in Inglalond.

It was a large house, built partly of stone, with a yard and a stable – similar to Harold's house back in Theodford. There were rooms for the more important folk and a large dormitory to house the rest of the warriors. Elric was put in the stable with the horse and the other servants.

Washing had been an occasional activity in my former life but

I had learned from Harold and Tostig that it was good manners to wash one's face and hands before appearing in company, so called for water to be brought to the room I shared with Valla. Kneeling on the stone floor in front of the bucket, I scooped water onto my face and under my arms, quite enjoying the feeling of being clean after the hot and dusty road.

'Let me try that,' said Valla, and to my amazement, flung off her cloak of skins and knelt, naked, beside me. She splashed water over herself as I gaped at her beauty and immediately felt the serpent uncoiling.

She finished rubbing the dust from her face and turned to me. I expected her to be angry with me for staring at her body, but she smiled and said, 'It is well that you find me comely Brand ... but you must wait. Can you accept that?'

'The waiting is hard,' I said, devouring her with my eyes but fearful that she would cover up at any moment.

'It will be worth it, I promise,' she said, washing her breasts and under her arms as I fought the urge to throw her to the floor. 'You will have all you desire ... as long as you keep your pledge to touch no other woman.'

'Why can't you set me a task?' I complained. 'The waiting would be less of a trial if I could work my way towards some fine deed ... with its due reward.'

'The waiting is the deed,' replied Valla. 'There is no other deed I require of you, and a fine thing it will be also ... to vouchsafe within me the power of Valla and then to father the next Valla from the vessel of my body.'

She turned to face me, water dripping from her breasts down her hard, flat belly.

'Don't you think that would be a fine thing Brand?'

'Yes,' I said thickly, my head whirling with lust, 'but to have you so close, but not to touch, is turning me witless.'

'I would take that as a compliment,' she said, standing and pulling the green dress from her satchel, 'but you must keep your wits. There is an ill feeling to this place.'

It was as though the sun dimmed, and I felt a sudden apprehension. Valla had already demonstrated her uncanny abilities and if she declared a place ill, then ill it was.

'Mind you, that could be said of any inn,' she continued with a shrug, and pulled the dress over her head, affording me one last glimpse of her favours.

'Shall we join the others?'

∞ ∞ ∞

I had never been in an inn before – not like the inn at Breahinga at least. The inn at Stybbor was just the front parlour of one of the villagers. I had been forbidden to enter but had seen inside often enough and it did not compare. The common room (as it was called) in Breahinga was as large as the hall in Harold's house at Theodford, but was filled with benches and tables and two roaring fire pits at either end (for light more than warmth in the middle of summer) and fat candles placed here and there. Harold had yet to join the company but Tostig and the rest of the men dominated one half of the room. The other half was packed with travellers and locals all gathered for the conclusion of business and the passing of news.

There was a smell in the air which at first I found unpleasant but then began to enjoy – a rich earthy smell of sour ale and old ashes, mingled with sweat and perfume. There was also the smell of meat roasting and my growling guts remembered how long it had been since breakfast.

There was also ale of course – a darker ale than I was used to, with a bitter taste, but after half a cup I was enjoying it and crying with laughter at Tostig's jokes.

'Here's another,' he cried. 'What am I?'

He supped long at his mug then, his eyes glinting with mirth, recited, 'I am a wonderful help to women, the hope of something to come. I harm no citizen except my slayer. Rooted, I stand on a high bed. I am shaggy below. Sometimes the beautiful peasant's daughter, an eager-armed, proud woman grabs my body, rushes my red skin, holds me hard, claims my head. The curly-haired woman who catches me fast will feel our meeting. Her eye will be wet.'

There was laughter, but it was an old riddle and before I could help myself, I blurted out the answer, 'An onion.'

If Tostig was momentarily disappointed, his humour was about to improve.

'That's not an onion,' complained Barding, a large oafish warrior with the strange northern accent of Tostig's men.

'Of course it's an onion,' laughed Tostig. 'What did you think it was?'

'I thought it was a man's cock,' complained Barding. 'The joke would have been much funnier if the answer had been a cock.'

Tostig howled with laughter as some of the men tried vainly to explain the joke to Barding, while I supped ale and felt my senses overloaded by so many tantalising smells and sensations wafting about the exciting room. It was a poor substitute for bedding Valla but at least it distracted me from that particular torment.

More ale was poured into my cup as huge platters of meat steaming from the kitchen were placed on the tables and the men gorged, while Valla ate daintily at my side.

'There is definitely an ill feeling to this room,' she repeated. 'I sense the presence of evil as sure as I know the approach of a storm. Can you not feel it in the air? It chokes the breath!'

If I hadn't been so bent on getting as much ale inside my skin as was good for me, I might have been more wary.

'What evil can be done to us among so many warriors?' I asked her, stabbing another cut of roast mutton with my father's knife and dragging it onto the wooden platter before me.

Valla shuddered and took a last sip of the ale.

'I have to get out of this room,' she said. 'And I believe that you also would be best served back in our chamber.'

'Will there be worthiness?'

Valla stared at me, with a flash of her old anger.

'No Brand ... not tonight. Not for a while yet.'

'Then I don't see the hurry in coming back to the chamber,' I replied, reaching for my cup and gulping down more of the dark ale, to which by now I was quite partial.

Valla's eyes narrowed and she looked about to say something, but she rose and left the table. And there was no mistaking the looks the men gave her as she crossed the room and vanished through the portal that led to the sleeping chambers.

'You're a lucky man,' said Tostig as he dropped into Valla's seat beside me.

I just nodded, as he filled my cup. In fact, I was tempted to tell him about my predicament with Valla but I knew what his advice would be, and it wasn't in me to rape her. Maybe that was my problem?

Then I remembered Valla's obsession with rape when I'd first met her and found myself smiling fondly. We'd certainly come a long way since then – married no less, even if only a sham *more danico* marriage. It gave me status in the eyes of the world and the privilege to see her naked in private.

'So what's she like in the sack?' asked Tostig, and I felt myself redden.

'Well?' he prompted. 'Do her eyes water when she peels your onion and puts it in her pantry?'

'Brand's too young to have an onion,' laughed Hereborn, Tostig's head retainer. 'He's only got a chive.'

Hereborn had his arm around the shoulders of one of the local whores, whose numbers seemed to be increasing as the night wore on. There were now several girls among the men, drinking, laughing and negotiating prices.

'I'll find out for you,' said the girl at Hereborn's side, and before I understood what was happening, she leant forward, thrust her hand inside my breeches and gripped my manhood.

'Onion,' she declared, as the men closest roared with laughter. The whore withdrew her hand, then kissed her finger tips and laughed, as a whirl of images confused me. Her hand on my manhood reminded me of Valla's hand when she'd threatened to geld me, and immediately I was hard again and reeling with ale and lust.

A whore? Why not do it with a whore, like the rest of the men?

At once, I was confronted with the pledge I'd made to Valla – to touch no other woman. But did whores count? I could see an argument for both no and yes.

The first of the men disappeared with his whore, and soon there was a steady stream of men going and coming, with the prices negotiated down as the same women were used and reused.

The most beautiful of the whores (not that she compared with Valla) was drinking and laughing with Tostig and yet to go outside –

no doubt he would take her to his chamber when he was ready.

More ale appeared in my cup, and I drained it. Then more appeared.

I stumbled outside to the latrine, which was just a hole surmounted by logs on three sides. Most of the men pissed against the stonework at the base of the building, and after taking two steps towards the latrine, I recoiled in disgust from the stench rising from the pit and joined the line of men pissing against the wall.

For some reason, the act of pissing in a line with my ale-sodden colleagues seemed like another liberating step in becoming a man. As the son of a thegn, most of my pissing had been private in the past and I felt a strange warmth towards my comrades – friend and stranger alike.

Onion, I thought, as I fumbled with my breeches and began to ease my burden. Then the memory of the whore's hand came to me and I hunched over self-consciously as someone pushed into the line next to me.

'Not from round these parts, eh?'

I looked up at a man not much older than me, his face boasting two large warts on his nose and cheek, and his eyes dull with ale.

'No,' I said, not much liking the look of him, and suddenly conscious of the fact that I knew none of the men in immediate proximity.

'I'm local,' he said, 'and we do like visitors at Breahinga. Fassbekka's the name, friend, and what might be yours?'

'Brand,' I told him, and turned away to concentrate on the end of my piss, but when I straightened up, Fassbekka had vanished.

I shrugged and headed back inside, once again wondering whether doing it with a whore was breaking my word to Valla. In fact, it occurred to me that she would probably approve – if my hungers were whore-sated, they'd be less likely to trouble her.

Back inside, among Harold and Tostig's men, I downed another cup and turned over this profound new thought in my mind. Yes, doing it with a whore was the answer, although maybe it would be best if Valla didn't know about it.

'You look lonely, traveller.'

I glanced up as a young woman sat at my side, dark of hair and thin, like Valla, but not so comely and fey.

'I am Grindel,' she said, 'and I would take your cares away … for a while.'

'My cares? I have no cares.'

'But you are a warrior,' she said. 'And all warriors have the care of their lords and the threat of death looming at every battle.'

In fact, that hadn't really occurred to me – that I might be killed in battle, and it sobered me a little.

'I am yet to face a battle,' I replied, reaching for my cup to drown the uncomfortable forebodings.

'I have seen it,' she said, reaching up to stroke the side of my face. 'Battle is terrible … like a butcher's yard but with men screaming instead of kine.'

'Battle is glory,' I told her, rather enjoying her hand as it went around my neck, and her other hand which caressed my thigh.

'Battle is glory,' she agreed, refilling my cup for me. 'And it is only proper that brave warriors should take their rewards between battles … for who knows what may befall?'

She handed me the cup and said, 'There … I have filled your cup. Will you not fill mine?'

I glanced about for an empty cup, then perceived the meaning behind her words.

'Erm … I have no coins,' I stammered, and wondered whether I was drunk enough to claim to Valla, should she ask, that the ale had been responsible for my actions.

'The service has already been paid for … by your friends,' said Grindel.

'Tostig,' I muttered, and drained my cup once again to drown the last of my better judgment.

'Come,' she said, taking my hand.

'Where are we going?' I asked thickly as she led me out into the yard, past the latrine and towards the darkness behind the stable.

'You'll see,' she said, laughing. 'It is not far … a comfortable place away from the eyes of others.'

It was pitch black behind the stable as I followed blindly, wondering whether holding her hand was already a breach of my pledge. And if the pledge was already broken, I might as well take advantage of the fact and enjoy myself. After all, I had been forbidden access to the sluts of my father's household since being promised to the church, so it had been at least two seasons since I'd had a woman – and I'd never had that many to begin with. A burning excitement began to course through my veins and I had to fight the urge to just throw her to the ground – mind you, I could tell that the ground that we stepped over in the dark would not be comfortable and there was a strong smell of horse shit. Horse shit, of course, was not as bad as most other excrement but I didn't want to lie in it, unless absolutely necessary.

'Where are we going?' I asked again, feeling very drunk but getting impatient.

'Hush,' she whispered, ' … nearly there.'

She pushed open a door which grated against a stone floor, and I heard the restive movement of beasts in the dark.

'There are fleece bales stored here,' she said, pushing the door closed again. 'It is more comfortable than the finest bed, and well suited to our purpose.'

Then her hands were pulling at my breeches. She untied the cord that kept them in place but as soon as my manhood was exposed to the night air, I felt a strange panic – that this was somehow a mistake, and that Valla would know and be upset about it.

'Wait,' I said, as Grindel's hand took hold of me in the dark.

'I cannot wait,' she said. 'You must fill my cup … as you promised.'

'I don't think I should. I promised Valla … '

'Please!' she begged me and pulled me down onto something wonderfully soft and comfortable which smelled of warm animals. I struggled vainly but the more I tried to get up, the more I seemed to be driven between her thighs as her hand guided me. And just as I felt myself brushing against the tight curls of her womanhood, I felt a sudden chill on my arse and knew the door had been opened. Somehow, I was convinced that Valla was standing behind me and threw myself off Grindel, just as something thumped into the bale beside me and Grindel screamed.

'Light!' snarled a man's voice, and a torch appeared in the doorway as I desperately struggled to my feet, pulling up my breeches. A very large and ugly man was holding a shovel and swung it at my head. Despite struggling with a surfeit of ale and trying to hold up my breeches, I managed to duck and jumped back where my foot landed on a pile of turd and I slipped to the ground.

'Light, I told you!' growled the man again and the torch grew brighter as another man entered the chamber, holding the torch high. In its light, I saw a farrier's rake and swept it up, just in time to fend another savage blow of the shovel. My assailant was far stronger and I knew my life was over unless I could escape or get help. I filled my lungs to shout for Tostig, but a hand whipped over my mouth from behind and, without thinking, I reversed the rake and thrust its point backwards where it connected well and caused a shriek. My main assailant was still swinging his shovel and while I managed to deflect another blow, I felt myself borne down under his greater weight and strength.

'You just don't want to die, do you?' hissed a voice as he forced me to the ground, his huge hand against the back of my neck and my face pushed hard into the filth of the floor. Then the edge of a blade was against my throat and I knew terror as he said, 'In case you were wondering ... we were sent by Malgard.'

Then there was a thud, and he fell on top of me and moved no more.

In my terror and confusion, I lay for a moment in total darkness, knowing not my fate. Then a voice enquired, 'Are you right lad?'

The voice was familiar, but I couldn't place it.

Then the weight above me was dragged aside and I sat up feeling drunk and dazed. The torch was lying in the doorway and a figure stooped and raised it, throwing a bit more light on the scene.

'Elric!' I said, as he placed the torch in a bracket by the door.

He gave me a sort of sneering mock bow and then examined the two men lying on the ground. One was a huge man, whose head was covered with blood. The other was curled up and clutching his guts. Grindel was still cowering half-naked in the fleece bales.

'Cover up lass, and get out,' said Elric, in the voice of a man accustomed to command. She gave me a last terrified glance and bolted into the darkness, as Elric dropped the large rock he was holding and picked up a vicious-looking dagger, and before I understood what was happening a great gush of blood covered the floor as Elric slit the giant's throat.

Then he held the reddened blade before the recovering smaller man, whom I recognised as the fellow with the warts who'd spoken to me while pissing.

'Talk,' said Elric.

'Nothing to say,' replied the young man, whose name I'd forgotten.

'You might need your sword, Brand,' said Elric, and I could have kicked myself when I realised my sword was still hanging in its scabbard at my side. I'd fought with a rake when I could have used a sword. I drew it at once and held the tip towards my would-be murderer's accomplice.

He eyed the sword and the massive corpse in its pool of blood, then licked his lips and said, 'Only met them today. They gave me drink and said they were looking for Brand ... they had a surprise for him.'

'Them?' I asked.

'Big man and small man,' said the accomplice – Fassbekka, that was his name.

'So where's the small man?' demanded Elric.

'Don't know,' snivelled Fassbekka. 'He were here a minute ago.'

Elric considered, then said to me, 'By his speech, he's a local ... but the dead 'un here's from foreign parts, away south.'

'He was sent by my uncle,' I said, shivering with fear and anger, and surprisingly sober once more.

'Him and someone else,' reminded Elric. Then he got Fassbekka to describe the small man – 'hair like dark honey' was all we got from him, and in fact he seemed a bit of a halfwit.

'I reckon he's telling the truth,' said Elric, wiping his blade on Fassbekka's tunic. 'But now we have to decide whether to kill him or let him go.'

I just shrugged, so Elric dragged Fassbekka's face close to his blade.

'You've made a big mistake tonight,' said Elric. 'You've attacked Brand ... a friend of the Earl Harold. The penalty for that is death!'

Fassbekka started to whimper as Elric continued in a terrifying voice.

'From this moment, your life is forfeit and can be taken at any time ... but if you lead us in the morning to the small man with the honey-coloured hair, we might forgive you. Now, fuck off!'

Elric aimed a kick as Fassbekka darted for the door.

Suddenly I felt drunk again, and slumped heavily onto a fat bale of fleece.

'Thank you Elric,' I said. 'I owe you my life.'

'Useless piece of shit,' he said, and I felt a hot flash of anger when I realised he was talking to me.

'I saw you come in with the whore,' he said, and it was only then that I noticed all the eyes on the edges of the firelight. We were in the stable, where the animals and servants were bedded down. 'And when you were attacked, I might have left you to it … except for your change of mind.'

'My change of mind?'

'You said you couldn't do it … that you'd promised Valla.'

'I did?'

'As soon as I heard those words, I realised that you have a bittersweet journey before you. Because I too have promised Valla.'

He sneered when he saw the hostile confusion on my face.

'Not *her*, fool. Her mother … Valla before her.'

'You knew Valla's mother?'

'Aye … knew her in every sense of the word. I'm your Valla's father.'

Chapter 10

Always Keep a Hand on Your Sword

It is a strange world that God has created. And yet sometimes we feel we've caught a glimpse of His Mind and Purpose. Aye, and His games.

That Elric, Valla and I should be thrown together by the chances of fate was too strange to be mere happenstance – there had to be a purpose behind it, some hand guiding the wheels of fate, and once again I was awed by the revelation – dimly though I perceived it.

Some of Valla's purpose also was now revealed to me – her desire to free the serfs for example, clearly with the aid and sanction of the Lady Swanneshals.

'I can't have Valla's father as my servant!' I exclaimed.

'Why not?' asked Elric.

'It is not seemly,' I protested. 'You should have a place of honour.'

'I'm happy with my place,' said Elric, grinning. 'Here in the stable with the other beasts.'

He proceeded to tell me of his own experience with Valla's mother.

'I met her in the wood on the morn of the summer solstice and fell immediately in love with her. Quite like your Valla she was ... a little wilder perhaps. Like you, I was chosen to be her future consort.'

'How long did you wait?'

'Long, and yet not long,' he replied, unhelpfully. 'The days were many, but leavened with the knowledge that I was her chosen man, and the life was pleasant enough. I loved her.'

'A man has needs,' I complained, ' ... and the rules are hard. Do whores matter?'

'I think you've answered that question for yourself,' grinned Elric and I swore with frustration. Then, reflecting on Elric's capture, I asked, 'Valla's mother ... she was with you when you were captured?'

He shook his head sadly. 'She is gone ... to a place I cannot follow.'

'She died?'

'Nay ... at least, I know not. But once the child is born, the mother feels the call and will eventually answer it.'

'The call?'

'Aye ... to seek the Place of Dreams. Don't ask me to explain it for I cannot.'

It was too much to worry about in any case. My eye fell once again on the body of the giant and I shivered, remembering his blade at my throat. The escape had been too near, and there was still the fellow with the honey-coloured hair to consider. I mentioned my fears to Elric, and then told him about the attack on my family, my meeting with Valla and all the rest up to the time he had attacked us in the dark.

'You took my hare!' he protested. 'You expect me to ignore an insult like that?'

'The hare was in my forest. It was therefore my hare,' I told him, suddenly feeling rather thick-headed – still whirling with ale and a thousand disconnected arguments. Fortunately, Elric returned to the subject that mattered most urgently.

'Malgard must want you dead indeed to send out slayers ... but he could not know that you had found the favour of the lords Harold and Tostig. I doubt whether you need worry about the honey-haired fellow for the moment ... he will have worked out by now that he is up against too many and will return to Malgard for further instructions.'

'You think so?'

Elric shrugged.

'It's what I would do in his position. He was sent out to kill one boy ... not a boy travelling in the train of the Earl of Wessex and surrounded by warriors. He will want to negotiate a much higher fee for a start and get extra men.'

My heart sank, as I realised that wherever I was headed I could never again take any man for what he seemed – at least while Malgard lived. Any man could be an assassin – I could trust no-one.

'That is the lot of any thegn,' laughed Elric, after I explained my fears. 'If you have what other men want, you must always be ready to fight to protect it. Your life is no more dangerous than it was and ever will be.'

It was hardly a reassuring thought, but I perceived that living with the threat of danger was the privilege of rulers and determined to rise to the challenge.

'Malgard has much to answer for,' I said. 'I will see him receive justice if it is the last thing I do … and when I come before the king and am confirmed as thegn of Stybbor I will also mete out justice to you Elric.'

'Will you indeed?' he said, his eyes hardening.

'Yes … in return for your years of trespass, and poaching the game of my father's wood, I will give you some hides of land and have you dwell there in peace and honour.'

Elric's eyes widened but then he stood and bowed.

'Furthermore, I release you from your bond. I will not have a serf for a father-in-law.'

'Thank you Brand,' said Elric, 'but perhaps it might be best if we tell no-one else of this arrangement for now … it would take some explaining, and I am happy enough to be a serf. Travelling in Harold's train is a simpler life than trapping coneys in the wood.'

He took the torch and glanced out the door.

'You'd best get back to Valla,' he said. 'As I have myself discovered, the time can come without warning.'

'The time?'

He gave me a rather pointed look and once again I felt a fool as I realised the import of his words.

'If it's any consolation,' said Elric, 'I think the time will come faster for you than it did for me.'

'Really? Why do you say that?'

'My Valla hated me when we first met … yours is clearly smitten.'

'Smitten? She insults me at every turn and has twice tried to geld me.'

Elric laughed.

'Ah yes,' he said, 'Valla does not care for rape and will take steps to prevent it. She remains smitten though … she would have left by

110

now were she not.'

'Not so,' I said. 'We made a bargain and her part was to come to Lundene with me.'

I explained the bargain and Elric shrugged.

'She doesn't need title or permission to dwell in the woods,' he said. 'The woods have always been and always will, and there is room enough for Valla. It is the source of her magic and it would take something very important for her to leave it ... even for just a while. That important thing can only be you.'

It was a surprising thought, that Valla might feel about me as I felt about her, and I wasn't quite ready to believe it after all her abuse. Still, she had said that when the time came, I should be the one to take her maidenhead. And she was my wife after all ...

The torch was dying so I resolved to worry about it later. I clambered up out of the comfortable fleece bales feeling drunk and bruised and stepped carefully around the body of the giant to get to the door.

'I still can't believe I fought him with a rake,' I said, with a small shudder.

'Yes ... always keep a hand on your sword,' advised Elric, 'you never know when you might need it in the dark.'

∞ ∞ ∞

I had no further use of my sword that evening. There was no-one at the inn who matched Fassbekka's description of the honey-haired man, and Valla was asleep when I stumbled into our small chamber. I listened to her slow breathing as I climbed into the bed next to her, feeling glad and virtuous that I had resisted the whore. Maybe my forbearance would somehow hurry forward the day when Valla would be mine entirely, although I was a little concerned about the Place of Dreams that Elric had mentioned.

Before I knew it, the light was streaming in through the window and I was waking to the sounds and smells of breakfast preparation, which reminded me of my family home and I felt a keen sadness. But how quickly I'd replaced my family with a family of my own – a wife at least.

Valla stirred and looked into my eyes.

'Something has changed,' she said.

I wondered if she meant the whore, but then realised the only possible answer.

'I met your father,' I said. 'I've released him from his bond.'

If she was surprised, she didn't betray it. She closed her eyes again and enquired, 'Is he still with us, or has he returned to the forest?'

'He remains, for now. I also told him I would give him land when I am confirmed thegn by Edward.'

Valla smiled.

'I wonder why he has stayed if you have given him leave to go ... but that was generous Brand. I hope you will not judge the gift wasted.'

'Why should I judge it so?'

'Let's just say that sometimes people give a gift ... hoping to receive something in return.'

'Such giving would be dishonourable,' I replied, feeling rather annoyed that my noble deed was being tarnished with base motive.

'And the gift in return wouldn't necessarily be desired from the first receiver,' she continued. 'It is conceivable that a person might give, for example, to a father ... hoping to receive a favour from ... let's say ... his daughter.'

Recalling Elric's theory that Valla was 'smitten', I edged myself closer in the warm bed that smelled so nicely of her natural scent.

'Should not a daughter be grateful?' I asked, 'when her father is honoured with a gift of land?'

'Yes,' said Valla, her eyes still closed but smiling, 'but there are limits to gratitude ... as we have discussed.'

I slid an arm under her neck and pulled her towards me, wondering when she would begin to struggle, but she lay there quite contentedly and I felt like I was handling the thinnest of eggshells that might crack at any moment.

She was warm and naked, and instantly my manhood felt like it must burst from the pressure of lust. I hadn't meant for it to come in contact with Valla's flesh, but she stiffened – and I thought she might scream – but she simply rolled over and said, 'I'm sorry Brand ... the time is not yet.'

I knew better than to start wheedling at her so I said nothing and contented myself with holding her.

'Tell me Valla,' I said after a few moments. 'Do you also feel the urge ... as I feel it so strongly?'

'The urge?'

'The urge to mate. It is a painful frustration so strong it gnaws me and robs me of wit and judgment. Do you feel it also?'

'Of course,' she replied. 'But I have a calling. There are few remaining like Valla. They have all faded because they could not control the urge ... as you call it.'

'You are truly a witch?'

She didn't answer, just lay in my arms with her back to me, her black hair tickling my nose but I bore it as any sudden movement might spoil the moment.

'I was put here, after two hundred and forty-two years to achieve some great thing,' she said, after a while. 'I don't know yet what that great thing is, but I must retain my powers until that day.'

'Your powers?'

'I don't wish to talk about it, Brand. Magic loses its potency when explained.'

'I will not ask again,' I replied, pulling her slightly closer, and for half a moment I felt her push herself against me and my head filled with delirious pleasure. But even as I responded, she leapt from the bed as though burned.

She did not talk to me for several hours.

Chapter 11

Our Peril and Our Loss

Malgard hurried through the stinking streets close to where Edward was building his new minster on the northern bank of the Temes. It was just before dawn and he had been advised by Cuthred, the king's factor, that Edward looked warmly on those who were up early for prayer as such bespoke a monastic persuasion.

'It is his greatest regret,' Cuthred had explained at their first meeting, 'that he was not a monk, and he holds the meanest priest higher in honour than any earl or thegn.'

It was valuable advice, and Malgard had paid – fifty silver pennies, with the promise of more once the thegnship was confirmed. Cuthred was a formidable ally (who had not questioned his tale) and Malgard needed allies after Gorik had brought the deeply troubling news that Brand was travelling with the sons of Godwin.

But if anything, that had unexpectedly strengthened Malgard's hand.

'You will discover, Malgard,' Cuthred had said, 'that friends of the Godwinsons do not easily find favour with the king.'

'But Edward named Harold Subregulus,' said Malgard. 'Surely the king honours him.'

'The king fears him,' said Cuthred, 'and fears the witan that supports him. If your enemy turns out to be a friend of the king's enemy, then the king will swiftly perceive that advancing your interest advances his own.'

It was an encouraging thought but still fraught with many dangers, reflected Malgard. Even if he was confirmed as thegn, it was still imperative that Brand be slain to prevent any kind of mixed message coming to the ears of the king and other thegns. Gorik had undertaken to arrange for Brand's death and Malgard grimaced as he wondered where he was going to find the money to pay for so many favours. The estates at Stybbor were no more than two hundred hides, plus rents on the village, the woods and some marshes that might be profitably drained. He had no desire to lose any of it after risking so much. Perhaps there might be further work for Gorik – and maybe even another like him if Gorik himself became too expensive, or learned too much.

The stink of the alleys was slightly relieved as he found himself in the large open space before the new minster where Cuthred had warned him the king might be found that morning, inspecting the work which soared above the surrounding district like a pure white bone sticking out of putrefied flesh. It was a building of great beauty and by far the largest Malgard had ever seen.

There were soldiers milling about the doors to the minster and the sergeant, a large, fat man with broken teeth and foetid breath, peered long at Malgard before consenting to send a message to Cuthred. But fairly quickly Cuthred himself emerged and beckoned for Malgard to follow.

After the stink of the streets, the inside of the minster smelled pleasantly of milled wood and sawdust. Great piles of masoned stone were stacked about the walls and only part of the floor had been laid. Scaffolds filled the chamber like the delicate skeleton of a great stone beast, and at the end of the vast room an arrangement of torches illuminated a spot where an aging man sat on a plain stool talking to two others.

Cuthred led Malgard to the edge of the light and waited until Edward's business with the engineers was complete. Once they had bowed and departed, Edward turned to gaze at Malgard. It had been only two years since Malgard had last seen the king and he was astonished at how Edward had aged in that time. The man looking up from the stool did not have the air of a ruler – indeed, he reminded Malgard of an elderly chaplain that he and Holgar had known in childhood who was given to long brooding silences and the sudden announcement of strange visions.

'This space in which we stand,' said Edward, apparently oblivious to the fact that he was sitting, 'will be the nave of my western minster.

It is only half built, but already I feel the presence of God. He approves, I think.'

'The minster does our Lord great honour,' ventured Malgard, speaking the words Cuthred had advised him to speak.

'Never enough though,' replied Edward, shaking his head sadly. 'We can never do enough to be worthy of His bounty.'

Cuthred cleared his throat, and Edward seemed to return to the present, looking at Malgard as though seeing him for the first time.

'My liege … may I present Malgard, son of Rathgar?' said Cuthred. 'Malgard bears grim tidings from the east of your realm.'

'What tidings are these, son of Rathgar?' enquired the king, and for a moment Malgard felt deeply ashamed of his actions. So kind and godly did Edward seem, that Malgard, for half a heartbeat, was tempted to confess his treachery and be shriven. But the moment passed and, prompted by Cuthred, Malgard told the story of the Viking attack on Stybbor and the death of Holgar, the thegn.

Edward's pale blue eyes never left Malgard's as he gave his account and Malgard felt himself shrinking, as though the eyes of the king saw truly despite his false tale. But when he reached the end Edward sighed.

'The Danes … too early did we rejoice their departure from this island.'

'It was not a total defeat sire,' said Cuthred. 'Malgard led the defence and won through to Lundene to warn us.'

Edward sighed again, then he said, 'Did we know Holgar?'

'Yes, my liege,' said Cuthbert. 'He stood with us at Gipeswic and Margate … his son Gram also was there. As was Malgard.'

'Alas,' said Malgard, now warming to his tale. 'Gram was slain in the raid.'

'This is grievous news,' replied Edward, 'and there is already much to trouble our councils.'

'But we thank you for your swift journey,' interrupted Cuthred, 'to let us know of both our peril and our loss.'

The aging king, reminded perhaps of his manners, looked up once again at Malgard. 'Thank you indeed Malgard. Is there anything we might do to aid the people of Stybbor?'

'They need leadership, my liege.'

Once again, it seemed to Malgard that the pale blue eyes of the king saw more than he was supposed to see.

'I see,' said Edward. 'Has Holgar no more sons to continue his line?'

'There is one other, the second son Brand. But he is not held in high esteem. Indeed, men say he is jealous of his brother and invited the Danes to attack, with the object of succeeding to the thegnship in his place.'

Malgard's throat felt constricted as he spoke the false words – almost as though God was causing him to choke on the lie. Surely the king must guess the truth and summon soldiers, he thought, but Cuthred came to his aid.

'Ambition and treachery,' he said, ' ... they are ever bedfellows.'

Edward was not quite ready to dispense with due process.

'There must be a trial,' he said solemnly, 'for these accusations to be proved, but in the meantime, the people must be led. You were Holgar's brother?'

'His only brother ... I had that honour Lord.'

'Malgard has brought a list of depositions,' said Cuthred, ' ... men who have sworn that Brand was seen leading the Vikings to the town and fighting on their behalf.'

'This is true?' enquired Edward.

'Grievous was the death of Holgar,' declaimed Cuthred, his voice ringing in the nave, 'but more grievous still was the treachery of his son, who had been promised to the church.'

The aging king was stricken, and he stared first at Cuthred, then at Malgard.

'A man of God did this?'

'I fear so, my lord,' said Malgard, the lies coming more easily with Cuthred's efforts on his behalf.

'A black evil,' muttered Edward, ' ... a black evil indeed when men who are most charged with showing humility and pious example are transported by ambition and greed. There are sworn depositions you say?'

'Yes, Lord,' lied Cuthred. 'The correct number in the proper form.'

'Then surely there is no need for a trial,' decided Edward, his voice rising and revealing something of his former strength. 'Let Brand

Holgarsson be declared outlaw. As for the leadership of the burghers of Stybbor ... the question ought to be referred to the Earl of East Anglia.'

'The lands in question are under the seisin of the Earl of Wessex,' advised Cuthred and a flash of anger passed over the face of the king.

'Harold?'

'Yes Lord,' said Cuthred, who then lowered his own voice. 'Might I suggest that it would be a comfort for you to know that at least one of Harold's vassals was loyal to the king above all others?'

'It would be a comfort indeed,' replied Edward, ' ... but there are proprieties to be considered.'

He seemed to struggle for a moment with an inner debate, then his mouth tightened as he made his decision. 'Very well ... will you Malgard, undertake to lead the folk of Stybbor in this their time of darkness?'

Malgard fell at once to his knees and kissed the hand that Edward extended towards him.

'I swear to lead them well ... and further I swear fealty to you my Lord and King ... a duty I hold higher than to any other Lord.'

Edward smiled grimly and proclaimed, 'Malgard, son of Rathgar, I declare you thegn and reeve of Stybbor. All lands, uses, profits and property that might have passed to Brand Holgarsson are hereby forfeited to you, my vassal. As for Brand Holgarsson, he is declared outlaw and may be taken or slain by any man who shall have our thanks and a bounty of twenty silver pennies.'

A sense of pure elation coursed through Malgard and, before he could help himself, a great belch of laughter erupted which he managed to turn into a cough.

Your pardon, sire,' he apologised, desperately fighting the laughter and tears of mirth rolling down his face.

'Your love and gratitude are noted Malgard,' said Cuthred, tightly. 'Now surely you want to get back quickly to Stybbor to repair the damage caused by the Danes.'

Malgard rose with relief, bowed, and all but ran from the chamber. When he got back outside the minster he rather startled the soldiers by bursting into loud hysterics and laughing until he fell to the ground like a man drunk.

'Edward's in good humour?' asked the fat sergeant with the bad teeth.

'Aye ... go inside and ask him,' laughed Malgard. 'He'll probably make you an earl!'

∞ ∞ ∞

I never quite knew where I stood with Valla, but my stocks continued to rise with the Godwinsons.

Elric had insisted that I take all the credit for the slaying of the giant in the stable, and when Harold and Tostig came out the next morning to inspect the body, they stared at me – their eyes reflecting a respect I didn't deserve.

'He attacked you from behind ... and yet you managed to defeat him?' said Harold in wonder, looking me up and down and obviously comparing my frame with that of the giant. 'There is more to you than meets the eye, Brand Holgarsson.'

'I was lucky,' I said, embarrassed, '... and I had some help, Elric –'

'All I did was distract him,' interrupted Elric. 'Brand fought him off with a rake and then cut his throat with his own knife.'

Tostig laughed.

'I saw you hit Elric with a rake that night in Theodford. Clearly Brand is a dangerous foe when there are farrier's tools at hand! We should use rakes in the shield wall!'

'I would rather learn the sword,' I said, seeking to steer the conversation back to safer ground. Tostig had promised to teach me swordcraft, although I had been practising as Carl suggested – spending hours at a time simply holding the sword out at shoulder height, to acquire sword strength and already I had noticed an improvement.

'And he was sent by Malgard,' mused Harold, still considering the body of the giant. 'I begin to perceive this Malgard is a viper ... ruthless and evil. We will help you get revenge for your family.'

'Aye, and for yourself,' added Tostig.

It was a comforting thought, and I felt a lot safer as we left that morning, despite the fact that we never saw Fassbekka again and had no further information with regard to the giant's honey-haired companion. Still, as a friend of the Godwinsons, I had no doubt that I would swiftly gain the favour of the king and that Malgard would be hunted down like the dog he was.

And speaking of which, four-legged Malgard no longer showed any signs of the damage I had wrought back in Stybbor. Valla's poultice had worked its magic and now he ran back and forth with the other dogs in the party, snuffling new scents and barking joyously in the late summer sunshine. Most of the warriors were feeling sick from ale and cursed him to be quiet.

Valla had little to say. She rode on the wagon with the victualler and master of arms, wearing the green dress despite the warmth and I wondered whether she wanted to cover more of her flesh than would be accomplished with the cloak of skins.

'She didn't find out about the whore, did she?' whispered Elric, with a nod at Valla.

I simply shook my head, not wanting to put into words my embarrassment regarding events at the inn.

'Then what's causing her mood?'

It was still a bit confusing – the idea of Elric being Valla's father was passing strange. Even stranger was the idea that he seemed to like me despite all that had happened since we encountered him and his friends in the woods.

'The fellow that died in the clearing,' I said. 'The man killed by Tostig for his defiance ... was he a friend of yours?'

Elric's usual cheerfulness vanished.

'The low are rarely noticed by the highborn,' he said. 'Why do you ask about him?'

'I ... I was just thinking about the morning of your capture,' I stammered, strangely embarrassed. 'And don't forget ... I've released you from your oath and bond. You may return to the forest if you wish.'

Elric smiled, 'You are a good man Brand ... or at least you will be. But if you don't mind, I'd prefer to travel with you for now. Even in the stables we eat better than I ever ate in the woods.'

I smiled, pleased to have his company. Although there was something about him that didn't quite seem right. For a start, he was fair-spoken for a low-born wood dweller, and seemed quite accomplished in the use of weapons and the ordering of men.

'Have you served in the fyrd before?' I asked him.

Elric glanced at me and then grinned. 'I don't suppose there's any harm in admitting it,' he replied. 'But I'd rather not talk about it, if you take my meaning.'

In other words, there was some disgrace in the manner of his departure. In all likelihood, he had run from a place of service and had no desire to be reclaimed.

My eyes lifted to take in my surroundings once again as we came to the crest of a hill that looked down over a wide plain. In the middle distance was a brown smear of low cloud, to which Harold pointed.

'Lundene,' he said, and I realised that the smear of cloud was in fact smoke – from how many chimneys? I wondered.

As usual, Harold was walking with Carl, questioning him long about his time with the Danes, during which he had learned much of their customs and politics. It had been thought among the lords of Inglalond that the Danes were spent as an invasion threat, but Carl was ever warning Harold that there were still some among them who regarded Inglalond – especially the north – as a tempting prize.

'There are even some,' said Carl, 'who would claim the throne should Edward leave no clear successor. The Danes and Saxons have inter-married over the years and there are some with at least a tenuous claim ... enough to raise men and fight, in any case.'

Harold took him seriously, but Tostig scoffed at the notion of Danes being a threat. 'The Danes are a rabble,' he laughed. 'Fearsome enough as raiders in small groups, but the leaders of the dragon boats will never form an army! They couldn't agree on the colour of turd.'

'You're probably right,' agreed Harold. 'They are a divided people but they fight well. If ever a strong leader emerged to unite them then we should look to our northern coastlines with some nervousness.'

'You and your coastlines,' laughed Tostig. 'Inglalond is safe from any foreign army. The real dangers are within ... and you, my brother, are the most dangerous man in the realm.'

'I am no danger to Inglalond,' replied Harold earnestly. 'Nor to Edward.'

'As long as he names you,' said Tostig.

'No!' insisted Harold. 'I care not whether he names me. I care only for Inglalond, united and peaceful. Would you have us return to the days before Cnut … with every second lord calling himself king and shedding blood over every stray field?'

'I would have the Godwinsons take their proper place,' replied Tostig. 'It is what our father would want.'

'Our father wanted an honourable peace,' said Harold, but it seemed that he spoke without conviction and Tostig pressed his point.

'How long must we live with the insult of our sister?' he hissed. 'When we were exiled he put her in a convent to rot in a cell … a stinking convent!'

The men had all gone silent, embarrassed by the anger of their lords but also intrigued by their words.

'*There* is Edward's revenge upon Godwin,' continued Tostig. 'He lies not with his queen, so no grandson of Godwin will sit upon the throne. What sort of man lets his own line wither to spite another's? Edward is no man I tell you … no man fit to rule, and that's why he names you Subregulus, to keep order as his lieutenant, but will not name you his successor! Even after the death of the aethel—'

'It matters not,' interrupted Harold. 'I am Edward's man and will not do aught against him, nor deceive him.'

'Then you are a fool,' snarled Tostig. 'He insults and deceives the Godwinsons … why should we not return the favour?'

'Because if we are to have peace, then someone must swallow his pride. I am prepared to do that for the good of Inglalond … and as head of our family, I insist you do the same.'

Tostig just laughed, and once again I had an uneasy feeling. I really liked Tostig, but something told me it would be best to stay on his good side. He would make a bitter foe.

∞ ∞ ∞

As we approached Lundene, the villages clustered more thickly together and almost before I knew it they had become continuous. Hovels and houses were built over and about each other like a tangle of plants all trying to reach the sun, and in places the rooves closed over our heads. The streets were occasionally cobbled but were mostly mud with a trickle of slime and turd down the centre. It stank abominably – even worse than Theodford – and the streets seemed to go on forever.

Fortunately, Harold had a large house with separate outbuildings on a couple of acres on the banks of the Flyot stream, close to where it flowed into the Temes. Like his place at Theodford, it was surrounded by a wall but made of bricks instead of thorns. Our party entered but I still felt closed in – the smoke from countless chimneys and forges obscured even the sky and Valla shuddered.

'This is an evil place,' she muttered. 'Can you not feel it?'

'I can smell it,' I replied.

The house was much larger than the house at Theodford, but was similar in make and style, save that it had two levels. The only two level building I had ever seen before was the monastery at Stybbor, where I would have been even now, learning conjugation and chastity, if not for the Danes and Malgard. It was an uncomfortable thought – I resented bitterly the treachery of Malgard but rejoiced in the freedom to be my own man. Mind you, I was still well-accomplished in chastity, I thought, as Valla and I were shown to our chamber.

Chapter 12

When All the Scrapping Dogs Are in the One Pit

The morning after he arrived in Lundene, Harold resolved to visit Edward. With him he took his minister Olwin and the monk, Carl, who intrigued him.

'Edward will like you, I deem,' said Harold. 'He is ever eager to meet godly men, and he will be interested in your story.'

'I do not enjoy the telling,' admitted Carl, 'but if the king wills it, my tongue is his to command.'

It was still early so Tostig was yet to rise, and Harold felt a pang of guilt that he was seeking an audience without his brother. But in truth, having once been a favourite of the king, Tostig was nowadays too ready to let his dislike for Edward show, which then made the king harder to deal with. It was simply easier without Tostig.

Close to the bridge, the stench of the streets was overborne by the tang of the river and the pleasant aroma of bakeries. Throngs of people gathered about the various stalls, mainly servants and wives buying bread for their masters, with animals and children scurrying at their feet ever ready to pounce on a dropped loaf or pastry. It was a noisy and lively scene and Harold smiled.

'When I see our people, here and in the countryside, happy in their daily lots, I am glad that we live on this island where the people are less vulnerable to attack by random raiders.'

'Brand might tell a different story,' remarked Olwin.

'The attack on Stybbor was hardly random,' said Harold. 'Mostly our people have lived in peace these last years ... the fyrd is not always summoned, and if it is, it is generally due to squabbles among our own lords.'

'That is the way of lords,' said Olwin. 'Like cats in a lane they contest every acre.'

'Perhaps,' agreed Carl, 'but cats risk only themselves and do not involve others in their contests.'

Harold stared at Carl thoughtfully.

'You are wise Carl,' he said. 'I admit that I hear still the summons of my father ... exhorting me from the grave ... calling me to take the throne. And yet many would die for my ambition. The people of Inglalond deserve peace.'

'The people of Inglalond will not have peace without a strong king,' said Olwin. 'Every day Edward continues without a clear successor, more who think they have a claim will start to dream.'

'And others,' said Carl, 'like Ulrik Dragontooth, will simply take advantage of our lack of order and vigilance.'

'If ever I come to lead the defence of Inglalond,' said Harold, 'I will build more ships to protect the coast. Alfred had ships.'

'Ships are expensive, Lord,' reminded Olwin.

'Burning villages and the death of innocents are more expensive,' said Carl, and once again Harold regarded him thoughtfully.

'I should have brought Brand,' said Harold. 'He would avenge his village and the deaths of his family.'

'There is still time for Brand,' said Olwin. 'The succession is more urgent.'

'True,' agreed Harold, perhaps a little doubtfully. 'I have much business with Edward, but I will speak for Brand and ask the king to intercede on his behalf. With any luck, this Malgard may even be in Lundene and can be swiftly apprehended. He is a very evil man I deem and I would have justice for Brand.'

'His cause is just,' agreed Olwin, 'and the raid on Stybbor will remind the king that his realm must be defended by a strong king.'

Harold smiled.

'Ever you intrigue on my behalf, Olwin. I thank you for it, but I will not act for my own part without the blessing of Edward ... nor will I go behind his back or deceive him in any way.'

The three arrived at Edward's hall close to the huge new church he was building west of the bridge on the north bank of the Temes.

Men went scurrying once it became known that the Earl of Wessex was waiting on the king, but it was some time before the king's man Cuthred appeared to lead them into Edward's presence.

'How fare you, Cuthred?' enquired Harold.

'Well enough,' replied the minister, whom Harold had never liked. 'Well enough when the burdens of office give me a moment's respite.'

'Surely the burdens of office are your greatest joy,' laughed Harold, determined not to let Cuthred's famous surliness sour his good humour. 'And speaking of office, how fares the king?'

'He grows older,' replied Cuthred, 'and he despairs of keeping the realm safe from so many dangers. That is why he has new friends I suppose.'

'New friends?' enquired Harold, but at that moment they came to Edward's door wardens and were announced.

The king sat on a high-backed chair, carved from dark wood, and raised up on a dais two steps above the stone floor. Leading to the dais was a long narrow carpet, brightly coloured and strangely decorated with patterns and human figures done in a style quite unlike anything Harold and his two companions had ever seen.

'Aah ... greetings my Lord Wessex,' called the king. 'I see you are interested in my rug.'

Harold, his companions and Cuthred approached the dais and bowed low.

'They tell me it comes from Persia,' continued the king, nodding at a pair of Norman knights who stood behind his chair, as though carrying on a conversation which had started some time before, ' ... a country far to the east. It is said to tell the story of a great warrior who became a holy man, but it is hard to discern any saintly act among so much fighting and fornication.'

'Perhaps the rug was unfinished, Lord?' said Harold, glancing at the Normans who stared back coldly. 'Or the end cut off?'

'We shall never know,' sighed the king, 'but in principle, it is a fine way to record deeds. I should have ordered such a rug to tell the story of my own reign ... save that there is no story to tell. I am neither warrior nor holy man.'

'You are both Lord,' insisted Cuthred, and Edward smiled.

'Nay Cuthred ... lie on my behalf to others if you must, but in my hall I would have the plain truth. My reign has been uneventful, mostly, and soon it will end.'

'An uneventful reign is the greatest bounty any sovereign can provide for his people,' said Harold. 'Your greatness, Lord, is manifest in the peace enjoyed by your subjects.'

'Alas … not all my subjects,' said Edward. 'The Danes have returned to sack and kill in East Anglia.'

Harold felt his shoulders twitch with a small thrill of danger.

'You have heard already of the attack on Stybbor, my Lord?'

'I have … but that is not why I summoned you to Lundene.'

The king glanced at Harold's companions.

'Did not Earl Tostig travel with you?'

'He did Lord, but the hour is yet early for the Earl of Northumbria.'

Harold's heart sank as he spoke – he felt he was betraying his brother in some small but meaningful way. He should have waited.

'I am pleased you came alone,' said Edward. 'It gives us an opportunity to talk.'

Harold's heart sank even further as he realised that events had come to a head, and he felt unprepared.

'Please leave us,' Edward announced to the hall, and the door wardens immediately ushered Cuthred, the two Normans, Olwin and Carl out of the chamber then departed themselves, leaving Harold alone with the king.

Edward sat in silence for a few moments, regarding Harold with his lips pursed, looking old and small.

'You have done a fine job as Subregulus,' began Edward. 'The kingdom, as you say, for the most part is at peace. But war will come when I am gone.'

Harold said nothing. He could tell from Edward's tone and manner that bad news was coming.

'I grow old,' continued Edward, 'and I feel my death not too many winters hence. It is like a dream that lingers on waking … departs with the day's routine but creeps back into my soul with the coming of night. One day the dream will not fade, and I will no longer be part of this world … save my bones.'

Edward was in a fey mood and Harold shivered once again, as though the king was about to speak his doom.

'I have no direct heir,' said Edward. 'The infant son of the aetheling has the best claim by blood, but I am aware he is not the witan's preference.'

'The witan will support whomever you support, Lord,' said Harold.

The king smiled and shook his head.

'While I live, they will ... but when I am gone my preference will seem less to their taste.'

And there it was – proof that Edward would not name Harold his successor. Harold remained impassive as Edward suddenly flashed with anger, 'Your father was my enemy. I will not have Godwin's seed take root on the seat of Inglalond! Even though it costs me my own dynasty!'

Harold said nothing, and Edward's anger abated, as though he was aware that his manners had been poor.

'I'm sorry Harold. You are, yourself, an honourable man but I sense your father still watching from the shadows and I will not give him victory even seven years past his death. I want your oath that you will support the aetheling's son Edgar in the witan.'

Harold swallowed drily, and looked the king in the eye.

'I think sire that you fear needlessly the spite of Godwin through the shape of his son ... but you are my king and I hold your command to be the equal of any oath.'

'Then swear to me,' insisted Edward.

'Very well ... I swear—'

'There is a further complication,' interrupted Edward.

Harold waited for the king to explain, but Edward seemed to be distracted once again by an internal conflict and took some time to continue. Harold found himself examining the beautiful stone vaulting held aloft by magic it seemed, until he realised that Edward was speaking even more softly than before.

'The Normans you met are emissaries of Duke William. I have been corresponding with him.'

Harold felt again the tingling across his shoulders and his hands closed into fists as the king said, 'Nothing has been promised, but if I were to die suddenly and Edgar still a child ... William claims a right to the succession. It is tenuous at best ... but I deem that he could prove to be Edgar's clearest obstacle.'

'What does he offer for recognition of his claim?' asked Harold, barely restraining his fury that the Bastard Duke of Normandy might be preferred to a son of Godwin.

'He offers peace ... and the possibility of extending our realm. It would be good to know that a part of the greater continent was also Inglalond.'

'Are we not safer as one people on our own island?' queried Harold.

'We are safer when all the scrapping dogs are in the one pit,' responded Edward with a flash of his former anger. Then immediately he subsided once again and returned to his inner conflict, leaving Harold confused, angry and beginning to see problems in the future which he had thought relatively uncomplicated until that moment.

'Nothing is promised,' continued Edward. 'I would prefer Edgar ... he has the clearest claim ... but he is very young and cannot be expected to rule for many years. I fear I do not have many years and that the succession will be determined between William and you.'

'I have said many times, Lord, that I will respect your choice for the peace of Inglalond.'

'Then swear it.'

Harold swallowed drily, troubled by many things – not least the insult to his family – but said, 'I swear to support the claim of the aetheling Edgar to the seat of Inglalond ... while he lives.'

Edward stared closely at Harold, as though he might require a supplementary oath, but then nodded.

'There is yet another matter I wished to discuss with you Harold ... the attack on Stybbor.'

'I know of it Lord. In fact—'

'I have appointed Malgard son of Rathgar as thegn and reeve of Stybbor,' continued Edward. 'It lies within the earldom of East Anglia, but the lands in question are linked with your own estate.'

'I am aware of that,' said Harold, 'but Lord ... there is something you need to—'

'Furthermore,' continued Edward, 'I have named Malgard's nephew, Brand Holgarsson, outlaw. He led the attack himself and sold his own father to the Danes.'

Harold was so astonished, he opened his mouth to speak, but no words could come.

'A man of God!' shouted Edward, his black humour restored. 'The crime is inconceivably evil … but for a man promised to the church to undertake such an enterprise is beyond my wit to comprehend! You will hunt him Harold. I have sent out word that I want this outlaw taken and made an example of for all Christendom to applaud!'

Harold was shocked into silence and Edward's eye's narrowed.

'Do you happen to know the whereabouts of Brand Holgarsson?' he asked.

'No,' said Harold.

∞ ∞ ∞

Despite the evil stink, the streets of Lundene were a riot of activity.

I walked with Valla through street after street of market stalls selling the wares of the town and the produce of its surrounding districts. Hundreds of people – in fact, thousands (if such numbers were possible) – flocked about the stalls shouting and pushing, laughing and swearing in an intricate merry dance. Pigs, horses, starving dogs and cats were all in the thick of it and Malgard trotted about sniffing at every new scent like a beast possessed.

'You really shouldn't call him Malgard,' reproved Valla. 'Malgard is an evil name.'

'It is a dog's name,' I replied and then cursed as Malgard rolled ecstatically in rotting fish guts – he'd be ripe tonight.

Valla laughed at the dog's antics and my disapproval. 'He's only doing what comes naturally,' she said, and I cocked an eyebrow.

'Why is it that Malgard is allowed to do what comes naturally, and yet I am not?'

'Because you are a man,' said Valla, 'with a high and noble purpose. A dog cannot choose his nature.'

It was the same argument we had had a hundred times but I never tired of it. And Valla seemed in an unusually happy mood so who knew what further inroads I might make in her resolve on such a day?

Harold's staff had sewn up all the rents in my brother's cloak – the light green cloak bearing the family device which he had worn on the day of his wedding and his death, and now I wore it proudly – feeling rather fine in the clothes Harold had provided, plus the boots I had taken from the dead Viking. And with Valla at my side in another gown furnished by the women of Harold's household, I felt a glow of happiness – I was a lord, walking in his finery with a beautiful wife among the streets of a great city. Life was good indeed and only getting better.

As we walked, Valla was examining the dagger she had claimed the morning after she had slain Olaf.

'It is beautiful work,' she said, 'I wonder who made it?'

'The runes are Danish,' I said. 'My father had one very similar.'

And in that moment I realised it was very likely my father's own knife – stolen by the Danes in the raid on Stybbor.

'What's wrong?' demanded Valla. 'You look like Malgard just pissed in your breakfast.'

And with the mention of his name, Malgard suddenly bolted up a lane leading away from the river.

'Hey! Come back!' I shouted. In fact, I was tempted to just forget him but Valla went after him, so what choice did I have?

'Stupid mongrel,' I cursed, looking up at the over-arching roofs which seemed to hold in the stink as they kept out the light. I was gagging with disgust as Valla ran into the tangled maze of lanes and alleys and within half a minute I was lost.

It was a cool and eerie feeling – just moments before we'd been surrounded by people, colour and clamour, and now there was a brooding silence. Some faces stared pale from the shadows but few were on the streets save the usual grimy children, dogs and rats.

I caught up with Valla where two alleys intersected and we debated which way led back to the river. All ways looked exactly the same, so it seemed the logical thing to go back in the direction we'd come from.

And as soon as we turned we saw them – four men carrying cudgels and watching us with obvious malice. They paused as we made eye contact, but then rushed at us and without thinking I pulled my sword from its scabbard.

Valla screamed as I stepped in front of her, threatening all four with the blade and they checked their run – none of them wanting to be first to test my skill. Funnily enough, I was immediately aware of how much stronger my sword arm had grown in just a week of practice. I felt power and confidence and stepped forward to threaten the closest of the ruffians who dared to assail us. Immediately the fellow to my right stepped past the point of my blade and swung his cudgel, but I managed to duck, and at the same time turned my original lunge into a backswing, which took him in the thigh. He grunted with pain and immediately backed out of the fight.

That still left three, all of them larger than me but none with swords.

'Run,' I shouted to Valla, who didn't move.

'Tostig! Help!' I shouted pathetically, knowing I was far from aid, but hoping to bring people out of their houses.

If anything the streets were emptier than before and the attackers laughed. The man at the back sneered, 'No-one can hear you Brand, so save your breath.'

With the use of my name I felt a chill of terror. These were no common footpads. The man who had spoken had a face of pure evil and his short hair had a strangely viscous appearance, as though it had been poured onto his head – like dark honey.

'Help came last time you attacked me,' I said, feeling the beginning of an ache in my sword arm. 'Why shouldn't it come again?'

Quick as a snake, the attacker on the right threw his heavy cudgel and before I could react, it fetched me a cruel blow on the knee and I staggered forward in pain.

The last thing I remembered was Valla's scream.

∞ ∞ ∞

Elric was enjoying being a servant. The hours were long but the work far easier than the hand-to-mouth life he had led in the woods.

It was a strange fate that had led him back to Valla. He hadn't seen his daughter since his own Valla had taken her away – to the place she had said he could not follow. And he had tried to follow but lost them in the mists and the woods, and the woods is where he had found himself, some years later, living with other outlaws until he remembered her only in dreams.

And then he had heard his daughter proclaim her name in the

darkness of the wood.

The following day he had known her at first sight, and she had known him despite the years that lay between them. She had been a child of less than 40 seasons when they'd parted, and now she was a young woman who reminded him achingly of her mother – clearly smitten by a young man who blazed with destiny.

And now Elric's own destiny was bound up with Brand's. There was little for Elric to do in the Lundene house – especially with Brand out walking – but in any case, Brand had released him from service. Of course, that release was not generally known, and if it was, he might well be claimed by Harold (whose Fighting Man device had been burnt onto his arm). So, for the sake of appearances, and for other reasons of his own, Elric laundered Brand's clothes and polished his gear. He swept out the room Brand shared with Valla and strewed the floor with fresh rushes. Then he went down to the kitchens to see what might be begged from the cook.

He was not the only one with that idea – Brand's dog Malgard was barking madly at the cooks and ignoring the scraps of mutton fat they had thrown on the floor.

'What's up Malgard?' asked Elric, and the dog jumped at his face forcing Elric to defend himself, then raced out the door.

∞ ∞ ∞

It was the pain that woke me. Not just the pain in my head, but also the feeling that my arms were being pulled out of their sockets.

Then the cold and the stench began to register, which somehow made the pain even worse.

But what finally caused my eyes to open in angry protest was the realisation that someone was pulling at the ring on my finger. It had always been overlarge for me and was pulled away before I could close my fist.

'Thank you Brand … I've been looking for this. I'll take that fine looking cloak also.'

To my amazement and horror, I was looking into the face of my uncle and sworn enemy.

'You piece of shit,' I tried to say, but the words were choked and

133

slurred. Even speaking was painful.

'You will rejoice to learn,' said Malgard, admiring my father's ring, 'that the king himself has named me reeve and thegn of Stybbor.'

I realised that the pain in my shoulders was caused by the fact that I was tied to a wall and I managed to stand, immediately easing that particular problem but my head was on fire and I felt like I was about to be sick.

We were in a small dark room, like a cellar, but it could never have been used for storage as it was far too damp and stank of filthy river water. There was a brazier of hot coals in the centre of the room and a single torch burning in a bracket above a low door. As my eyes adjusted to the dim red light, I saw Valla lying trussed on the floor at my feet. There were other shadows shifting about behind Malgard.

I opened my mouth to speak, but Malgard slapped me hard in the face.

'You will speak when invited to, boy,' he snarled. 'I haven't finished explaining the depths into which you have fallen.'

He slipped the ring over a finger on his left hand.

'Fits perfectly,' he said. 'Clearly it was destined to be so. I was fated to be thegn and you were fated to die in a sewer and be turned into pig shit. That's a proper fate for an outlaw.'

I just stared at him in angry bewilderment and he laughed.

'Yes ... outlaw,' continued Malgard. 'You were outlawed by the king when he heard about your evil part in the attack on Stybbor. That a man of God could do such a thing seemed to perturb him greatly ... he was quite upset about it, and very angry.'

'You arsehole!' I slurred, finally managing speech, but he smacked me again in the face.

'What did I say about speaking when invited?' he asked mildly.

'The king will learn the truth from Harold Godwinson,' I said, ignoring his rules.

'Yes, I was quite concerned about that possibility,' said Malgard. 'But if you are no longer around to make the claim, then Harold will soon forget your matter ... aaah, what have we here?'

All my and Valla's belongings were heaped on a small bench and Malgard pulled Valla's dragon-hilted knife from the pile.

'This was mine,' he laughed, '... given to me by Holgar, but the last time I saw it, it was stuck in his chest. I wonder how it came here.'

I roared with rage and leapt at him, and Malgard laughed in my face as the ropes held me back.

'He died badly ... your father,' said Malgard, examining the knife closely, '... although your death will be far worse and will end, I think, with this family heirloom stuck between your ribs.'

With that he slapped me hard again and I seemed to see stars as my head thumped against the wall. Then two men pushed past Malgard, dragged Valla off the floor and threw her over a bale.

'Leave her!' shouted another man. It was the honey haired turd who had led the attack in the lane. He pushed the others aside and stooped to examine Valla's face. She had a rag tied around her mouth which he tore away and immediately she screamed, but he struck her hard in the face and she was shocked into numb silence.

That woke me up. A cold murderous rage came over me, and I felt strangely calm, looking quickly about the room and taking in all possibilities to aid our escape. I was aware of a sharp edge to the mortar near my right wrist and began gently rubbing the rope that tied me against it. It was unlikely that anyone would notice in the flickering semi-darkness, but the attention of all the men was now on Valla, sobbing as she lay on the bale.

'Allow me to introduce Gorik,' said Malgard, indicating Honey Hair. 'He is an assassin of great skill, and I rather think he admires your lady.'

Gorik tore at Valla's dress and she resisted for about two seconds until he slapped her twice again. Then she just lay there in tears as he ripped the dress down the front to reveal the thin but beautiful body against which I had slept for the last six nights.

'Well, well ... you are a pretty one,' said Malgard, as the other men shuffled forward and Gorik pulled down his breeches. 'Like a perfect flower, but we shall pluck you ... petal by petal.'

'You filthy piece of shit!' I shouted, my voice finding strength in rage and terror, but Gorik just laughed.

'You think I'm filthy now?' he said. 'Wait till you see what I get up to with your pretty lady!'

Desperately I rubbed harder at the mortar, despite the fact that it was tearing my flesh as well as the rope. A trickle of blood ran down my arm and dripped off my elbow, but it was easy to ignore the pain in my anger as Gorik, already rampant, knelt on the filthy floor and pushed Valla's knees apart.

'No!' she sobbed, as Gorik seized Malgard's dagger and laid its tip against her breast.

'Shut your mouth and open your legs or I'll slice your fucking tits off!' he snarled.

Malgard laughed.

'Are you enjoying this Brand?' he asked. 'Gorik of course won't be the last. Your pretty lady will have many husbands today, and you will watch them all.'

They were all watching Gorik as he poised over Valla and shouted at two of his men to hold her legs apart.

'You're a fucking mouse cock Gorik,' I said. 'You won't even touch the sides with a shrivelled up piece of mouse turd like that!'

'Hold her still!' shouted Gorik, ignoring me.

'Don't know why you're trying to plough a woman in any case,' I continued, my voice getting louder in my fear and fury. 'Don't you get ploughed yourself every night by Malgard? Isn't that what you prefer, Mouse Cock? Malgard's cock up your arse, while you squeak for more?'

With a terrifying roar, Gorik abandoned Valla and lurched up from the floor. I couldn't twist aside as his fist thumped into my guts and then smashed me in the face so that my head whacked again against the wall behind me.

Gorik then turned away and walked over to the brazier where he pulled a red hot poker from the coals and approached me – his face twisted with evil wrath.

'Mouse cock, am I?' he snarled. 'At least I've got a cock, which is more than you'll have in a moment.'

He held the poker before my face, and I could feel its heat from more than a foot away.

'But before we take your cock we'll take your eye,' he said. 'Just the one, for now, because I want you to see what I can do with this mouse cock of mine.'

And with that he lunged the poker at my left eye, but in that instant the last of the rope broke and I managed to grab the poker half way up its shaft and deflect it from my face. The heat, some eighteen inches from the burning tip, was still searing but I managed to hold on and tear the poker from Gorik's grasp. Then I reversed it on him and he screamed as the brand took him on the side of the face.

In the immediate uproar, as men came at me with knives, I alternated between swinging the poker to keep them at bay and applying the burning tip to the other rope securing me. It caused further grievous injury to my left hand and wrist, but I was suddenly free and stepped forward, swinging the poker and standing over Valla, who swept up the dagger Gorik had dropped.

Gorik had run screaming from the room but Malgard was shouting at the other men to attack me. It was hard to see how many there were in the half darkness, but I strode forward and pulled another branding iron from the brazier then kicked it over, scattering coals towards Malgard who shrieked and ran for the door. The scattered coals, unfortunately concentrated all the men in half of the room which meant they were all between me and the door, and it was suddenly much darker. The room filled with smoke and then one of my pokers was swept from my hand by a cudgel I'd not seen in the dark. Bodies pressed around me and then a terrible scream filled the chamber. Then another, and I realised the men were turning away from me – to a new danger. Immediately I stepped forward and caused more screams myself as the brand found more flesh to burn. One of my victims twisted aside and fell onto the coals where he screamed horribly and the small room stank of scorched meat.

'Brand!'

I couldn't see through the smoke and the press of bodies, but it was Elric's voice.

'Elric!'

'Force them onto the coals!' he shouted, and at once I moved to my right to herd the last two of the attackers towards the coals on my left. One of them tried to slip past me but Valla with a shriek of vengeance leapt from behind me with the dagger, forced him to stop and my poker came down hard upon his head which split like an over-ripe fruit.

Suddenly the room was much brighter and I realised that, despite the dampness of the chamber, one of the bales had caught alight, and the smoke was much thicker.

'Get out!' yelled Elric as he drove a sword through the guts of the last attacker, who had fallen to his knees in an effort to surrender.

'Get out!' he shouted again and I dragged Valla through the carnage of flesh, slipping and choking and our eyes stinging. Up a flight of wet stairs, we found ourselves in a filthy hovel like an old fisherman's shack. There were a few greasy bunks and a central table littered with bowls and flagons and the fly-blown remnants of a joint of mutton. To my surprise and disgust, Elric seized the joint as we fled the hovel and found ourselves back outside – where Malgard leapt about us happily. Elric tossed him the stinking joint and he tore into it, his tail wagging with frenzied joy.

Then the pain hit. Both of my hands were blistered from handling the hot irons, and my right arm was torn from the sharp mortar, but I was alive and exultant. I roared with victory as smoke poured from the burning house of my defeated enemies and Valla threw her arms around my neck and clung to me fiercely.

'Thank the dog!' shouted Elric as the street filled with anxious neighbours carrying buckets, rakes and axes to stop the flames spreading to their own shacks.

Ignoring Malgard's angry growls, he picked up the joint again and carried it away, beckoning Valla and I to follow as Malgard yelped for his prize.

'Thank the dog,' Elric repeated, as we pushed through the crowds and found a street heading down towards the river. 'He was barking his head off and wanting someone to follow … that's how I found you. This is yours by the way.'

He handed me the bloody sword, plus the scabbard.

'I found it upstairs before I ventured down … came in useful. Did you see that last fool, trying to surrender?'

Elric laughed and shook his head.

'Fine with me if they don't want to fight … makes 'em much easier to kill.'

The pain was really gripping me now and I couldn't take the sword.

'Hold it for me,' I said, indicating my ruined hands. And that's when I remembered the ring.

'Fuck!' I shouted. 'Fucking Malgard! He's got my ring!'

Elric hadn't seen Malgard, or Gorik, when he'd stormed the house, and there's no way they'd still be there. I shrugged and continued walking. The king would give me a new ring when he learned what had happened.

∞ ∞ ∞

'You cannot go to the king,' said Harold.

'Why not?'

'Because he has named you outlaw, and will not relent.'

Back in Harold's house, my wounds had been tended as well as the art of his physician allowed, although Valla had insisted on dealing with my burns herself, mixing a filthy balm out of some mysterious ingredients, which seemed mostly to be mutton fat.

'Can we not explain to him the truth of Malgard's treachery? Is he not just?'

'His ears are bewitched,' sighed Harold. 'His minister Cuthred I deem has the mastery and favours Malgard. I did not press the matter for I did not wish the king to know your whereabouts. Indeed, I broke my own word and lied on your behalf.'

I stared at Harold in misery, but held my tongue, perceiving how deeply he felt about the matter.

'I lied because to do otherwise would have resulted in a greater evil,' continued Harold, and my heart went out to him. His was a most noble spirit and I felt once again a profound insight, as though again I was privy to the Mind of God, blazing through the vessel of Harold.

'I cannot thank you enough, my lord,' I said. 'Please allow me to return the favour by serving among your housecarls.'

'That would please me also Brand,' he smiled. 'But for the moment you must be hidden. Travel with me by all means, and learn to use your sword, but the name Brand must be buried, for now.'

∞ ∞ ∞

In bed that night, Valla lay for a long while with her arms about me and her face buried against my neck. I was unable to touch or hold her in return, but lay on my back in a state of bliss despite the pain of my wounds.

'I cannot begin to express my gratitude,' whispered Valla, after a long contented silence.

I could think of a way she might begin, but it would have been churlish to say so. Of course, my manhood was straining upwards against the coverlet like a tent pole, and Valla's hand moved down my chest, my stomach – her fingers like feathers – and I gasped as she held me. This time without the gelding knife in her other hand.

'Would you save me from rape,' she asked, 'just to do the deed yourself?'

'I would.'

She laughed softly, and her hand began to move.

'There are other ways, my darling,' she whispered, and the pain in my hands seemed like nothing at all.

PART TWO

Chapter 13

The Last Words of Ygrene

The bale of fire was hurled into the night sky, struck the keep tower in a spectacular display of burning shards and then sank out of sight behind the stockade wall.

The stockade was the fastness of Dafydd ap Rhiwallon, one of Gruffydd ap Llewellyn's cousins, but Dafydd was absent, at Gruffydd's camp no doubt, and it would cost him.

His family were within and nearly a hundred men had defended the stockade, but it was going to fall – like all the others had fallen in Harold's spring and summer campaign against the Welsh. Gruffydd called himself a king, but that was not to Edward's liking so the Godwinsons had brought their housecarls – Harold from the south, Tostig from the north – and had raised the fyrd.

As the rightful thegn of Stybbor, I should have been among Harold's closest, but by virtue of Malgard's treachery I had been outlawed, so was hidden in the fyrd. But in the three years since I had come into Harold's service, I had learned to fight and had seen much violence. At 17, I was taller than most and almost in the fullness of my strength. Indeed, I found fighting to be simple. Carl had been right when he'd taught me the importance of sword strength – he with the strength to hold up a shield and use a heavy sword for longer would always prevail.

I had even developed my own style of fighting – keeping my foe at bay by holding the point of my sword towards his face and waiting for him to tire himself with slashes which I simply avoided or fended with my limewood shield. Inevitably, my foe would stumble, or overextend, and then I would strike – at sword arm or throat – whichever presented itself.

Another bale of fire rose sparking into the night, soared over the wall and burst in a great wash of light which then faded to a sombre flickering red. Again the throwing machine was righted and its winches squealed as the ropes were tightened, forcing the great lever downwards until the scoop might be loaded with another burning bale.

I could fight in the shield wall, but I preferred open combat where strength and speed and cunning were more likely to be rewarded. The shield wall, for all its honour, was more prone to chance. One could be felled by a stray spear or sword thrust deflecting off the poorly held shield of a neighbour, or even have one's feet pulled from under by peasants with long hooked bills reaching from behind the enemy shield wall.

Fortunately, in battles of greater renown, I was forbidden to stand with the housecarls in order to prevent my recognition during the shouting of names and lineages prior to engagement. My battles were fought on the edges of the shield wall, but these were bloody affairs and could have a major impact on the outcome. If the enemy's shield wall could be threatened from the flank, it would quickly fall apart, and I had never been beaten in such a battle. Harold and Tostig valued my prowess and bade me wait until my name could be cleared.

'Harold will be king after Edward,' Tostig frequently declared, '... and Edward grows old. When he is gone you can confront Malgard, but please allow me to be present when you do. I would love to see his face when he realises you still live and that he no longer enjoys the king's protection.'

Harold, Tostig and Elric had spread the rumour that I had perished in the burning house where I had defeated Malgard's assassins and killed my first man in battle – whose head had been crushed with the poker I'd wrested from Gorik's hand. My scars had been grievous, and slow to heal, but heal they had and by strange coincidence, the men of the fyrd named me Branded Hands (or Brand for short) without ever connecting me with the outlawed thegn of Stybbor.

Elric also fought at my side in Harold's battles. At first he had been my mentor, but in the new fighting season of 1063 I had felt my prowess and confidence grow, and now I had emerged as a natural leader. As a servant, Elric's place should not have been in the battle, but such was his own prowess with sword, spear and bow that no-one questioned the matter. In fact, I had freed him but he stayed for the adventure and to be close to his daughter.

As for that, my relationship with my 'wife' had strengthened and deepened in the three years since I had saved her from rape in a stinking cellar on the banks of the Temes, but it was yet to deepen in the way I wanted it to. To the world we appeared to live as man and wife, but in private she retained her maidenhood despite the many tricks she devised for satisfying my lust. There were also times, she told me, when she could barely contain her own powerful urges, but if she were to become with child, the source of her magic would pass to the daughter in her womb.

Not that she displayed much in the way of magic, except in the manner of healing, and her herbs and ointments were much sought after by the men of the fyrd. Even Harold's physician would at times consult her in the use of herbs or the making of balms, and she travelled with the fyrd, refusing to leave my side and making me happy in the process. Although there was no denying that I looked forward impatiently to the full consummation of our 'marriage'.

Flames suddenly leapt up and brightened the night beyond the stockade wall and Harold raised his hands to cease the battle. He stood before the gate under his twin banners – *The Red Dragon* of Wessex and *The Fighting Man* (his personal standard) and called for Dafydd to surrender before he burn with all his household.

'Dafydd! Yield the fort and your family will be spared!'

'Dafydd isn't here!' called a strangely accented voice. 'He is with the king.'

'There is no king,' returned Harold, 'save King Edward in Lundene. Swear allegiance to him now and I may spare you.'

There was an eerie silence for a few moments, but then flames became visible over the wall and some screaming could be heard. Suddenly the gate was thrust open and Harold's men fell back. A large man appeared in the doorway holding a huge axe, which he flung down and walked forward, palms raised and empty. Harold inclined his head and bade the man stand next to him as dozens of his followers darted out of the burning fort, throwing their weapons onto a rapidly growing pile as they came.

The leader's name was Garryd and he walked back towards the flames, shouting, 'Ygrene! Come quickly and bring your child!'

There were more screams, but no further fugitives ran from the flames.

'Ygrene!' shouted Garryd, his eyes filling with tears as he was forced back by the heat.

Then a woman appeared at the gate bearing a child, the fire all about her and licking at her clothes and hair. As we watched, her long red mane kindled and she pointed at Harold, calling loudly in the strange tongue of the Welsh. Then she spat in his direction, turned her back and walked calmly back into the boiling horror of flame.

'What did she say?' asked Harold, as Garryd stared stricken with grief at the roaring bonfire that had been home for over a hundred people.

Garryd would not translate Ygrene's last words, but he didn't really need to – and over the next hours her words were repeated a thousand times.

'I see your doom invader ... when a new star lights the sky then all that is yours will be taken away. Your house will be burned as mine burns, and all your deeds forgotten. Only your death will be remembered.'

It was well known that people on the brink of death were given strange visions and women especially had the power of prophecy at such times. Harold was deeply troubled by the last words of Ygrene.

Valla also was moved by the manner of her death.

'She felt no pain,'

'She must have felt pain ... the heat was unbearable, and we were thirty paces from the gate.'

'Nay,' said Valla, in wonder. 'In the passion of her death she moved and spoke calmly. She must have had great power to master the flames, even as they consumed her.'

'If she had power, why didn't she use it to save herself?'

'Maybe she did,' said Valla.

Then later as we lay together in a roll of fleeces, I discovered the reason for Valla's preoccupation with Ygrene's words.

'She mentioned the star ... the new star. What do you think she meant by that?'

'There's no such thing as a new star,' I replied.

'Sometimes I see a strange new star in my dreams,' said Valla. 'Only, it is different to other stars … and moves.'

'Some stars move … Mars and Venus move.'

'The star of my dreams is different, and much bigger than ordinary stars. It has long hair, like a woman in the wind.'

'A hairy star,' I laughed and Valla squeezed my balls, causing my laughter to cease abruptly.

'This is important Brand.'

'Alright,' I gasped, forcing her hand away from my balls, and she began to stroke my thigh, which usually meant she was about to proceed to further ministrations.

'I've dreamt of the star and now Ygrene foresees it in the moments before her death,' she continued, stroking my thigh and trailing her fingers along my stomach. 'It can only mean doom.'

'How do you know that the star of Ygrene is the same as your hairy star?' I said, rolling onto my side and cupping my hand between Valla's thighs.

Normally, she would push my hand away, but that night she kissed me fiercely and pulled me on top of her. Almost before I knew it my manhood was throbbing at the gate of her maidenhood and her hand was guiding me home.

But I found myself resisting. I too could see the future, and what I saw was Valla with child and leaving me for the Place of Dreams.

'Brand,' she whispered, nuzzling at my neck and writhing beneath me. 'I am ready for you.'

Her hand pulled me down but still I resisted – tormented by the thought of losing her – tormented also by the fact that I was resisting what I had longed for, ached for.

'Please Brand … my love … be one with me.'

On hands and knees, I held myself rigidly still and said, 'I'm going to lose you, aren't I?'

'What do you mean?'

'One day, when we have a daughter, you will leave and take her to the Place of Dreams … as your mother took you.'

Valla lay still and was silent for a while. Then she said, 'If I go, then I will return to you when my task is complete.'

'Like your mother returned to Elric?'

The moment passed, and I distracted myself (as I had done many times over the last three years) by allowing my thoughts to turn to Malgard. I took some pleasure in the thought of him growing soft and complacent in my father's home while I grew tall and strong and battle-hardened, but while the king lived I was not ready to take my revenge.

Malgard would keep, unlike Valla who was clearly still restless. Once again her hand reached between my legs and once again I held it still.

∞ ∞ ∞

The next morning, the fort was a charred and smoking ruin. Harold stood with Garryd and Carl (whom he had appointed his personal chaplain) and hung his head in grief.

'I am charged with a task by the king,' he said, 'but I take no pleasure in the death of innocents. Nor do I see the need for such deaths.'

'She was proud,' said Garryd, 'and preferred the ruin of her flesh to the ruin of her pride.'

'I would have treated her with honour and restored her to her husband … on condition he laid down his arms and no longer supported Gruffydd.'

'He never would have done so,' said Garryd, 'and doubtless Ygrene wished to avoid becoming a gaming piece that might be used against her husband. Her death confirms Dafydd's allegiance to his cousin.'

'And makes a bitter foe for me,' replied Harold. 'So be it. I have many foes.'

'Your friends outnumber your foes Lord,' said Carl.

'That is so, for which I thank the Lord,' said Harold. 'But it takes only one foe to kill a man.'

'Not while I live,' growled Garryd.

Garryd had sworn an oath to Harold and all his followers likewise. The vanquished often made such oaths in return for their lives but Garryd appeared to genuinely mean it.

'Believe not Lord that you have many foes among the Welsh,' he said. 'You are known to be a man both of honour and prowess … and Gruffydd Ap Llewellyn is a fool. We might have lived in peace within our marches, but he wants to antagonise Edward by calling himself king.'

'King of the Sheepfuckers!' laughed Tostig, joining the conversation.

Harold stared sternly at his brother, but Garryd laughed grimly.

'The Sheepfuckers,' he said, 'will be on your side if you can rid them of Gruffydd and promise them peace.'

With that he strode away, and Harold turned to his brother.

'Garryd is a good man, and will help us keep the peace when Gruffydd is destroyed.'

'Keep the peace,' sneered Tostig. 'Since when were the sons of Godwin interested in peace with Sheepfuckers?'

'The sons of Godwin are interested in peace with all men,' insisted Harold, barely able to mask his irritation. 'If I am ever to be king, brother, then it must be achieved through building bridges … not burning them down.'

'But I like burning bridges,' laughed Tostig. 'Even if I must stand on the bridge as it burns, I will do so if it brings down my enemy.'

∞ ∞ ∞

Valla moved among the women and children who had been last to leave the burning fort, many of whom had been scorched. She had mixed up a large batch of her stinking sheep fat balm to soothe their hurts, and of course she wasn't talking to me. In the past I had inspired her fury when she believed me capable of rape, but that was nothing compared with the wrath that descended after I'd refused to lie with her.

First she had teased.

Then she pleaded.

Then she became angry and insulting, even suggesting that maybe I'd prefer to be with Olaf Pighammer.

And when I laughed, she raged.

And then she cried.

'Forgive me Brand … you were right. Tonight was not the time but I felt the need so strongly. The power would have passed from me.'

But for all her penitence and gratitude, she was still distant and cold the next morning, as though I had done her great insult in preserving her powers. Perhaps in a thousand years time women will be less of a mystery to men.

One of the most sorely afflicted by burns was Guinned, one of Ygrene's sisters who had barely survived the fire and was grieving piteously for her sibling. Valla applied the balm gently to the horrible burns on her arms and legs, causing me to remember the pain of my own branding three years earlier. Guinned's burns were far worse than mine, but she bore the pain stoically in honour of her sister.

'You remind me of Ygrene,' she suddenly said to Valla, and for some reason I felt a thrill of doom – of warning perhaps.

'Ygrene?' asked Valla.

'You have the skill, don't you?'

Valla paused in her work and looked the girl in the eye.

'I have skill with healing,' she said with a glance in my direction, as though wanting to end the conversation.

'It is more than that,' replied Guinned. 'I feel it in your hands and see it in your eyes.'

Valla resumed her tender application of the balm – Guinned's right side and breast had also been burned.

'I feel Ygrene's death less bitterly now,' said Guinned. 'Now that I know you live. I feared Ygrene was the last.'

Valla suddenly turned on me.

'Brand, I need more nettles … could you fetch me some please?'

I glanced into the pot and saw there was still plenty of the balm, and knew that she wanted to speak with Guinned privately.

As I turned away to fetch the unneeded nettles I felt the sky darken so was surprised to look up and see the sun shining in a flawless field of blue.

∞ ∞ ∞

'Where do you want to go?'

'A cave.'

That afternoon, Valla repeated the conversation she'd had with Ygrene's sister, who was now sleeping peacefully under the shelter created for the more grievously wounded – most of whom were women and children. We had suffered almost no casualties during the short siege.

'Guinned bade me go to see Myrrthn in his cave … Ygrene's tutor.'

'A tutor in a cave?'

'So she said. It is two miles to the west … along the river, then a path when we reach the beech tree … withered into the shape of an aged man.'

'A withered beech … '

'Then down into a small hollow … made of stone. His cave is there.'

'Why does she want you to see him?'

Valla seemed strangely distracted, and I knew there was something she wasn't telling me.

'Myrrthn must be told of Ygrene's death. It is a courtesy.'

'Then why not send a servant … or one of Guinned's own people?'

'She asked me to do it,' said Valla, 'and I said I would. You don't have to come.'

There was little chance of that. These were dangerous hills at the best of times, but after a battle when the stray Welsh would be thirsting for vengeance, it was asking for trouble to walk alone more than fifty paces from the camp.

Elric and I donned our fighting gear and waited by the river path for Valla to join us. We had a strange relationship, Elric and I. He was almost the same age as Harold but seemed much younger. He and Valla never seemed to acknowledge their own relationship, but clearly liked each other, and I felt a great sadness for him that he had been sundered from his own Valla.

'Do you think you may ever see her again?' I asked suddenly. We hadn't discussed that topic for a while, but he knew immediately who I meant.

'I believe so,' he said, after a pause, then walked a few paces down the path to try and see around the next bend.

In his fighting gear, Elric did not have the look of a serf. Like me he wore sheep leather boots wrapped with thongs over heavy woollen hose, a tough leather jacket, reinforced in certain places either for protection or to assist archery. Elric was a very fine archer – as good as Valla – and together they had taught me some of their art, but I was much better with the sword and, as I grew, was coming to like using the battle axe I had taken from Olaf Pighammer. I was also becoming accustomed to wearing Angdred's shirt of rings – it was still a bit large for me but it gave confidence. If you are less worried about the thrusts of others you can better concentrate on guiding your own to where they might do most damage.

As was my habit, I pulled the sword from its scabbard and held it out straight at shoulder height. I could do this effortlessly now, for long periods, knowing that the practice had saved my life on several occasions and was likely to do so many times into the future. In order to balance I held the axe in my left hand, but it was much heavier and I could not keep it up as long.

The sword I had named *Revanche*, meaning 'vengeance' in the Norman tongue that both Harold and Carl had been teaching me. The tongue of politics they said. The axe I simply called *Pighammer*. It was a brutish thing, like its former owner, and terrorised any who came near when I began to swing it in a fight. That's when Elric and I made a strong team – an axe wielder, at the end of his stroke, must leave himself open to counter strokes but with Elric at my side with sword and shield to protect my flank we could carve great furrows in any mass of men. Truly, I feared no man and no battle.

One other weapon I had also. After that dreadful night in the cellar by the Temes, Valla had returned to me the silver hilted dragon knife which Malgard claimed had killed my father. The knife now lived in a sheath concealed in one of my boots and I had sworn an oath to use it only on one man. The knife had no name, for no name could possibly do justice to the depth of my hatred.

My reverie was disturbed by Malgard racing towards me, snout down and coursing while Valla followed looking beyond beautiful in a light summer gown. She carried a covered basket and smiled at me, and despite my misgivings we turned away from the camp in Malgard's excited wake.

It was a pleasant afternoon as the three of us set out along the path, Elric ten paces ahead with an arrow nocked as Valla and I walked hand-in-hand enjoying the music of the stream, the calls of birds and the sweet/warm smell of the season. Valla's favourite flowers –

bluebells – clustered in vast carpets and the drone of bees was like a music of subtle enchantment.

'This is a fine country,' I remarked, but Valla didn't answer – just squeezed my hand and I realised she was nervous.

'What's wrong?'

She gave me a tight smile and shook her head, and my careless reverie of moments before was replaced by a sense of foreboding.

'Is there some danger you've not told me about?'

'I don't know,' said Valla. 'I'm not sure what to expect.'

I released her hand and drew *Revanche* silently from its sheepskin scabbard.

But the birds continued to sing and the stream continued to whisper and chuckle – and gradually the sweet/warm spell came over me again.

After the best part of an hour we came to a tall, dead beech – grey with age and uncannily shaped in the form of a man. It seemed to be pointing up the narrow track that led away from the stream and, if anything, I felt even more relaxed. Elric and Malgard didn't pause to wait for us, just turned onto the track as though they'd gone that way a thousand times before.

The track led upwards for a few hundred paces, into thickening woods with rocks and roots forming a natural stairway. The sweat was beading as the work became harder and I wondered whether I truly needed the shirt of rings on such a peaceful errand.

Up ahead, Elric had paused and as we came up to him I noted the trees had cleared ahead, the reason being that we stood at the brink of a stone hollow – a ring of rock walls less than a hundred paces across and round almost as though fashioned by men. There were numerous caves in the wall and outside the largest a small fire was set with a few fish skewered on withes roasting. There was no-one in sight, but clearly the setter of the fire was not far away.

Another natural stair of cracked and broken stone led down into the hollow where a spring trickled out of the wall near the bottom, filled a large stone basin which splashed into a low cave and vanished.

We approached the larger cave where the fire was set, and there was a sense of peace that hung over the hollow like the smoke that rose from the small fire but stayed within the circle of stone. The smell of the roasting fish was overpowering, and I suddenly felt incredibly hungry.

'Eat!' cried a voice from the cave. 'Eat, and welcome to it.'

It was a strangely high pitched voice, and a small man appeared in the entrance – almost naked – clad in skins with a necklace of bones and covered with blue tattoos – mainly of spirals and interwoven serpents.

'Eat!' he repeated, gesturing at the fire and coming closer.

Before I could help myself, I had pulled three withes out of the fire, passed two to Valla and Elric and started tearing at the delectable fish that tasted like heaven. Elric also ate hungrily but Valla just stared at the man.

'You are Myrrthn?'

'I am,' he said. 'You are not hungry, like your companions?'

Valla didn't answer, and I noticed a pile of sweet smelling bracken – freshly culled and laid out as though to make a bed in the open air and I dropped my axe and sword and sat to finish my fish. Elric sat beside me, blinking and yawning stupidly. I would have laughed except I was far too sleepy to laugh.

∞ ∞ ∞

Valla was unconcerned when Brand and Elric fell into a deep sleep.

She was still unconcerned when the smile vanished from Myrrthn's face and he examined the sleeping men closely, sniffing at Brand as though he could tell his alignment and history in the same way Malgard did with other dogs.

'I was asked by Guinned,' said Valla, 'the sister of Ygrene … to bring you sad tidings. Ygrene is dead.'

'I have seen it,' said Myrrthn.

'You were there?'

'I have seen it,' he repeated, but would say no more.

He sat, on the opposite side of the fire and bade her sit beside him.

'You can eat the fish,' he said. 'It will not affect you as it did your friends. You have the skill.'

He pulled the last of the fish from the fire and began to eat himself, always with his eyes on Valla.

After a while he said, 'You have done well.'

'I have?'

'Very well. Any maid who lives among warriors and retains the skill must have power indeed.'

Valla stared at him frankly, partly irritated by his ill manners, partly fascinated.

'I have a very understanding husband,' she said, embarrassed, and at the same time marvelling how the best part of three years in Harold's household had turned her into something approaching a lady. Until she met Brand, she might have passed for a member of Myrrthn's clan.

'Do not be shamed,' said Myrrthn. 'These are important matters and must be discussed openly by two such as we. There are few left … I had great hopes for Ygrene but the tragedy of her death is leavened by your arrival.'

'What could my arrival possibly mean for you?' asked Valla, suddenly fearing that her happy life was about to be disrupted.

'You know,' chuckled Myrrthn. 'Oh yes, you know … you have managed to preserve your power and now the time approaches when you must use it. So you are frightened.'

'I'm not frightened,' said Valla, 'just confused. My mother said I must retain the power, but she never told me for what purpose.'

'And has it been hard to retain the power?'

Valla felt herself blush, but then the embarrassment lifted as though such personal intimacies were no more significant than eating or drinking.

'I was sorely tempted,' she said. 'My husband has endured my celibacy, but only last night I was overcome with desire and wished to give myself to him … but he would not.'

'The curse of love,' said Myrrthn, almost spitting with contempt, 'is the reason most women of power lose it. They try to justify their weakness with blandishments … say love is the greatest magic of all. They are wrong.'

'Was Ygrene a woman of power?'

'She was a woman of great power, but it passed to Raewyn, who burned beside her mother.'

'Ygrene shone with glory,' said Valla in awe. 'She noticed not the heat and spoke calmly and strongly … even as the fire took her hair and clothes.'

'It was the power of the child,' sighed Myrrthn, 'pouring out all at once to extinguish pain … but now it is gone. There are so few left like unto you, Valla. You are precious.'

'Precious to whom?'

'To those who would have the old ways remain potent in this land … the spirits of tree and brook and stone.'

'I am also precious to him,' said Valla, feeling a wave of fondness for Brand who lay in the bracken with a smile of contentment on his sleeping face.

'As I said, it is the curse of love,' sneered Myrrthn. 'If you stay with this man, you will surely feel the urge again and his forbearance may not be as strong next time. The power will pass sooner or later … sooner I think.'

'If only I knew what my purpose is to be,' cried Valla. 'It is hard to hold on to something when you know not what it is held for.'

'Your purpose is clear,' replied Myrrthn. 'To defend and preserve the old ways … the old world.'

As he spoke, his voice became strangely musical. A window seemed to open in her mind and much that was hidden was made clear.

'Yes … I see that,' breathed Valla in sudden awe.

'The world changes,' encouraged Myrrthn. 'This new god they bring from across the sea is killing all that was rich and green and growing. Like a pestilence it lays low the spirit of the old gods … the spirits of tree and brook and stone. They can only survive while the people honour and nourish them.'

'I have seen them,' said Valla in wonder. 'Like a waking dream … small bright creatures in sunlit glades or floating in eddies of hidden streams.'

'They sense your power,' said Myrrthn. 'They do not reveal themselves to many. Occasionally they take pity and aid a lost child and sometimes they might even take action to thwart or avenge an act of evil … but singly their influence is weak and grows weaker. United, they could be invincible.'

Pictures formed in Valla's mind as Myrrthn spoke, and she felt as though she was watching scenes from an epic history.

'Soon an army will land in ships bearing the red cross of the killer god. You can prevent it. You can raise the power of wood, brook and stone to keep this island free of outside influence ... make it a bastion for the old powers and the old ways.'

Myrrthn pulled a blade from somewhere and laid the tip at Brand's throat.

'What are you doing?' cried Valla, half-wrenched from her enchantment.

'It would be best if temptation was removed,' said Myrrthn. 'But in compensation for his life, I could send him to a heaven of unutterable bliss, if you wished it.'

'No. Please ... let him live. He is a man of great honour and has done only good to me despite trials that would have been far beyond the resolve of weaker men.'

'Then you must leave him,' said Myrrthn.

'Leave him?'

'Now ... before he wakes. You are too precious to lose.'

Even as Myrrthn spoke, Valla's heart was filled with all the love for Brand she'd been holding back almost from the moment she'd met him. In that moment she knew she couldn't go another night in his bed without doing what came most naturally.

'I ... I can't leave without saying goodbye,' she said, feeling flustered and forced untimely into an impossible choice.

'You must,' insisted Myrrthn. 'Your desire's so strong I can smell it. To spend another moment in his company will surely lead to you rutting like animals, and the power will pass. The task cannot wait for your daughter ... the killer god is coming in many ships ... and he is coming soon.'

'But he'll think I've abandoned him.'

Myrrthn's eyes narrowed.

'Already you doubt your purpose ... two hundred and forty-five years you have prepared for this task and after only a few seasons with this profane and brutal man you are ready to betray the gods ... betray all the mothers who sacrificed so much to give you the honour of the task! Betray Ygrene!'

'...Ygrene?'

Myrrthn spat into the fire and Valla realised that night had crept over the conversation. It was suddenly cold.

'Do you think it mere coincidence that Ygrene died when you happened along?'

'What?'

'Even now, she watches and she hears. Consider well before you betray her trust.'

Valla felt a rush of fear, but also of something else – something she had sensed but not properly understood before. Myrrthn waved a contemptuous hand toward Brand and Elric.

'All these fools with their swords and squabbles over the right to rule. Rule what? Other fools! Theirs is not the true conflict. The great battle of our times will be fought between gods. The killer god is coming ... our gods need a champion to unite them. It might have been Ygrene's daughter but she felt your power and knew you had a better chance of mustering the full power of the old gods. You would betray her sacrifice?'

'No,' said Valla. 'I will accept the task ... do the thing for which I was prepared.'

'That is well,' said Myrrthn, 'but the acceptance of your task requires a sacrifice of your own. That is why you must leave your husband ... until the task is done.'

'I can return to him?'

'When the task is done,' repeated Myrrthn.

'He won't know I mean to return,' said Valla, her heart already rending for the hurt she must do. 'He'll think himself alone and may despair ... or seek the comfort of others.'

'He will not,' said Myrrthn. 'He would seek you until the end of days ... if you leave a message.'

'So I may speak with him after all?' she asked, brightening.

'Urrgh ... the animal stench is strong on you,' complained Myrrthn, his face twisted with disgust. 'Nay ... no speech, but you can send him a dream, if you wish. A dream of your creation passed into his sleeping mind. I can arrange it ... lie next to him.'

Valla sat by her husband and smiled fondly. Beautiful he now seemed and filled with a noble purpose and spirit. There was greatness in him and the desire to share his life and bear his sons was suddenly overwhelming.

'Lie down,' repeated Myrrthn, impatiently. 'And think of the messages you want me to send to him. I will do the rest.'

Valla lay by Brand, kissed him on the lips and snuggled against him with one arm around his neck. She closed her eyes and allowed the carnal thoughts that had been growing in her mind of late to be fully expressed.

'Ooh, he's a lucky man,' laughed Myrrthn, his voice growing distant as though part of a dream himself, and Valla felt like she was moving – entwined with Brand but flying with a roaring in her brain, and her heart as light as a sparrow.

'There is a price for this,' said the voice, but Valla was too intent on her message to take much notice.

'A price?' she dimly wondered.

'His continuing celibacy,' chuckled Myrrthn. 'You may return to him when the task is done, for good or ill … but only if he has remained faithful to you.'

'He will remain faithful,' she murmured, even as she poured her love into the dream union, her heart filling with impossible joy.

'He will remain faithful,' she repeated.

'He will remain … '

Chapter 14

A Vulnerable Gaming Piece

I awoke from the most beautiful dream – strangely vivid, and so strong it felt more like a memory of things that had truly happened, and did not fade as dreams tend to fade.

In the dream, my refusal to lie with Valla had been overborne by the sweetness of her lips and the strength of her resolve, and my long wait had been worth it, a thousandfold.

So when I found myself looking up at a bright blue sky from a bed of sweet-smelling bracken, with Elric snoring gently at my side, I felt first surprise then the stirrings of alarm.

I leapt to my feet, staring about at the caves in the ring of stone, but somehow I knew she was gone.

'Valla!'

The fire by which we had lain had long gone cold and the stone hollow felt as though it had been abandoned for years.

'Valla!'

My voice echoed mocking from the walls and Elric grimaced and moaned. Then he looked up at me in shock.

'Brand!'

'Valla's gone.'

We gathered up our weapons and made a brief inspection of the larger caves, but it was a futile gesture. She was gone, as was the dog Malgard and the man – Myrrthn – and the whole incident of arriving in the hollow, eating the fish and falling asleep seemed like a bewitchment.

There was no point staying in the empty hollow so we trudged over to the stairs, washed our heads and drank from the clear, cold spring water in the basin, and left for Harold's camp. I hoped that she might have returned that way herself but knew I was deceiving myself. She would never have returned without me.

'It was hard waking this morning,' murmured Elric as we arrived back at the beech man who pointed up Myrrthn's path. 'Such a dream I had ... as though my Valla had never left.'

As he spoke, I remembered further details of my own dream – details of such intense passion they defy my powers of description – but an urgent message she left me also, which filled me both with sadness and with hope.

'Wait for me Brand. I promise I will return and never leave again, but first I have been given my task, for which I have long prepared. You will come to find it is allied with your own task but I can say no more for now. Stay faithful Brand. Lie with no other woman and I may return to you for the fulfilment of our life together ... for good or ill. There will be a sign. You will know it when you see it. Know that I am coming. It will not be as long as you think.'

'The Place of Dreams,' I sighed, tempted to take my axe to the beech man.

'The Place of Dreams,' repeated Elric, and we trudged in silence back to the camp.

∞ ∞ ∞

The camp was being struck as we returned and, as I expected, Valla had not come. Elric and I went looking for the kitchen but Skalpi, one of Harold's housecarls, called to me urgently.

'Brand ... there is a council within our Lord's pavilion. You are summoned.'

'I am?'

If I were recognised as the thegn of Stybbor then a summons to a Lords' Council would have been my natural due, but as a man named only for the scars on his hands I had no rights nor dues, save Harold's favour which he usually took care not to show in public.

Harold's tent was the only one still erected and I hurried over with Skalpi. The guards stood aside to admit me and I entered the large tent – as big as most houses inside and hung with many banners. Harold, Earl of Wessex, Subregulus of Inglalond, sat in a carved oak chair and behind him hung on crossed staves were *The Red Dragon* and *The Fighting Man*. Standing in a half-circle around him were some of his brothers and housecarls – Aethelnoth and Eadnoth the Stallers – and other lords, including Tostig, Garryd and Leofwine, Earl of Kent. Kingly Harold looked, yet not a king.

'Ah … Brand,' he said as I stood with Skalpi on the end of the semi-circle. He beckoned me closer and in some confusion I approached him, conscious of the stares of his council.

'In every army,' announced Harold, raising his voice slightly, 'there are two types of leaders … those born to it, such as ourselves, and those whose courage, natural talents and popularity mark them out as men whom others will follow. Brand is such a man and it is time his service was rewarded.'

He stood and pulled a leather thong from around his neck upon which was strung a bronze and silver token – *The Fighting Man* of his banner.

'By this device,' said Harold, 'will men know that Brand is a captain of the fyrd and to be obeyed by all seasonal warriors.'

Then he placed the thong around my neck as the housecarls all grinned and acclaimed me, making me feel honoured but oddly embarrassed.

Harold resumed his chair and said, 'Stay Brand … we were talking of the next step in the campaign. As a man who knows the mind of the fyrd your counsel is valuable.'

A servant brought me a cup of wine, which caused my stomach to groan audibly with hunger, but I drank, if only to put something inside me. Then I heard a voice speak with authority, and was amazed to realise it was my own.

'The fyrd cannot fight the Welsh. The Welsh are hidden and fight in threes and fours … striking quickly then retreating to their secret places deep in the woods where armies cannot go.'

This led immediately to interjections of agreement and dissent and the debate continued without me for a while as the servant refilled my cup and I swilled it down, feeling even hungrier than before. In fact, Harold's campaign had been marked by success after success as forts were taken with few casualties, but the head of the snake was alive and dangerous. Gruffydd ap Llewellyn remained at large and while he did the Welsh would continue to harry the lands closest to their borders.

'But never Aelfgar's lands,' snarled Skalpi (ever one of the more belligerent types).

Aelfgar was the twice outlawed Earl of Mercia. As an outlaw myself, I was aware that such could be imposed unjustly. I was also aware that some accused Harold of supporting Aelfgar's outlawry due to some dark design of his own, but I reckoned I knew Harold as well as any and could not believe him capable of such politics.

The conversation passed on to consider all aspects of Aelfgar's history and motivations. Most damned him but Tostig seemed amused by the debate.

'I travelled with Earl Aelfgar and his sons to Rome, two years ago,' he said, 'and found him an amusing companion. Do we really care what he gets up to with the Welsh?'

'Your lands are far from Wales, Earl Tostig,' answered Harold. 'There are others with lands on Gruffydd's borders who take a less tolerant view of Aelfgar's activities.'

'It is Aelfgar that fills Gruffydd's head with destiny,' muttered Garryd. 'If it weren't for Aelfgar, Gruffydd might have been content within his marches. Aelfgar is also Gruffydd's general … and father in law.'

'Perhaps Aelfgar wishes to blend Mercia and Wales into one country surrounding Wessex?' mused Leofwine, a young, red-bearded man and another of the Godwinson brothers. 'It would be a heavy blow against us were he to succeed.'

'He will not succeed,' said Harold with a warm smile acknowledging Leofwine's care on his behalf. 'But it seems to me that if we cannot fight the Welsh in a single decisive battle, and if Aelfgar is Gruffydd's general, then our strategy must be to remove Aelfgar from the game.'

There was a silence as Harold's words were pondered.

'We must fight as the Welsh do,' said Leofwine. 'Send a small band of Welsh assassins into the heart of Gruffydd's camp to kill Aelfgar and the game will be close to an end.'

There was a further silence as this unusual strategy was considered.

'The Welsh cannot be asked to perform such a service,' said Harold. 'It is too great a strain on their loyalties. Any assassins must be Saxon.'

'It would be no simple task Lord,' said Garryd. 'There are signs and passwords that must be used to get through the forest ... and even if a troop of non-Welsh speakers could get close enough to Aelfgar to murder him, they would have little hope of getting out again. You would be asking such men to make the ultimate sacrifice.'

'What if the troop consisted mainly of Welshmen?' I found myself asking. 'Could they not give a good enough account of themselves to get into the camp, taking with them a couple more with the main task to complete? Getting out again could be arranged if the task were done secretly enough.'

'It seems we have a volunteer,' laughed Tostig, but no-one else laughed.

Harold stared at me a few moments, chin in hand. Then he turned to Garryd, 'Well Garryd ... will it serve?'

'I can find you men whom I would trust to get slayers into the camp at Rhuddlan,' said Garryd, 'but the killing will be hard and the escape harder. Any men you send will have to know that their chances of getting out again are slim.'

'What if the camp were attacked by a larger force ... at a prearranged hour?' I asked. 'In all the confusion the killing and the escape might be accomplished without anyone knowing until it was too late.'

'You just said the camp is in a place where armies cannot go,' said Eadnoth. 'How do we arrange an attack if we cannot use the army?'

'It would not have to be a meaningful attack,' I replied. 'Just enough to distract the Welsh and think themselves under attack. Twenty men might achieve it...especially if mounted.'

There was one argument that Tostig had won with his brother – his interest in the Norman way of fighting, mounted on large horses, had become fashionable among the earls and thegns. Harold led a cavalry of some 60 mounted knights on his summer campaign against the Welsh, and while it was rare that the cavalry caught the Welsh in the open, they were certainly effective when they did.

'Mounted men could certainly aid the escape of the slayers,' agreed Garryd. 'We might also attempt to get boats in but those would be stranded if the fight went against us ... '

His words trailed into silence as all turned to Harold for his judgment.

'Becoming quite the strategist Brand,' mused Harold. 'That is why you are a captain of the fyrd.'

He sprang up out of his chair and started pacing back and forward in concentration. Then he stopped abruptly and said, 'I like it ... with the exception of two details. If the opportunity arises to kill Gruffyd before Aelfgar, then that should be the main priority.'

There was a murmur of general agreement, and then Harold placed his hands on my shoulders.

'Also,' he said, 'I don't want you to go, Brand.'

In fact, I hadn't volunteered, but everyone seemed to assume I had. It was a dangerous mission with only a small chance of survival – even if the plan was carried out well. But it was also obvious to me that I was one of those in Harold's army with the best chance of at least accomplishing the killing, if I could get close enough to Aelfgar.

'Who else can you send, Lord?' I heard myself ask. Was I mad?

'You have become an important part of my army Brand ... you are not expendable.'

'All soldiers are expendable, Lord,' said Aethelnoth. 'You must balance the cost of losing Brand against the gain of Gruffydd losing Aelfgar.'

It was a well made point and I could tell by the mood of the tent that I was now a vulnerable gaming piece in the great game of Wales. Some of the men gathered about me grinning and clapping me over the shoulders. Well, I had brought it on myself.

∞ ∞ ∞

'It's because of Valla, isn't it?'

Elric was appalled at the turn of events, but insisted on coming with me.

'No, I don't think so,' I said, uncertainly.

'Just because she's gone to the Place of Dreams doesn't mean you must cast your life away in some noble gesture,' he said. 'What about the dream ... and her promise to return?'

'Has your Valla returned?' I countered.

'No … but I never had the dream message that you received. I have hope that your Valla will return. Mine will not, so the task should be mine.'

I laughed.

'Just because she's gone to the Place of Dreams doesn't mean you must cast your life away in some noble gesture.'

Elric stared at me, then grinned and we laughed together.

'We shall both go,' I said, 'and fare the same together … hoping that both our Vallas may return.'

And at that moment Earl Tostig approached and gestured at Elric to leave.

'You are a brave man,' said Tostig, ' … as I have always said.'

'Thank you, Lord.'

'Lord?' he laughed. 'We are equals, you and I … especially on the battlefield! Walk with me.'

He spoke in a friendly enough voice, but a small thrill of warning shivered between my shoulders. Nevertheless, it was impossible to refuse so I followed him into the forest by which we had camped since the beginning of the siege. As ever, the sound of birdsong made me lighter of heart and I dismissed the vague, unworthy suspicions I had of Tostig Godwinson.

'You know Brand, the mission is hard. No-one would blame you if it failed.'

I stared at him, the small thrill of warning returning.

'What do you mean?'

'None would blame you,' he repeated, '… but some might reward you.'

'Reward me? For failure?'

'Maybe even me.'

He stood in the shadows, half concealed with the ghost of a smile on his lips – like, yet unlike, his elder brother.

'There are vast lands within my earldom,' he said. 'Stybbor is a small and tame place with no fighting to occupy a man. You deserve better. I will give you a thegnship in the north of my country and help you extend it into the land of the Scots.'

As he spoke, I had an urge to accept. What fun it would be to go north with Tostig and harry the Scots – carving out an estate for myself in the process – but I could not let Harold down.

'I can't betray your brother ... not wilfully.'

'Well ... maybe you will fail through no fault of your own,' smiled Tostig. 'The reward will be the same ... if Aelfgar lives.'

'You want Aelfgar to live ... even though Harold wants him dead?'

'He is a friend of mine,' said Tostig, with a wave of his hand as though the thwarting of his brother's plans were nothing. 'We earls are all political and ever change our allegiances as the times warrant. Harold and Aelfgar have fought on the same side in the past ... should Aelfgar die simply because he knows the truth about the aetheling?'

'The aetheling?'

My head was spinning with confusion. Tostig's eager words sped past me in a persuasive torrent and I knew not which argument to pursue.

'Scotland is a vast country,' continued Tostig, 'with only Scots to defend it. You and I could create realms up there, Brand. You would build an army and, when the time is ripe, come marching back to Stybbor at the head of your own host ... Malgard would shit his breeches to know that nightmare awaited him!'

So attractive was the prospect that I truly wanted to accept, but instead I said, 'Harold is my Lord and he has asked for Aelfgar's head.'

The look on Tostig's face was difficult to make out in the shadows under the trees.

'Well ... you are a good and faithful vassal, Brand ... eager to carry out your Lord's will. That is a fine thing. But going into the heart of the enemy's camp is a hard task ... perhaps the feat will be beyond you?'

I said nothing – too confused to trust myself to make coherent speech.

'And if it so proves, then you shall have an estate in Northumbria ... ten times as large as Stybbor.'

With that he was gone and, moments later, Elric stepped from behind a tree.

'What was that about?'

'Trouble,' I replied.

Chapter 15

A Truth You Do Not Want to Learn

We stole through the forest in the hour before sunrise. Light glimmered beyond the horizon but it was still dark under the trees. Elric and I were accompanied by four Welshmen, one of whom (Gawayn) spoke the Saxon tongue well enough. They were Garryd's men and had sworn an oath to serve Harold – but surely these same men had sworn an oath to serve Gruffydd and I found myself reflecting on Tostig's words about changing allegiances. Was an oath worth nothing?

If the Welsh decided their oath to Gruffydd was stronger when back in his camp then Elric and I would rue our error. The Welsh were notorious for devising long and painful executions as a warning to others.

One of the men, with an unpronounceable name and a strange red stain on his face, walked about ten paces ahead, occasionally whistling softly like a birdcall, while the rest of us walked with drawn weapons, scanning the forest for enemies. But no-one answered the birdcalls and no shaft sped from the trees.

We had left Harold's camp about thirty hours previously, walking at first along the same stream bank I had taken with Elric and Valla the previous day. When we got to the strangely shaped beech, towering ghostly in the moonlight, all of the Welsh made the sign to ward off the evil eye and I asked Gawayn about the man in the hollow.

'No-one knows,' he replied.

'No-one knows ... what?'

'Who he is ... where he came from. Many years he's dwelled in the caves. Avoid him if you can … do not look at him or speak with him. None who do escape.'

'We escaped,' I said. 'Elric and I ate his fish and slept by his fire.'

Gawayn considered me for a moment. Then he said, 'Did you speak with him?'

And after going over the incident in my head I said, 'I don't believe I did. Only Valla spoke with him.'

'So where is Valla?' he asked, and I had to think about that.

Nevertheless, he spoke urgently with his fellows and they all stared at me in open distress and an argument briefly ensued. Red Stain in particular was gesticulating and muttering angrily – pointing both at the beech man and at me. But after a while they shrugged and resumed the journey, which a mile or so after the beech man led away from the stream and up into the hills along narrow twisting goat tracks. Two rising suns illuminated a land of great beauty with much exposed rock – the bones of the mountains – and numerous waterfalls splashing down into steep, misted gullies into which no-one had set foot since the dawn of time.

'Who is … or was the aetheling?' I asked Elric on the second morning.

Elric picked his way carefully along a cliff top track which looked like it must form a waterfall in wetter weather. Many of the rocks were green and slippery and the drop to our right would certainly be fatal.

'The aetheling, Edgar, is just a child' he replied after reaching a point of comparative safety. 'His father was the son of old Edmund Ironside … Edward's half-brother … but he died when Edward brought him home.'

'Where had he been?'

'In a land far to the east … raising a family safe from the politics of Inglalond.'

'And why did Edward want him here?'

'To be king after Edward. He had the strongest claim and was escorted home by Harold … but as soon as he set foot on these shores he died.'

I had to think about that also. Then lowering my voice, I said, 'Tostig says that Aelfgar knows the truth about the aetheling.'

'I heard,' muttered Elric, 'and let me assure you Brand that, if he does, then it is a truth you do not want to learn.'

'Is Tostig saying that Harold killed the heir to the throne?'

'Would it bother you if he did?' laughed Elric, who never ceased to amaze me with his intimate knowledge of the affairs of the great. 'You, who are about to kill a king yourself?'

'There's no king of Wales,' I replied, 'Gruffyd's just a pretender.'

'Yes,' agreed Elric. 'And Harold's just an earl.'

After a couple more hours negotiating cliff tops, we dropped down into a wide valley filled with trees, crossing several streams on our journey to the valley floor where a small but vigorous river flowed north and westward.

'We are over the spine of the hills,' said Gawayn. 'It is not far from here.'

We followed the right bank of the river where the trees were less thick and surreptitiously I pulled one of the small pieces of red cloth from my pocket. I had been leaving these here and there along the path we had taken so that Harold's following party would be led to Gruffydd's camp and be able to feign an attack at the appointed hour, which was the following dawn. However, I hadn't told the Welshmen about the coming attack and didn't want them to know I was leaving a trail. With an eye on Gawayn to make sure he wasn't watching, I dropped the scrap of rag and continued in Elric's wake.

After a couple of miles, the trees began to cluster more thickly and I found myself speculating about the Welshmen. Elric and I had sheathed our swords but they all carried drawn weapons. If we were going to the camp of friends and believed ourselves clear of the Saxon forces, then surely their weapons should be sheathed. It was wearying to carry a sword and no man did it unless he expected an attack – or was guarding prisoners.

I slowed my pace and noted that the two men behind us slowed also to keep us hemmed in.

'Are you tired?' asked Gawayn.

'A little,' I replied. 'How far to the camp?'

'Rhuddlan? Not far. You can rest in an hour or two.'

'I need a rest now,' I said and immediately turned down to the river and knelt in the coarse sand and rounded pebbles to splash water over my face and swallow a few cold draughts. Presently Elric joined me and in the Norman tongue (which we had both been learning) I muttered, 'Treachery ... be ready.'

Elric gave no indication he had heard me and, like me, splashed the weariness from his heart and limbs with cold river water. I stood and stretched, noting that three of the Welsh hemmed us against the river and all had drawn swords. The fourth – the tallest of them – stood a little further back and stared forward along the flats to where the forest curved around us to meet the river again.

'How many sentries have we passed so far?' I asked Gawayn, who stared at me before answering.

'None,' he replied. 'There are always folk in the forest ... but none attached so far to Gruffyd's army.'

'Are we being watched even now?' I asked, uncomfortable with his acknowledgment that he had seen forest dwellers when I had not. He just grinned at me, and that's when I saw the red scrap of cloth in his hand.

Without further word I flung the rock I had picked up from the river bank, taking Gawayn flush on the nose as I swept my sword from its scabbard to confront Red Stain to my right. I was just in time to parry his own stroke and heard the ring of swords behind me – clearly Elric had also managed to draw in time. Gawayn, blood dripping, was shouting at the tall man on the edge of the fight as Elric and I closed together to keep the river at our back and one flank free. Red Stain backed out of the fight, grinning as the Welsh all muttered together in their incomprehensible speech.

Gawayn's nose was smashed flat and was clearly giving him trouble. He spat blood at me, but then managed a grin of his own as he pulled more of my red scraps from his pocket.

'No-one will come,' he laughed. 'You are now at Gruffyd's mercy, so throw down your swords.'

Elric and I snatched a glance at each other and I saw his confidence.

'Why would we throw down our swords,' I asked, 'when it's only four Welsh against two Saxons. We've faced worse than that and won.'

'Plenty of times,' agreed Elric, suddenly lowering his sword. 'In fact, why don't you take them without me Brand ... should make the challenge a little more even, and you could do with the exercise.'

'If you wish,' I said and leapt at Red Stain, forcing him back towards a large rock, and then swept my sword at his colleague – a left hander. Gawayn shouted in Welsh at the tall man who strode towards Elric.

What I really wanted was time to reach for the battle axe strapped on my back. Or the shield, but two weapons were better when taking on multiple foes. I leapt again at Red Stain who took another hasty step backwards and tripped on the rock. Immediately I turned to the left hander, knowing I could concentrate only on him for the precious seconds it would take Red Stain to get up again. I stretched my neck towards him, knowing he would swing, and he did, my sword taking him in the elbow as I leapt back again. Left Hand was howling as I turned again to Red Stain running at me – his lips drawn into an animal snarl and his teeth white against his rage. I stepped to my right and kicked him hard in the knee as he went past, feeling something crack, and he went down squealing.

I glanced over to see how Elric fared and was surprised to see him just standing, unmolested. Gawayn however lay in two pieces on the ground, and the tall man stared down at his body.

The fight was over.

∞ ∞ ∞

The tall man's name was Cynan. When he realised Gawayn meant to prevent our mission, he had taken five seconds to side with Elric and I, but lacked the Saxon speech to inform us.

Instead he let his actions do the talking and had, to Elric's amazement, swept Gawayn's head from his shoulders while I disabled the other two, both of whom glared at us with bitter hate. Left Hand was dying – his arm was half off and blood was pulsing into the sand to pinken the water a few feet from where he lay. Even as we watched his eyes turned to glass and dulled. Red Stain however was grey faced in pain, his knee bent at an unnatural angle.

'What do we do with him?' asked Elric, but before I could answer, Cynan's sword swept again. Red Stain hadn't seen the blow coming so died easily. Then, without another word, Cynan started collecting large stones.

'Hide … must,' he said in broken Saxon, pointing at the bodies, which Elric expertly searched and produced a small pile of weapons –

none of which we needed, but it suddenly struck me as a good idea to take their shields. The Welsh devices and designs were quite different from our own, and it should have occurred to me before. Gawayn also had a small purse of coins, which I offered to Cynan, but he just spat so I tossed them to Elric.

They should've formed the shield wall, said Elric. 'We might've been fucked if they'd done that.'

'Welsh aren't used to fighting in the shield wall,' I replied. 'Ambush and run is their way ... not much use when they have to stand and fight. Besides, Cynan wouldn't have joined them so we would have won anyway.'

Ever with an eye on the trees, Cynan dragged the bodies down into the water and, with the aid of weapons and stones, managed – with our help, once we understood what he was doing – to weigh them down. Soon the bodies were quite invisible. Cynan had dealt them all further deep wounds to the belly and I understood he was preventing them from bloating in death and floating to the surface.

'He's done this before,' said Elric, with an approving grin.

It was about three hours after sunrise and the day was cold. We drank water (upstream from the bodies) and ate food that had been carried by Gawayn and his men – dry bread and a strip of salt mutton.

Elric and I debated the wisdom of returning – at least part of the way to distribute some of the red scraps – but the thought of being watched doing so by people unseen did not seem wise. Also, I had no desire to return to Harold with my mission untried.

We spent some time gauging the extent of Cynan's Saxon and he learned impressively quickly so that communication rapidly improved.

'Go Rhuddlan ... I speak only,' he said. 'You kill Aelfgar...I kill Gruffyd.'

He certainly had no love for the self-proclaimed king of Wales, which was reassuring, and after a couple of hours we continued on our way – Gruffyd teaching us a small number of Welsh words such as Yes, No, Thank You, and I Don't Know, which might prove useful in the enemy camp.

In fact, I now felt a great deal more confident. I'd always felt a bit uncertain of Gawayn and Red Stain – being only with men I trusted made me feel as though I had a lot more control.

We passed into a deep forest, keeping the river to our left and continued along a trail that twisted and turned through ash, larch and pine, and presently I smelled the first tang of salt that reminded me of the southern wind back home.

'The sea is close,' I remarked, feeling suddenly homesick for Stybbor. Then there were other smells – wood smoke and roasting meat – and noises in the distance, of people. I began to see people coming and going through the trees, even children running about carefree so confident were the Welsh in the security of their forest fastness.

But if the Welsh were relaxed, I was not. The trees thinned and we found ourselves approaching another stockade of spiked fences surrounding a moveable village of tents and shanties abutting the river, which was noticeably wider this close to the sea. The gates were open and the men guarding were all laughing at some jest as we approached – I tried to seem relaxed, as a real Welshman would have been.

Cynan hailed the guards, who regarded us without much interest. The leader had long black hair, braided like Valla's, and I felt a pang of distress to be reminded of her. And perhaps he saw me staring for he aimed a torrent of incomprehensible Welsh at me, which I tried to ignore, but others stepped into my path on the very point of entry to the village.

Cynan began to answer on my behalf but the leader silenced him with a word, put a hand on my shoulder and asked me what was obviously a question. The only word I understood was 'Gruffyd', but if it was a question, then maybe he'd be happy with a one word answer. I had two possible Welsh answers to use but the wrong answer would mean a fight to the death against impossible odds.

'Yes,' I said, and saw the relief on Cynan's face.

The leader nodded, clapped me over the shoulder, and we entered the camp of Gruffyd ap Llewellyn – who called himself king of Wales.

Chapter 16

A Magical Place

Valla sat naked in a glade in the mid afternoon.

Myrrthn also was naked but she did not fear him. He sat on a rock before a pool, his back to her, and sang a low song in a tongue she barely understood. A few words she remembered from her mother but the music once again seemed to paint pictures in her mind.

They had come to what Myrrthn told her was a sacred place.

'One of the last remaining places where the old wights are willing to show themselves to folk of flesh and blood. We must prepare ourselves, to show that we are worthy.'

The preparation involved drinking a bitter concoction of mistletoe and mushrooms. As Myrrthn warned her there was stomach pain, but when it passed she felt an exhilaration and the light seemed to take on a special quality – glowing but soft – and any movement seemed to leave a trail in its wake. Butterflies, blue, black and gold flickered about the glade and for the first time Valla was aware of their tiny lives as important. In that instant she heard Myrrthn laugh as a creature flickered about his hand and another landed on his shoulder.

A splash from the pool and she saw a frog swimming away like a tiny human and she sensed his power. Myrrthn laughed again and Valla realised she herself was laughing.

'You see them?' asked Myrrthn.

'Yes.'

A ladybird landed on Valla's finger, climbed up to the tip as she held it raised, then flew off into the golden light above the pool which seemed to be pulsing with a life of its own.

'This is a magical place,' said Myrrthn. 'Do you understand?'

'Yes.'

For the first time since they had undressed he turned to face her and patted the rock next to him. Valla edged forward so that, like Myrrthn, she sat with her feet in the water which was strangely warm. Tadpoles swam about her, many with hind legs, and she found herself laughing at how oddly they moved.

Myrrthn spoke to her about the strange, connected lives of the pool, trees and under fern. Lives with purpose, connected to all things, connected to her.

'But the killer god disconnects us from the land,' he said. 'Takes away the true meaning of rock, leaf and brook so these things are no longer valued for themselves but swept away to make more room for the killer god and his legions. Would you have this swept away?'

'No,' breathed Valla, profoundly distressed at the idea.

'Will you do all in your power to prevent the killer god coming in many boats to these shores?'

'Yes.'

A butterfly, glittering blue and silver-black, hovered in the air before her and Valla felt an awe – felt a presence and seemed to see a human face and hands waving in a way that almost had meaning – a message she could almost grasp.

'Then you must learn to use your power,' said Myrrthn.

∞ ∞ ∞

Gruffyd's camp was little different to any other camp of men on the march, although Rhuddlan seemed semi-permanent with a river wharf and quite a few shacks and shanties amid the many tents, but even the walls were temporary and could be pulled apart in a few hours and carried to a new location. It was little wonder they were so hard to bring to battle.

Cynan obviously knew the camp well enough and led us to a place where a number of canvases were hanging from poles or trees and just needed staking. Elric and I immediately grasped what was required and once Cynan was satisfied we knew how to stake a tent he said, 'Talk no man ... get food.'

With that he departed and, feeling a little light-headed, I found myself laughing as I hammered the last of the pegs into the ground.

'What's so funny?' muttered Elric, with the ghost of a grin himself.

'This is madness,' I said, 'and yet, here we are … in the heart of the enemy camp.'

'Too easy,' agreed Elric. 'We mustn't expect it to stay easy because it won't … especially if you really want to … erm … do what needs to be done.'

I was conscious also that the speaking of Saxon would be a highly suspicious activity so switched to Norman, which was less likely to be recognised – and I needed to practice because Harold frequently used the Norman tongue and encouraged all his housecarls to learn it. 'When Edward is gone there will be need to treat with the Normans,' he would sometimes say. 'I need men who speak their tongue, so learn it well Brand, if you would be of use to me.'

There were few things I wanted more, so was happy to learn, and Elric learned also which was just as well in a place such as Gruffydd's camp where to be discovered as Saxon would mean torture and death.

That's why I was laughing so nervously. The camp seemed so peaceful – and yet there were men here who had lost everything to Harold and would be only too happy to take their vengeance on his spies. I wondered whether Dafydd had heard yet the news of his wife Ygrene and her fiery death. Then thinking about Ygrene made me remember Valla and once again I was tormented by the manner (and the fact) of her departure.

Somehow I knew that she had gone to perform the task she had been prepared for, but I would be reunited with her on condition that I lay with no other woman. Well, that was simple enough – I wanted no other woman – but how long would she be away? I turned to consider Elric, building a fire near the entrance to our tent. He had been abandoned by his own Valla …

'Elric?'

He glanced up from his work as the flames began to catch.

'Your own Valla … did she put a condition on her return?'

Elric's lips thinned and he heaped more kindling on the small blaze.

'Yes. The same condition as your own.'

'And … have you remained faithful to her?'

Elric pulled some small boughs from one of the many piles about the camp and arranged them over his fire.

'You know I have not,' he said, 'but once the loaf is cut ...'

Elric shrugged and fed his fire with more kindling to get the small logs properly caught. Then he said, 'Do you remember the day we met?'

'Of course.'

'One of the Rocker women had pledged herself to me. She was alone. I was alone. In hope of Valla's return I resisted for a time but ... in the clear light of day, after several years alone, it seems like foolishness to waste the well-meant love of a good woman when there seems little or no chance that the other will return.'

He stared into his fire for a few moments.

'And now, through my weakness, I have made it certain that the other will not return.'

∞ ∞ ∞

Cynan returned, with a loaf of fresh bread and some news.

'Gruffydd here ... Aelfgar here.'

I realised at this point that I didn't really have any sort of plan to achieve my mission. I had just thought to get close and strike at Aelfgar when the opportunity presented itself. This plan now seemed inadequate – not least in giving us some hope of escape – and I started to consider our surroundings.

'We need to prepare for our escape,' I said.

'The river?' suggested Elric. 'We could strike before dawn and make our way into the river. That way we will leave no trace for their dogs.'

The Welsh were noted for hunting with dogs, and there were many at Rhuddlan – large and fierce – and the camp was frequently interrupted with their disputes.

'There is still a need to prepare for Harold's arrival,' I said. 'Gawayn may have taken the red markers away but there are still others that know their way to Rhuddlan ... we should prepare for the likelihood of a covering attack.'

'We should also prepare for no covering attack,' said Elric, '... so how do we prepare for both?'

The three of us shared Cynan's loaf which was soft and fresh with an oddly nutty flavour – very pleasant when you got used to it. After eating also some more of the salt mutton and washing it all down with silty river water, I felt the need to shit so went looking for the nearest latrine.

'Talk no man,' warned Cynan, but he needn't have worried. I picked my way past a lane of tents that looked also semi-permanent given the numerous augmentations and ornamentations, and found a latrine protected only by a short wicker fence. It was far more public than I was used to, and it stank – my three years in Harold's frequently travelling army had done nothing to inure me to the stench of turd – but I was at least used to the lack of privacy.

Like many latrines this one was simply a hole in the ground with a triangle of logs at the top to enable three men to shit with their backs to each other. I picked the log facing the salt breeze, dropped my woollen hose and perched on the rough-hewn pine, and as I did so two men entered the wicker enclosure. I had my back to them and paid them little attention – until they started speaking in Saxon.

'I weary of this place,' said a voice, and I just resisted the instinct to turn. It would not be wise to reveal myself as a Saxon-speaker. I sensed the men sitting either side of me and heard them loudly commence their ablutions.

'We are not blessed with many choices, Edwin,' replied an older voice and I stiffened.

'Still ... I will be glad when we can leave. There is no couthness here ... no proper songs, comfort or decent food.'

'I like their songs ... but you can leave whenever you wish. It is only I who am declared outlaw,' said the elder voice, confirming my suspicion that my companions were none other than Aelfgar and his son Edwin.

Suddenly I was struck in the arm and I turned half to my right to see a man glaring over his shoulder. There was plenty of grey in his hair and beard but he retained some muscle and vigour it seemed.

'You!' he said. 'Do you understand my speech?'

I had the wit to shrug, then in Welsh I said, 'I don't know ...'

The man stared piercingly for a few more moments, then forgot me.

'It wouldn't surprise me if Harold had spies in the camp,' he said. 'Even assassins … it's what I would do in his place.'

'You are safe here, father.'

'Not for much longer … Harold and Tostig's forces are joined now. If they but knew it they are only two days march away.'

'They cannot come at us here … not in numbers enough to worry us.'

'Which is why they will send assassins,' finished Aelfgar.

The three of us sat in silence for a few moments, then Edwin said, 'We should return to Mercia and beg the king's pardon. You've done it before.'

'Aye, that has to be the last resort … but Gruffydd would not be pleased if his general left on the eve of the storm.'

'Gruffydd is a fool,' muttered Edwin. 'His own men scorn him.'

'A fool he may be,' said Aelfgar, 'but he has the wit to know his limitations … which is why he needs me … or thinks he does. He has me watched … he is worried I will run.'

'We should take a boat,' said Edwin. 'The river is fast and the coast is not far. We could slip away tonight and be in Mercia in days.'

'Tempting,' said Aelfgar, 'but you're forgetting Tostig.'

'I'm not forgetting Tostig,' said Edwin, 'I just don't trust him.'

'Neither do I … but I trust him to at least look out for his own best interests. He has the land of an earl but a royal ambition. The goodwill of Mercia is valuable to any future king.'

They were gone before it occurred to me I had a dagger in my boot – even if that dagger was reserved for my uncle.

∞ ∞ ∞

'Aelfgar was right there … unprotected … and you let him live?'

Elric was scornful.

'Naked as his own mother … and you let him live.'

'His mother?'

Elric stared at me in mock pity.

'You never heard of the Lady Godgifu?'

Cynan looked up sharply and grinned. 'Coffantree.'

'You see?' laughed Elric, 'Even Cynan knows the story … and you do not.'

'What story?'

'Aelfgar's mother rode naked through Coffantree … to spite her husband, Leofric.'

'Why would she do that?' I wondered.

Cynan said something I didn't catch and laughed – and it suddenly seemed like the two of them were teaming up at my expense.

'Enough of your naked riders,' I snapped. 'We have a difficult and dangerous problem here, in case you've forgotten.'

'I'm not the one who's forgotten,' said Elric. 'We could've been on our way already if you'd had the wit to murder Aelfgar when his back was turned.'

I knew he was right. The truth was, I was so interested in Aelfgar's and Edwin's conversation it hadn't occurred to me to kill them until they were gone.

'Clearly they have been talking to Tostig,' I said. 'What could that mean?'

I had repeated the entire conversation for Elric's and Cynan's interest – although Cynan had remained fairly blank. His interest was Gruffydd.

'It means a potential alliance,' said Elric. 'to support Tostig in a royal claim.'

'But Tostig supports Harold,' I said. 'No-one has greater ambition for Harold than Tostig. I've heard him say so many times … even though Harold says he will respect Edward's choice … that he will not seize the crown if promised to another.'

'The witan will approve no king other than Harold,' said Elric, 'so eventually he will have no choice … unless he would see the country plunged yet again into war.'

'We're at war now,' I said. 'We're always at war.'

'Proper war I mean,' sneered Elric. 'Not these pointless scraps in the wilderness as a few lords squabble like hens over a toss of barley.'

We sat in silence as the evening closed in. There was a huge cauldron of stew being prepared and we caught occasional whiffs on the breeze, causing my stomach to growl in anticipation.

'If Harold refuses the crown … maybe Tostig would have it for himself,' I guessed. 'It would explain why he wants Aelfgar to stay alive. Northumbria and Mercia combined is a formidable realm.'

'Tostig is also on friendly terms with Malcolm of Scotland,' said Elric.

'Is he?' I said. 'Well why did he offer to carve me an estate out of Scotland?' I wondered, but Elric shrugged.

'As Aelfgar said, Tostig has a royal ambition. The promises of royalty are ever political and perilous.'

'Although less perilous than the danger we face right now,' I remarked, and again there was silence. I now felt myself wallowing in a mire of intrigue and was sorely conscious of my status as a pawn – an under-informed and hesitant pawn. It seemed that whatever path I chose regarding Aelfgar, I would be disappointing a future king.

After a while we noticed men moving towards the cooking fires as though some silent signal had gone out and we joined the straggling procession, armed only with short daggers and wooden bowls.

There were more men in the camp than I'd realised – perhaps many had been out on patrol during the day – but I guessed there had to be several hundred. There were plenty of cooking fires about the camp and over a hundred men were sitting at benches around the cooking area as the queue snaked its way towards the cauldron. Cynan exchanged brief words to a few of our companions but Elric and I remained silent until a thick stew was slopped into our bowls and we took a small loaf from one of the several baskets.

'Thank you,' I said, in Welsh, grinning at how useful my ten-or-so words of Welsh had proved.

Most of the benches were full and we were making our way towards a comfortable-looking log away from the centre of activity, when a large and friendly-looking man stood and beckoned us to join him and his two even larger fellows at one of the tables.

I paused in alarm, but there was no way I could ignore the friendly gesture.

'Thank you,' I said, now painfully aware of how useless my ten-or-so words of Welsh would be in any prolonged exchange.

Fortunately, Cynan was sharp of wit and immediately took over the conversation, gesturing at Elric and I and saying something that caused our new companions to laugh. Nervously, I dipped the bread into the stew and was amazed at how nice it tasted. That nutty bread again – and the stew was probably venison, although there was other meat in it, pease and something like onions but sweeter. I gave the meal most of my attention while occasionally scanning the crowd for a glimpse of Aelfgar.

The noise grew louder as men (and some women) filled the benches and all other places to sit, including the ground around the firepits. If I ignored the stray words of Welsh here and there the buzz was exactly the same as any other evening meal I had attended in the company of fighting men – shouts of laughter, short disputes – until the singing started.

I had never heard anything like it.

A group of a dozen men began to sing and there was immediately silence from all the rest. I didn't understand the words, of course, but the way the voices blended in such sweet melody seemed to convey somehow a meaning, and I found myself travelling a journey in my head – flying like an eagle over mountains and rivers – then down to the sea that I had seen more in my dreams than in waking reality. The song was like a dream, and now I saw ships – many ships full of warriors and they were coming for us. But then the music changed again and I saw myself with Valla, living simply together in a small house with a garden, and the scene was so beautiful I felt my heart must break for sorrow and loss.

And yet, I felt strangely uplifted as the song ended and I opened my eyes. There was much applause and congratulation of the singers, and then I saw Aelfgar standing near the fire with his son Edwin, and another man – perhaps fifty years of age – whose arms were covered with tattoos and golden rings, like those worn by the Danes. He had long grey hair and the bearing of a leader. With him was a young woman – tall and very fair with golden hair and dressed in linen, but wearing also a cloak of skins against the cool of the evening – summer though it was.

A chant commenced among the men, 'Gruffydd, Gruffydd, Gruffydd ... ' and I found myself joining in – blending in speech with those around me and still much affected by the music of the song.

Presently the grey-haired leader raised his arms for silence and the chanting subsided. He began to speak in a low growling voice and the men began to mutter and snarl. I was keenly aware of how impossible my position was, as the men around me became angrier in response to Gruffydd's address. My heart and stomach were fluttering as they did before battle, but unlike a battle the enemy were not aware of me clashing sword against shield or shouting and showing my arse. They were not aware of me at all, but if they did become aware …

Then Gruffydd stood back and gestured at Aelfgar, who stepped forward and began an oration of his own in Saxon, which was then translated – sentence by sentence – by Gruffydd. It was an awkward business and the men didn't seem to be paying much attention, which Aelfgar clearly resented because after a couple of minutes of thanking them and praising them, he then said, 'All hail King Gruffydd … you ignorant sons of sheep!'

And before I could help myself, I laughed.

In that moment, the passing of time seemed to slow. Aelfgar turned to me like a striking snake, his eyes piercing as I realised my error. Cynan was staring at me white-faced, then he leapt to his feet, pointing at me and shouting.

Suddenly everyone was staring at me and then hands reached for me. I swept them away angrily and thumped my fist into the face of the first who tried to take me, but something hit me from behind and, before I knew it, I was at the bottom of a ruck of a dozen furious Welshmen – aware that my life was effectively over.

Chapter 17

A Dangerous Game

'So … Harold sent spies. I expected as much.'

Aelfgar, seemed grimly amused, but not so amused that he tried to prevent Gruffydd's men from casual violence as they prepared a brazier. I knew what that was for.

Elric and I were tied to heavy poles inside the largest of the more permanent buildings within the camp – just a large shed really, with woven rush mats on the ground. I hadn't seen what happened to Cynan.

That he had denounced us was certain, but I clung to a hope that he had done that out of necessity when I had so foolishly revealed myself, and that he might still do something to aid our escape. It was a forlorn hope. A better hope might lie in a possible attack on the camp in the morning – if we lasted that long.

Gruffydd was also present, as was Aelfgar's son Edwin, and it was Edwin who was most responsible for the violence – punching or kicking Elric or me every now and then as he oversaw the red coals forming. I had a broken nose and bloodied mouth, but Elric had a broken arm and shouted with pain every time Edwin gave it another savage twist.

'So where is Harold?' demanded Aelfgar.

'Two days march,' I said through thick and bleeding lips, seeing no point in concealing what they already knew – or thought they did.

'And who are you?'

My eyes were fixed on the floor which was stained a reddish brown around the poles. I had heard terrible stories about the games the Welsh liked to play with prisoners, but no amount of steely resolve to accept my fate could prepare me for the horror of my predicament.

I opened my mouth to answer but there was a brief commotion at the door and another man was allowed entry – shouting in furious Welsh, his face streaked with tears and his eyes filled with retribution. I didn't need to be introduced to guess that this newcomer must be Dafydd Ap Rhiwallon – husband of Ygrene – and my fear was greater even than the time in the basement on the Temes, when I faced a similar peril with Malgard in charge. Without another word, Dafydd strode towards me and pulled a dagger from his belt, but he was restrained by Edwin and shouts from Aelfgar and Gruffydd.

Dafydd stood glaring at me, as Gruffydd spoke urgently to him, but then Gruffydd's voice changed and Dafydd grinned – and I felt a rising terror as I gathered that something had been promised for later.

But if I relaxed a little about punishment postponed, I was in error, for Dafydd swung a vicious punch at my groin and my eyes filled with a watery pain. Then I heard Elric yelp again and in the midst of the fear and madness I began to think clearly.

'I repeat,' said Aelfgar, 'who are you? What is your name, boy?'

'Brand Holgarsson.'

'Brand Holgarsson,' repeated Aelfgar, as though trying to place me. 'So whom did Harold Godwinson send you to kill … Gruffydd, or me?'

'I wasn't sent by Harold.'

There was an angry shout from Dafydd, who was once again restrained by Aelfgar. But if I thought that Aelfgar was protecting me, I was corrected when he pulled a long, iron rod from the brazier – its handle wrapped in leather but its end glowing dull red.

'I normally prefer these implements hotter,' remarked Aelfgar, 'but in a camp such as this we have to make do.'

He brought the glowing tip towards my broken face and I could feel its heat from a yard away. A foot away it was almost unbearable – and I had seen the results of such injuries – faces blistered and twisted out of shape, for those who survived the hideous burning pain.

'You weren't sent by Harold, you say,' sneered Aelfgar. 'Who else would send a Saxon slayer into Gruffydd's camp?'

Despite my fear of the burning rod I managed to look Aelfgar calmly in the eye and said softly, 'I was sent by Tostig.'

My words had some of the desired effect for Aelfgar's eyes

widened, for a moment, but then he continued, 'Tostig is the brother of Harold ... if you were sent by the one then equally you were sent by the other ... to spy and kill.'

'Not so.'

'And what of your companion?' demanded Aelfgar, turning suddenly to Elric. 'What tale would he tell of your mission?'

I doubt whether Elric guessed what plan I had but he was alert enough, despite his pain, to confirm that we had been sent by Tostig.

'So what was Tostig's message?' demanded Aelfgar, ignoring more shouted anger from Gruffydd and Dafydd.

'I wasn't told,' said Elric. 'Only Brand was trusted.'

Aelfgar examined the iron rod, which had dulled to grey, and thrust it back into the brazier. Then he seized Elric's broken left arm again, getting a yelp of pain for his effort.

'The message from Tostig,' insisted Aelfgar as Elric howled, while I struggled desperately against my bonds. I could barely move, so expertly was I trussed, and there were no convenient sharp objects as there had been in the cellar that time. I felt my mind must snap with the terror of imminent pain and death, when Aelfgar dropped Elric's arm and said to Edwin, 'We shall give the coals more time to heat the tools. You stay ... while I discuss with Gruffydd and Dafydd how best to profit from this situation.'

There were furious objections from Gruffyd and Dafydd who clearly wanted to get on with the business of pain and death, but Aelfgar spoke urgently in Welsh and they were eventually persuaded.

We were left with just Edwin for a sentry.

∞ ∞ ∞

Edwin didn't speak with us, despite my several attempts to engage him. He had a skin of wine from which he constantly drank and hummed a tune as though out riding on a summer's morn without a care in the world. He heeded me no more than the pair of moths that flickered about the several torches – and rose from his chair only to top up the brazier with fresh wood from time to time.

After half an hour or so, the door opened and Aelfgar returned, looking back over his shoulder as he entered. He spoke no word to

Edwin, but pulled the rod from the brazier which was now glowing a bright pink.

'How's the arm?' he enquired.

'Better,' replied Elric. 'Thank you.'

I gaped at Elric, then my hopes soared as I perceived that the last time I thought Aelfgar was twisting Elric's arm, he was in fact pulling it back into place. That could surely only mean that he was interested in my subtle bait.

'Well,' he demanded, standing before me, 'I have only a few moments before the others return … what message from Tostig?'

'Harold has this place surrounded,' I said, 'he will attack soon, but Tostig sent us to get you out of the camp. You and Edwin. I was given passwords and promise of safe passage for you … all others will be slain.'

Edwin now took an interest in me, but Aelfgar said, 'Harold is two days away and cannot come against Rhuddlan in numbers. The scouts have confirmed this.'

'I swear it. Harold's army is coming as we speak … brought here by secret ways, by Welshmen sworn to his service. Tostig is your only hope.'

'I knew it!' exclaimed Edwin, all calmness gone and his voice rising. 'Harold will surely overrun this place … we should leave at once!'

'Peace Edwin,' hissed Aelfgar, pulling at his beard as he pondered my news.

'What are the passwords?' he demanded.

'They shall be revealed as needed,' I replied. 'Knowledge of the passwords is our own safe passage.'

'What proof do you carry?' asked Aelfgar. 'How do I know I can trust you? I sat next to you at the shithole this afternoon and you said nothing.'

'I didn't know you were Aelfgar in that moment,' I replied, already prepared for that question. 'Tostig bade me be certain before revealing my true purpose … and why else would I be here if not to bring you to safety? Two men cannot hope to attack Gruffyd's camp.'

'Maybe not … but they might hope to slay in secret. Either Gruffydd or myself.'

Aelfgar drew Edwin to the far corner and there they muttered together for a minute or so. It was clear that Edwin was the more nervous of the two and seemed to be urging his father to do something, but Aelfgar remained unconvinced. Thoughtfully, he slid the burning rod from the brazier once again and approached me.

'I have been trying to remember everything that Edwin and I said at the latrine this afternoon,' said Aelfgar, 'and it strikes me that you may have heard enough to be tailoring the information to your present plight.'

He brought the searing rod to within a couple of inches of my face.

'This is a dangerous game you are playing Brand Holgarsson.'

'No more dangerous than your own game,' I replied, 'playing kings against each other.'

He might have resented that, but laughed grimly.

'Perhaps ... but the game stops now. What proof can you show that you are Tostig's emissary rather than Harold's killer?'

'There is only my word,' I said, 'but I offer you this token ... an attack is planned for the hour before dawn. When Harold attacks ... in just a couple of hours ... you will know I have spoken truth. You will know also that you have left it too late to get away, for surely Gruffydd will expect his general to lead the defence.'

Aelfgar's lips twisted into a bitter smile and he brought his own face within a couple of inches of mine – sharing the heat of the rod – which he suddenly thrust back into the brazier with a curse.

'You have an answer for everything,' he snapped. 'But Gruffyd and Dafydd want you dead, so how do I keep you alive for long enough to discover if you speak truth about the attack?'

'Tell them I am Harold's son.'

'What?'

'Tell them I am truly a bastard son of Harold ... and very dear to him. I am therefore worth more alive than dead.'

'Why would they believe such a story?'

'I am a bastard son,' I said thinking furiously, 'I wasn't sent but came of my own volition to try and win my father's regard.'

'By doing what?'

'By killing Gruffydd ... or you,' I added, and found myself grinning despite the danger, and the pain of my broken mouth.

'That's not enough,' said Aelfgar, getting angry in his impatience.

'There is also this … look under my shirt. The token.'

Edwin strode forward and pulled at the woollen garment I wore under my leather jerkin, revealing Harold's gift. He pulled it free and both men gasped when they recognised *The Fighting Man* – Harold's personal device in bronze and silver.

'You truly are a son of Harold?' demanded Edwin, and I laughed.

'Nay … just a captain of the fyrd,' I replied, ' … but a good friend of Tostig all the same.'

Once again, Aelfgar drew Edwin into the corner for a muttered conversation, and I was sure that they were now convinced by my desperate lies – or nearly so.

Edwin was sent away, and presently returned with Gruffydd and Dafydd and a violent argument in Welsh raged for some time. Gruffydd examined *The Fighting Man*, still hanging outside my jerkin, and then spoke excitedly to Dafydd – causing Aelfgar to shake his head adamantly. I could guess that the story of my lineage had been believed, but seemed not to have had the desired effect. Instead of wanting to use me as a hostage they were eager to avenge Ygrene by killing a son of Harold.

Dafydd gazed at me, fingering a long, thin blade, while Aelfgar spoke urgently to Gruffydd. Then the two Welshmen spoke again and Dafydd grinned – and they left the room.

'You had better not be wrong about Harold's attack,' said Aelfgar softly. 'Dafydd plans a very nasty end for you, Brand Holgarsson. Indeed, I believe they hope to use you in negotiations with Harold … but still take their vengeance upon you. That is Welsh diplomacy.'

Aelfgar sent Edwin to retrieve their weapons and valuables for flight, while I lamented the loss of our own weapons – still in the tent, wherever that was. No doubt I could steal another sword or battle axe in the Welsh camp, but a man gets used to his own weapons and *Revanche* and *Pighammer* were precious to me. It would be harder to kill with unfamiliar tools.

'How long until dawn?' asked Elric, his face still white against the pain of his arm.

Aelfgar put his head out of the door to sniff at the night and check the sky.

'Hardly more than an hour it seems,' This side of the hills, the light comes long before the sun.'

Aelfgar was nervous I sensed – and it stood to reason. He had already betrayed Edward twice, and was now about to betray Gruffydd. I was curious as to why a man elevated to Earl would be so willing to jeopardise such fortune, so many times.

'You and Tostig must be great friends,' I remarked, suspecting that such a lord would ignore the question, but he must have been nervous indeed for he was almost amiable as he said, 'We travelled to Rome together ... Tostig and I ... and my sons Edwin and Morcar ... and Burgheard, who did not return. Such a journey affords many opportunities for intimacy, so yes, we are friends ... and glad of it I am in this wretched place.'

Aelfgar glanced out of the door again, looking for Edwin, then he said, 'So why would a captain of Harold's fyrd be an emissary of Tostig? My safety will not be one of Harold's priorities, so surely you are acting against your own lord's interests.'

'That may be so ... but Harold had no particular duty for me and has not declared anything regarding your person ... beyond the outlawry of course. And I have some sympathy for outlaws.'

I told him my own tale and Aelfgar became quite personable in his responses, expressing disgust for the actions of my uncle.

'And Harold has gone three years without getting revenge on your account?' he exclaimed. 'You should be working for me. Malgard would have died screaming long ago.'

'Harold will not do aught against the wishes of Edward ... while he lives,' I replied. 'But I am nearly old enough ... and skilled enough now ... to do something on my own account. But even if I did, I am declared outlaw and would be in no position to take back my thegnship ... until Harold is king.'

'You may wait longer than you think for that,' said Aelfgar, as the door opened again and Edwin slipped inside with a large heavy sack. I was interested in Aelfgar's last comment, but with Edwin's return the room temperature changed and I chose not to pursue it.

'Hide that outside,' said Aelfgar, indicating Edwin's sack. 'Quickly!'

'Why?' asked Edwin.

'If Gruffydd were to enter now ... he would take one look at that and know we meant to run. Get it outside … but close, if we need it.'

Edwin left again with the heavy sack, and Aelfgar rolled his eyes as the mood of trust and friendship deepened yet again.

'I was Earl of East Anglia for a time,' said Aelfgar. 'I think I knew your father … a large man with red-blonde hair, like yours. His badge was a boar's head.'

'You remember well,' I replied.

'But I don't recall Malgard …'

'Taller and thinner than my father … with a scar on his cheek from the shield wall at Margate, so he claims. I believe he cut himself shaving. Have a look in the top of my left boot.'

Aelfgar gave me a queer look, but such was the mood of trust now between us that he stepped forward and rolled down the top of my boot, revealing the silver-hilted dagger I kept there.

'Take it.'

Aelfgar pulled the dagger free and examined it closely.

'It is a beautiful thing,' he said, 'with a wicked point.'

'My father was murdered with that knife,' I said. 'I keep it for vengeance against my uncle and will use it against no other man.'

Aelfgar laughed. 'I truly hope … for your sake, Brand Holgarsson … that Harold attacks. If he does not you would be best served using this knife on yourself, for Dafydd loved Ygrene very deeply and would slake his agony though your own … for many hours.'

'Harold will come,' I said, keenly aware of the missing red markers.

'The danger will come in the first moments of the attack,' said Aelfgar. 'Gruffydd would use you as a gaming piece against Harold, but Dafydd wants you dead. He may send a killer to prevent your escape if an attack comes.'

'Then you had better choose sides quickly,' I replied. 'You can only get to Tostig … and safety … through me. So you'd better keep me alive.'

The friendly atmosphere of the last little while was suddenly gone, but I was confident that Aelfgar had made up his mind – as matters currently stood – to seek sanctuary through Tostig. I had won his trust.

In that moment a horn blew in the distance.

Then many horns responded, much closer, and there was shouting around the Welsh camp.

'You spoke the truth,' said Aelfgar with a relieved smile and strode towards me with my own knife. In a matter of seconds he had cut my bonds and then attended to Elric as I flexed my arms and fingers to relieve the stiffness.

Through cracks in the wooden walls I could see fires springing up throughout the camp and the shouts became more urgent and were coming closer.

Without a further word I swept the long, iron rod from the brazier, still glowing pink.

'Where is Edwin?' muttered Aelfgar, and those were his last words. I almost felt sorry for him as I smashed the iron rod into the top of his head, and then again to make certain as he hit the ground while blood and hair sizzled into steam on the end of my rod.

'I truly believed you myself,' said Elric, picking up the knife where Aelfgar had dropped it. 'You should be a skald with playacting powers such as yours.'

I stole to the door, expecting Edwin to return at any moment, but was amazed to find myself face to face with Cynan, who slipped grinning through the door with all our gear wrapped in a cloak.

The camp was in total uproar and Cynan pulled out his own sword. 'Gruffydd,' he said, and was gone.

I took my knife from Elric and replaced it in my boot, then we followed Cynan, leaving Aelfgar, Earl of Mercia, lifeless in a black pool of blood.

∞ ∞ ∞

Harold had done far better than I hoped. A number of small ships managed to enter the river, closing off that route of escape, and some fifty men had attacked the main gate. Torches were streaming towards the fight and, after quickly binding Elric's arm in Aelfgar's belt, we joined the defenders.

For some stupid reason we were both laughing as we ran through the dark – me clutching *Pighammer* and Elric his sword in his good hand – surrounded by furious Welshmen who knew not we were enemies.

When we reached the gate there had to be more than fifty men about the low spiked walls defying the attack and without a word I plunged into the middle swinging *Pighammer* left and right with Elric at my side watching for counter-attacks. In the semi-dark and confusion the Welsh failed to mark me and within seconds I had cut my way to the gate and pulled the locking bar free. Then I turned back into the fray, hunting foes as Elric dragged the gate half open and shouted for Harold.

Finally, I was marked and a huge man with a long sword ran at me in the half light, summoning others as he came – but mostly they were wary of *Pighammer* cleaving through wide arcs to kill or maim any who got too close. This was where my countless hours of practice – simply holding the weapons out at shoulder height – really mattered. I was no taller or stronger than the man with the long sword, but I had the wind to use my weapon longer.

The light was growing as more torches joined in a half circle about the gate and the man with the sword and I were left to fight alone. I was no longer swinging wildly but using the axe-head to parry his thrusts and slashes at the haft of my axe. That is ever the main strategy fighting axe with sword – to break the hardwood handle to render the weapon useless. But *Pighammer*'s haft, besides being thicker than most, had also been reinforced for a foot below the head with iron rings. It was a heavy and fearsome weapon and I watched the fear grow in the eyes of my opponent when he saw that all he had done was blunt his own weapon in trying to hurt mine.

He was getting tired also. The tip of his sword was no longer pointing at my throat as he held me at bay and his face gleamed with sweat as the half circle of Welshmen shouted and encouraged him. His movements became laboured and more predictable – ever in the same patterns he moved, but they got slower, and tighter. Without further thought, I swung my axe and let go of it, so that the top of the axe-head took him in the shoulder. He staggered backwards as I dragged my own sword – *Revanche* – from its sheepskin scabbard.

As I approached him I could tell that his sword arm was useless, and then there was a great shout as Harold's men came pouring through the opened gate. The swordsman dropped his weapon as others fled back through the camp, pursued by whooping Saxons eager to blood their swords on a beaten foe.

'What of Gruffydd?' asked Harold, appearing at my side.

'He is here,' I said, suddenly exhausted as I perceived that I had survived my mission. The swordsman fell to his knees and spoke words I couldn't understand, although the meaning was clear. I lowered my sword as the screaming and shouting arose all about us.

'You fight like a demon with that axe,' said Harold. 'I wouldn't care to face you.'

'Brand is one of the very best in the fyrd,' agreed Tostig, who had also appeared. 'Have I not said so since the day we met him in the forest near Theodford?'

'Tostig has ever been your champion Brand,' agreed Harold, clapping me over the shoulder and nodding his acknowledgment of Elric.

'But come … what news of Aelfgar?' asked Tostig.

'Aelfgar is dead,' I replied, and the scowl on my champion's face was like the first tremor of thunder beyond a suddenly black horizon.

Chapter 18

Visions of the Hidden World

Gruffydd escaped.

The portable walls of his Rhuddlan camp meant that it was simple enough to open up a breach and judging by the numbers slain or captured, at least a hundred and fifty went with the self-proclaimed king of the Welsh.

'The river is denied him … he'll have made for the mountains,' said Garryd, and the signs seemed to bear that out. Harold sent scouts and it was soon confirmed that Gruffydd had fled into the mountains to the south and west heading to the fortresses of Dolbadarn or Dolwyddelan.

'They are very strong places Lord,' explained Garryd to Harold. 'A small number of determined defenders might hold out long against a great army … an army that needs to be fed.'

Nevertheless, and despite the lateness of the season, Harold was determined to press his advantage. Further ships arrived and many men had disembarked to swell the numbers already at Rhuddlan to nearly five hundred. These were joined by a force of Tostig's housecarls who'd come in from the northwest, swelling the army under Harold to not far short of a thousand. They were all given bread and salt meat to carry – enough to last a week if spared, and supplemented wherever possible off the land – so we took off in pursuit, only hours behind Gruffydd.

I discovered myself to be very popular after the successful raid. It seemed everyone had heard of my feat in gaining entry and opening the gate, but I was oddly reticent regarding the death of Aelfgar. In normal circumstances I would have revelled in the notoriety, but the mood of Tostig was sour and he was very different from the affable lord who had always taken my part. I could hardly bear to meet his eye.

This was noticed by Elric, as we marched along the path Gruffydd had taken through the forest

'It seems you guessed correctly regarding Tostig's ambition.'

Furtively I glanced about to make sure none were within earshot.

'Perhaps. Say nothing more for now.'

But Elric couldn't help himself.

'You've made an enemy out of a friend, Brand. The way he looks at you behind your back … it catches the breath … it turns my blood cold.'

'He'll get over it,' I said, without much confidence.

'He's more the son of Godwin than Harold is,' said Elric, 'which means he'll never get over it unless you find a way to appease him … do him a favour bigger than the loss he now feels.'

I was yet to sleep after the night's exertion and found myself yawning as the path grew perceptibly steeper. Through occasional gaps in the forest roof we caught glimpses of the mountains rising up before us and I felt dismayed by the prospect of the climb when I so desperately needed rest.

'Of course, the worst problem,' continued Elric, 'is what this means for Harold. If Tostig is scheming against him, he needs to know.'

Exactly the same question had been troubling me from the moment I overheard Aelfgar at the latrine.

'I don't believe Tostig is scheming against Harold,' I said, glancing again over my shoulder. 'I do suspect though that if Harold refuses the crown, as he always says he will, Tostig may feel justified in taking it.'

'He may have started thinking that way,' said Elric, 'but once a man imagines the crown on his own head … all sorts of justifications become possible.'

'I'm not getting involved in a fight between the Godwinsons.'

'But if they do fight you'll have to choose sides,' insisted Elric – still giving voice to my own fears. 'If you warn Harold now … '

'I make a deadly enemy of Tostig when Harold confronts him.'

'But if you don't warn Harold now … '

'Then I run the risk of Tostig prevailing … with no Harold around to protect me.'

Eventually Elric came to the conclusion to which I had come myself.

'Safer to do nothing … for now.'

'Yes,' I agreed, 'but we will watch Tostig closely.'

As we advanced there were occasional arrows from thickets or behind rocks – which slowed us considerably, but confirmed we were on the right track. By evening we had crossed the river west, climbed out of the forest and were camped along an uplands field well away from the mountain wall to our left. Garryd had advised Harold to avoid the shelter of cliffs as the heights were perfect for the dropping of large stones – a favourite tactic of the Welsh in high places.

Wrapped in a blanket, too exhausted for sleep, I found myself thinking again about Valla – and Elric's Valla. Could it be that Elric had prevented the return of his own Valla through fucking the Rocker woman?

It didn't seem to make any sort of sense, but in case it did – was I ever likely to be tempted?

I lay there, remembering the young wenches of my father's household with whom I'd rutted constantly until promised to the church on my fourteenth birthday. But the more I tried to picture them the more they seemed to turn into Valla, with whom I was yet to consummate. I realised that I had no carnal memories worth keeping save those with Valla – such as they were – and in that moment knew I could never be tempted by another.

With that thought, I relaxed – and slept like a stone until morning.

∞ ∞ ∞

The fortress at Dolwyddelan was formidable – up on a knoll within a high valley approachable only by steep and narrow paths and utilising the natural fortifications afforded by sheer rock faces. It had a good water supply and it was said that Gruffydd was victualled well enough to see off any siege if the besiegers were not replenished. As soon as we established ourselves about the knoll and ascertained that Gruffydd was indeed locked up inside, Harold sent foraging parties to raid any holdings within the region – and while a steady supply trickled in, it would hardly be enough to sustain a lengthy investment.

'We need to get inside,' insisted Harold at a council of housecarls on the third day of the siege. 'Gruffydd laughs at our discomfit, secure in his belief that he can outlast us. But I will not return to Edward without Gruffydd's head.'

It was strange to think that only seven days earlier I had been in council with the same men as we pondered the problem of Aelfgar. Once again I stood in a half circle with Skalpi, Leofwine, Aethelnoth and Eadnoth the Stallers – and other lords, including Tostig and Garryd. Yet another younger Godwinson was also present – Gyrth, Earl of East Anglia, older than me but with little of my battle experience. That didn't stop him being as belligerent as any other there, and he immediately volunteered for every plan suggested, no matter how foolhardy.

'Nay Gyrth,' laughed Harold, as yet another hopeless plan was proposed by Skalpi, which was little more than marching up to the gate and challenging Gruffydd to single combat.

Tostig had seemed to recover somewhat from his dark mood in the wake of Aelfgar's demise, but he was certainly not his old cheerful self.

'We cannot bring the throwing machines up such steep and narrow paths,' he said, 'but we have engineers … could they not build more with the materials at hand. There is good timber in this valley.'

'It would take time,' replied Aethelnoth, ' … more time than we are likely to have.'

'Still, it is better than doing nothing,' said Harold. 'And the sight of us preparing siege engines may affect morale within the fortress and convince them we have resources enough to do the job.'

After some thought he added, 'Build ladders also, but don't let those be seen. We might attempt an escalade on a moonless night.'

Shortly afterwards he ended the council but as the lords and housecarls left the pavilion he called me and bade me walk with him to survey the fortress.

'I haven't thanked you,' he said, 'for your work in Rhuddlan.'

I just nodded, gazing at the fortress as if to perceive weaknesses unmarked by others.

'It was fine work Brand, and raises your value still more within the fyrd ... there are few so valuable to me now. Do you understand what that means?'

I supposed it meant that he would reward me, but to my vague unease he said, 'It means you could be singled out by my enemies. Anyone who wished to weaken my position would do well to have you slain.'

'But you have no enemies lord,' I replied (hoping it was true). 'Surely your only enemies are Inglalond's enemies ... such as Gruffydd.'

'Would that that were so,' laughed Harold, as we climbed to within bowshot to examine the walls and gate of Dolwyddelan. 'Nay Brand ... all lords have enemies. You yourself have seen that a thegn's seat can be taken by treachery ... so can an earl's, or even a king's. And treason can arise suddenly in the heart of any man.'

I couldn't help but feel that he was gently testing me, but presently he asked about the exact manner of Aelfgar's death and his eyes widened in astonishment as I poured out the tale – leaving only the details regarding Tostig.

'But why would Aelfgar protect you against Gruffydd and Dafydd?' he queried. 'It makes no sense.'

'I understood that Aelfgar had been outlawed in the past ... and yet made his peace with Edward,' I said. 'I rather overstated the size of our army ... and hinted that reconciliation might be possible again and further hinted that keeping me alive might aid his cause.'

'Keeping alive a spy would aid his cause?' asked Harold, doubtfully.

'Forgive me lord ... I also told him I was your bastard son and very dear to you.'

Harold stared at me, then barked with laughter and threw an arm around my shoulders.

'At last I understand your reticence,' he said. 'I could tell there was something you were leaving unsaid ... so that is the way of it.'

He grinned and shook his head while surveying the fortress, and the sky darkening in the east.

'I would be pleased to have a son such as you,' he said, to my great embarrassment. 'Brave, resourceful, intelligent, strong at arms ... best of all, reliable. A lord needs to rely on other men, so he needs to know those he can trust ... not just always to take his part but to succeed.

Lordship is about winning Brand … never forget that.'

'Yes lord.'

'So … Brand the Reliable … how do I get inside this fortress?'

I pondered for a few moments, gazing up at the high walls that I would hate to climb in the dark, knowing that knives, stones and worse awaited me at the summit.

'Maybe you don't need to get inside,' I mused. 'Maybe Gruffydd's peril is already in there with him?'

I told Harold about Cynan and my belief that he had probably gone with Gruffydd's men.

'Cynan ap Iago?' asked Harold, with sudden excitement. 'The son of Iago ab Idwal?'

'I know not, sire.'

Suddenly Harold laughed again. 'Iago was lord of Gwynedd before he was slain by Gruffydd … Cynan is his son and will avenge his father given the opportunity. How sure can we be that he is inside?'

'We can't,' I replied, marvelling that I had been eating and sleeping with yet another lord denied his birthright through treachery, like myself.

'Perhaps not,' agreed Harold, 'but I like your suggestion that we need not enter to conquer. The Welsh are a notoriously divided people … how might we help them to remember their own grievances against each other?'

I gazed once more at the fortress and the many soldiers lining its walls. Then, I turned back to our own camp and saw in the distance that already trees were being felled to provide timber for throwing machines and ladders, and that the activity had been marked by the watchers on the walls.

'Tostig's idea was a good one,' I said. 'It will give the Welsh reason to believe we intend to stay. As time passes and we remain in numbers far superior to their own, building engines to attack them, the pressure will rise inside the fort and their own divisions may be remembered. What if we were to help that memory by sending heralds to tell them it is only Gruffydd we want … that all others may go free if Gruffydd is delivered up to us?'

Harold grinned and once again threw his arm about my shoulders.

'That is the exact strategy I have conceived myself over the course of our conversation. We shall try it.'

I grinned in return, pleased to have been of service to such a great lord.

'When we leave this place, with Gruffydd's head,' continued Harold, 'I shall give some thought to your proper station.'

'You mean my revenge on Malgard?'

'I mean considerably more than that young Brand Holgarsson. After Edward dies, there will be a need to revise many things ... not least the earldoms. Say no more for now, but I believe you may be worthy not just of Stybbor, but of all East Anglia.'

I was speechless as Harold turned and strode back down the steep path. Not so much because he had offered me an earldom, as for what such an offer meant.

The offer could only be made by a man who had decided to be king.

∞ ∞ ∞

The gates of Dolwyddelan opened and a small number of Welsh lords approached us. Gruffydd was not among them but, to my rising excitement, Cynan was. Indeed, he led the others, and that fact alone gave me almost certain foreknowledge as to what was about to pass.

'Cynan leads them?' asked Harold.

'He does, Lord.'

By this time the tale of my slaying of Aelfgar had become common knowledge and my reputation soared within the fyrd. Even among the housecarls, though not officially one of their number while the name Brand Holgarsson was outlawed, my standing was very high and I found myself naturally to Harold's immediate left as Tostig stood to his right.

There were six of the Welsh and they paused about five paces before us. Cynan stepped forward and placed a large covered basket at Harold's feet, then he stepped back and rejoined his fellows.

'Who among you speaks our tongue?' asked Harold.

'I do sire,' said the oldest of them. 'I am Huw ab Wellyn of Caernarfon.'

'What would you have me do?' asked Harold.

'Leave us in peace,' replied Huw, 'to rule ourselves in acknowledgement of Edward's overlordship … as we did before Gruffydd.'

'Who will rule you?'

Huw turned to Cynan who was glaring a challenge at Harold.

'Cynan ap Iago,' said Harold, striding forward and offering his hand. Cynan stared at the hand, then slowly accepted it. Then he spoke in Welsh to Harold and his words were translated by Huw.

'Cynan ap Iago, king of Gwynned and Wales, greets Harold, Earl of Wessex and thanks him for assisting in the return of the crown to its rightful house.'

'Is that why we were here?' growled Tostig, but Cynan continued, promising friendship between Inglalond and Wales if we respected his borders.

Harold listened patiently, then he said, 'Men of Gwynned … you are here because your last leader brought you to here and you followed, through no fault of your own, because that is the duty of vassals. But Gruffydd was wrong. There is no crown of Wales … not even a crown subject to Edward. Call your leaders any name you will, except king, and we shall have peace.'

These words were translated by Huw and Cynan's eyes narrowed, but then he shrugged and stepped forward, and raised the lid from the basket.

We had all known what would be inside – the blood leaking from the bottom was proof enough of that – but Harold bade me look, being the last to have seen Gruffydd. I nodded to acknowledge Gruffydd's presence, then I nodded at Cynan, who nodded in return. Then he gestured to one of his fellows who produced a horn and blew a long note in the direction of the fortress. Immediately, I reached for my sword – half expecting an attack – but instead of an army, Edwin, son of Aelfgar, emerged from the gate festooned with chains. His face was bruised and bloody and clearly there had been a dispute.

With Edwin, besides his guards, was the woman I had seen with Gruffyd and Aelfgar at Rhuddlan. Queenly she was, and very fair – tall, golden-haired and beautiful as though she had stepped from the staves of a song of elves and faeries. Thus, for the first time, did Harold Godwinson, Earl of Wessex, Subregulus of Inglalond, behold

Edith, daughter of Aelfgar, Earl of Mercia, widow of Gruffyd ap Llewellyn.

∞ ∞ ∞

Tostig was outraged.

'Marriage to Edith? You can't be serious!'

The argument was quite public, before the council of housecarls in Harold's pavilion. Some men of Harold's status would have been profoundly insulted by the words, but Harold could never be angry with Tostig – not for long, at any rate.

'Quite serious,' said Harold.

'But you already have a wife,' spluttered Tostig. 'How can you insult the Lady Swanneshals? The mother of your sons!'

'She is a wife *more danico*,' said Harold. 'She has always known that one day I would take a political wife, and I see here an opportunity to bind Wessex and Mercia … the two greatest earldoms … by marriage.'

'And what of Edwin?' demanded Tostig.

'That is for Edward to decide,' said Harold.

Edwin had been released from his chains and given a small pavilion of his own, befitting a provisional earl. He knew I had slain his father but in accordance with the law, such killing was doubly authorised by both his allegiance with Gruffydd and the fact of his outlawry. Harold had required him to acknowledge the legality of the slaying as a condition of his release, and he had done so with very poor grace. His mouth forgave me, but his eyes promised vengeance.

Not that I was too concerned about it. I had seen Edwin under pressure and imploring his father to creep away from Rhuddlan. I judged myself his superior at arms and had little fear of him, but Elric reminded me that he was an earl (or likely to be confirmed as earl) with the treasury of an earl and access to slayers of his own. Once again, I had to be wary of all men, as who knew what might be concealed behind a friendly smile.

A friendly smile I had not expected was Tostig's.

The day after the death of Gruffydd at the hands of his own housecarls (Cynan had dealt the killing blow) we were preparing to return to Lundene. I had collected coarse sand from a river bed and was scouring my shirt of rings – admiring the sun glinting off the polished metal – when a shadow darkened my work.

I looked up to see Tostig grinning at me and felt a shiver across my shoulders.

'Brand,' he said, 'I've not yet congratulated you on the success of your mission.'

I didn't really know what to say. I had reason to suspect Tostig's ambition had outstripped his brother's, and yet I was also aware that Harold might have changed his mind about the crown. This had the potential to turn two close siblings into bitter rivals.

'Thank you Lord. I know Aelfgar was your friend and I liked him myself in our brief acquaintance ... but Harold gave me a duty.'

'Speak no more of it,' said Tostig, 'but walk with me Brand. I would have your counsel on a hard matter.'

My heart sank, but what choice did I have? I shook the sand from my hauberk and wrapped it in an oiled goatskin. Then I rose and followed the Earl of Northumbria down towards the stream which sparkled in the cool, bright sun.

'Rarely have I seen a man rise so quickly,' said Tostig. 'You have done well.'

'Thank you Lord Tostig ... but truly I seek nothing for myself save the chance to serve your brother and live the life of a fighting man.'

'You were destined for the church, were you not?'

'I was. My uncle's treachery did at least save me from that dull fate.'

'Aaah, your uncle. What has become of him?'

There was something vaguely disturbing about the question, and the tone of Tostig's voice, but nevertheless I answered, 'I know not. I presume he continues to flourish at Stybbor ... ill-prepared, I hope, for the day of my return.'

In fact, after my last conversation with Harold, I had already started daydreaming about arriving in Stybbor as Earl of East Anglia, with a dragon-hilted dagger in my hand. It was a delicious fantasy, ending in blood.

'We will all look forward to that,' laughed Tostig, 'but your return is not certain.'

I glanced at him, wondering what he meant.

'The matter upon which I wanted your counsel is bound up with your own interest,' said Tostig. 'The question of Edwin ... and his brother.'

'What have they to do with my interest?' I queried, already having a fairly good idea.

'Can you not guess?' asked Tostig, and laughed when he saw the look on my face. 'Yes ... they will say nothing in public, but the sons of Aelfgar will not let their father go unavenged.'

'Does that mean they will have revenge against Harold?' I asked. 'Or Edward? I may have done the slaying, but it was done on the order of the king and his deputy.'

'Edwin will know that,' agreed Tostig, 'but he is a small man and will be satisfied with a target he deems within his measure.'

'I am hardly within Edwin's measure,' I sneered. 'I could fight him left handed with a farrier's rake and still have the head off his shoulders.'

'No doubt,' agreed Tostig. 'But men such as Edwin do not fight duels with slayers of renown ... they use assassins and care not if one, two or even ten fail. An assassin will get you in the end, and Edwin can afford to wait.'

'Unless I get him first ... '

Tostig grinned.

'And thus we come to my own problem ... did I not tell you it was bound up with your interest?'

'The death of Edwin is also in your interest?'

Tostig did not answer for a moment, but considered me as though wondering how much to reveal of his purpose.

'My interest is ever the advancement of the house of Godwin,' he said. 'Harold and I have long planned to share Wessex and Mercia ... leaving other parts of the realm to Leofwine and Gyrth ... and gradually tightening our hold, irrespective of what puppet of the line of Cerdic might be king. But now Edith has bewitched my brother and through marital obligation will confirm the son of an outlaw in what should be my place.'

My head was whirling with this revelation. Something wasn't quite right – Tostig had been ready to treat with Aelfgar to unite Northumbria and Mercia, yet now he wanted Edwin killed. In that moment I perceived that his true desire was to prevent a union of

Wessex and Mercia under Harold – effectively cornering him in the north. If he objected to that he truly was seeing himself as a rival for the crown, as Elric had guessed.

'I have no cause to challenge Edwin,' continued Tostig, 'but all men know he is likely to attempt murder against you. If you were to slay Edwin, all would know it was in self defence and none could hold it against you.'

'Except perhaps Edwin's future brother in law …'

'Harold will never believe murder on your part,' insisted Tostig. 'He holds you in the highest esteem and will swiftly forget Edwin once he is gone and replaced with a son of Godwin.'

'There are no other sons of Aelfgar?'

Tostig waved the question away.

'There is Morcar … younger even than Leofwine. He is no viable option.'

So this was the way of life among the great – murder and conspiracy and the opposite of all the courtly virtues they revered in song. Tostig could tell I was struggling with it all and said, 'Come Brand … you are a fighting man. You should be aware by now that striking first and striking hard is the best way to stay alive.'

'A fighting man strikes in the service of his lord,' I replied. 'I don't think Harold would want this death.'

'Don't think Harold squeamish,' laughed Tostig. 'Convenient political deaths have ever advanced the house of Godwin. Harold himself escorted the aetheling safely from Saxony … only to see him die within days of setting foot in Inglalond.'

Again I felt the hair rise on the back of my neck as the conversation strayed into areas I did not wish to go.

'Harold slew the aetheling?'

'I said not so,' smiled Tostig, ' … and yet the aetheling died within days of being beyond help. I've never questioned Harold closely about it, and surely there are slow ways of killing that look like sickness.'

'Poison?'

'Who knows?' replied Tostig. 'There is another matter also.'

Tostig glanced about to ensure we were not within hearing of any other, then lowered his voice. 'As you are aware, Harold now hopes to wed the Lady Edith … Edwin's sister.'

Tostig said no more, but waited for me to make the connections for myself.

'Harold will need the consent of her family,' I said. 'And the head of her family is now her brother Edwin ... '

'Edwin who wants you dead,' said Tostig.

' ... No!' I said, perceiving at last what Tostig was trying to tell me.

'Oh, Harold would prefer you alive ... I'm sure,' said Tostig, 'but if the choice had to be between you and Edith ... for the political stability of Inglalond ... then even Lord Harold ... wise in law and fairest man in the realm might look the other way when Edwin seeks his vengeance.'

'No,' I repeated, shocked to my very core that Harold might prove false.

'Now you understand the problem,' said Tostig, 'and how our interests are aligned.'

I just stared at him, utterly mortified by his revelations. Then I glanced over at Harold's pavilion where he happened to be speaking with both Edwin and the Lady Edith. Tostig followed my eye and said, 'A happy family they make already.'

∞ ∞ ∞

Elric's arm was bound tightly – held in place with staves shaped to his arm and wrapped once again in Aelfgar's belt. Four days after breaking it still throbbed with pain but he could flex his fingers freely which, according to Harold's leech, was an excellent sign.

'Your strength will return,' he said, 'as long as you do nothing reckless to re-injure the arm before it heals.'

He gave Elric some herbs to help with the pain and asked me where Valla had gone.

'Your wife has an excellent preparation for the dulling of pain, but will not share her secret. Such would help your friend better than I can do, but steep these herbs in hot water and breathe the vapours. Then drink the water when it cools and your pain will be relieved for a time.'

We thanked him and left, heading up the slope above the knoll on which the fortress of Dolwyddelan stood with its gates wide open.

With a cold breeze defeating the wintry sun, we sat huddled in heavy woollen cloaks and I repeated my conversation with Tostig.

'You're fucked,' was Elric's assessment.

I was inclined to agree, but still refused to believe that Harold would permit my death for political or marital expedience.

'Mind you,' I said, 'Lordship is all about winning ... he told me that himself.'

'Winning ... and always choosing the winning side,' agreed Elric.

We watched as the last of the camp was taken apart. It had been a successful campaign and the fyrd was preparing to disperse and return to their homes for the harvest. Tostig would head north with his housecarls and Harold intended to go to his house at Bosham in the south, but first we would visit the king and place Gruffydd's head on a spike on Lundene Bridge.

'So which is the winning side,' I asked, 'Harold's or Tostig's?'

'Tostig has the advantage at the moment,' said Elric, 'because Harold doesn't know he has a rival.'

I wasn't entirely sure that was true, but for the sake of argument let it stand.

'What would happen if I killed Edwin ... as Tostig wishes ... and all knew it?'

'It would depend on the attitude of the Lady Edith,' said Elric, '... and how much love she has for her brother. All know you are Harold's creature so she would assume the killing was done on his order. If she wants to be queen, then maybe she will just ignore it ... but if her concept of family honour is strong enough, she may demand a sacrifice.'

'And if I slay Edwin but no-one knows it ... or can prove it?'

'You make Tostig happy,' mused Elric, 'but maybe you embarrass Harold. Most will assume it was your work.'

'Which means I must wait for Edwin to send his slayers, but do nothing in my own defence.'

Elric laughed.

'As I said ... you're fucked. But I doubt whether Edwin's your biggest problem.'

'So what's my biggest problem,' I demanded, thoroughly wearied by the subtle perils of politics.

'I feel a storm coming,' said Elric. 'Tostig hides it for now but with every passing day I sense him hardening his resolve to take the crown for himself. That won't end well.'

I agreed with Elric that a war between the Godwinsons would be catastrophic for Inglalond, but it was not my biggest problem.

My biggest problem was Valla. I had at least been distracted from the problem when hunting Aelfgar in the camp of the Welsh, but now the fighting was over I was utterly tormented by Valla's absence and felt the love of her more keenly every hour.

∞ ∞ ∞

'I sense a change,' said Myrrthn.

Valla and Myrrthn sat, naked as ever, in the mouth of a cave near the peak of Yr Wyddfa – tallest mountain in Gwynned. A fire blazed between them with greenish flames as Myrrthn fed it with herbs and powders. Again they drank of the elixir Myrrthn brewed from mistletoe and mushrooms, and again Valla sensed the invisible portals opening to show visions of the hidden world.

'What change?' she asked in a musical voice, spanning the worlds.

'A new power rises in defiance of the killer god … a strong leader … but he needs our help.'

Valla stared into the flames as Myrrthn spoke for some time describing arcane aspects of battles in the mists of time and the great battle to come.

'Not yet,' cackled Myrrthn, 'but soon. Oh yes, the killer god believes he has the power to sweep all before him on these isles … but he will not find it a simple matter. Oh no … the storms and furies defy him still and they will do what they can … if we support them.'

'Support them,' repeated Valla.

'An enchantment is called for,' said Myrrthn, staring into the flames. 'A great spell … the greatest spell ever woven since the beginning. You and I shall achieve it, and the isles will be safe from the killer god for a thousand years.'

'Others will be needed,' said Valla.

'Oh yes … others will be needed, but not now. In the far future, others will take up the battle when these isles are a fading bastion for

the old gods amid a tempest of ignorance and fear. But for now …
the task is ours alone.'

'Others will be needed,' insisted Valla, and Myrrthn was silent for
a time – staring into the flames until he cackled again with delight.

'You see deeper than I ever dreamed,' he breathed. 'Oh yes … Valla
sees deeply. But only one other will be needed.'

'Only one,' she agreed.

PART THREE

Chapter 19

A Bond of Silence

Harold had not been in Lundene for many months so was impressed by how far the work had proceeded on Edward's new minster on the north bank of the Temes, west of the city. Masons worked on scaffolds soaring so high into the heavens that the whole structure looked unworldly – supported by God somehow – for how else could such a building be permitted to stand?

Harold's musings were interrupted by the king's minister, Cuthred, who greeted him warmly at the door, immediately putting him on guard as Cuthred had ever been antagonistic to the sons of Godwin.

'Good news from Wales, I hear.'

'Aye,' agreed Harold, not wishing to engage with the man.

'The king is pleased … greatly pleased my lord Wessex.'

There was no need for torches inside the building, not least because the building was unfinished, but Harold perceived that the chapel would always be full of light and was awestruck by the way the early morning beams shone down onto the altar – already in place at the western end of the chapel as though God himself were bestowing a blessing.

'How is the king?' asked Harold, and Cuthred's mood became sombre.

'He ages … ever more quickly, Lord … and is troubled by dreams and portents.'

Cuthred's frankness and apparent friendliness were unsettling, causing Harold to wonder what had changed since he had last been at court. He approached the altar, where Edward sat nearby on a hard stool, surrounded by large men arrayed for war and with their hair curiously shaved at the back.

Normans, thought Harold, irritably. The king had ever more emissaries from Normandy –since Gyrth and Leofwine had been ransomed with the Duke for the good behaviour of Godwin and his elder sons – and Harold felt his anger rise again at memory of that humiliation, and the dealings Edward had advised regarding the succession.

Only one of the attendants was not a soldier and he seemed to be the leader of the group – a churchman by his tonsure and robes. Harold felt his hackles rise as he recognised the Bishop of Fecamp – a man to whom Edward had given land in Sussex despite the fact he was clearly an agent of the Duke of Normandy, whose interest in Inglalond was becoming disturbing.

More disturbing still was the way the Normans seemed to close protectively around Edward as Harold approached, but it was not the manner of vassals protecting their lord – more the manner of dogs protecting a bone.

Harold chose to ignore the Normans and strode to within five paces of the king. Edward looked in better health than Harold had feared from Cuthred's warning, and certainly he spoke with vigour.

'My lord Wessex ... I have already heard from your herald and I thank you for your work in Wales.'

Despite his words, Edward seemed to be keeping his anger in check.

'Is there some aspect of my work that displeases you, sire?'

Edward gazed at Harold for a moment, then indicated the Bishop.

'You have met Bishop John of Fecamp?'

The Bishop bowed but managed to convey an insolence as though bowing to a Fool at Carnival.

'I have met the Bishop,' said Harold.

'Bishop John tells me,' said Edward, 'that you plan to marry the sister of Edwin of Mercia.'

Harold was stunned by the revelation and how quickly the news had travelled. He turned to the Bishop whose eyes glittered black with amusement.

'Your friend Eadnoth was full of news,' explained the Bishop, ' ... as full of news as he was of ale.'

'Well?' demanded Edward.

'I have seen the lady, sire,' admitted Harold, 'and regard her as a fitting bride for the Earl of Wessex.'

'I do not,' replied Edward. 'It is important to keep the parts of my kingdom in balance ... and allowing the strongest Earl in Inglalond to add Mercia to his fief would send the wrong message to the realm.'

'What wrong message would that be, sire?' asked Harold, furious that such an argument should be held before the Normans.

Edward seemed to perceive that his manners were wanting, and as swiftly as his anger flared it faded.

'Forgive me Lord Wessex ... you have journeyed long and swiftly to bring me news of victory in Wales, and I thank you for it. But I have another task for you.'

Edward seemed to slump in his seat and muttered to himself as Harold waited to learn what was required of him. One of the Norman warriors was grinning and Harold turned to the Bishop, who was also grinning. The king is weak, thought Harold. He makes Inglalond look weak and he fires the ambitions of our neighbours.

It was a startling realisation. Harold had occasionally heard rumours of claims made by the Kings of Norway and Denmark to the crown of Inglalond. He had also heard rumours of a claim by Duke William – The Bastard men called him – but had never seriously entertained those claims because how could they ever be enforced? Harold knew he was the choice of the witan but if Edward named another lord of Inglalond as his successor, Harold would have supported it to the death. A choice from beyond Inglalond though?

'My lord,' said Harold. 'May I have a word in priv—'

'I have been giving thought to the succession,' interrupted Edward. 'My death, perhaps, is not for some years but I grow older and there is need for certainty.'

'The last time we spoke,' said Harold, deeply humiliated to be having such a conversation in public, 'you made clear that you wanted the aetheling's son Edgar to succeed.'

'And so I do,' agreed Edward. 'But he is young and there must be provision for his minority should I die before he is of age.'

'I will protect him,' said Harold.

'Like you protected his father?' asked the Bishop and Harold swore with a fury that no amount of courtly politeness could withhold.

'Sire, forgive me,' he apologised, aghast at his outburst, 'but I protest that we have this conversation before men with no interest in the succession.'

'All men have an interest in the succession of Inglalond,' said Edward, ' ... in particular our neighbours.'

'I, of course, am more than a neighbour,' said Bishop John, ' ... as my hides in Sussex will attest. But let us speak of happier matters sire ... you have good news for the Earl of Wessex.'

Edward stared at him for a moment, then seemed to recover himself.

'That good news is bound up with the subject we were already discussing ... the succession.'

Edward turned to Harold and said, 'The other reason we were displeased with your plans regarding the Lady Edith of Mercia is that we have agreed another marriage more suitable for the future peace of Inglalond.'

'Oh yes? And what marriage might that be?'

'You are to marry Adeliza ... the daughter of Duke William.'

Harold all but staggered backwards, so strong was his outraged response to the news, but he mastered his temper.

'And what does Inglalond receive in return for this maiden of Normandy?' he enquired.

'Protection,' said Bishop John. 'As you are doubtless aware, there are many who covet the crown of Inglalond. This marriage guarantees the Duke of Normandy's allegiance.'

'None would dare to attack Inglalond in the knowledge that Normandy watched over us,' agreed Edward. 'And you yourself, Harold, have always said your greatest ambition was for the peace of Inglalond and her subjects. This marriage ensures it.'

Harold had a vision of Normandy watching over Inglalond like a buzzard watching over a wounded lamb, but held his tongue.

'So it is arranged then,' said Edward. 'In the spring you will travel to Normandy and there marry your bride and bring back oaths of friendship and protection from Duke William.'

Harold bowed, furious at the grin on the face of the Bishop of Fecamp, and strode from the massive chamber full of the glory of God.

And yet, by the time he reached the door he found himself relaxing.

He had at last made up his own mind about the succession.

∞ ∞ ∞

Elric and I spent a pleasant autumn and winter at Harold's house at Bosham on the coast. It was the first chance I'd had to relax in some time and, while I missed Valla dreadfully, I took much pleasure in the simple life of the household – chopping wood for fires, hunting and fishing, training at arms and taking long walks along the seashore or through the woods. And with every passing day the threat posed by Aelfgar's sons seemed to fade.

Elric, of course, spent every available moment in the arms of the wenches of the household or the village inn and I doubt not that he fathered several children that winter, but for me there was no attraction in the idea. I wasn't even concerned with my vow to Valla – I simply wasn't interested.

When not engaged with hunting or falconry, Harold spent much of this time closeted with the Lady Swanneshals and their many children – the eldest of whom were Godwin, named for his grandsire, and Edmund. They were only three years younger than I and I took some part in their training and doubted not that they would make strong warriors one day.

Godwin, in particular, became my friend and often accompanied me on my rambles. I enjoyed his company but, if one thing did hang over the house like a bird of ill omen, it was Harold's impending nuptials to Adeliza of Normandy, and young Godwin's conversation would ever turn that way.

A favourite place to walk was the hill overlooking the harbour at the east end of the bay.

'This is a poor place for a harbour,' said Godwin, one cold but sunny day toward the end of February, 'the bay fills with sand and silt and the men wanting to board the boats must wade through mud and shallows. We should have chosen a place with deep water where we can step on and off boats with no more difficulty than entering a hall.'

'It is a safe harbour,' I said. 'Sometimes you have to put up with a little inconvenience for the sake of safety.'

'But why not have safety and convenience?' he demanded. 'If I were planning a town I should want both a safe harbour and a place of embarkation where men were not required to get mud on their hose.'

I laughed, amused as ever by his serious manner of speaking.

'Well, maybe that's the way it was when the town was settled,' I said. 'Things do change with time.'

'I dislike change,' muttered Godwin, and there was a silence. Then, as I knew he would, he said, 'What will happen to my mother when my father marries the Norman woman?'

'Nothing,' I replied. 'She will continue to live here in peace and honour … as will you.'

No sooner had I spoken, the Lady Swanneshals appeared on the path below us and called. Godwin waved happily to his mother while I sat staring out to sea – toward the Norman coast where Harold was due to travel with the change of season.

'Godwin,' called his mother, gliding the last few paces to our vantage point where, many years prior, some forgotten mason had carved a bench from a boulder facing the sea.

We stood to greet her and she said, 'Godwin … I have found you. Your father wants you back at the house.'

Immediately the two of us began to leave but the Lady Swanneshals touched me on the arm and said, 'Stay a moment Brand.'

Godwin looked from her to me and back again, as though he guessed there would be something worth hearing if he stayed, but then he shrugged and left us – racing back down the path with a vigour that made me realise I was getting older.

Swanneshals sat on the bench and bade me sit also. I had never before been alone with her and felt just slightly uncomfortable. She was certainly a beautiful woman still, for someone who had borne so many children, and must have been almost thirty years old. She would have been young indeed when married *more danico* to Harold before Godwin was born.

'I have missed Valla,' she said.

Very little had been said by others regarding Valla's absence – I suspected that Elric had warned people not to ask me about it, but such warnings would not include the Lady Swanneshals.

'I miss her also.'

'It is good to see a man and woman love each other so deeply,' she said. 'It moves the hearts of all around to see such love ... you are a lucky man.'

'There are two types of luck,' I replied, unable to prevent the bitter edge entering my voice. 'Lucky I was to find her, but that good luck is now reversed and I have to wonder whether I would have been luckier never to find her in the first place.'

'Nay,' she replied. 'I understand somewhat of your condition. It was explained to me the night we met.'

I turned from my examination of the sea to regard her – serious but light of heart – beautiful but earthly – full of jest and wisdom, and I felt that here truly is a Queen fit for Inglalond. All men could love such a Queen and my heart filled with sadness that she would never sit crowned by her husband's side.

'We have never spoken of that night,' she continued, 'although I expect you may have wondered at the time.'

I found myself smiling and said, 'You helped Valla free the captured serfs ... I had forgotten that.'

Swanneshals smiled also. 'You bit my hand in the darkness ... and I saw you staring at the bandage the next morning, but you said nothing. Already we had a bond of silence.'

'A bond of silence, my Lady?'

'To leave unsaid those things that best remain hidden.'

I wasn't entirely sure what she meant, but nodded – fearing where the conversation was leading. Swanneshals lifted her gaze to the south and east.

'Normandy is close,' she said, '... a land of enemies. I sometimes imagine the sea before us filled with ships ... bringing an army to destroy us.'

'Valla dreamed of the same thing,' I said, and then wondered how I knew that, for she had never mentioned it.

'Valla has the gift,' agreed Swanneshals.

'They cannot come though,' I said. 'Ships are expensive and however many they might carry, we would still have ten times ... a hundred times their number on the shore ... led by your husband.'

221

'My husband?' queried Swanneshals. 'It seems I am no longer to have a husband.'

I had not meant for the conversation to go down that path and sat in embarrassed silence as she continued staring towards Normandy.

'Will you do me a favour Brand?' she asked.

'Of course, my Lady,' I said, my heart sinking in anticipation of what secret service she might request, putting me in conflict with Harold.

'It is only a small favour,' she said, as though guessing my fear, ' ... yet it may seem large before the end. Be his friend. Stay true to him no matter what ... he will need such friends.'

Once again I found myself staring at her, as though she had revealed for a moment some awesome power and insight and I wondered how Harold could even consider marriage to another.

'Of course,' I repeated. And what else could I possibly say?

Chapter 20

Nowt But A Codpiece

'I have been given my task Brand. You will come to find it is allied with your own task but I can say no more for now. Stay faithful Brand. Lie with no other woman and I may return to you for the fulfilment of our life together ... for good or ill. There will be a sign. You will know it when you see it. Know that I am coming. It will not be as long as you think.'

On the morning we were to leave for Normandy I woke from the most powerful dream. It was my usual dream of Valla but so strong I could barely believe it just a dream and lay some while in disappointment. But then the sounds of rising and the smell of fresh bread wafting through the house banished the dream disappointment and I rose with excitement as I recalled our impending journey.

Elric was already in the kitchen, seated at the table with some of the other men and I found myself considering his changed circumstances. No words had ever been said, but Elric's status had risen as steadily as my own despite the fact that he bore Harold's mark on his arm – burned over the scar I had dealt him the night we met. It just goes to show that prowess at arms counts for more than a man's birth.

'What are you grinning at?' he demanded, as I sat to his left and pulled a large bowl of steaming pease and pork fat towards me.

'Nothing,' I laughed. 'Just happy to be alive.'

There was a distinct contrast of moods in the house – those travelling were in high spirits while those remaining were dour as though their world was ending. Godwin sat at the table white-faced with humiliation, rubbing his eyes to hide the evidence of tears. He had wanted to accompany us but been refused. For his safety,

Harold had insisted, but Godwin perceived that he would be an embarrassment to his father, given the reason for the journey, and felt the shame deeply. The Lady Swanneshals did not appear at breakfast.

An hour later we assembled with our gear in the courtyard.

'How's the arm?' I asked Elric.

'Strong,' he replied, flexing his fingers. 'It's mended really well, thank the gods.'

'Gods?' enquired Carl, who was also travelling.

'God then,' grinned Elric, simultaneously crossing himself and making the sign against the evil eye. Carl stared but chose not to chastise him further.

It was a strong group of housecarls and selected fighters who were to make the journey. Skalpi was there, large and belligerent as ever. Also Aethelnoth and Eadnoth the stallers and others who had been on the Welsh campaign, but neither Leofwine nor Gyrth – who had previously been held ransom by William and had no desire to return.

The high spirits of the travellers were bubbling over once free of the sombre household and I found myself laughing for no reason. I stood, as Carl had taught me years before, with axe and sword extended at shoulder height, marvelling at the muscle in my arms. I had been a skinny youth but seemed to be getting bigger and stronger all the time. Even the shirt of rings fitted me snugly now, whereas in the past I'd been obliged to tie it around my waist to stop it slipping. As for *Pighammer*, it was a brutish and heavy instrument which I wielded as lightly as a willow wand – none would dare stand before me if I felt like killing and had Elric at my side.

The only man in poor spirit was Eadric, the sailing master, who stared anxiously towards the bay and swore with frustration.

'What ails you Eadric?' boomed Harold, emerging from the house and back to his usual good humour, apparently.

'We've missed the tide,' scowled Eadric. 'No point leaving now.'

'Excellent,' said Harold. 'I had a mind to farewell this land with a feast so let us go at once to the rooms prepared.'

Eadric stared at him, then shrugged as Harold laughed, 'Forgive me, master steersman. I should have taken you deeper into my counsel regarding the day ... when will be the next tide? Ten hours? Eleven?'

'Ten,' agreed Eadric.

'Then that gives us nine hours for revelling, let us go!'

It occurred to me that the Lady Swannehals had not appeared to farewell us, as was her custom, but I supposed that was not surprising given Harold's mission. Still, I would have preferred all things to happen in their normal course before departing on a journey and felt just a small shiver of uneasiness – which I immediately banished for the foolishness it was.

There were twenty-nine in the party, counting servants (plus dogs and Harold's favourite falcon), and we trooped down to the harbour where the innkeeper had prepared a room above his house with a view over the bay which housed a small fishing fleet – all of which had departed for the day. We surrendered our weapons to the servants for carriage out to the ships still at anchor, a hundred yards offshore.

After the non-appearance of Swanneshals, I was in a mixed mood myself despite the excitement around me. I was eager indeed to experience a sea journey to a strange country, but at the same time full of forebodings on behalf of the Lady Swanneshals. Fey she had seemed in the final days, as though she shared something of the skill she claimed for Valla and had already witnessed events yet to come that would be hard for Harold. This thought again made me wonder how Harold could countenance any woman but Swanneshals and at some time during the feast, when I had already had more ale and wine than was good for me, I found myself talking to him amid the noise and laughter of the travellers.

'How long have you been married to the Lady Swanneshals?'

It was an accidentally aggressive question thanks to the wine clouding my wits, but Harold seemed not to mind.

'How long? Fifteen years … I think.'

'And yet you must have another wife?'

Some men may have taken offence but Harold slapped me on the back and laughed as though it was the funniest jest he'd heard in a month.

'No wonder she likes you, Brand. I'm glad you take her part.'

If I was confused before I was astonished by his mood and answers now.

'But ... do you not love the Lady Swanneshals?'

'More than my life ... but not more than Inglalond.'

No doubt I stared in drunken confusion – certainly I felt thick-witted and stupid as the greatest man in Inglalond, save the king, placed his drinking horn on its stand and explained to me the subtle complications of his condition.

'You are yourself married *more danico* but may in time rise to an Earldom ... we have discussed it.'

I nodded, embarrassed to speak openly of such rewards.

'But if you wish to pass on the Earldom ... or even the thegnship you will take when Malgard is dead, to your sons ... then you should be Christian married. The church increasingly has influence in this.'

Immediately I knew Valla would refuse a Christian marriage, and in that instant was certain that God was testing me again. I wanted to turn this new realisation over in my head but Harold was talking. 'There are many dark tides to pass beneath the bridge ere I can relax and enjoy my dotage. And I have sons to produce to settle the line.'

'But has not the Lady Swanneshals already given you sons?'

'Of course she has ... but they must be the right sons. The church will not easily recognise them, and there are other considerations ... But speaking of tides, I can tell from Eadric's face it is time we left.'

He jumped up and called for his falconer while I gazed drunkenly down from the upper gallery in which we had spent the day feasting and had the odd feeling that this was a key moment in my life – that God Himself was staring at me with a vision keen as the sun piercing clouds. I even held my hand up to shield my eyes but the clouds that had rolled in from the south-west were dark and free of visions.

The three ships were over a hundred yards away across the mud flats. The words of serious young Godwin came back to me and I found myself smiling as the excited housecarls and others started clambering down the steep stair towards the mud. Already Skalpi was floundering drunkenly up to his knees and it occurred to me how I might keep my nice green tunic dry. At the bottom of the stairs I removed my boots and hose, then pulled my tunic over my head and wearing nowt but a codpiece began striding through the muddy shallows.

'Brilliant!' exclaimed Harold, and soon all the others, except the thoroughly muddied Skalpi, were following suit and we arrived at the ships with dogs and hawks and as clean as one could reasonably hope.

Harold's ship was the largest and would have been the best part of forty feet long with a wooden stair built into the side. It took all of us some time to clamber aboard in water up to our waists and several fell laughing into the sea as we attempted it, but eventually Harold's well fed and thoroughly drunken housecarls and fighters were sprawling about the decks as Eadric and six of the servants pulled on long oars to get us into deeper water.

We had all but missed the tide so the going was not easy, but when we finally left the bay a westerly breeze pushed us towards Normandy and I had to say that my admiration for Eadric the steersman soared. The ocean was such a mysterious and dangerous place, yet Eadric had tamed it and moved assuredly – his hands on the steering oar, his eyes on the sky. He was finally in a good mood and I found myself enjoying the sensation of movement on the water – which seemed less daunting with Eadric's confidence.

'Not bad,' said Elric, as I leaned on the gunwale, looking back at the shore in the fading light. 'I've got us a place in the bow.'

There was little cover on the ship. Only one canopied space above deck, so we had the choice of sleeping in the hold with the bilge and the rats, or on deck with the weather. It was only early spring, so still cold, but most preferred the deck, wrapped in cloaks with oiled skins pulled over the top as protection against rain and sea.

We ate a meal as the darkness fell, then drank until wine dulled the last of our wits and fell snoring one by one into our damp blankets – heedless of what the morn might bring.

Chapter 21

Arriving Unannounced in a Strange Land

'Why are these people so stupid?' wondered Malgard, as Gorik and his soldiers tore apart the hut of a family who were clearly hiding grain.

The husband and wife were forced to watch, the husband already bleeding from a broken nose and mouth, as their home was dragged to the ground with hooked bills and axes, and the hearth smashed with hammers.

The woman began to cry again and Malgard raised an eyebrow as Gorik immediately strode over and smacked her hard in the face. Malgard hated women crying and Gorik took care that he would not have to hear it.

She stopped. Or at least, her whimpering was soft enough to be ignored, but Malgard moved ten paces for good measure to watch the soldiers in their work.

'Here it is,' called one of the men, scraping in the hearth, and all crowded around to see the hidden cavity opened. A slab was levered up and Gorik got down on his knees to peer into the hole. He reached inside and pulled out a small sack.

'So,' said Malgard to the couple, 'you have nothing left for the taxes, you say? Let us see the truth of it.'

Gorik upturned the sack and a dozen or so withered turnips fell onto the ground at Malgard's feet.

'Please lord,' cried the man. 'It is the last of our winter store … there is nothing else. We already paid our taxes … doubly so … and there is nothing more to give!'

Malgard kicked the man in the face and then stamped on his hand, feeling a satisfying crack.

'Take those for the pigs,' snapped Malgard, pointing at the turnips, then he turned and strode towards his palfrey, held by a nervous page.

An hour later, back in his large house at Stybbor, Malgard raged about the hall – which was too cool as they had burned all the seasoned wood and were forced to try logs still green and young.

For the first two years of his thegnship he had lived well. Once he'd been installed by the king and with the last of Holgar's line confirmed dead, he had returned to Stybbor and imposed his will – drastically raising taxes to repair the damage from the Viking raid, but also to afford the opulence his status as reeve and thegn demanded.

He had brought Gorik from London to become his sergeant and the small but vicious man had waged a war on Malgard's people to screw every last grain and fleece from them to swell the thegn's hoard.

But there was never enough, and what little there was, was spent quickly. Malgard had no patience for the advice of those that told him the land could only produce so much and that he ought to live within its means as Holgar and his fathers had done. Such advice he considered treason, and there was only one punishment for treason.

Clearly the peasants had stopped producing as much as they'd done in the past and an example needed to be made – mutilation, or some public floggings perhaps? He would have preferred executions but even Malgard knew there had to be some peasants left to do the work. Of course, there had been some executions. A number of families had simply disappeared – walked away in the night – but those recaptured had been beheaded as an example to anyone else with itchy feet.

There was no denying that the shire of Stybbor was approaching crisis point. Men were needed to do the work and the once thriving land was falling into ruin. Gorik had suggested an alliance with Danes to raid some neighbouring shires and, while Malgard had initially rejected the idea, he was coming to see it as the only feasible answer – in the short term at least.

As Malgard brooded on the problem, one of his remaining soldiers announced a visitor. Dressed well and obviously from Lundene, the man approached Malgard's chair in the hall and bowed deeply.

'Malgard, son of Rathgar ... I am Torvald, I bring you greetings.'

Malgard smiled, his mood much improved at receiving due honour from a richly accoutred stranger. It somehow emphasised how well he was regarded by the rest of the world and deflected him from the laziness of his peasants.

'From whom do you bring greetings, Torvald ... the king?'

'Nay lord.'

Torvald glanced over his shoulder at the soldier who had brought him, and Malgard pointed to the door. When the soldier had gone, Torvald bowed once again and said, 'I bring you greetings from Tostig, Earl of Northumbria.'

∞ ∞ ∞

My head was like a blacksmith's shop and my mouth like a cess pit when I woke the next morning, and before I knew where I was the vomit erupted from my guts like blood from a stuck pig.

In the depth of my misery I slowly gathered that others were also being sick and the movement of the ship was no longer pleasant but more a form of torment that made the head reel. Eadric and his sailors were unaffected and strode about the ship slopping buckets of water over men and vomit to clean the decks. Harold also seemed unaffected but I knew that he had spent much time at sea and that was no doubt the reason for it.

We were all given a salty broth with herbs in it and after an hour or so I began to recover and take some interest in our surroundings. The water was not rough, but neither was it placid. The land behind us was a white and green smear in the distance and the land before us looked oddly similar to the left, but faded and disappeared to the right – to the south.

Harold bade the sail be furled and we sat in the middle of the ocean, drifting as the current took us while Harold took counsel under the canopy he shared with Eadnoth, Aethelnoth and Skalpi – the most senior of the housecarls. Eadric, Carl and I were also invited and I listened in amazement to the latest news.

'I have received two messages in recent days,' said Harold. 'The first from Edward who confirms our mission ... that I am to marry William's daughter and submit myself to his authority … in Normandy. William will be ranked highest in Inglalond behind the king and the aetheling, Edgar. As a token of his acceptance of the arrangement, William is to furnish us with a relic for the consecration of Edward's new minster … it is a relic that Edward admired before he returned to Inglalond to be king himself.'

'In truth,' said Aethelnoth, 'that is not quite the way of it.'

Harold cocked an eye at him and there was the ghost of a smile on his lips.

'How so Aethelnoth?'

'The placement of the words "In Normandy" … did not the message say: go to Normandy and place yourself under William's authority?'

'Is there a difference?'

'A fairly significant difference,' said Aethelnoth but Harold waved him into silence.

'Those are details with which we need not tax ourselves in this moment,' said Harold, and there was laughter from all but Aethelnoth, who looked pained, then shrugged as Harold continued, 'The second message concerns the Count of Ponthieu … one of William's vassals. It seems he has rebelled against his oath of fealty … or is about to.'

There was a silence as this piece of news was considered. Then Skalpi said, 'Do we know where Ponthieu lies? It would not be wise to land there.'

'Would it not?' asked Harold.

'Nay … we could be held and ransomed … or worse. Guy is notorious and sees a man solely as a pile of coins … and I'm not rich enough to be ransomed.'

'There are many such pirates and slavers on that coast,' said Carl, with some feeling, and there was another silence as all remembered his past as a thrall.

'Ponthieu lies in the northern part of Normandy,' said Eadric, gesturing with his arm in the direction it lay. 'Close to Flanders.'

'There is also this,' said Aethelnoth, 'if we were to land in Ponthieu it might be mistaken by William as support for Guy … poor behaviour from a future son-in-law.'

'Well,' said Harold, with an odd smile, 'we shall have to be careful to land in the right place.'

Harold turned to his falcon, hooded to prevent its terror of the open sea, and spoke soothingly as he fed it small strips of raw meat. Effectively dismissed, I suddenly felt much better and hungry myself.

After putting some day old bread and cold meat in my belly I sat in the bow watching the eastern shore with vague misgivings. There were many stories of shipwreck and other perils befalling travellers on that coast, although we were in numbers enough and armed enough to defy most brigands. The feeling returned, stronger than ever, that I was again being tested by God, but the nature of the test was unclear. That it was bound up with Valla, I was certain and the further we sailed from Inglalond the more keenly I felt her absence.

The water was suddenly white about the bow and I turned to see the sail unfurled and Eadric leaning on the oar. Clouds rushing up from the west pushed a wind before them and the three ships raced across the water veering slowly to the leeward.

To the north.

∞ ∞ ∞

In the mid-afternoon, pushed by strong winds and barely ahead of a storm, we entered a wide bay and sought refuge up a large river. Beyond a breakwater on the southern bank we found a harbour of sorts with just a few small fishing boats and anchored some forty yards from the sandy bank. We saw no-one ashore, although no wise man would be abroad with such a storm about to strike.

The boats and the few shacks I could see looked exactly the same as what you might see in Inglalond, which was both reassuring and disappointing. I'd expected a different country to be stranger than that. Harold scanned the harbour, deep in thought, and eventually decided we would make landfall to discover where we were.

The anchor was drawn up and Eadric's sailors pulled on the heavy oars to bring us onto the beach. The anchor was then secured and we leapt out of the ships with swords and shields to hunt for locals. Not that we meant them harm – it is simply best to have a weapon to hand when arriving unannounced in a strange land.

The shacks were mainly smokehouses and the ground was thick

with fish scales and bones. Tangled ropes and nets lay in a large pile with broken casks and other debris typical of a fisher village – the only thing missing was the villagers. An ear-splitting crack of thunder suddenly split the sky open with lightning and rain and we piled into two of the smokehouses to stay dry, using the racks as uncomfortable benches to wait out the rain. There were no torches so it got quickly dark, but it was at least warm with so many bodies huddled together. Eadric muttered to himself but Harold was in high spirits as though enjoying a game. The dogs were delighted to be spending so much time with him and he showed them a good deal of affection – until one of them squatted and shat and the stench was overpowering. I couldn't bear the stink and pushed past the other men out of the door and into the rain, where a flash of lightning revealed a large group of mounted men in armour bearing down on the village.

Immediately I shouted the alarm and the others poured out of the smokehouses with sword and shield and Harold called for the shield wall.

But it was beyond hope. We had only eighteen fighters and eleven servants. They had sixty or seventy men all in good chain and bearing the same device. Before we could stop them they got between us and the ships and the time for fighting was over. The time for negotiation was at hand.

A man on a large black horse – I had never seen a horse so large – moved to the fore of the threatening group of men and called out in Norman, 'Who are you and what are you doing here?'

His manner of speaking was different to the style of Norman I had been taught by Carl and Harold, but I was curiously delighted to be able to understand the stranger so well.

Harold spoke up, 'I am Harold ... Earl of Wessex. We are sheltering from the storm and mean no harm.'

'Mean no harm when outnumbered, I suppose,' said the horseman. 'Perhaps if there were only fisher folk about you would be less courteous?'

'The Earl of Wessex has no quarrel with Norman fishers,' laughed Harold. 'But you were speaking of courtesy ... I have given my name, you should give yours in return.'

The horseman moved his horse closer and counted us. 'Eighteen?

There are no more? You invade my land with just eighteen?'

'This is no invasion,' said Harold, quelling Skalpi's indignation with a hand, '... as I said, we were on a fishing party off the coast of Inglalond but were blown by the storm which now drenches us all the way to here. And where might we be?'

'A fishing party?' enquired the horseman. 'You intended to fight fish with swords?'

Some of his men laughed at that, but so did Harold.

'Nay, the swords are not for fish ... but no man travels without weapons these days.'

'Men travel without weapons in my domain,' said the horseman, 'unless I give leave. Please place your weapons in a pile and then take ten steps back.'

There was no choice. Harold stabbed his sword into the ground then leaned his shield against it. One by one we followed his example then stepped away from the growing pile.

'Now you shall accompany me to my house, where we will decide what is to be done with you, Harold the Fisherman.'

Again some of his men laughed, but Harold did not.

'You are yet to tell me your name,' said Harold. 'I accept no man's hospitality until I know his house and lineage.'

'You are hardly in a position to dictate terms,' said the horseman, 'but you are in the village of Hunefloth on the Seine River in the county of Ponthieu. As for my name ... if you are truly the Earl of Wessex, then I am sure you have heard it.'

So, Skalpi's fear had been realised. We were in the hands of Guy de Ponthieu and could expect to be imprisoned, pending ransom.

'And if you know my name,' continued Guy, 'then you must know my reputation. You will be named and assessed for ransom. And if not ransomed, you will be executed ... as a warning to all stray fishers.'

Once again his men laughed, and we fighting men were surrounded and marched off through the torrential rain towards no clear future – the servants were left under guard at the ships. One concession only did Guy make. Harold was allowed to bring his dogs and falcon.

Chapter 22

The Way of the World

Guy's fortress near Belrem was similar to Harold's house in Theodford – stone base with wooden walls surrounded by outbuildings and fully encircled by a high bank crowned with stakes and thorns. We were locked in a small stockade open to the skies and nowhere to sit save the stinking, muddy ground. Rain continued to pour down on us as I naturally started looking for means of escape.

The walls were only about ten feet high, so might be scaled, but were constructed from sharpened stakes. It would be difficult indeed to get over the top – and what would you do on the other side if you did? Four armed men guarded the stockade and plenty more guarded the gate.

Harold was spared the stockade, and also Carl as a man of God. They were taken into Guy's house and doubtless treated well enough while the rest of us shivered and grumbled.

'Why did you bring us here, Eadric?' demanded Skalpi. 'How could you not know this was Ponthieu? Call yourself a steersman? I call you a witless bonehead!'

'You are the bonehead,' replied Eadric, unruffled. 'Is it not clear that Harold wanted to come here?'

'Wanted to come?' demanded Skalpi, and when Eadric nodded smiling, Skalpi swore with disgust.

'Well, Harold himself is a bonehead if he wants to come to Ponthieu with just eighteen fighters,' raged Skalpi. 'This journey is madness!'

I had to admit it looked that way as we sat in the stinking mud with the rain pouring down, but I had too much confidence in Harold to despair.

'And now I need to shit,' moaned Skalpi. 'Guards!'

The guards ignored him until he pounded on the gate and shouted, 'There's nowhere to shit or piss in here! Bring us a bucket!'

'The ground is for shitting,' laughed one of the guards. 'It's good enough for pigs.'

'That's why it stinks in here,' muttered Elric.

'Call me a pig, will you?' shouted Skalpi. 'You'll fucking regret that you slimy Norman turd!'

With that Skalpi leaned into a corner, reefed down his sodden breeches and shat copiously. Then, to our amazement, he picked up his own steaming turd and flung it over the wall, and by the enraged disgust on the other side had found a mark.

'That was clever,' remarked Aethelnoth, as the guards shouted for assistance. Outside we could hear men assembling and weapons being drawn.

'Be ready,' growled Skalpi, reaching for the ground again, and I winced with revulsion. Even still, I stepped to the side of the door, and when it opened, Skalpi flung the rest of the turd through the gap and there were more shouts of disgust. Then a man burst through the door but saw me not as I seized him by the sword arm and swung him into the wall behind me. In two seconds I had taken his sword and Elric was pounding his face. Another was through, but I stepped behind him into the doorway to defy any more entrants, meaning there were two guards in the stockade – one stunned and bleeding, and the other armed but surrounded by angry Saxons, not least of whom was Skalpi who kicked him viciously in the knee.

Moments later, Skalpi was at my side, also bearing a sword as we defied the massing guards.

'We have two of your comrades,' shouted Aethelnoth, 'try to enter and they die!'

∞ ∞ ∞

'So,' said Guy, Lord of Ponthieu, 'you are the Earl of Wessex ... richest man in Inglalond. I'm very pleased to meet you.'

Harold sipped the wine that had been poured for him and Carl and was surprised at its excellence. He was also surprised at the richness of the room, hung with tapestries and smelling sweetly of herbs and incense.

'You are less pleased to meet me, I suspect,' continued Guy, 'but that is the way of the world I'm afraid. Careless folk who end on my shore must pay until I am satisfied that they have nothing left to pay.'

'You need money of course,' said Harold, apparently untroubled by his predicament.

Guy considered him, as though surprised at his insouciance, then shrugged and said, 'All men need money.'

'But none have so sore a need as those who take up arms against their lords. My ransom could raise such an army that the Duke of Normandy would never know a day's peace until he had accepted your terms.'

Guy was silent for several moments, sipping wine and pondering.

'If you know that,' he said, 'then I begin to wonder whether your landing in my country was an accident.'

'Of course it was an accident,' said Harold, with an eye on the servants standing by the door. Guy followed his glance, then waved the men outside. When they were gone, Harold said, 'You are correct, my lord de Ponthieu ... my arrival was by design, but I wish it to appear an accident.'

Guy's eyes narrowed and he said, 'You are very curious, my lord Wessex ... but you presume too much on my indulgence, unless you have something to offer of greater value than your ransom ... and that of your men.'

'I hope you may judge it so,' said Harold. 'And it is this ... I offer you my friendship.'

Such was Guy's surprise that he snorted wine through his nose and onto his fine white tunic. He brushed at his front in tight-lipped annoyance, and said, 'No doubt the friendship of the Earl of Wessex has a value ... of sorts ... but I am a shallow man and do not well perceive subtleties. I prefer gold.'

'Gold comes and goes,' said Harold, 'but friendship remains. You will be besieged before too much longer.'

'Perhaps,' agreed Guy. 'But I am not the only lord to object to the Bastard's rule. William fights on several fronts, as he has done all his life. It is the price he pays for his lineage.'

'That may be,' said Harold, 'but I am reliably informed that all except you are now back in the fold and have accepted William. Indeed, it is the reason I came here.'

'I never entirely left the fold,' said Guy, 'It seemed prudent to keep a foot in William's camp. But suppose you are correct … and suppose I accepted your offer of friendship … what immediate practical benefits would there be?'

'Ransom,' said Harold, as though such were obvious, 'but a ransom of my choosing.'

Guy turned to look for the servant, then remembered he had been sent away so stood and poured more wine himself.

'And what ransom would you choose to pay?'

'Men and ships,' said Harold. 'It is what you most need and I have them in plenty.'

'Men and ships,' repeated Guy. 'Interesting.'

'You could achieve much with a thousand Saxon warriors,' said Harold. 'Maybe even the Duchy of Normandy for yourself … with adequate politics and timing?'

Guy was silent for a long while, stroking his chin. At last he said, 'A thousand warriors could certainly tip the balance in my favour … but how would I control them? They are loyal to you and you might suddenly decide your fortune would be better served on another side.'

'Why would I come here and imperil myself to make a false offer?' said Harold. 'Our interests are aligned.'

'They are?'

'King Edward has arranged for me to marry William's daughter,' said Harold.

'Aaah,' said Guy, 'at last I begin to perceive your subtle Saxon mind. You do not wish the wedding to proceed?'

'I do not wish to disappoint my lord Edward,' replied Harold, 'but if I am held captive … alas, I cannot come to my betrothed.'

Once again, Guy poured wine for Harold and Carl (who had said nothing).

'It would be a sore blow to William,' reflected Guy. 'He has made no secret of the fact that he expects to be named Edward's heir. And you becoming his son-in-law would bind you to his house. I can well understand that you might find that … limiting.'

'What is that noise?' interrupted Carl, and all three sat silently for a few moments until the sound of shouting outside registered.

'It seems our colleagues are not getting along,' remarked Guy, rising from his seat, and in that moment a wet and muddy soldier entered the room.

'My lord … the prisoners in the stockade are rioting and have abducted two of our men.'

'They must be very resourceful,' remarked Guy, unperturbed. 'Let us see the way of it.'

He gestured for Harold and Carl to follow, and strolled from the room – pausing to admire a tapestry on his way.

Outside, the rain had eased, but the yard was a sea of mud. Harold stifled a laugh when he saw Brand and Skalpi defying the numerous guards. Indeed, if it were possible he would have wagered money on Brand and Skalpi being able to withstand Guy's guards forever.

'You see,' said Harold, 'a thousand such warriors would be valuable for a man with your concerns.'

Guy shouted at the guards and they stood down. One man gestured angrily at a stain on his shoulder and tried to remonstrate with Guy but a further word from his sergeant and the man was silent.

'Come out!' shouted Guy, and the call was repeated by Harold. One by one, Harold's party emerged cautiously from the stockade and assembled shoulder to shoulder, like a shield wall without shields.

'At the urging of your lord, I have changed my mind,' said Guy. 'You are no longer to be confined.'

Guy spoke to the sergeant who nodded and started shouting orders at his men and some servants near at hand. All raced to do the lord's bidding.

∞ ∞ ∞

Once again I woke with a thunderous head and poisonous gut, which was little wonder after the evening before.

We had been given fresh linen shirts and hot water for bathing. We had then been invited into Guy's hall where two wild boar roasted over a vast central fire pit and other meats and pastries were laid out in great plenty. Best of all was the wine. I had tasted nothing like it and gulped eagerly to get my share.

'Don't get drunk,' warned Elric. 'For all we know this is just a ruse to make us incapable.' But Elric had matched me cup for cup and in the cold light of morning was groaning like a woman in childbirth. I would have laughed except for the toxic thudding in my own head, and I forced myself to unwrap the layer of skins and get up.

We had spent the night in a barn, although I had no recollection of entering and stood blinking outside in the pale dawn, pissing against a wall. Others were stretching and moaning and Skalpi appeared with bloodshot eyes and vomit through his beard, causing me to laugh despite the pain it cost me. He pulled a full bucket from the hands of a servant, placed it on a bench and thrust his head in for several seconds before bursting out in a spray of mist and gasping – substantially cleaner and surprisingly sober.

'Aah,' he sighed, 'now I am myself again. Where are the kitchens?'

The servant offered to lead so those of us already risen got the best of the freshly prepared fare. It was quite different to what we would eat in the morning back in Inglalond but pleasant enough – the bread was soft and white with a plain flavour but a lovely texture. There were many other strange looking and oddly flavoured items on the table, including salted cucumbers and soft cheese, but strangest of all was a cream they called mustard with a fiery taste that went well with meat and bread. There was also a very pleasant drink that seemed to be warmed wine with spices.

'So what do you think of Harold's deal with Guy?' asked Aethelnoth, who had already been seated when we entered.

'If it allows us back to Bosham without paying a ransom,' said Skalpi, 'it's a good deal.'

'How is a deal that obliges Harold to disobey the king and fight William in any way a good deal?' enquired Aethelnoth. 'No good will come of this.'

'And we won't all be permitted to return,' said Eadric, sitting at the bench beside Aethelnoth. 'Mark my words, Guy will want hostages … those he deems closest and dearest to Harold will have to stay until the host returns.'

'Well, put me down to stay,' said Skalpi. 'The wine is excellent, and the women very beautiful.'

He tried to reach for one of the serving girls but she eluded him with a smile and Skalpi returned to his breakfast with a shrug.

'I'll catch her later.'

The room was filling up also with Guy's retainers, who were surprisingly cordial after the fight in the stockade. Only the fellow with the bruised and cut face who had been first through the door seemed sullen in our company, and in order to forestall his animosity I attempted to make friends.

'You are a brave man,' I said to him. 'First into the stockade to take on sixteen Saxons.'

I offered him my hand and he looked at me, then looked over at Skalpi with a sneer, and said, 'I will take your hand, as it has not been used for flinging merde.'

Several men laughed but Skalpi shrugged once again, without pausing at his breakfast. 'A soldier must use whatever weapons are at hand. You would do the same.'

'I would not!'

'Then you would die,' said Skalpi.

'Death is more honourable than throwing excrement,' insisted the Norman.

'I'm sure that's true,' replied Skalpi, 'but honour is a matter of expedience sometimes ... not least when your hosts refuse the courtesy of a bucket to piss and shit into.'

There was more laughter, including from some of the Normans and Aethelnoth seized the moment.

'Come, we are to be fighters together ... we should be friends. I am Aethelnoth.'

He named the rest of us at the table, and then the Normans introduced themselves. Even the fellow with the bruised face (whose name was Richard) seemed at least civil by the time we were finished our meal and we trooped outside together as though all divisions had melted away.

Outside in the yard a bolt of sacking had been unrolled onto the muddy ground and our confiscated weapons were laid out – guarded by several of Guy's men.

'They're giving our weapons back,' said Elric, 'but we'll have to swear an oath to Guy.'

This was disturbing news.

'What oath?' I asked, but Guy, Harold and Carl emerged from the hall and all followed them over to where the weapons lay. We stood about them – Saxon and Norman – in a great semi-circle while Guy inspected the weapons, and among all that hoard, the weapon that took his interest was *Pighammer*.'

'My God!' swore Guy, hefting the axe. 'This is a brute of a thing. Which of you uses this?'

I stepped forward but at that moment there was a cry from the gates. All turned, and through the open gate we could see a troop of horsemen approaching.

'Shit, damn and fuck,' muttered Guy, just audible enough for me to hear him.

There were some thirty horsemen approaching in two columns, all in chain and carrying long lances. As I glanced about the Normans were looking angry and some were scurrying for weapons.

'My lord?' enquired the sergeant, but Guy waved him away and strode to the gate, still holding *Pighammer*. Seconds later the first of the riders clattered into the yard and we all stepped back to clear a large enough space for the giant horses that steamed and blew in the cool morning – trotting about and looking magnificent as the riders slowly assembled themselves. It was an arrogant display and deliberately designed to insult Guy, I would have thought.

If he was insulted, Guy didn't show it. He stood before his doors, grasping *Pighammer* by the neck with its end in the ground – a threatening pose. The leader of the troop, a bareheaded man with the back half of his head shaved, like most Norman warriors, walked his horse up to Guy and gave him the merest of bows from the saddle.

'Count Guy de Ponthieu,' said the horseman, 'I understand you are entertaining guests expected by my lord, Duke William … who is also your own liege lord.'

'It is my Christian duty to entertain all guests who end on my shore,' replied Guy, 'but they have only arrived in the night … someone has made the journey very swiftly to your Master to give him this news.'

The leader leapt down from his horse, but my attention was taken by the strangest thing I had ever seen. One of the horsemen was only half a man – a dwarf riding a smaller horse than the others, but dressed exactly the same – even the same half-shaved head, marking him a warrior, but surely it was some kind of Norman joke. Indeed, some of the Normans laughed as the dwarf clambered down from his horse and was lifted off his feet when he tried to lead it by the reins.

'I was told you would ask that question,' sneered the leader, oblivious to the comedy. 'I was also told to answer it, so yes Lord Guy, you have spies in your midst and all you do is swiftly known in Duke William's court. Where is Harold?'

Guy was holding *Pighammer* in a way that suggested he would dearly like to put it to use, but the moment passed and Guy gestured for Harold to step forward.

Harold drew himself up and stared at the troop leader, who was marginally more polite than he had been with Guy.

'I am William fitzOsbern and deeply honoured to meet the Duke of the Anglais,' he said and bowed. 'We have a long way to go so must ride. There are only four spare horses, so choose three men and we shall leave in an hour.'

With that he strode into the hall, leaving Harold and Guy speechless. If they were truly to form an alliance against William, this was the time to start with over a hundred against thirty, but the appearance of William's men (and possibly the confirmation of spies in his court) had rocked Guy's confidence. Harold took *Pighammer* from Guy and walked over to me.

'You will need this,' he said.

Chapter 23

A Warrior and Warlord at the Peak of His Powers

The half man's name was Turold and he claimed to be William's nephew.

'That makes me royal,' he declared as we trotted along on huge horses through the pleasant fields of Normandy in early spring. It was remarkably similar to the lanes and fields of Wessex and East Anglia with hundreds of peasants and other labourers busily ploughing and sowing amid tree blossom and wild flowers, and the air filled with birdsong and the burr of bees.

Harold had selected Skalpi and me to come with him, and because he could not (or would not) choose between Aethelnoth and Eadnoth the stallers, he bade Elric come also, knowing him to be cunning, resourceful and an excellent fighter. The others were to remain guests of Guy until sent for.

'Royal?' I queried, glancing over Turold's head at Elric as we rode three abreast.

'Yes … William will be king soon enough, so I'll be a king's nephew.'

There was something odd about Turold. He had none of the haughty arrogance of the other Norman knights, but was almost childish in his boastful manner, as though making up for his lack of height with noise. It was the most natural thing in the world therefore for Elric and me to amuse ourselves by inspiring him to ever greater and more unlikely claims.

'So … it would be possible,' said Elric, ' … if the right people died somehow … for you to become king?'

'Of course it would,' said Turold, as though such were the most obvious thing in the world. 'That's what being royal means … in line for the crown.'

'King Turold,' I said, pretending astonishment. 'So who would have to die?'

'Well … William for a start,' said Turold, thoughtfully. 'After that, Robert Shortpants … Richard … young William … he has other sons and daughters. Then there is his brother, my father … he's a bishop so he'll step aside for me … '

'Your father's a bishop?' laughed Elric.

'Maybe he'll be the next pope,' I said.

'Maybe,' agreed Turold.

'Imagine that!' exclaimed Elric, '… father and son ruling all of Christendom!'

'And all that needs to happen is just a few convenient deaths,' I said. 'Maybe their house could burn down at Christmas?'

'Turold!' shouted the leader, fitzOsbern, from just in front of us. 'If you have not the wit to perceive when men make a fool of you, then hold your stupid tongue.'

'We were just talking,' sulked Turold, and there was silence for a while, until Turold muttered, 'fitzOsbern thinks he can talk to me like one of his common soldiers. He will learn different when I am his liege lord.'

There was an impressive degree of malice bubbling away in Turold and while I laughed I was also mindful that it would be unwise to make an enemy of him.

'You said William will be a king,' I said. 'King of where?'

Turold looked startled, and then cunning as he answered, 'Who knows? He might just get the pope to declare Normandy a kingdom instead of a duchy. The pope usually takes his advice.'

I glanced over my shoulder to where Harold was riding with Skalpi and hoped he had heard the exchange.

'So who exactly is your father?' I asked.

'William's brother Odo … bishop of Bayeux. Greatest man in Normandy.'

'Do you get on well with him?' enquired Elric.

'Of course! What sort of question is that?'

'Where I come from,' said Elric, 'men such as yourself tend to be … actors.'

'Actors?'

'Or they live in the woods. I heard of a large community of dwarfs living in the forest near Lincoln.'

'I don't care for the word dwarf,' threatened Turold, displaying more of that fine malice, 'and I would caution against its use in my presence.'

fitzOsbern shook his head and spurred his horse to put some distance between himself and Turold. Elric and I once again caught each other's eye over Turold's head and I had to clench my teeth to prevent laughter.

'As for my father,' continued Turold, 'I am so high in his esteem that he has arranged a noble wife for me. I am to be married.'

'Is your fiancée also a dw— … erm … is she of similar stature?' asked Elric.

'Nay, she is higher than me in body, but my stature is greater than hers … thus we are well enough matched. She is very beautiful.'

'What is her name?' I asked.

'Emma,' replied Turold, and for the first time there was a passion in his voice that was not his usual sly conceit.

'She's a lucky girl,' said Elric, and I had to turn away to prevent Turold seeing my struggle not to laugh.

'Tell us about William, your uncle,' I said, raising my voice slightly for Harold's benefit.

'The Duke?' said Turold. 'You will meet him soon enough … Rouen is not far.'

We had been riding some hours and I was getting sore at the top of the thighs, being unused to horses, so that was welcome news.

'Is it true,' I asked, 'that his protector was murdered before William's very eyes in his own private chamber … when he was just a boy?'

'You heard about that?' laughed Turold.

'How did William escape?' asked Elric. 'How does a warrior get killed when a young boy survives? It makes no sense.'

'It will make sense when you meet him,' said Turold. 'Like all in my family, my uncle cannot easily be killed. He has survived assassins and countless battles. His prowess is legendary and his bearing would daunt even your famous Arthur.'

At that moment a herald at the front of the column blew on a long horn and seconds later there was an answering blast in the distance.

'Welcome to Rouen,' said Turold.

∞ ∞ ∞

Rouen was a good sized town. Smaller than Lundene, but larger than Gipeswic, it was remarkable for its clean and orderly streets – at least, those streets closest to the Cathedral and William's palace. The lower part of the town was the usual shithole.

There was much more use of stone here than back in Inglalond – a beautiful whitish stone that gleamed pink in the setting sun as we approached from the south. Many folk filled the streets as we passed and fingers were pointed.

Twice we were passed by small troops of horsed warriors – so disciplined they barely glanced at us despite the curiosity they surely felt – and I was a little in awe of their martial deportment. Still, I doubted not that, if it came to a fight, *Pighammer* would even up the score. With that thought I sat taller in the saddle (despite the pain in my thighs) so the Normans would see a Saxon lord in the fullness of his strength and violence. They would think twice before upsetting me.

Harold also, I noted, rode high in the saddle with his falcon on his glove, looking every inch a Saxon prince with his fine moustache and flowing hair in contrast to the half-shaved Normans who couldn't decide whether they were warriors or priests.

Near the top of the hill, William's palace was the most glorious building I had ever seen. Other worldly it seemed with its fully stone walls and tiled roof, with a watch tower rising over all and decorated with Roman style vaulting. Even the courtyard was paved with stone and the hooves of the horses sparked as they clattered under another archway bristling with archers.

'William likes archers,' said Harold, gazing about the courtyard and up at the Cathedral – the only other building we could see from inside the high walls.

'Death from distance,' said fitzOsbern, as though explaining a mystery to a child.

'Where is the honour in that?' demanded Skalpi, with a snort of contempt. 'I look into a man's face when I fight him.'

'When you're not flinging turd over walls,' said Elric, and I laughed.

Skalpi grinned also but said, 'Archers just shoot into the shield wall and know not who they strike … and the meanest peasant can bring down the noblest thegn or earl!'

'Still, I can see how teams of archers might create an advantage,' said Harold thoughtfully. 'If the world changes we would be unwise not to change with it.'

That was an interesting thought and I found myself pondering its many meanings as we dismounted, and finally I could stretch to relieve the stiffness and soreness of riding.

Grooms and farriers led the horses away and a falconer relieved Harold of his hunting bird. The soldiers formed up behind us facing the large double doorway where further soldiers stood guard. I suddenly felt very exposed and vulnerable as Skalpi and I stood either side of Harold, with Elric to my left. All swords were sheathed, but *Pighammer* was unslung in my right hand.

And then we waited.

Only Turold had entered the hall, nodding at the guards who heeded him not and I smiled again at memory of our conversation. He was an odd fellow – indulged due to his father, which in itself was strange. The clergy were increasingly forbidden to marry in Inglalond and their offspring were regarded as a bit of an embarrassment, so either it was different here or Turold's father was too important to be scorned.

Still we waited, and the courtyard was strangely silent. Such places typically were full of noise but the silence and stillness of the guards was unsettling. Even the dogs trotted about without barking – nosing at hands and feet, but otherwise obedient to the rule of the cloister.

Servants emerged with torches, which were placed in brackets either side of the door. Other torches were lit in the entrance way and we were aware of how cool and dim it had become. The sky was violet and a homely peace settled over the town.

Then horns rang out and a chamberlain dressed in red and gold strode from within and welcomed us to the Palace of Rouen – seat of William, Duke of Normandy. The men behind us shuffled forward to form an honour guard either side of the door and then we were beckoned inside – allowed to keep our swords, but I was bade to leave *Pighammer* at the door.

It was a beautiful hall and possibly the cleanest chamber I had ever seen. The entire room was made from that white stone with rugs on the floor in place of rushes and the walls were hung with arrases and tapestries depicting hunting scenes, pastoral scenes and even the fables of Aesop.

At the end of the room, on a dais, sat the Duke. Others stood behind him and to either side but Turold sat on the edge of the dais, looking proud enough to burst.

William was a large man who stared at Harold like a cat with a mouse. He had red-brown hair, also shaved at the back, and a chain of gold glittered on his massive chest. Whispering in his ear as we approached was a churchman and I heard Harold mutter angrily as he walked beside me.

'You know the priest?' I asked, in a low voice.

'Aye,' said Harold but there was no more as we had arrived at the base of the dais.

'Welcome and well met!' said William as we bowed before him. The closer we came, the larger he seemed – a warrior and warlord at the peak of his powers. A bastard he was by birth but with a nobility and natural authority that made Harold, barely younger than William, seem a boy in comparison.

'Thank you lord William,' said Harold, 'we are honoured to come before you. Indeed, I brought a gift for the hour of our meeting but alas … it was taken by your falconer.'

'There will be other gifts,' said William. 'We have a lifetime for gifting, do we not?'

Harold gave a tight smile then introduced the rest of us, naming us all as captains of the fyrd – even Elric. In turn, William named those about him including the priest, who was in fact a bishop.

'I believe you know John, Bishop of Fecamp,' said William. 'He has been much honoured by Edward.'

The bishop bowed, grinning an insolent grin that announced his intention to be part of the unfolding drama. The church claimed the pre-eminent power, after all. It wasn't as much recognised in Inglalond, but that happy country was far from the pope and separated by the Channel. Perhaps it lay differently in other parts of Christendom?

William had named his wife, Mathilda, but of the two other women present, neither were Adeliza – Harold's betrothed. One, however, was a dark-haired beauty who reminded me achingly of Valla and I remembered my certainty on the ship that God was about to test me again. She met my eye and smiled as she was named by William the Lady Emma. I glanced down at Turold who was glaring at me and once again I was struggling not to laugh.

'No doubt,' said William, 'you are anxious to meet your bride. A banquet is being prepared but first you shall be taken to the rooms prepared for you to make your toilet. Go ye hence and we shall commence in one hour the giving of gifts.'

'Come,' said Emma stepping forward, 'I have chosen rooms for you.'

Servants appeared at our sides and we followed the Lady Emma down a passageway to a large wing of chambers.

'Are we guests or prisoners?' asked Skalpi and Harold laughed grimly.

'Both,' he said.

'Bastard,' muttered Skalpi.

Chapter 24

A Harmless Interlude

Like the hall, the bedchambers were incredibly clean and smelled sweetly of flowers floating in basins. Bowls of warm water also were provided and we were bid undress and wash. Combs and shaving gear were also there for those that wished, and clean linen hose and tunics. After washing and shaving my new and wispy beard, I felt wonderful putting on clean clothes. Then presently we were summoned and returned to the hall where two long benches were set up below a high table.

Harold, attired in red and gold like William, was directed to the high table but the rest of us were seated together at the top of the lefthand table and glass goblets were placed in front of us, filled with the local red wine. I hadn't drunk from a glass goblet since my brother's ill-starred wedding day, and felt again that pang of loss – and no little guilt for the fact that my revenge against Malgard was not yet taken. That time would come.

As it had been in Ponthieu, the red wine was delicious and, despite Elric's usual warning not to get drunk, we were soon laughing and singing as the benches slowly filled with William's folk.

Turold sat opposite Skalpi at the head of our bench and next to him, directly opposite me, was his betrothed, the lady Emma.

'Why do you stare?' she asked, and immediately I apologised, feeling embarrassed and strangely thrilled.

'Forgive me, lady. You are so like my own wife it robs me of my wits.'

She smiled at that and I found myself grinning at Turold who glared with open hostility.

'You are young to be married,' said Emma, and I perceived that she was somewhat older than me – perhaps early twenties. Turold would have been about the same.

'I am nearly eighteen,' I said. 'That is not so young in my country.'

'I suppose not,' said Emma. 'Indeed, I was married myself the first time at fifteen.'

'But we don't like talking about that … do we,' interrupted Turold, and the merry buzz of the table paused for a moment to allow for him.

'No, you don't,' agreed Emma, getting a flash of dwarfish anger for her trouble.

At that moment William entered the hall with the Bishop and all stood until they were seated next to Harold. With William also were his wife Mathilda and his daughter Adeliza, who was to be married to Harold. Beautiful she was, but very young.

'How old is Adeliza?' I asked Emma.

'Fourteen,' she replied, and I found myself feeling sad for the Lady Swanneshals, being supplanted by a child for the sake of politics.

Yet more of the wine was poured into my glass and I decided I didn't care about Turold's feelings.

'Why do you wear the back of your head shaved?' I asked him.

Turold considered me – clearly wondering whether I was making fun of him, then said, 'All warriors shave their heads thus … knights at least.'

'You are a warrior?' I asked him, allowing the doubt I truly felt to enter my voice.

'You really don't want to find out,' said Turold, baring his teeth and revealing that malice I had sensed before, but I laughed openly.

'You'd have to get up on a stool to fight me,' I said, 'but I'm ready when you are.'

The table erupted with laughter, and I was surprised to feel something touching my leg.

∞ ∞ ∞

'So … you were blown north by the storm and landed in Ponthieu,' said William.

'Aye,' said Harold, dismayed by the tender years of Adeliza. Some men rediscovered their youth in the arms of a child bride, but Harold Godwinson was not such a man.

'The Count has a reputation, you know,' said William. 'Most are careful to avoid the Seine at all costs.'

'Well, the storm had other plans for us,' said Harold.

'The storm was God's plan,' said the Bishop. 'But was it your plan to go to Ponthieu?'

'I have already said it was not,' replied Harold, allowing the edge of his dislike for the priest to show.

'Come, Harold,' said William, with a reproving glance at the Bishop. 'You have arrived safely, which is the main thing. What opinion did you form of Guy?'

'I had barely time to form an opinion,' said Harold.

'And yet you spent two hours closeted with him ... and at the end of that time your men were released from a stockade. You had made an agreement, had you?'

'An agreement to let my men go, yes,' said Harold, cautiously.

'Ah, your men,' said William. 'They will be brought here over the next few days. We need all the men we can find.'

'You do?'

'Yes ... there have been disagreements among my local lords which I am obliged to resolve. Indeed, I heard that Guy might be getting ideas to join the local coalition ... which is why I feared for your ... safety ... when I heard you had landed in Ponthieu. He may have held you in ransom and forced me to give concessions.'

'Forced you?'

'Of course. You are to marry my daughter ... I could have been forced to pay his ransom to recover you, but fortunately Guy did not press his suit and must therefore still be loyal to me. Would you agree?'

'William,' said Mathilda, his wife, ' ... allow your guest to eat and drink before you press him with politics. This is supposed to be a family occasion.'

'And how is family separate from politics?' laughed William. 'But you are right, my honey sweet ... where are my manners?'

At that moment there was a commotion from the top of the nearest table and Harold glanced over to where Skalpi and Brand were red-faced with laughter as the dwarf, Turold, leapt onto the bench with a drawn sword.

∞ ∞ ∞

'Turold!'

All turned to where Duke William stood, blazing with anger.

'What have you been told about fighting in my hall?'

All the wind seemed to fall out of Turold's sail and he pointed mutely at me.

'Apologise at once or leave the hall,' said William, and Turold – eyes bright with malice – thrust his short sword back into its sheath and stepped down off the table. Then he bowed stiffly, resumed his seat and began drinking heavily.

'I accept your apology,' I said, laughing. And then I felt something rub against my leg again. I glanced at the Lady Emma and realised, to my small embarrassment, that it must be her foot sending me a message.

'Oh I'm sorry alright,' said Turold quietly. 'Sorry you ever came to Normandy and sorry for whatever steps I might take to achieve your destruction. You make a fool of me at your peril, friend.'

The foot rubbed harder against my leg and I wondered: was she trying to warn me against antagonising her fiancé? Or was it something else. There was the faintest of smiles on her face, but she was turned to her neighbour on her left.

'Come, put aside your anger, Turold,' I said. 'No harm done and this is a time for celebration, is it not?'

Turold ignored me and gulped wine, but Emma's foot stroked slowly up and down my leg. Then she turned to me and said, 'So, Lord Brand, tell me about your wife.'

'Valla? She is very beautiful … dark haired, like yourself, but slightly younger.'

'Ah yes,' said Emma, 'I am a woman of experience. All men should know such a woman … to teach them.'

'… Teach them, my Lady?'

'Teach them how best to please a woman,' she replied and I glanced at Turold, but he was drinking and muttering to himself and clearly hadn't heard her.

'Most men are selfish,' she continued, 'caring only for their own pleasure ... but a woman must be pleased also or where is the incentive for her to engage again in the future?'

'The incentive lies in pleasing her husband,' replied Skalpi, and I was slightly astonished at the turn of the conversation. This was the kind of talk one might have with a whore, but never with a noble woman – not in Inglalond at least.

'A wise husband is best pleased by an equal relationship,' said Emma, with a glance at Turold and I laughed despite myself.

Turold seemed to launch out of his drunken reverie at the sound of my laughter and glared again at me.

'Don't talk to me about equal relationships,' he slurred – drunk quicker than any man I'd ever known. 'I am the nephew of a Duke ... you are the third daughter of a Count's youngest brother. Where is the equity in that?'

'I am a niece ... you are a nephew,' she shrugged, her toes tickling my ankle.

'I am a better nephew than you are a niece,' insisted Turold, his voice rising and I glanced at the high table to see whether William had noted the disturbance.

'You have to make up the difference in other ways,' said Turold. 'I shall expect it on our wedding night.'

'You go on expecting then,' said Emma and I laughed aloud as Turold roared with fury but was quickly seized by William's men and ejected shrieking from the room.

'I have to go,' sighed Emma, rising from the table and curtseying to us, and then to William and Harold.

Then she was gone, although the shouting of Turold could still be heard for some time, blended with other sounds of revelry and violence.

∞ ∞ ∞

I was having once again my dream in which Valla was finally given to me completely. The sweet carnality left me overwhelmed ... breathless, but suffused in the smell of her body ... breathless ...

Only gradually did I emerge from the dream because in the darkness it felt as though the coupling of the dream continued – inexpressibly delightful. And then in my confusion I dreamed I was indeed awake and yet my manhood felt like it was tightly held in a woman's most intimate embrace. I tried to sit up but my face was met by warm flesh and a glorious smell. Naked thighs were planted either side of my chest.

Slowly, I put together what in fact was happening and my head whirled with the strangeness, and yet the wonderful sensations. Tentatively, I put forth my own tongue and found tight curls. Taking the thighs in either hand, I pulled myself up and buried my face in that heavenly smelling flesh while at the same time feeling her mouth move up and down in simulation of the sex act which I hadn't known for nearly four years. Only Valla's hand had ...

'Stop!' I cried hoarsely, twisting myself aside and throwing my companion off me.

'What is the problem?' asked a voice, and I knew it was Emma.

'I cannot ... I am sworn to another.'

'So am I.'

There was a pause, as my mind whirled with faith and lust.

'Your wife is far away ... across the sea,' whispered Emma, 'and this is just a harmless interlude. A dream perhaps? Who can tell in the darkness?'

'Valla will know ... and I promised.'

'How can she know? It is not as though we are coupling in the usual way. We Frankish ladies long ago discovered this means of giving and seeking pleasure. It is discreet and children cannot be gotten.'

Her presence and perfume were overwhelming me as I sought to recall my promise to Valla. Could this Frankish method of pleasure be somehow an exception?

I felt Emma begin to kiss my thigh again and certainly I desired her to do more, but I said, 'I promised to touch no other woman ... this is surely touching.'

'You are not touching,' said Emma, 'you are being touched. Now be still and enjoy.'

I felt her move on the bed and her knees were once again planted either side of my chest. Her heavenly scent was once again in my face and I remembered her words at dinner – that it was important for a man to give pleasure as well as receive it.

What choice did I really have?

Chapter 25

The Normal Rules Regarding Men and Women

Beams of pink light filtered through the tree tops as Valla and Myrrthn walked in the dawn to the edge of the forest near Ceaster with Malgard trotting eagerly ahead, nose to the ground.

They were clad in skins but went barefoot as the frosts of winter and early spring were no longer crisping the ground white.

Where the trees failed in a line of stumps, Myrrthn waved his arm to take in the entire valley neatly planted with barley and wheat – dotted here and there with houses, shacks and vegetable gardens, with a church on the far ridge.

'You see,' said Myrrthn. 'The killer god in all his majesty … lord of his creation.'

Valla made no reply, but the orderly fields looked strange after so many days in the forest, as often as not naked and steeped in Myrrthn's elixirs.

'You see how the house of the killer god is like a watch tower … a sentinel guarding the tamed and broken.'

'Yes,' said Valla.

'These orderly fields are the same as the men who tend them,' sneered Myrrthn, ' … put in their place by a god that kills the wild, natural ways and must have order and sameness. In his own image he creates them … orderly and lifeless.'

'Yes, I see,' said Valla, and it truly seemed sad to her. The freshly hewn stumps nearby were like broken bodies strewn on a battlefield – cut down in ignorant, bloody violence.

'This is what they want for the whole world,' seethed Myrrthn, working himself into one of his passionate rages. 'Everywhere the wild things gone, and order in their place.'

It was a shocking thought – that everywhere could be made orderly and the secret places all banished and Valla felt a kind of despair, and a fury that such a black evil could be permitted.

But then Myrrthn laughed.

'Come,' he said. 'I will show you something.'

He led her back into the wood and her heart soared again as she passed through fern and forest and felt the greenness enter her soul. After twenty minutes or so they came to a partial clearing in which the ruins of a stone building mouldered under vines and grass with trees bursting through the remains of the roof like a crown on a corpse.

'You see?' said Myrrthn, and Valla felt a joy of relief.

'They cannot conquer forever,' she breathed, and Myrrthn cackled with delight at her insight.

'This was one of their temples ... a hallowed place for the killer god in all his victory and glory. But now it lies in ruin ... it is possible. Oh yes, it is possible for the wild to reclaim the tame. You yourself were wild, but becoming tame when I met you ... just in time, was it not?'

'Yes.'

Myrrthn climbed the thickest part of the crumbling wall and stood above the ruined church with his arms raised in triumph.

'I did this!' he shouted. 'I ... Myrrthn ... brought low this place and made it fit once again for all wild creatures.'

A stray beam of sunlight picked out Myrrthn's face and he held up his hands as though cupping light like water. Small birds flitted through slanting beams and two red squirrels chased each other about the bole of a tree, uncaring of Myrrthn and Valla.

'It can be done, you see,' he said, in a softer voice, as Valla climbed up to join him.

'Yes.'

'But our task will be much harder. Not just one church in one valley ... our task is to restore the entire island to the wild and the fae. A mighty spell is needed.'

'All of Inglalond?'

'That is the tame name,' admonished Myrrthn, ' … you must unlearn it. But before we can achieve the task, there is a great peril before us.'

'Yes,' agreed Valla.

'Ships,' said Myrrthn. 'The killer god is coming in ships bearing the cross of his mission … and he is coming soon.'

'I have seen it,' agreed Valla, as the sunbeams were snuffed out by cloud, and she was overcome by a profound sorrow.

∞ ∞ ∞

When I awoke I was alone with my guilt.

I was partly assuaged by the fact that I had not coupled with Emma in the normal way with the full locking of loins. And the fact that the incident had occurred in a different country was surely also a leavening factor.

Earlier, as we lay in darkness I had asked her, 'Why did you come to my chamber?'

'Because I like you … and because I hate Turold.'

'When are you to be married?'

'Never, if I have my way.'

'Will you have your way?'

There was a pause, and then she said, 'Perhaps. He is the family embarrassment, but William likes him.'

'He does? It didn't seem so when he was ejected from the hall tonight.'

'Turold is frequently ejected, but always allowed back because he is Odo's son … and also because he is a bastard.'

At that point her hand had started moving down my belly and suddenly held me.

'I shall name this Turold,' she said. 'Then, when you hear me say I wish to kiss Turold, you will know to expect me in the darkness.'

I laughed at what seemed one of the funniest jokes I'd ever heard and was excited by the idea of repeat performances, but at the same time I was aware that I was betraying the spirit, if not the letter of Valla's demand that I touch no other woman. This first time had been accidental as I emerged from a dream, but to do the same thing apurpose – to positively plan, anticipate and execute the same acts would be to take the matter to a new level.

I realised I had become hard in Emma's hand.

'Oh … Turold wants to be kissed again,' she said, and I groaned with a fairly novel blend of ecstasy, mirth and guilt.

But alone in the light of morning, I resolved that there would be no repeat. I washed my face in a bowl of cold water and opened the shutters on a cool, crisp morning. My window overlooked the edge of the town behind the cathedral and then planted fields for several miles to the north and west until a forest filled some low hills. It was a rich and pleasant land and I was not surprised that it was so frequently in dispute.

I walked through the white stone halls in search of breakfast and everywhere people were strangely courteous and formal. Breakfast was similar to what had been served at Guy's fortress of Belrem and Elric as usual was already seated with Skalpi – wolfing into the meal as though it might be his last.

To my small consternation, Turold was also present seated with Emma. His banishment had been only temporary, but he wore a shiny black eye as evidence of his struggle.

'And how is Turold this morning?' I asked, but he ignored me in rude contrast to the courtesy of the others.

'Surely you know better than anyone else,' smiled Emma.

I nearly burst into laughter as I perceived her game and decided to share it.

'He looks a bit sticky with his eye closed shut, but he's been in a fight.'

'He gave as good as he got,' agreed Emma. 'Every time he was knocked down he stood up again. I don't think anyone could drain all the courage from Turold.'

Turold suddenly looked so ridiculously puffed up and proud that I couldn't help myself. The repressed laughter came squealing out as I collapsed onto a bench next to Elric who stared at me in smiling confusion. I tried to compose myself while reaching for bread and soft cheese, but the laughter would not be denied and I howled.

'I think Turold deserves a reward for his courage,' said Emma, fondling Turold's hair. 'I shall kiss him until he bursts with happiness.'

Well that really set me off and Elric and Skalpi stared at me in amusement as I half collapsed against Elric's shoulder, tears of mirth rolling down my face.

'Come,' said Skalpi, 'a merry jest is being played here … will you not share it Brand?'

'There is no jest,' I gasped. 'I simply had a dream … a strange dream, which now strikes me as very funny.'

'All the better,' said Skalpi. 'It is often said that portents are revealed in dreams … a dream so powerful as to make you laugh like a sot must be portentous indeed.'

'Yes, come Brand,' said Emma, 'why don't you share the dream?'

'Very well,' I replied, dabbing at my eyes and reaching for the mustard. 'I dreamed I was eating a pie. It tasted wonderful and yet it smelled strange.'

'You must always be careful when eating pie,' replied Emma.

'Yes,' I agreed, 'but it seemed as though what I tasted and what I smelled were two different things … like eating hare but smelling a gamy fowl.'

'I don't see why that would make you laugh,' complained Skalpi. 'Eating a hare pie?'

'It depends on the nose,' said Emma, her eyes sparkling with mischief.

'Aah, I think you have it,' I said. 'I believe it got stuck for a while … in a place that reeked like a tannery.'

The sudden change in mood was like being unexpectedly drenched in snow melt. The laughter ceased and Emma's face went white. I turned to see Harold and William standing in the doorway, William staring at me as though he'd caught me murdering his children.

'You were saying?' he demanded.

'Nothing, Lord,' I stammered in confusion, wondering what I had done to offend. Only Turold was smiling.

'Brand was telling us about his dream, Lord William,' said Turold, with an evil grin, ' … and about his disgust for tanneries.'

William stared piercingly at me, then turned and strode away – leaving the room in a sombre silence.

∞ ∞ ∞

'His mother was a tanner's daughter.'

Harold had summoned me outside for a stroll after a breakfast finished mostly in silence – silence but for the delighted cackling of Turold.

'A tanner's daughter?' I echoed, aghast at the idea that William thought I had deliberately mocked him.

'I have already apologised on your behalf,' said Harold, 'and swore you did not know of his mother.'

'Is William satisfied?'

'He is mollified,' said Harold, staring at the forested hills that lay in the direction of Inglalond, 'but not entirely satisfied. He wants you to swear an oath.'

'Gladly,' I replied.

'Wait until you know what the oath is,' advised Harold. 'He wants us to fight for him and part of the reason he is ready to forgive you is that I told him you were one of the best fighting men in my army.'

'Well … I'm always up for a scrap,' I said. 'Who does he want us to fight?'

'A fellow by the name of Conan is causing problems for one of William's kin to the south … in the land of Brittany,' said Harold, 'but the reason I wanted to talk to you is this … I'm not displeased that there is now a point of conflict between William and you.'

I groaned, aware that I was once again a pawn in some subtle game of politics.

Harold glanced about to ensure none were listening.

'I do not wish to marry William's daughter,' said Harold. 'She is too young, but there are other reasons.'

I waited for him to explain, hoping that he might say that his love for the Lady Swanneshals was too strong to be compromised by a Christian marriage, but if that was his reason he kept it to himself.

'If there is conflict between William and my men,' he said, 'it gives me an excuse to argue with him until we cannot agree about anything … including the marriage. Then we will return to Inglalond, with nothing decided for the future.'

'I see.'

'Do you?' grinned Harold.

'I think so … you want to—'

'Nay, put it not into words. It is enough that you understand that it pleases me for there to be conflict between you and William. Don't anger him too sorely, but find ways to keep him irritated. There is something else also ... '

He smiled oddly as I waited for him to explain further.

'The Lady Emma.'

'What about her?' I asked, with a sinking foreboding of what would be required of me.

'I think she likes you.'

'I am married.'

'You are a thegn, with the prospect of becoming an earl before too much longer ... that means the normal rules regarding men and women are relaxed in your case.'

I just stared at him, not entirely sure what he was asking.

'Emma is betrothed to the dwarf Turold,' explained Harold. ' ... William's nephew. There is a strange relationship between William and Turold. William is constantly embarrassed by the dwarf but family ties are strong ... as they always are for bastards ... and I think he sees Turold's condition as somehow akin to his own.'

'He does?'

Harold glanced about again to check none could hear us.

'I think so. William's has been a most epic struggle from a bastard born of a tanner's daughter up to Duke ... a somewhat harder fight than a dwarf born of a bishop, waiting to be a count ... as they call earls over here.'

'But what has all of this to do with me?'

'Well, you know best,' said Harold, with that odd smile again, 'but if Turold were to become enraged and scandalised, it would be another point of dispute between William and me ... especially if I refused to censure your behaviour. William is very courtly regarding romance and would not want his daughter marrying a man who approved of infidelity.'

If my head was whirling before it was spinning dangerously now and liable to leave my shoulders. The political danger was unmanning, and yet being directed by the greatest man in Inglalond to pursue the Lady Emma was exciting, not least as such direction surely compensated for any promise I had made to Valla.

'Very well,' I said after collecting my wits. 'I shall fuck Emma in the service of my country.'

'Thank you Earl Brand … but not yet. I don't want any arguments until after the Brittany campaign. I want William to see how well we fight.'

Chapter 26

The Truth of Property

Early that afternoon there was a weapontake in the town and we in the palace were arrayed for war in William's livery. Fine chain hauberks – strong, but marvellously light – were given us, and other leggings and pieces which strapped or bolted on also. I refused all weapons, preferring my own, but they did insist on a long spear as we were to ride into battle on horses, which was a strange idea and I felt awkward about it.

'Watch how you swing your sword, Brand,' laughed Skalpi, 'You'll have your horse's ears off!'

'Watch yourself,' I replied, reflecting that Skalpi's advice would be difficult to follow in the chaos of battle.

Elric looked strangely well suited to the Norman armour, but it was Harold who looked magnificent – every inch a proud and noble warrior and sat his horse well despite his preference for fighting on foot. *The Red Dragon* of Wessex he had left at Bosham, but his personal standard – *The Fighting Man* – he bade me bear for him. Such was usually Eadnoth the staller's office but he was yet in Ponthieu with Aethelnoth and the others and our campaign lay to the south-west.

The other piece of gear we were given was a godsend – hose for riding that were reinforced with soft leather about the inner thighs, and I understood that long hours in the saddle would not prove the torment they had in the past.

Arrayed in our gear we assembled in the courtyard where William gave an account of his grievances against Conan and why we must travel to a place called Mont St Michel between Normandy and Brittany to get redress. He was very convincing, and even I who had

266

little interest in local politics felt offended on his part and ready to exact his vengeance.

Then, up on his enormous red warhorse, he passed through our midst and under the arch of his Rouen palace and in well-ordered ranks we followed him – me beside Harold, proudly bearing *The Fighting Man*, but already aware of how irritating that duty was liable to become during the long hours of riding ahead.

We paused outside the town to collect the infantrymen – William's version of the fyrd, and several thousand strong. William gave the same speech for their benefit, and once again we were on our way. I found I could balance the staff of Harold's banner in my stirrup, leaving one leg dangling, but at least I could just hold the banner straight rather than expend energy holding it aloft.

As I've remarked before, it was a pleasant countryside through which we marched – fields were neat and bordered with hedgerows. Even the copses and forests seemed planned, as though everything in William's duchy had been specifically placed for best effect. But if their fields were better ordered than ours, their peasants were not – these people had a sullen air about them and often I saw provosts – men with whips who enforced the labour. The ceorls and serfs in Inglalond needed no such compulsion, but got about their work in good spirit. I found that thought a little saddening – men should enjoy their labour.

That train of thought had me speculating about Elric once again, so I paused to wait for him. Very fine he looked, with only the snaggled teeth detracting from his otherwise knightly bearing.

'You've come a long way, Elric.'

He glanced about the fields, then said, 'I was just thinking the same myself. You see these people working like slaves … in fact some of them probably are slaves. And yet, my own condition … living in the woods as an outlaw … was way beneath them.'

We rode along in silence for a while as I reflected on all I knew of Elric, and then realised there were large gaps in my knowledge.

'You never told me,' I said, 'how you became so skilled at arms. Clearly you had fought in the fyrd before I met you.'

Elric didn't answer for a while, but then laughed softly, 'I thought we had a silent agreement never to discuss that.'

'We did?'

He considered me for a moment and said, 'I know you well enough now to know you won't betray me ... I was a sergeant for the Thegn of Norwic.'

He paused to allow me to digest that piece of news, but then there were questions and to my slight astonishment I gathered that Elric had been born nephew to a thegn and had therefore grown up learning arms. He had served as a retainer to his uncle but had left that service after meeting his Valla. Then, after she left for the Place of Dreams, he had sought her and eventually taken a new position with the Thegn of Norwic, where after acquitting himself well was promoted to sergeant.

'The son was the problem.'

'The thegn's son?'

'Aye ... second son. A piece of shit if ever there was one ... and jealous of my standing with his father.'

'So ... '

'So he accused me of a crime which, I believe, he had done himself and forced his father to choose between us ... he chose to believe me.'

'Hah!'

'But this went ill with the son ... as you might guess ... and he came for me in the night. Tried to murder me in my bed.'

'Oh no,' I said, ' ... and you killed him instead?'

'And then I panicked,' admitted Elric. 'I should have gone straight to the thegn and taken the odds to his justice ... but foolishly I ran, with another who also witnessed the attack.'

'But this was madness,' I cried. 'Why run when you had a witness to your own self-defence?'

'The witness might not have been believed,' said Elric. 'He was my brother.'

'What? You never told me you had a brother.'

'You knew him,' said Elric.

I stared for a moment, and then with a sinking heart I guessed, 'Not the fellow slain by Tostig on the morning we met?'

Elric's eyes blazed, then he glanced forward and back to ensure none were close enough to hear us, 'That is why I stayed after you granted my freedom. I wanted to be close enough to take my vengeance if the chance arose.'

I glanced forward to where Harold laughed with Skalpi, then lowered my voice, 'You mean to kill Tostig?'

'I have nearly tried it on several occasions,' said Elric. 'In Wales, when he spoke with you privately about letting Aelfgar live ... I had an arrow nocked and aimed at his back from ten paces ... but to let fly might have involved you.'

'How so?'

'You would have chased into the forest to find the slayer and almost certainly you would have seen me, thus forcing you to choose between me and Harold. I would not put such pressure on our friendship.'

I actually found myself laughing so outrageous did Elric's tale seem.

'Mind you,' said Elric, 'the way the brothers Godwinson parted after the Welsh campaign suggests to me that there will be blows between them before the end. I might yet be able to combine my vengeance with my duty.'

'Never,' I replied. 'There is too much love in Harold for him ever to see Tostig as a foe.'

'Be that as it may ... there is too much hate in Tostig and it takes just one to make a foe. I'd bet my balls on them fighting ere the end.'

'Tostig is Harold's greatest champion,' I protested, but even as I did I remembered our conversations in Wales and wondered whether there might be some peril in Tostig's soaring ambition.

There was a silence for a time as I struggled with the enormity of what I had just learned. In truth, I should be warning Harold that Elric meant to murder his brother, but I knew I could never do that – just one more matter to trouble my conscience. And with that thought I returned to my latest quandary – whether my behaviour with Emma meant I had broken my vow to Valla.

I suspected not, for a range of reasons, but I also knew that should I lie with her again, on purpose, I would no longer be able to argue my innocence – neither to Valla nor myself.

∞ ∞ ∞

Conan had retired to the castle and abbey of Mont St Michel on the coast – one of the best fortresses I had ever seen, and certainly the most beautiful. It was built high up on a rocky promontory and the approaches were flooded twice a day by the tides. A besieging army might spend an eternity there as the defenders were well stocked and could bring in extra supplies by sea.

Of course, taking on his liege lord from such a position had no future, so Conan would be forced eventually either to fight or to slip away by sea and lose everything. I expected him to fight and I was correct to do so, for on the third morning of the siege, just as the tide was lowest and the castle walls were glowing pink from the sunrise at our backs, the gates opened and a host poured forth to take us unawares. The horsemen, Conan at their head, ploughed through the front of William's army and could have escaped if that was their purpose, but instead they made for William's pavilion and were soon ringed by his army – ill-prepared and unarmoured, but in numbers enough to surround the horsemen and slow them down.

Harold and I, with Elric and Skalpi also, seized our weapons and were immediately at the front of the fray – fighting our way through Conan's knights toward the leader with the plumed helmet. I was swinging *Pighammer* in great cleaving arcs that none could face. Men and horses quailed before me and the others with swords stabbed at eyes and slashed at sword arms. We were forcing them back towards the sea and William's army pressed around us, hemming knights and infantry alike against the shore where they must surrender or die.

William appeared beside us, also bearing a bloody sword, and shouted for Conan to give up, but a madness of pride had taken him and he spurred his horse at William. Harold leapt in front of him and slashed at the horse's face, causing it to rear, and Conan was thrown to the sand.

Men pushed forward with raised swords but William shouted at them to leave Conan be. Yet such a madness was on Conan that even then, when all was clearly lost, he still preferred to fight. He dragged himself to his feet and again came at William, sword swinging, but again Harold stepped in front of William and parried Conan's blade and bore him back. They were both large men and a circle formed about them as elsewhere the battle ceased. Hundreds of voices urged the two warriors who stalked each other – Conan with the advantage because Harold was without armour.

But Harold kept Conan moving and the advantage of armour turned to Conan's bane. He tired and Harold soon had him on his knees and his sword was lowered in defeat. Harold looked to William, who signalled for Conan's helm to be removed. Conan reached up himself to remove the snouted helmet and we saw a surprisingly young-looking man with blonde hair and piercing blue eyes – staring with hate at William.

'Why have you attacked my cousin, Ruallon of Dol, and attempted to seize his lands?' demanded William, but Conan was defiant, even in surrender.

'The lands were taken from my family, as you well know. I was attempting justice to retrieve them. And even if you slay me it will not change the truth of ownership … not if Ruallon keeps them for a thousand years. They will still truly belong to my family and all here will know it.'

'No man can truly claim to own something which he has not the strength to hold,' said William. 'That is the truth of property.'

Conan was put in chains for William to ponder his doom and Conan's army – mostly unfought – had surrendered with his fall. Several of William's men had been sent to the fortress to make it secure but then a commotion sounded and all looked to where two of William's knights had waded too far into the incoming surf to pursue the last of Conan's soldiers. Now – trapped in the treacherous sands and weighed down by armour – they had only seconds before the tide swept over them. Without a word, Harold ran into the surf, and without further thought I followed, to aid if I might.

Unhindered by armour and strong as a horse, Harold dragged the knights from the water even though one had already gone under, yet both would surely have drowned if he hadn't acted so quickly. I might have aided him even then but stood back to enable all to appreciate the fullness of his deed. And they acclaimed him. A goodly part of William's army had witnessed the rescue and they cheered loudly – in particular William, who stood forth from the host and embraced Harold.

'Thrice am I indebted to Harold, Duke of the Anglais,' he cried and all were quiet to hear his tribute. 'The rescue of my knights is but one of the services he has rendered. A braver service occurred just minutes ago as he stood twice between my body and Conan … but best of all, he has agreed to wed my daughter Adeliza, thus blending our houses and smoothing my way in Inglalond. No man deserves more of me and I shall see that he is honoured as he merits.'

Harold bowed, while I pondered the meaning of the words 'smoothing my way in Inglalond'. Then Harold was led back to William's pavilion and wine was poured for the captains, including me, Elric and Skalpi. All of us were praised by William, even me despite my accidental reference to the tannery.

'I thank God that you are on my side, Brand,' said William. 'To see you swing that axe was terrifying. None could withstand you.'

'There are many thousands like him in Inglalond,' said Harold, 'but Brand is certainly one of the very best.'

'Many thousands?' echoed William. 'I should like to see them … all arrayed in formation for battle. A terrifying thought.'

'Only those who approach with malicious purpose need be terrified,' said Harold. 'Mostly they swing scythes and follow ploughs … but every man in Inglalond can fight.'

I had the sense that they were conducting two conversations at once, but William called for chests to be brought outside the pavilion. The first was opened and inside were some items of war gear of the highest quality. A hauberk with gold and silver rings among the iron was given to Harold, and a helm also, inlaid with silver and gold to show William's device.

'These are but a token of my esteem and signify that you are my favoured man,' said William, 'but as I said at our meeting we have a lifetime of giving and receiving to look forward to, do we not?'

'I'm sure we do,' replied Harold. 'As you give in Normandy, so shall I in Inglalond.'

A hard gleam came for a moment to William's eye but, if he meant to speak, he thought better of it and allowed more wine to be poured by servants.

Then the second chest was opened. Inside was yet another chest – beautifully carved and inlaid with silver and pearls.

'This chest is from the sacristy at my brother's church at Bayeux,' said William. 'It holds bones sacred from the foot of Saint Peter … the foot that was uppermost when he was crucified inversely by the pagans. Long has it been coveted by Edward of Inglalond and will form the centrepiece of his new minster on the Temes. It will also form part of Adeliza's dowry … thus will Edward, and future kings, ever be grateful to Harold Godwinson.'

Harold bowed and the rest of the day passed in pleasant aftermath. It had been a short but hard battle and all of us had cuts and scratches which we bathed in seawater and bound in damp linen as Valla had taught us to do. Then we returned to William's pavilion where a day-long banquet was prepared and served for the captains and favoured warriors.

The next morning, the army – injured more by hard drinking than hard fighting – began its homeward journey but William wished to pause in Bayeux to introduce Harold to his brother the bishop. Conan was still in chains and was locked in the bishop's palace while William considered what to do with him, and in the late afternoon a large contingent appeared from the north-east.

Adeliza and other of William's people had been summoned to meet him in the hour of victory and she stood behind her father as he prayed in the large, red-brick abbey that soared into heaven. But while her father gave thanks for the victory, ever her glance strayed towards her fiancé who, by the set of his jaw, was well aware of the attention and liked it not.

After the devotions, we were taken to yet another banquet at which William's brother, Odo, presided. A huge man he was, bigger even than Skalpi, and to my surprise greeted us dressed in armour polished black, which was strange gear for a priest. When I remarked upon it he informed me that his greatest joy was to fight, which struck me as even stranger as men of God were usually men of peace.

'I was bound for the monastery myself,' I told him, 'but one of the reasons I avoided that life was so I could live and fight with warriors. I didn't know the two lives could be blended.'

'There are rules governing the fighting,' said Odo. 'As a man ordained, I am not permitted to shed blood.'

'So how do you fight?' I asked, genuinely perplexed by the idea of a priest at arms.

'With that,' he grinned, pointing to where a huge, black mace hung on the wall between two crucifixes. 'God's work can be complex, so I achieve it with whatever tools are necessary.'

He was an unnerving man and I was glad to let him attend to the great ones – leaving me on the outer with the less than great. Turold was present and so was Emma. I had been drinking the rich red wine of Normandy for some hours and, the instant I saw her, felt the serpent twitch between my thighs.

Glancing at my arm, I saw the linen wrapped and thought inevitably of she who had taught me to wrap it so, but she was not here – and the woman I had been ordered to pursue by the man who would be king, was smiling at me over the head of her fiancé who sneered at the sight of my numerous bandages.

'Oh there you are Turold,' I laughed, careless of his prickly dignity. 'We missed you in the fight, but you've made it in time for the feast I see.'

All who heard me laughed, with the exception of the dwarf who scowled black murder. In that moment I remembered he was Odo's son, and again I reflected on what an unusual churchman he was – fighting and fucking were all part of God's work, apparently. I would have been less reluctant to join the church in Normandy.

'I have just had words with Odo's chamberlain,' said Emma to me and my Saxon companions. 'He had put you all in the same dormitory … but I informed him that you were lords of high favour and distinction and that it would be a grave insult to your dignity. I insisted upon separate rooms and it seems that, as the future wife of Odo's son, I have some influence.'

'It's a shame you couldn't arrange just the one room for you and me,' said Turold and she laughed.

'You must be patient for your wedding day,' reproved Emma with a smiling glance in my direction. 'But if Turold is very good, he might get a kiss tonight.'

I had to turn away to prevent them seeing the laughter on my lips, but Elric was staring at me with a worried frown.

Later, when I went outside to piss, he sidled up next to me.

'Tell me it isn't so,' he said.

'Tell you what isn't so?'

Elric stared at the splashing ground for a few moments, then said, 'Please tell me you haven't been fucking Emma.'

'I haven't been fucking Emma.'

'But you mean to.'

'I shall do my best to avoid it,' I replied, glancing over both shoulders, 'though Harold himself has asked me to get close to her.'

Elric rearranged his clothing and wiped his hands against his tunic. Then he said, 'I'm not even going to ask why he would require such a service … you are mired in politics I fear, and no doubt Elric will need to snatch you away to safety at some point. But clearly she likes you. You and Emma seem to share a secret joke as only lovers do, and I am not the only one to mark it.'

On the one hand, it was a warning of danger. But on the other hand, it confirmed that I was achieving exactly what Harold wanted.

'If tongues should wag,' I replied, 'so much the better.'

I turned to re-enter the hall but Elric held me by the shoulder.

'Don't forget Valla,' he said. 'I would not have you make the error I made.'

I felt a flash of irritation, but shook it off – he deserved better of me than that.

'I haven't forgotten Valla.'

∞ ∞ ∞

'Turold hates you,' giggled Emma.

We were lying in the darkness of my chamber which adjoined her own. She had come in the middle night and woken me in the same manner as she had done the first time, although it took longer to rouse me from my wine-fuelled stupor. But once awake I took full advantage, exploring her with lips and tongue as she explored me. I ached to turn her onto her back and push inside her, but – I had drawn the line and would not cross it. She did not ask me to, but I could tell from the way she positioned herself that she would welcome my manhood within her and it took all my forbearance to resist the urge to let it happen.

But what did happen was exciting enough and my head reeled with the lust and the fun of it – not least that she was Turold's fiancée and the thought of him discovering us made me shake with laughter.

'Why should he hate me,' I replied, 'when I am so kind to his fiancée?'

'He would love to be so kind,' she replied, 'but a black cat will claim the keys of Rome before I take that imp for a husband.'

In fact, the reason for her dislike was nothing to do with his size.

'He is a little man in more ways than one,' she complained. 'He … well, you have met him. He is small-minded and tiresome … worst of all he is boring. The thought of spending my days listening to his pointless triumphs and petty grievances turns my mind to merde. That's why I like you.'

'Because I don't turn your mind to merde?'

'You make me think only of this,' she said, reaching for that which she called Turold. 'It is fun, no? Especially to do it in secret.'

'Would it be possible,' I mused, 'to do it in front of many people without them knowing?'

'In front of Turold?' she smiled. 'Perhaps I could hide beneath a table and kiss you thus, while you spoke of serious matters with him?'

'It would not be easy to remain serious,' I said, and groaned with pleasure as she teased me once again to attention.

A little while later, when we were able to speak, she said, 'I want to do it.'

'Do what?'

'I want to kiss your Turold while you speak with mine … we must find a way.'

She was absolutely enchanted with the idea, but I didn't believe she was serious.

'You still haven't told me why Turold hates me.'

'Isn't it obvious? He resents your stature.'

'Then he may as well resent every man in creation.'

'Not your height, fool … your standing. He is jealous of your friendships with the great ones … and you not even a knight.'

'I have nothing without Harold's patronage.'

'Not so,' she said. 'Even Harold envies you.'

It was so outrageous an idea that I laughed aloud, which was not wise for those trying to be discreet in the dead of night in a crowded palace.

'That's ridiculous,' I said, in a more cautious whisper. 'Harold is the strongest man in Inglalond … after the king.'

'And yet he envies Brand … a man still young but proven in battle and with one clear purpose … to claim what should have been his.'

I had told her of my great quest – to drive the silver-hilted dagger into Malgard's heart and reclaim the thegnship of Stybbor, which I would give to Elric if ever appointed earl.

'I believe Harold to have that same purpose.'

'His father's purpose perhaps,' said Emma. 'Harold would be happier led than leading.'

'Hush!' I admonished. 'Let not these words be said again.'

Shortly afterwards, as the wolf light stole through the shutters, it was time for Emma to leave. I rose to check the corridor, and as I opened the door found myself face to face with Turold.

'Turold!' I said, loud enough for the room behind me. 'What do you want?'

Without a word, he tried to push past me, but I held the door against him.

'Who have you got in there?' he demanded.

'There is no-one here,' I laughed. 'Get ye gone foul imp.'

He started shouting and shoving against the door and presently a couple of soldiers appeared, in no great hurry, as though they knew that any alarm raised by Turold was unlikely to matter.

'He has a woman in there!' shouted Turold to the men. 'I demand access.'

'There are plenty of other women,' yawned the taller of the two soldiers. 'Get your own.'

Turold was almost beside himself with fury.

'I don't want a woman you fool! I want to see his woman! I heard her voice!'

'I don't have a woman,' I said, 'but I would like one if there are women to be had.'

The guards shrugged and Turold flung himself at my door again, shrieking to be allowed in.

Suddenly the next door up the corridor was flung open and Emma, dressed in a mantle, emerged demanding to know what the noise was all about.

Turold gaped at her, and was immediately sullen and silent.

'What is wrong, my lord?' she enquired, calmly.

'Nothing,' said Turold, giving me a look of venomous hatred as he turned and strode away in the grip of his wounded dignity.

The soldiers shrugged again and followed Turold. I had half a mind to beckon Emma back into my room but we had evidently had a close call. I grinned at her, then closed the door. My shutters were open and I looked outside to examine how Emma had achieved the return. The rooms were on the second level so she had been obliged to perform some feat of acrobatics to get from my window to hers. There were exposed beams and embrasures enough for a skilled person to manage such a feat and clearly she had that skill.

In the east the sky glowed pink and gold. It was going to be a special day.

Chapter 27

The Nature of the Test was Obscure

We were required to attend a mass before breakfast, led by Odo, and I sat in the second row of the abbey, trying not to laugh at the sight of Turold with another black eye and split lip.

The mass was overly long for warriors wanting breakfast and I could hear my belly growling before the end. Odo gave a long sermon about the need to pursue the enemies of God into whichever land they might go and it occurred to me – indeed it shocked me – that Odo's religion was both political and convenient. I had never realised until that moment that it was possible for men to do all manner of evil or politics in the name of God. This was a dangerous line of thinking, I knew, and again I had to wonder whether God was testing me. If so, the nature of the test was obscure, but I was gladder than ever that I had not gone into the monastery and become subject to the authority of men like Odo who clearly harnessed the name of God to their own private purpose.

At last it was over and as we filed towards the kitchens I could see that yet another carnival was being prepared on the lawn beside the abbey. They were great ones for celebrating these Normans.

Harold fell in step beside me.

'So,' he said, 'I heard about Turold's tantrum this morning…did you have her in your room?'

'Of course. As you bade me.'

'Brand the Reliable,' he laughed. 'No test is beyond you.'

'Save one,' I thought sadly, but hoped that by refusing to fuck in the normal way I was yet hanging on to a thread of my promise to Valla.

'I need the affair between you and Emma to be more widely known … can you manage that? Today if possible?'

'Your word is my command,' I laughed, and Harold grinned shaking his head.

'I am lucky to have met you Brand Holgarsson,' he said. 'I believe we will be friends for many years and do great things for Inglalond.'

He slapped me over the shoulder and strode forward to talk with Skalpi. Then Elric was at my side.

'I saw her.'

' … Saw who?'

'I saw Emma go out your window while the dwarf was shrieking this morning.'

I could sense the disapproval in his manner, but reassured him that I had not fucked her, and in any case, I had been ordered by Harold to pursue her.

Elric shrugged, but was clearly unconvinced.

After breakfast we watched the preparations for the carnival continue, including the construction of a stage for entertainments. There were numerous booths about the stage in which special foods or wares were prepared, and one of them gave me an idea which made me smile. It was a very small stage where puppets might perform and I laughed aloud in anticipation.

'What's funny?' asked Elric.

'Oh … nothing,' I replied, grinning.

'You're up to mischief. That much is plain.'

The first wine of the day was poured and Elric said, 'When shall we return to Inglalond?'

'You don't like it here?'

'I like it well enough,' said Elric, 'but I prefer our food … the ale is not the way I like it.'

'The wine is superb,' I replied.

'It is,' he agreed, sipping, 'but it doesn't compensate for the malice I feel, always beneath the surface of their courtly manners and pageantry.'

'Oh, that,' I laughed.

'It's always like this at court, I suppose,' he reflected. 'Being in a strange country with a strange court just makes it seem darker. But when shall we leave?'

'I know not. I understand there is some important ceremony to take place this afternoon. I suppose we shall leave soon enough once all the players are satisfied with their politics.'

'And if they are not satisfied?'

I turned and grinned at him – impressed with his capacity to always see the heart of the problem.

'In that case we will leave even sooner.'

∞ ∞ ∞

Shortly after breakfast there was a clatter of horses and we looked up to see a sight that was welcome indeed. Aethelnoth, Eadnoth and all of the others who had been left behind in Ponthieu rode into camp and I felt a weight lift from my heart. Harold strode about laughing and greeting them, a muttered word here, a slap on the shoulder there, and even though we still numbered only eighteen fighters, I felt the balance had moved subtly in our favour. I was delighted to reacquaint myself with my colleagues and share our adventures over numerous cups of wine.

There were many entertainments over the course of the day, but the main event was due to feature a chest and a table set up before the main stage. The chest was the one from which William had produced the beautiful chain and helm which he had given to Harold after the battle at Mont St Michel. The table was draped with a cloth but was otherwise bare.

In fact the entertainments did not take place upon the stage. That was where William's seat was raised with Harold to his right, his wife Mathilda to his left and Adeliza to Mathilda's left. Skalds, jugglers and acrobats took their turns to beguile the great ones and there were many speeches regarding William's magnificence, Adeliza's beauty and Harold's bravery and nobility. Odo seemed to be in charge of all ceremonies and yet he certainly drank more than any warrior – not that it seemed to affect him.

Around the middle afternoon, Odo rose again and waved the musicians to silence. He stood between the table and the chest and made further tribute to his brother, then called upon Harold, Duke of the Anglais, to make the oath required of him by Edward on behalf of Inglalond.

Harold rose from his seat beside William and there was a keen and breathless silence as he approached Odo. Then Odo held up a jewelled sword and informed us that it was William's sword, blessed by the pope himself, and that Harold should make his oath touching the sword, which was then laid on the covered table.

'Come Harold,' said William, 'what oath would you make before all of Christendom?'

'I will swear,' said Harold, one hand resting on the large and ornate chest representing William's house and the other on the sword, 'before these witnesses here, in Normandy, to be the man of Duke William …and to do his bidding as befits a loyal son in law.'

William stared hard at Harold and opened his mouth to speak, but at that moment Odo gave a shout and swept the cloth from the table. Beneath the table was the chest of saintly bones from the sacristy and Odo cried in a terrible voice, 'Behold! The oath was made upon the sword of William, Harold's new liege lord, and the relics of Saint Peter which will be kept in the most sacred cathedral of Inglalond. The oath is therefore doubly binding before God and let all men know that Harold has so sworn!'

There was a deep silence, and William looked troubled, as though something had not quite gone as planned, but then there was cheering and he forced a smile, and stepped down to embrace Harold. The music resumed, servants appeared to refill our cups, and Emma gave me a wink and slipped away. The sun was westering but the light was yet strong and the breeze balmy. The wine made me feel full of jest and utterly invincible, and in that mood I stepped behind the curtain of the little puppet stage and began to put on a show.

Immediately there was a roar of laughter from Elric, Skalpi and some of the Norman warriors and they all gathered closer to hear my tale.

'Gather round!' I cried, in my best imitation of a skald's storytelling voice, 'for I shall sing you the tale of Turold and the Troll!'

More warriors hurried over carrying horns and cups, their faces split with grins as the name of my story was repeated by my delighted audience.

'Once upon a time, there was a little town called Bayeux ... the people were happy except for one terrible problem ... can you guess what that was?'

'No! Tell us!' shouted Skalpi, and there was more laughter.

'Alright,' I said, 'the people were afflicted by a troll who lived in a cave on the edge of town, and every month he would catch one of the local children for his pantry.'

'No!' objected my audience.

'Yes indeed,' I replied, 'and the town was running out of children so they had a special meeting to decide what to do about the troll.'

I didn't bother trying to use the many puppets to illustrate my story, but I did use my fingers to indicate a crowd. 'What shall we do?' I asked in a frightened voice.

'We need a champion!' I replied in a different voice. 'Let us send for the mighty Turold ... greatest warrior in all of Normandy!'

Skalpi was crying with laughter and many of the Normans were having trouble standing, they were laughing so hard.

'Did you call me?' asked a figure I portrayed with my thumb. 'For yea, I am Turold ... hero of the age ... slayer of mice and eater of chickens!'

I wiggled the thumb hero up and down the stage as more warriors hurried over to see the commotion, and that's when I felt hands pulling at my breeches.

'Turold!' cried my finger crowd. 'You must go to the cave and save us from the troll that dwells within and eats our children.'

'And what shall be my payment?' asked thumb Turold. 'For trolls are dangerous, and it may be that I am eaten myself ... even though there is less meat on me than most children.'

'You shall have a kiss,' I replied, in yet another voice.

'A kiss from the lady Emma?' exclaimed thumb Turold. 'There is no greater prize in Christendom! Bring on your troll at once!'

My breeches were pulled down past my knees and lips went around my manhood, causing me to groan with pleasure – which I then had to incorporate into my story as the growl of the troll in his cave.

'Who approaches my cave?' I demanded, making a cave tunnel with my left hand.

'It is I, Turold, greatest of warriors. I have come to punish you for eating children.'

It was all I could do to stand as Emma's lips moved long and slow along the length of my manhood.

'Why don't you come into my cave?' I squeaked, barely holding back the laughter and the impossible pleasure. Fortunately the audience was laughing too much to notice.

'Here I come!' shouted thumb Turold, as Emma seized my balls and sucked so hard I felt my knees trembling and mighty spasms began to surge through my loins. Without noticing, I abandoned the play to hold Emma still, and in that moment the real Turold burst through the audience brandishing *Pighammer*, which he smashed onto the stage before me.

He did me no damage but the stage and the booth collapsed, and I was revealed – half naked with Emma kneeling before me. There was an astonished gasp, but then a roar of delighted laughter, as though my audience believed the revelation to be the intended climax of my show. But Turold was enraged and I just had the wit to disengage and catch the haft of the axe as he swung it at Emma's head.

'Whore!' screamed Turold. 'Bitch! Treacherous fucking slut!'

I pulled *Pighammer* from his grasp, but I was knocked aside by an equally enraged Odo who dragged Emma to her feet and gave her such a slap as to nearly take her head off. I was about to attack Odo in her defence when I was hit from behind and dragged to the ground.

'Lie still you fool,' hissed Elric in my ear.

∞ ∞ ∞

William and Harold stared at the commotion among the drunken warriors – falling about in fits of laughter while Odo dragged the Lady Emma by the arm to William's seat.

'This piece of sluttish filth is no longer betrothed to my son!' growled Odo, pushing her onto the ground.

'Thank God for that,' spat Emma, who received another vicious slap for her trouble.

William had not seen the scandalous revelation but when Odo described what had happened he was incensed.

'You will be flogged and branded as a whore,' said William to Emma, ' … then sent into exile from all of my lands.'

'It is better than marriage to Turold,' said Emma, but that was the last thing she said as Odo clouted her so hard she lay still with blood trickling from her mouth. At a flick of Odo's hand, she was carried away by soldiers.

'Where is the man involved?' demanded William.

The Norman warriors, who had only moments before been howling with laughter at my tale, now parted like Moses' famous Red Sea to leave me bearing the brunt of William's fury.

'He is one of yours,' said William, turning to Harold. 'How will you punish him?'

'Punish him?' enquired Harold. 'What has he done to merit punishment?'

William stared at Harold in shock and the angry silence deepened.

'He has dared to defile a woman intended for my family,' said William. 'If you cannot see the harm in that you are not the man I thought you were.'

'He is a warrior,' shrugged Harold. 'Such men take their pleasures as they can. It was the Lady's responsibility to stay chaste.'

'You swore an oath to be my man and take my part,' said William, ' … not ten minutes ago. Do you defy me already?'

'I am not defying you, Lord William,' said Harold, calm despite the thunderous mood of his host. 'I am merely trying to understand what crime you perceive Brand Holgarsson to have committed.'

With the mention of my name, William's anger seemed to seethe even hotter.

'What crime?' he shouted. 'He insults and mocks me, and then he defiles the women of my household! If you are not insulted on my behalf then I must judge you complicit!'

Harold glanced over to where his men had all gathered about Brand and felt his confidence soar.

'Come, Lord William,' said Harold, 'the day we punish warriors for expressing their natural urges is the day they cease to follow us. Would you have me punish Brand for breathing, or needing to sleep? A fighting man has needs and if Turold is unable to curb his betrothed then he must suffer the penalty.'

Odo stamped his foot with rage and took a step towards Harold, who remained calmly seated. But William rose to his feet with a face like doom.

'By God, I will have no son in law who sits by and watches me insulted!'

With that he left the dais, followed by Odo, Mathilda and a tearful Adeliza who stared achingly at Harold before being dragged away by her mother.

'You swore an oath!' shouted William in a passion of fury.

'So I did,' muttered Harold. 'So I did. In Normandy.'

Chapter 28

Like Dogs With A Cornered Hind

'Stay faithful Brand. Lie with no other woman and I may return to you for the fulfilment of our life together ... for good or ill. There will be a sign. You will know it when you see it. Know that I am coming. It will not be as long as you think.'

Once again I woke from my frequent dream of Valla, and after a few moments of peaceful happiness was suddenly wracked with guilt as I recalled my behaviour with Emma. True it was that I had not lain with her in the accepted sense, but I had allowed her to distract me and sought pleasure with her – and if given the choice again I would certainly have resisted her charm.

Elric said little on our voyage home, which also unnerved me, but Harold was in excellent spirits and frequently summoned me to his side to share a cup of wine and talk about the future.

'So ... I return to Inglalond unmarried,' he said, with a foot in the bow gazing towards the white cliffs. 'This has been a most favourable fishing trip.'

Instead of going back to Bosham, we made straight for the Temes and rowed slowly up the river against the flow. All of us took our turn at the oars and I was tired and sore by the time we reached the pier at Wapping and were able to step back onto a friendly shore. Horses were found and we went to Harold's Lundene house where there was much rejoicing, for the servants and housecarls there had not seen their lord for nearly a year.

That night we were joined by Harold's younger brothers, Gyrth and Leofwine, and their faces were grim as they retired to a private chamber with Harold, who intended to seek an audience with the king the following day. Elric, of course, was quite expert at extracting the news brought by the brothers from their housecarls.

'Tostig,' he muttered as we sat at the large table in the kitchen with some of Gyrth's men – all of them young and full of excitement to be visiting Harold.

'What's he done?'

'Stirred up a hornet's nest in the north. Thegns are objecting to his rule … and his burdensome taxes.'

'There is a petition before the king,' informed a young soldier with a badly broken nose who had been listening to our muttered conversation. I had a notion to tell him to mind his own business, but curiosity got the better of me.

'What petition?'

'They are begging the king, in his wisdom, to relieve Tostig of the earldom and appoint another who will respect the laws of Cnut.'

'And the tax measures,' added another. 'Tostig has gone mad with greed … taxing the thegns four, five and six times the customary rates for hides and caricurates.'

'Don't forget the murders,' added yet another. 'Every time someone goes to Tostig to complain they end up mysteriously dead. The thegns won't stand for it anymore, and there's already been an uprising.'

'What did I tell you?' whispered Elric. 'Tostig's ambition has the better of his judgment, and this is just the beginning.'

It should have been cause for grave concern, and yet Elric wore a grin like a split melon.

∞ ∞ ∞

Harold, accompanied by his younger brothers, Gyrth, Earl of East Anglia and Leofwine, Earl of Kent, was admitted to the chamber where Edward sat with his minister Cuthred and Bishop John of Fecamp. Harold felt his hackles rise at the presence of both men, but the Norman bishop in particular angered him.

None rose to receive him and Harold marvelled at the king's decline. He looked to have aged ten years in the six months since Harold had last seen him. His movements were slow and his voice even slower, but the simmering anger burned hot as ever.

'So Harold … you have returned from Normandy. What news of

William?'

Harold had no doubt that the recent events at Bayeux would already have been reported to Edward by Bishop John.

'My Lord,' said Harold, 'I made my oath as you bade me, but I am sorry to report that we had a disagreement.'

'Over what?'

Harold had no desire to describe the incident involving the outlaw Brand Holgarsson, but suspected Edward would already have been informed. Hopefully the bishop did not know the name of the man involved.

'It was a trifling matter which—'

'It was a matter of honour,' interrupted the bishop, 'in which you refused to take the part of your newly sworn liege lord.'

'And the relics?' asked Edward. 'Where are the bones of St Peter which were promised for my new minster?'

'William did not release them, sire. I made the oath ... in Normandy, as requested ... but William broke trust and did not permit the marriage nor the release of the relics.'

Edward was silent for a few moments, staring at Harold as though trying to perceive an unsavoury subtlety.

'So where does this leave the succession?' he finally asked, to himself.

'I have already sworn to recognise the throne right of the aetheling,' said Harold. 'I will protect him and see that he comes into his inheritance.'

The bishop snorted with derision, but said nothing as Harold stared a challenge at him.

Then Edward groaned – a groan of defeat and despair and all his anger seemed to vanish.

'I am so tired,' he complained. 'Old and tired ... and the realm I hoped to leave in peace and prosperity is falling apart before my aging eyes.'

'The realm is strong,' replied Harold. 'We have many soldiers and ships enough to protect us from external attack.'

'It is not external attack that troubles me,' spat Edward in a sudden fury. 'It is the sons of Godwin who have manoeuvred themselves into positions of power and now threaten to tear Inglalond apart like dogs with a cornered hind.'

'Sire … I—'

'What do you intend to do about Tostig?' demanded Edward, interrupting rudely.

'I will carry out my king's instructions,' said Harold.

'Will you? And what if my instructions are that Tostig be relieved of the earldom and sent into exile?'

'Then that is what I will do, in your name,' replied Harold.

'Then do it!' shouted Edward. 'Report back here when it is done and perhaps I will think better of you.'

∞ ∞ ∞

Malgard could scarce believe his eyes.

He had heard from Tostig Godwinson's own lips that Brand lived despite the reports of his death in the burning house four years prior, but he had not quite believed him. It was impossible that Brand had survived such an inferno – and yet, here he was – grown into a large and seasoned warrior and clearly a favoured man in Harold's household.

Malgard sat with Gorik in an upstairs room of a small inn opposite the gate of Harold's London house where he could watch the comings and goings, and two days after the reports of Harold's return, his vigil was rewarded with a sighting of the man he'd believed perished. Brand, now the image of his elder brother Gram, was alive and returned to trouble Malgard's dreams.

'Follow him,' said Malgard to the small man fingering the long, puckered scar on the right side of his face.

'Follow him and learn his habits … but try nothing for now. He looks a formidable warrior and we must make absolutely certain this time.'

PART FOUR

Chapter 29

Split Our Family and You Split Inglalond

It was getting cool again as we reached the outskirts of Yorvik – a walled town more Danish than Saxon, not least in its smell. Like all great towns it stank disgustingly of turd, but there was also a stink of rotting meat and fish which tended to be concentrated in designated areas in places like Lundene or Rouen. In Yorvik the shit was everywhere.

Anger also.

We travelled in a party of some two hundred warriors and had been aware of eyes in the forests and upon the hills as we passed.

'Brigands … in Northumbria?' Harold had remarked.

'They are the housecarls of thegns displaced by Tostig,' said Carl. 'Or that is my guess.'

'Tostig has done much damage to the country,' sighed Harold. 'It will be hard work to put right.'

Also travelling with us (to my small distress) were Edwin, Earl of Mercia, and his younger brother Morcar. Morcar was white-faced and sweating as we approached the gates of Yorvik which were guarded by men still faithful to Tostig. I had been privy to some of their conversations with Harold so understood his fear. He was only a year or two older than I but was facing the prospect of a manly task.

Not that the task was widely known as we were allowed through the gate at dusk by sullen soldiers and marched through the cold and stinking town. The houses were tumbled so closely together it reminded me of Theodford in East Anglia, and the rats so numerous that the cats had tired of the novelty and heeded them no more than the children shitting in the streets heeded our party.

Tostig's hall was seated on a low hill rising above the worst of the muck and was protected by a low wall of stone and a group of his housecarls at the gate. Once again we were greeted without any enthusiasm (or respect) but allowed through the gate to where at least some preparation had been made for our arrival. Many tents had been erected for the soldiers and others were led to a large barn. Harold, Carl, Elric and myself, and a handful of others, continued towards the main hall where we were greeted by Tostig's chamberlain and shown to rooms down the right wing of the house.

I was sharing a room with Elric and we were given clean (but cold) water. Since our time in Normandy, I had adopted Skalpi's method of washing so thrust my head into the bowl and was immediately refreshed. Elric was a little less boisterous but was also quickly clean and we sat either side of the large bed, wondering whether we would be called or whether we were simply expected to make our way to the hall in our own time.

Elric seemed far less at ease than his usual implacable self, but I knew this was the first time he'd been in Tostig's presence since he had admitted to me that Tostig had killed his brother and he had sworn vengeance.

'So what do you mean to do?' I asked him.

'Nothing … for now,' said Elric, knowing exactly what I was asking.

There was a silence between us, then Elric said, 'As I told you before, there will be trouble between the brothers Godwinson. Tostig will regard anything less than full support against his rebel thegns as treachery … at which point they will come to blows and Harold's policy will suddenly be aligned with my own.'

I had to concede there was a fair chance of Elric's prediction coming to pass, but Elric then said, 'So what do you mean to do?'

'Me? What do you mean?'

'Edwin,' he said, lowering his voice.

'Aah … yes, Edwin.'

I had not missed Edwin's murderous looks, and he had clearly grown into his earldom. He was a far more confident young fellow than the poetry loving wastrel I had encountered in Gruffyd's camp at Rhuddlan.

'I think he will try nothing for the moment,' said Elric. 'He has more than enough to concern himself at the present ... and Harold makes no secret of his regard for you. But once Harold and Edith are married ... presuming they do marry ... Edwin will no longer have to behave himself. That is when you will need to be on your guard.'

Once again I was impressed with Elric's deep understanding of the ways of the court, but my growling stomach compelled me to seek the kitchens so I put all intrigue and politics from my mind and went in search of something to fill my belly.

Intrigue and politics did not stay long out of my head. As Elric and I stalked the corridors of Tostig's hall there was a tension in the air and knuckles whitened on the spears of sentries as we passed.

'They all know,' muttered Elric. 'Tostig's men expect trouble ... and there are only two hundred of us.'

'There are more than two hundred,' I replied, barely above a whisper.

Elric glanced at me, but at that moment we emerged into the main hall where the tension was almost visible. Tostig and Harold sat either side of a long table – Harold flanked by Gyrth and Leofwine. All others, including the sons of Aelfgar, stood in a semi-circle back far enough to respect their privacy, but from the look on Tostig's face the conversation was not going well.

∞ ∞ ∞

'I thought you were coming here to strengthen my hold,' spat Tostig at Harold, 'not to prise it loose.'

'It is the king's decision,' said Harold.

'The king,' sneered Tostig. 'Since when have the sons of Godwin given a tinker's fart for the king?'

'I have always honoured the king, brother ... but even more I honour the law and custom that give safety and certainty to our people. You do not honour the law, which is why you have come into conflict with your own thegns ... and why Edward sees fit to relieve you of Northumbria.'

'And who does he propose to put in my place? One of Aelfgar's brats?'

'Morcar,' agreed Harold and Tostig barked with laughter.

'Morcar? Has he even left his nurse's teat?'

Harold turned and summoned the brothers Edwin and Morcar to the table.

'Good God!' laughed Tostig. 'Even now his knees knock together as he approaches! How will you take my earldom boy when you can't stand in my presence without shaking?'

Morcar said nothing, but looked to Harold for guidance.

'He has the will of the king on his side,' said Harold, 'therefore he has all the support he needs. Your earldom is finished brother.'

Tostig thumped the table.

'By God it is not!' he shouted. 'Do you seriously believe you can come up here with just two hundred men to put a boy in my place so you can marry his sister?'

'That is not the reason,' sighed Harold, who had expected the accusation.

'Really?' scoffed Tostig. 'Do you look me in the eye and swear you will not marry Morcar's sister?'

Harold reddened and was silent, and Tostig laughed in bitter triumph.

'Ha! I knew it! You and the brats of Aelfgar have conspired to supplant me. And I suppose it was Edwin who unsettled my thegns with promises and lies and caused them to rebel. That is what many believe in the north.'

'Then they are mistaken,' said Harold, ' ... and in the minority. Your own thegns have petitioned the king for your removal and a return to the laws of Cnut and customary tax levels. That is the reason for your removal and anything else is mere coincidence.'

'Coincidence,' laughed Tostig. 'I call it ambition. Harold's ambition that saw Gruffydd and Aelfgar killed and now Tostig supplanted to gain the hand of the Lady Edith. You have been determined brother.'

'I can hardly marry into my own family,' replied Harold. 'If I do marry the Lady Edith it will be a political marriage for the good of the realm ... and for the house of Godwin.'

'Don't dare mention our father!' thundered Tostig. 'Edward was his enemy and here you are doing Edward's bidding when the only proper way to honour Godwin's memory would be to unite the realm under his sons and wipe out any gutter rats that stand in our way. Even now we could put this argument aside and simply announce you king! Who would dare oppose it?'

'I will not take the kingdom by force … and I will not be king without the blessing of Edward and support of the witan.'

'Then you are not fit to be king,' sneered Tostig. 'And maybe that is why the Bastard is claiming you swore an oath to be his man.'

'So I did,' replied Harold. 'But only in Normandy … a place to which I have no intention of returning so the oath is worth little.'

Tostig shook his head and said, 'I suspect William perceives the oath to extend beyond Normandy … at least as far as Lundene.'

'He can perceive all he likes. It will avail him nowt in Inglalond.'

'You will need my support when he comes,' said Tostig, suddenly grim, and Harold felt a quiver of premonition across his shoulders.

'You do have my support brother,' said Harold, 'but not so far as to defy the king. There will be other earldoms … in places where you are less unpopular.'

Tostig laughed again.

'Accept this humiliation now and then receive my reward later like a good little lap dog? Never!' he roared, then rose from the table and pointed at his brother.

'I lay this doom upon you Harold Godwinson … split our family and you split Inglalond. Split Inglalond and you will never be king!'

∞ ∞ ∞

We didn't sleep that night.

All expected Tostig to fight so Harold pulled us out of his hall and we retired to a field outside the gates of Yorvik where Harold's pavilion had already been raised, as though he had known the inevitable outcome of any confrontation with his brother.

There were a good many comings and goings during the night – mainly comings, for as the wolf light stole over us I perceived that our two hundred was swollen to several times that number. Edwin's army of Mercia had arrived throughout the night and Tostig – if he meant to make a stand – would have been dismayed to see our numbers from his walls.

When the sun was risen, Harold bade his heralds blow upon their horns, and then the army advanced. Harold, Gyrth and Leofwine rode horses, as did the brothers Edwin and Morcar, but the rest of the host was on foot, save two. Eadnoth and I carried *The Red Dragon* of Essex and *The Fighting Man*, so were given horses to carry those banners. I more than half expected a fight so was wary indeed as we approached the gates, but the soldiers simply stood aside and Harold passed through with young Morcar just behind him and we rode through the quiet town to the square before the minster. Then, when all the army had assembled, Harold bade the horns be blown again and announced in a mighty voice that Edward, king of Inglalond, had declared Tostig Godwinson outlaw and relieved him of the earldom. In his place he had appointed Morcar, son of Aelfgar, and let all here acknowledge that choice.

To my surprise there was tremendous cheering. People came pouring out of the houses as word spread that their lord had been replaced and a spontaneous celebration was soon under way. The townsfolk of Yorvik were singing and dancing – ale was produced from nowhere and open air kitchens were set up in minutes. Morcar was grinning widely as he perceived his popularity, but Harold was troubled and sent soldiers to find Tostig. He was nowhere at hand and men were saying he had left in the night with only twenty of his most trusted housecarls.

'Downriver he went, Lord,' reported one of the local soldiers in a thick accent difficult to understand. 'But he'll be back, mark my words. In no happy mood he were.'

Morcar stood upon a platform in the centre of the square and announced a return to the laws of Cnut and a reduction in local taxes, and swore to be a just and temperate lord. The cheering that greeted these words was deafening and Harold said to those closest, 'Here is a lesson for any man who would rule others. It saddens me to see Tostig's fall so celebrated.'

'He was most unwise in his judicial caprice,' agreed Carl, who had heard the news from the local clergy, 'and zealous to the point of greed in his exactions. Such will ever be resented.'

'Money is the liquor of government,' said Harold. 'We must have it, but drink too deep at our peril.'

He looked east to where the river Ouse wound its way towards the coast.

'Should we chase Tostig downriver?' he wondered aloud. 'There were more things I wished to say to him and I fear the mischief of his resentment.'

In the end it was decided that as no-one was truly sure of the direction of his flight there was no point in following.

'What'd I tell you?' muttered Elric. 'The next time Harold and Tostig meet will be with swords in their hands.'

'Perhaps,' I agreed, 'but where will Tostig find an army? He has few friends in Inglalond.'

'There are other armies,' said Elric. 'If I were Tostig I'd be going straight to the Bastard to offer my services.'

'He'll go to his brother in law first,' I replied.

'Flanders?' snorted Elric. 'He won't find any ambition there. Normandy's the place to get his vengeance bubbling ... or Denmark. The northern Danes in particular.'

It was a troubling prospect but, the way things stood, Tostig's unpopularity suggested that he would find friends difficult to come by.

Which meant our borders were safe.

Chapter 30

A Lesser Evil

We stayed a fortnight in Yorvik to see Morcar fully established in his earldom. Harold spent many hours instructing him and Edwin on how to govern and bade them also pay close attention to the coast.

'The Danes are ever a threat,' reminded Harold, 'but Tostig is our chief concern. Nothing would surprise me ... and he has returned in triumph from exile in the past.'

'That was with you and your father,' reminded Edwin, but Harold took no solace.

'He has seen it can be done ... and will judge himself the inheritor of Godwin's spirit. Aye, he will return ... sooner or later.'

It took us the best part of another fortnight to return to Lundene and when we did, at the beginning of November, Harold was unable to see the king. Edward was ailing and kept to his chamber, and soon the rumours arose – the king was dying.

'And so we come to the main action,' Harold remarked to his small council – the stallers and chief housecarls, and me. 'I will now speak openly of what many have surmised for all my adult life ... who shall be king after Edward?'

'You and none other,' said Gyrth and there was a murmur of agreement.

'But the aetheling Edgar's claim is better than mine,' replied Harold, 'and I have sworn to support his claim. I will not be charged faithless by any man.'

'The aetheling is a child,' snorted Eadnoth. 'The witan will be nervous and divided ... even if you are installed as his minister and protector.'

'Does it matter if the witan is nervous and divided?' asked Harold. 'The aetheling will take only a few years to grow into kingship.'

'The Bastard will strike next year,' said Skalpi, and there was a silence as this was digested.

'He won't come,' said Leofwine. 'We are too many for him ... he would need allies here and who could he possibly get, besides Tostig perhaps?'

'The Bastard will come, I tell you,' insisted Skalpi. 'Have we not spent months with him last summer and learned somewhat of his mood? He made much of your oath Harold ... he will expect you to support his own claim and charge you perfidious if you do not.'

Harold laughed.

'I swore to be his man in Normandy. I said nothing of Inglalond, except to say that I would return all favours and honours over here should he ever visit ... in circumstances that would make me his liege lord.'

'If that's the oath you swore,' said Skalpi, 'I doubt it was the oath William heard. He will come and damn you as faithless if you do not make him king.'

'What do you think Brand?'

I was shocked out of my reverie to be asked a direct question, but answered as my instinct suggested.

'He has ambition, Lord, or why would he say that he needs you to smooth his way in Inglalond? I heard him say that more than once.'

'But why should he believe he has any claim?' demanded Gyrth. 'He has no royal blood in Inglalond.'

'Half his blood is tannery blood,' laughed Leofwine, getting a smile from all but Harold.

'I suspect William believes himself to have been promised the throne by Edward,' I said. 'Certainly Edward loves the Normans and is ever attended by them ... that bishop of Fecamp is always at his side ... and William's ... whispering in their ears like a back lane cutpurse. It would surprise me not to learn that William has had reports from the bishop that appear to promise the throne, and it pleases him to believe them.'

'I believe you have guessed the way of it,' said Harold. 'It all fits and explains much else. But will William attempt an invasion if I support the aetheling?'

'My Lord and brother,' said Gyrth, 'I love Inglalond more than my life, so speak no treason … but you must not support the aetheling. I implore you to take the throne yourself. It is the ardent wish of the witan.'

'But I have sworn to support him,' replied Harold. 'The only way I could become king is if the king himself changed his mind about the succession and appointed me with his own hand. But he would cut his hand off before appointing a son of Godwin.'

'Then must we stand by and watch Inglalond invaded and torn apart for the sake of a little honour?' demanded Skalpi. 'It is a lesser evil to break faith and thereby keep our country.'

'It is a simple thing to advise another to break faith,' smiled Harold, 'but I am the one who must bear the taint of it throughout history and I would not be remembered as Harold the Faithless … Harold the Usurper.'

'If Brand is right,' said Skalpi, ' … and I am certain that he is … it means the Bastard will make a claim for the throne, but will he actually try to take it? Surely that is the main question.'

'If Harold is on the throne then I swear he will not dare,' insisted Gyrth, 'but if we commit the error of crowning the aetheling, then well may we look to the southern coast for William's ships.'

'I have made my position plain,' sighed Harold. 'If that means war, then we must prepare ourselves.'

He rose and stared out the multi-panelled window as the rain increased its violence against the glass.

'Where is Tostig?' he wondered aloud.

∞ ∞ ∞

Tostig marvelled at the beauty of William's palace at Rouen. The white stone shone in the mid-morning sunlight – the very picture of modern engineering – and Tostig was almost ashamed of the stone and timber hovels they called houses back in Inglalond. Much would change when he returned in triumph.

He passed under the arch with his retinue and was welcomed by a chamberlain at the door and bade to wait in an annex. Bowls of warm water were brought for the laving of hands and faces muddy from the road, and a small fire burned in a wide hearth. It was not much of a welcome, reflected Tostig, but better than nothing.

Eventually, the chamberlain informed him that William would see him and one other.

'Come Malgard,' said Tostig, 'you speak their tongue and have earned the honour.'

Malgard nodded but finished his toilet before joining Tostig at the entrance to William's hall. But even Malgard, usually careful to retain an aloof dignity, gaped with wonder at the majesty of the chamber. Tall white columns rose to meet a stone arched ceiling and hung with tapestries. A wide red carpet led to a dais upon which were raised two thrones, where William was seated with his wife Mathilda.

As Tostig approached he perceived that William was a large man in the fullness of his strength – very similar to Harold he seemed, and Tostig felt a flash of bitter anger, which he managed to suppress as he bowed before his host.

'Tostig Godwinson,' remarked William. 'I will not deceive you ... the name Godwinson is not welcome here.'

Tostig straightened up and replied, 'My Lord ... not all sons of Godwin are as faithless as Harold. I was hoping to make amends for my brother's poor conduct.'

'Indeed?' remarked William. 'And how would you achieve such a thing?'

'By ruling Inglalond as your vassal after Edward is dead.'

William stared at Tostig, and was silent for some time. Then he gestured at Malgard.

'Who is your companion?'

Tostig glanced at Malgard and replied, 'Lord ... allow me to introduce Malgard son of Rathgar ... a thegn of Inglalond whom I shall raise to earl after Inglalond is under your shield.'

Again William was silent as he considered, then he summoned the chamberlain.

'Have the guests and their men housed and prepare a table.'

Then, turning back to Tostig, he said, 'We shall talk again in an hour.'

Tostig and Malgard bowed and left the room.

∞ ∞ ∞

Malgard squeezed his eyes shut and rubbed at his temples. He was afflicted with a sickening headache but, for the first time since he had taken up with Tostig Godwinson, was starting to feel confident he had made the right decision.

The invitation had come as a great surprise. Malgard was amazed to learn that Earl Tostig even knew of his existence. But it soon became clear that Brand had become a man of influence in the court dominated by Harold, which meant Malgard's name was known and trouble would surely come for him in Stybbor – sooner rather than later. Malgard needed friends and Tostig had seemed a strong friend – and a man after his own heart when it came to squeezing wealth from his vassals. But the incident with Harold in Yorvik, followed by the cool reception in Flanders by Tostig's own brother in law had rocked Malgard's confidence.

That confidence was now partly restored with their reception in William's country. Even the fact that it was less than fulsome was somehow reason for belief that their fortunes had turned. William was a strong and immensely powerful ruler – his provisional or guarded support was far more substantial than the enthusiastic endorsement of lesser men and Malgard, despite his pounding headache, felt his doubts and burdens easing.

A further reason for confidence was Gorik. Malgard had left him in charge at Stybbor but he had also been given the task of watching Brand and waiting for an opportunity to strike. Malgard had been surprised to learn that Tostig also hated Brand – although for reasons he couldn't fathom. But he had provided money to pay for further slayers if needed by Gorik.

Yes, Tostig was a difficult man to fathom in many ways – and disturbingly changeable in his moods. One minute he could be merry and joking – and then for no apparent reason he would fly into a rage and strike at those closest. Mind you, he had shown Malgard nothing but respect so far, but a man so intemperate would eventually crack. Malgard knew that his turn would come to bear the brunt of Tostig's anger.

Perhaps if Gorik succeeded in ridding the world of Brand, it would be better to return to Stybbor as though nothing had happened and very slowly restore his fortunes under Harold – or whichever puppet king was put in place by Harold. Yes, that was certainly a viable option – and possibly the most likely given Gorik's skill.

Then again, there was a solidity and inevitability about the majesty of William. If anyone could take the throne of Inglalond, then William was the man and it would be wise to make himself useful to such a ruler.

Another wave of pain and nausea surged through his head and guts as there came a knock at the door, which opened to admit a serving girl. Ragged and beaten she looked, but Malgard could sense beneath that a beauty and powerful spirit. She placed a bowl of warm water on a table and curtsied with just enough of a dip to preclude a charge of insolence. Then as she made to leave the room, he moved between her and the door.

'What is your name?'

' … Emma.'

'Emma, lord,' admonished Malgard with a smile.

'Emma, lord,' she repeated, her eyes downcast.

Malgard examined her closely, feeling strangely aroused.

'There is something about you, Emma … something I like.'

She tried to step around him, but he held her back and said, 'Stay a while and tell me about William's household. My name is Malgard.'

'Malgard?' she looked up at him quickly, and at once he knew.

'Aah … you have heard of me?'

She didn't respond, but her blush was answer enough.

Malgard turned to the door and locked it, removing the key.

'Have a seat, Emma,' he said, indicating the bed, 'and tell how you heard of my name.'

She neither sat nor spoke and Malgard grinned, sensing her fear.

'Yes, there is definitely something about you,' he mused. 'You have too much dignity and poise for a servant … despite the rags and dirt. Here … '

He indicated the bowl of water she had brought.

'Why don't you wash your face so I can see the real Emma?'

'There is nothing to see,' she snapped. 'The real Emma is gone … and I am not permitted to wash.'

'Not permitted?'

'It is said that I am a filthy woman and that my filth must remain evident so that none ever mistake me again as virtuous.'

'Who says such an unkind thing to such a pretty girl?' asked Malgard, intrigued and enchanted by her.

'Duke William.'

'I am sure there is some mistake,' said Malgard, taking the sponge from the bowl and squeezing it. Then he approached her and began to wipe her face. She did not resist but stood with her eyes closed as Malgard, almost tenderly, removed the dirt, revealing a fading yellow bruise by her right temple but also a face of astonishing beauty.

'You are beautiful,' he breathed. 'Why don't you remove the rest of your clothes and allow me to wash you completely?'

She didn't move, but neither did she resist when Malgard lifted the ragged smock over her head, leaving her completely naked.

'Beautiful indeed,' breathed Malgard, feeling an ache in his groin he hadn't felt for years.

He washed her very thoroughly and she said not a word. When the job was complete he bade her sit by him on the bed.

'Now, Emma … please tell me exactly how you heard my name.'

'Brand told me about you.'

There was a look of pure contempt on her face, and before he knew it he had slapped her and jumped off the bed as though burned. She stared defiance at him and suddenly Malgard could no longer control the violence burning within. He pushed her face down on the bed, then tore his own breeches off and dragged her towards him. She didn't resist but he didn't care. Forcing himself into her, Malgard felt a wild exhilaration as though he were fucking Brand himself – mounting him and showing him the true depth of his downfall.

'You are truly a filthy woman, Emma,' sneered Malgard, quickly approaching climax. 'A filthy, filthy woman and so you are a perfect vessel for all my disgust … my loathing … and my hatred for Brand. It is I … Malgard … who shall prevail … and Brand … who will die … in the filth … and mud … as he should … have done … when I murdered his father.'

Malgard's words came out in short angry bursts as he thrust the last of his hatred and bitterness into her, then pushed her away. In fact he was tempted to break her neck – that would have been the perfect ending to their tryst.

But Malgard was a practical man. He had not enjoyed a woman so much in years and was already looking forward to the next time.

'Get out,' he said, unlocking the door. 'Get out ... but bring another bowl of water when I am ready to sleep later.'

She dragged herself off the bed, pulled the smock back over her head and left the room giving Malgard such a venomous look that he roared with laughter.

His headache was completely gone.

∞ ∞ ∞

'It cannot be done.'

Two hours later, Tostig and Malgard sat with William and his senior retainers – chief of whom were William fitzOsbern and a bishop named John with whom Tostig was familiar from Edward's court.

'Inglalond is too strong,' said William. 'I know I am Edward's choice for the crown of Inglalond, but how can I press my suit if Harold opposes me?'

'Inglalond is strong,' agreed Tostig, '... but divided. A strong leader with the right allies could prevail.'

'And you are that leader?' enquired William.

'With your blessing and support,' said Tostig, 'I could lead an army from the north while you attacked from the south. It would give the parties opposed to Harold a banner to rally by.'

'Opposed to Harold,' echoed William. 'So he does expect to be king ... despite Edward's promise to me?'

'He says not,' said Tostig, ' ... even though he knows he is the witan's choice. But Harold is still the man to be faced, whether he fights for the aetheling Edgar, or on his own account.'

'The witan,' sneered fitzOsbern. 'How does a group of lords prevail over the choice of the king? It is madness! Blasphemy!'

'It is the way they do things in Inglalond,' sighed William. 'I will do away with the witan if ever I cross the sea. But Harold will not support the aetheling.'

The last comment was so surprising that all paused in their deliberations and waited for William to explain himself.

'If Harold truly supported the aetheling,' said William, 'he would have had no qualm in swearing an oath to me. The oath would have enhanced the aetheling's position and obliged me to protect him if that was Edward's dying preference ... whatever he might previously have promised the Duke of Normandy.'

William allowed himself a rare smile and said, 'Nay ... Harold thought himself clever in avoiding the marriage that would have bound him to me. It frees him to take the crown when Edward is gone, but in so doing, he has also freed me from supporting the aetheling, if that be Edward's written will.'

William laughed, and the others stayed silent – perceiving the Duke was in one of his rare inclusive moods.

'Now, when Edward dies, Harold will manage the politics of the witan and have himself declared king. And I need only remember Edward's promise to me ... and Harold's oath ... and may legitimately claim that any alternative arrangement is void. I, William of Normandy, should be the true king of Inglalond.'

There were growls of support from the Normans at the table and Malgard felt excitement – to be sitting at a table where such mighty destiny was being forged. There were huge opportunities in such a massive undertaking as was implicit in William's words.

'But, as I said before,' said William, his mood suddenly deflating, ' ... the enterprise of Inglalond is too hard, if Harold opposes it.'

There was a gloomy silence as they understood that William would not challenge Harold, but Bishop John of Fecamp cleared his throat and said to Tostig, 'Who are the magnates opposed to Harold?'

Tostig's head was still whirling slightly with the possibilities outlined by William, and indeed felt slightly foolish that he had not come to the same conclusion. It even occurred to him that his interests were best served by being back at Harold's side, but nothing could forgive Harold's betrayal at Yorvik and Tostig controlled his anger with an effort.

'There are many in the north,' he replied, 'who would oppose Harold. And Malcolm of Scotland is my friend. He will aid us.'

'But if there are so many in the north who would take your part,' said William, 'why are you here now in exile?'

'I was betrayed,' snarled Tostig, his malice bare. 'My own brother stole upon me like a thief in the night … bringing the army of Mercia.'

'It is a formidable army?' enquired fitzOsbern, with a glance at William.

'It is led by a child,' said Tostig. 'Were I not taken so unaware I should achieve its destruction easily … especially if men knew the choice was between Harold and me … with you at my side.'

William considered Tostig and then lifted his eyes to the ceiling in contemplation.

'It would be a difficult and expensive business,' he said at last, ' … an invasion of Inglalond. And I have seen Harold in the field … he is a good leader of men. No matter how many I brought with me, he would have the advantage both of numbers and position.'

'He has no horses,' said Tostig.

All of the Normans glanced up in sudden interest.

'No horses?' enquired fitzOsbern.

'A handful perhaps,' conceded Tostig. 'Many times I urged Harold to fight as the Normans fight … on heavy horses built for the task but he prefers the shield wall.'

'Archers?' asked William.

'All men can use a bow,' said Tostig, 'but Harold has no tactical groups of archers … indeed he regards the use of archery in war as dishonourable.'

'Does he indeed?' remarked William. 'Although I am intrigued to learn Harold has *any* concept of honour after his behaviour here.'

'There is also this, Lord,' said Malgard, speaking for the first time. 'You do not need to defeat Harold's army. You need only to defeat Harold. The rest are just mice and will quail without their leader.'

William stared long at Malgard, then turned to the bishop. 'What is your opinion of the other magnates?'

'I agree there are none capable of leading … other than Harold,' said the bishop. 'Of course, it may well be that Harold supports the aetheling … but he is still the man we need to remove. He would lead any defending army, whether on the aetheling's part or his own.'

'Even though he swore an oath to me!' snapped William, in a flash of wrath that took Tostig and Malgard by surprise. 'He should be supporting *me* in Inglalond.'

Then as swiftly as it appeared his anger was checked.

'I am a practical man,' said William, calm once again. 'I admit I coveted Inglalond but gave up on the notion once Harold revealed his perfidious nature. There is much to lose.'

'But much to gain,' said the bishop. 'Inglalond is a wealthy land.'

'I have not the soldiers,' said William, 'and neither does he,' he added, nodding at Tostig.

'What if the pope were to learn of Harold's oath to you?' mused the bishop. 'I have told you many times that you are Edward's choice above Harold. Indeed I have heard Edward demand of Harold that he support you. Surely that gives you a higher claim than the Earl of Wessex to the throne and if he will not honour his oath then he is perfidious indeed.'

'And that helps me … how?' asked William.

'The pope is already vexed with the Anglais,' continued Bishop John, 'and will not give a pallium to recognise the choice of Archbishop Stigand. With the support of our friends such as Lanfranc … and even Hildebrand in Rome, the Holy Father might be persuaded that Harold is a foresworn oath breaker and that your claim … based on Edward's promise which Harold swore to recognise … is the better one.'

'I still don't see any practical benefit,' said William, his impatience turning to anger.

The bishop remained unruffled.

'With the pope's blessing, Lord, you could appeal to all of Christendom. All the greatest knights and mercenaries from here to Hungary would flock to your papal banner. I estimate you could lead an army of more than ten thousand into Inglalond … ten thousand professional fighters against Harold's fyrd of farriers and farm lads.'

'Horses … archers … professional infantry,' urged Malgard, ' … use them strategically just to kill Harold and the battle is won.'

William got up from his chair and paced back and forth between the table and the darkened window like a caged beast in the circus of Rome. Then he paused at the window and stared into the night.

'And how exactly do you fit into this?' he demanded, turning back to Tostig.

'Well,' said Tostig, with a glance at Malgard, 'you will be busy with your own realm. I thought to rule Inglalond in your name.'

'How thoughtful of you,' laughed William. 'How very noble and generous to do me such an honour. I win a realm and you rule it in my name.

'No!' he suddenly shouted, thumping his palm on the table. 'If I take on the enterprise of Inglalond I shall rule it myself. You I will recognise as Earl of Northumbria, if ... *if* you provide me with an army in the north. If you can't do at least that then you are not worth a pinch of shit, so why should I give you anything?'

'I can bring an army from the north,' insisted Tostig, 'but I want Mercia also.'

'Do you?' said William, bringing his face close to Tostig's. 'Well, you'd better bring an army big enough to convince me!'

Chapter 31

A Form of Treason

All through December the earls and thegns of Inglalond assembled in Lundene for the Christmas court. In normal circumstances, most of the earls and perhaps a third of the thegns, who numbered in their hundreds, would attend, but with news spreading that the king was dying the numbers were far greater than usual and I kept an eye out for my uncle. With Edward on his deathbed, I had little fear that my charge of outlawry could be made out, so was just about ready to denounce Malgard and challenge him if he showed his face.

The other thought that intrigued me was the true nature of Harold's ambition. In council he would constantly say that he would not take the kingship unless Edward gave it to him, but my private conversations with Harold frequently suggested he still hoped to be king. How else could he speak of giving me an earldom if the crown was not in his thoughts?

Elric had no doubt.

'He will manage it somehow,' he laughed. 'Harold means to be king...he just wants the formalities to appear in order.'

I wasn't entirely sure of that, and could not conceive of any way the king might be persuaded to name Harold as king after himself. In the meantime, the normally festive period of December darkened into deepening gloom as the king ailed – attended ever by his wife, Harold's sister. It was said that she grieved sorely for her husband, despite his ill treatment of her in the past, and sat by his bedside for long hours ministering to his needs and recording his words in case he said anything of import for the realm. It was reported that the king kept having the same dream in which two monks appeared before him. They were godly men known to Edward in his childhood and they reported to him that God was angry with Inglalond, for its people were impious and its rulers divided.

One ruler, at least, was doing his best to heal the rents in the fabric of Inglalond. Harold wedded Edith, the sister of Edwin and Morcar, in a quiet ceremony just before Christmas. Harold's mother and sister refused to attend the feast, to Harold's pain. I was there with the rest of the stallers and closest housecarls, despite my outlawed status, and was surprised at the subdued feeling. There was an air of hopelessness and if not for the unstinting industry of the many servants I believe the realm might simply have collapsed under the weight of despair.

Elric, at least, was ever in good cheer.

'I'll never forget my life in the woods,' he said, heaping his trencher for the third or fourth time. 'While there are warm halls, ale and women at hand I'll not be downhearted.'

I laughed at that, but was affected by the general mood. The king had done nothing right by me, but he was still the king and cornerstone of civil society. If only there was clarity over the succession then the general mood might have been lighter.

Harold presided over the Christmas court and every day I sat with Elric in the wings, watching to see whether Malgard arrived. It was said that nearly every thegn in the land had come to pay their respects to Edward and see the new king, whoever he might be.

For a couple of days the aetheling Edgar was present with his uncle and some more distant relatives. He was a lad of about eight or nine and small for his age, recalling little of his grandsire, Edmund the Ironsides. White faced and trembling he sat on a dais to Harold's left, unable to meet the eye of nearly all who greeted him, but at last he was sent away for his health.

'Harold wanted them to see the aetheling,' whispered Elric. 'He wants all the realm to know that choosing Edgar is impossible if we are to live unmolested by William.'

Once again I was surprised by Elric's insight into the minds of our leaders, and had no doubt he was correct – duplicitous though it seemed of Harold, of whom I found such politics difficult to believe.

Still, if scaring the earls and thegns had truly been Harold's motive in displaying the aetheling, his plan could not have been more effective. As soon as Edgar departed Harold was visited constantly by embassies and delegations representing all the nobility of Inglalond and urged to take the throne for himself.

'It is almost a form of treason if you do not!' swore Edwin of Mercia. 'Nothing will encourage the Bastard more than a child on the throne he claims for himself.'

But Harold would not be swayed and the mood of the court sunk ever lower with the impending death of the king and the confusion that must result.

Two days after Christmas Edward stirred himself and joined the court, but all marked how frail he seemed. Elric was all but laughing aloud.

'This too is Harold's work,' he said. 'Having shown the nobles a child, he now shows them a dying old codger, while he sits alongside in all his noble grace and power.'

Harold certainly looked every inch the king while Edward appeared to have one foot already in the world of ghosts – shaking and mumbling and requiring his wife's constant attention. Soon he was removed back to his chamber and the demands that Harold obey the witan and be king after Edward were shouted openly.

'He will manage it, I tell you,' grinned Elric, unaffected by the gloom. 'How can he refuse the command of his nobles?'

The New Year passed and the story of the king's recurring dream had grown. Apparently the monks that appeared in the dream would inform him that God was angry with Inglalond and would send foreign devils with fire and sword to punish the impiety and division of her people.

'But will not God be merciful?' asked Edward, in his dream.

'Inglalond will not be restored to her proper state,' declared the monks, 'until a tree split in half by lightning is repaired and grows green again.'

And because such a thing was impossible without God's intervention, the mood of the court became fey. As the crisis deepened, Harold summoned me on the freezing fifth night of the New Year.

'Come with me Brand … the king approaches the end and there are words that must be said and heard by witnesses enough to establish the truth of all that passes.'

They were strange and portentous words to which I did not trust myself to respond. But I followed him, and to my great surprise he led me to Edward's privy chamber where the king had weakened to the point that both archbishops of Inglalond attended him – Stigand of Caunterbury and Ealdred of Yorvik. Such could only mean that the king's death was close and I was both alarmed and embarrassed to be invited to his bedside. Harold's mother, sister and two of his brothers were present, Gyrth and Leofwine. Aethelnoth and Eadnoth also were present, plus Edwin and Morcar (ignoring me) but not their sister, Harold's new bride. The king's physician was present but he sat with his head in his hands looking as sick as Edward. Other churchmen also were present, including Carl – one of Harold's personal chaplains – and I found myself reflecting on how much had changed since I first met him in the forest, wearing a thrall's collar and looking himself like a fighting Dane.

There was a low chanting coming from the two archbishops and I realised, to my dismay that it was the last rites they administered as Edward lay grey-faced and mumbling with Edith his wife washing his brow. Stigand it was who took charge at this point. As his brother bishop continued the Latin, Stigand spoke to the king, and said, 'Edward, king of all Inglalond ... our Lord in heaven now summons you, and so the time has come when you must name the man to succeed you on the throne.'

Edward stared at him, his expression unchanged, but managed the words, 'I have chosen ... all know it.'

'The aetheling Edgar is a child ... not yet ready to rule. Who will you name before him?'

'I chose William of Normandy to be his protector,' replied Edward in a wheezing whisper that turned into a gasping cough.

When the king was at peace again, Stigand said, 'William refused your commission, Lord. He would not swear to Harold to recognise the aetheling and did not deliver the relics you desired for your new minster.'

Edward's eyes suddenly glistened with tears. 'All is in ruin,' he cried. 'Clearly I have lived a life of sin for surely God would have made my passing untroubled had I not.'

'You are as close to being without sin as any mortal man,' replied

Stigand with a gentle smile, 'but although you have not left a son, you can at least ensure the continuity of your realm and the estates of your family.'

'My wife,' replied Edward.

'William will not honour her,' said Stigand, his voice rising slightly, 'but her brother will.'

'Harold?' asked Edward, as though the idea had truly only occurred to him in that moment.

'Harold is strong,' encouraged Stigand, turning to glance at the tall man standing at the end of the bed, clad in silver mail – the very picture of Saxon strength and nobility. 'Harold will keep the kingdom safe until the aetheling is ready … or, if the king were to determine otherwise in the most solemn moment of his life … '

The kings eyes moved slowly from Stigand, he turned to Harold and beckoned him closer. Harold knelt by the king and took his hand, withered and frail as a feather.

'What does the king command of me?'

'You will honour your sister?' asked Edward.

'I always have and ever will,' replied Harold, his own eyes glistening with grief.

Edward went silent for a while, and though the tension in the room was like a full-drawn bowstring, he heeded it not.

'My heart forebodes that all choices are ill,' said Edward at last. 'But if I can guarantee the honour and estate of my wife Edith … whom I confess, I have not treated as she deserved … then I will at least do that.'

He pointed at Harold, 'You also, Harold, deserve my confession. I have not treated you as you deserved … and now God punishes me for it with a body wracked before its time. You will honour your sister?'

'I will,' repeated Harold.

'Then into your hands I commend my kingdom,' said Edward, 'but only—'

'Behold the king!' interrupted Stigand, and the release of tension was like the bursting of a storm.

'Behold the king!' cried the stallers and churchmen, with only Edith looking upset at the head of her husband's bed.

Edward groaned such a note of pain that it surely seemed he uttered from across the threshold of death, and in that moment a cock crowed out in the darkness and a tinge of light limned the edges of the window panels.

'The rain has ended,' said Stigand, 'and a new dawn graces your kingdom, Lord. God shows His approval of a good and wise decision.'

But Edward spoke no more, and Edith began to weep softly.

And Harold swept from the room, calling at once for his council.

Chapter 32

Poachers and Other Criminals Condemned

If I'd been embarrassed to be present at the death of one king, I was not surprised to be present at the coronation of the next.

Only six hours later, Harold, the second of that name, Godwinson, stood in the nave of Edward's new west minster decked in royal robes, his brow anointed with oil, his head crowned. The king of Inglalond.

I stood in the fourth row with Elric and Skalpi as we acclaimed the king, standing between the archbishops Stigand and Ealdred and looking reborn as a creature of God – glowing in the magical light pouring through the vast coloured window to the west. So holy and magnificent was the sight that I remembered with guilty discomfort my doubts regarding the truth of God in our lives – only a few years back. Now I knew better. Now I knew that God was real and was in awe of all His works – not least His manner of testing me, His most imperfect servant.

Again and again we acclaimed King Harold, and the joy of the witan overflowed like too much wine. Edward's dying act had been to name Harold his successor and the witan had instantly endorsed it for Harold was strong and Inglalond was now united under him – truly united in a way it never had been before because all knew only Harold Godwinson could hold it together and defend it from the Bastard.

Indeed, Harold commenced his defence of the realm immediately. He spent several days hearing disputes and giving his judgments, but at the same time he held war councils and sent men forth with orders for building works and arrangements regarding the fyrd. Edwin and Morcar were sent back north with orders to fortify their coastal towns and establish networks of watch towers at the mouths of all important rivers. The same was done along the southern coast – or rather what had already been done was improved as Harold had been Earl of Wessex for some years and had already made the south secure.

He issued orders for the building of more ships, coins were struck with his image, and while those coins bore the inscription 'Pax', foundries turned out axes, swords and spears in such a frenzy of activity as had never before been seen on such a scale. In only a month Inglalond bristled with arms – soldiers were everywhere – in Lundene at least – and, knowing that the fyrd when summoned could number as many as thirty thousands, there was no need to fear anyone.

'William will have spies in our midst,' reckoned Harold. 'I have banished that Bishop of Fecamp and confiscated the land given him by Edward, but he will have eyes and ears at his command and news of all we do will soon be known in Normandy … which is well. I want William to know that he can never challenge the might of Inglalond.'

'He'll have to get here first,' laughed Skalpi.

'Do not underestimate him,' warned Harold, with surprising earnestness. 'I learnt much of his mind in our time together and I swear he covets Inglalond and will take it if he can.'

For me, Harold had a special job. He drew me aside one morning, a month into his reign, and said, 'I have not forgotten my vague promises in respect of an earldom.'

I was embarrassed by his words and hoped he did not suspect I had been waiting for that very reward.

'It is enough for me to be at your side and making myself useful,' I managed to say and Harold boomed his usual laugh.

'Useful? You are more than useful, Brand the Reliable … but you shall have your proper station … when the time is right.'

That was a relief. I'd half expected him to make me an earl on the spot and was not dressed for it. We were standing in the yard of his hall which adjoined the minster and in the first week of February it was unseasonably warm. I was wearing only a linen shirt and leather jerkin and was warm from archery practice with Elric, who had made himself scarce at Harold's approach.

'My brother Gyrth is currently Earl of East Anglia, in which your thegnship lies. I think I will probably give him Wessex and you East Anglia, but not until I know that there is no threat from William.'

'You know,' I said, ' ... we have been so heavily occupied the last few years, I have hardly given Stybbor a thought ... except my dreams of revenge against Malgard.'

'Ah yes, Malgard,' mused Harold. 'He did not attend the Christmas court ... nor my coronation.'

'He did not Lord ... and I was greatly looking forward to seeing him.'

'I'm sure you were!' laughed Harold. 'In fact, I think it is time for you to correct that state of affairs. You should take a hundred men to Stybbor and arrest him if it might be done.'

Instantly my heart leapt and I punched the air with a shout of imminent vengeance.

'But not just any men,' said Harold, with an odd smile.

'What do you mean?' I asked, detecting something strange in his manner.

'What did you notice about the Norman army ... their manner of fighting?' asked Harold.

'Well, they prefer horses to their own feet and do not use the shield wall as we do.'

'What else?'

I thought for a moment, remembering our campaign with William in Brittany.

'Archers,' I said. 'They make much use of archers.'

'They do indeed,' agreed Harold. 'And organise them in teams. I want you to create me a team of archers to deploy as the Normans do ... to weaken the shield wall, or any other placement of soldiers ... or even cavalry before it reaches our own position.'

The possibilities were suddenly huge in my mind and I was impatient to start immediately. However, I perceived a problem straight away.

'It takes time to make an archer,' I said, 'and most of your regular soldiers are not trained to it.'

'Correct,' agreed Harold, 'which is why I want you to scour the local gaols and stews for poachers and other criminals condemned.

Let them be pardoned if they have skill with a bow and will serve you.'

I was aghast at this turn, but Harold gave me a dozen hardened warriors to keep my recruits in check. And of course there was Elric.

Like Valla, Elric was a master bowman and delighted with our assignment. Skill with a bow was not esteemed among warriors but regarded as a peasant's art. I, who had witnessed at close hand what Valla had achieved as a fifteen year old girl, had a somewhat higher regard for archery and was keen to investigate its strategic possibilities. But first we needed to find our archers.

We started with the gaols and dungeons of Lundene. Few people stayed long in a gaol as serfdom, mutilation or execution were the norms. Anyone locked up was usually awaiting one of these so we had no shortage of prisoners keen to transmute their sentence to service in my archery troop. But first they had to pass Elric's test.

At each location a butt was set up with a red outer circle and a yellow centre circle. The butt was placed thirty paces away and each prisoner, closely attended by armed guards, was given three arrows. To pass the test they needed to get two out of three inside the red circle or one in the yellow. It was a feat beyond most but steadily our numbers grew and more than one had put all three arrows in the gold. But at one location on the eastern outskirts of the city a fellow due to be hanged the following morning missed the butt completely with his first two arrows, so was required to hit the bullseye with his third. He took careful aim, then turned with his arrow aimed directly at my chest.

Immediately swords were raised around him and Elric thrust a shield in front of me, but I pushed it away and said, 'What do you mean to achieve with this action? It will only see you killed today instead of tomorrow.'

'What is a day?' he replied. 'I have not learned the bow so cannot pass your test … but I doubt even I could miss from five paces, so add me to your troop or die.'

I studied the man. Young, wiry, filthy – with dried blood in his hair but eyes burning with determination.

'I believe you mean to do it,' I said, and waved aside one of the soldiers who had crept to within striking distance behind him.

'Nothing surer,' replied the man, and I noted his hands were steady, betraying none of the strain he must have been feeling.

'I'll make a deal with you,' I said. 'As a reward for your resourcefulness and bravery, I'll allow you to join if you can at least hit the butt with your last arrow.'

He stared at me a few moments, then turned back to the butt.

'Relax,' I told him, even as the pent up tension flowed out of me. 'Picture the arrow in the centre of the butt and release.'

Seconds later an arrow thunked into the butt, just clipping the gold. The man stared in wonder at his handiwork, as Elric strode forward and punched him hard in the guts.

'Welcome to the archery troop,' said Elric as the man collapsed groaning into the mud. 'You even think about pulling another trick like that and I'll cut your fucking throat.'

∞ ∞ ∞

A week later we had our hundred. Harold provided bows, arrows, knives plus a handful of bowyers and fletchers to make and repair the weapons and even a wagon and horses to carry cooking gear and whatever else we could need to get quickly from place to place as might be required. With myself, Elric, my twelve marshalling warriors and the servants there were a hundred and thirty of us bivouacked in a field north-east of Lundene. There we trained for another week, established which of the archers had the best skills and which could best understand the various offensive and defensive tactics we meant to employ in war when it came. We quickly came to appreciate how devastating a concentrated flight of arrows could be, so the main tactic was the selection of targets, co-ordination of shooting and retreat. I split the archers into five teams of twenty under five leaders, one of whom was the young fellow who had threatened me with an arrow.

Walt was his name, and he quickly impressed with his intelligence and ability to spot a target or a threat. We had the teams compete against each other in a series of contests and Walt's team emerged victorious – not least in the provision of meat which was mostly hunted in the fields and forest around us.

There were only two desertions in that time – a father and son who slipped off in the night and were quickly forgotten. The rest of them, felons to a man, seemed surprisingly proud to be part of a new troop under the king's banner. 'Death from distance' became our motto (suggested by Elric, remembering one of William's men) and before I knew it the men had invented marching songs that boasted of the damage we would do to anyone who challenged us (and lauded also the bravery and brilliance of their leader – much to my embarrassment).

As for marching, the men were delighted to receive their first assignment – a hike into East Anglia to retake the lands of their captain and arrest the evil Malgard – usurper and murderer. It was a romantic notion and the stories (started by Elric) about the campfires got the men into quite a passion, again, much to my embarrassment. I was greatly touched by the men's affection and it just goes to show how quickly a felon can be reclaimed if you give him a job and a bit of self-respect.

We stayed at the inn at Breahinga, where nearly six years previously I had eluded Malgard's slayers while being tempted by a whore. One had been killed by Elric but the other had escaped and I had to think for a moment to remember his name – the honey haired fellow. Gorik! That was him – and the last I'd seen him he'd received a searing poker to the face for his trouble. No doubt he was dead by now.

I asked for news of Stybbor but it was a small and remote place and none at the inn knew of it, despite it being only two or three days march to the east, depending on weather and roads.

It was a bitterly cold day at the end of February when I started to recognise landmarks that told me we were only hours from my home village and started to feel excitement.

'Do you mean simply to march in?' asked Elric. 'Or do you wish to scout the village and hall first for signs of strength?'

'We will go carefully,' I replied, 'but we also go quickly. I do not wish any rats to escape the trap.'

'It may be that we ourselves walk into a trap,' said Elric, and while he was right to advise caution, I sincerely doubted that Malgard could match our strength and I wanted him caught before he could lock my father's hall against me and force a siege.

I began to know uncertainty when we passed the first of the abandoned hovels. A house I had known on the western edge of my family's domain had more or less collapsed and was overgrown with bramble. No animals clustered in its yards.

Further houses were in similar condition along the road and the fields that should have been bare and ready for planting were also overgrown. There was a sense of abandonment and I began to feel a strange fear – even that the Danes had methodically slaughtered all in the district on that evil night my family had been destroyed.

Finally we saw smoke above the trees and knuckles whitened on bow staves as we approached the village of Stybbor.

Only the monastery looked the same. The rest of the village looked as though it had been trampled flat and then the wreckage used to build a pathetic collection of huts and shanties to house the starving handful that remained.

Clearly there were no soldiers around to defend Malgard's position. Elric blew on a hunting horn and maybe thirty people – ragged, filthy and underfed – trickled from the various hovels.

Surrounded by my men in a wide half-circle, I bid the villagers approach and then announced, 'I am Brand son of Holgar … the rightful thegn of Stybbor returned. Where is the usurper Malgard?'

Most didn't seem to know what I was talking about, but recognition and wonder flickered in the eyes of some and then a voice I recognised said, 'Malgard is gone.'

I turned and gave a cry of joy.

'Brother Waldo! You still live!'

Waldo had barely changed since the day of my brother's wedding. He was thinner and more ragged, but the bushy white eyebrows and ice-blue eyes were exactly as I remembered him and I strode forward to embrace him.

'You still live also young Brand,' he gasped as I squeezed the breath from him. 'We thought you dead these five years. How is your Latin?'

'Not as good as my Norman,' I replied, as more starvelings and monks emerged to swell the bedraggled throng.

'So where is Malgard?' I asked after the general celebration had diminished when the villagers understood that the son of Holgar had returned to put the village to rights.

'He's not been seen for six months,' said Waldo, who was now abbot after the death of Brother Oldred two years prior. 'But much evil he did in the days of his rule.'

The village and lands had supported over three hundred people in my father's time but there would have been less than a hundred still scratching a living there now. I sent two teams of archers out to hunt and forage while the rest of us set up an outdoor kitchen on the green in front of the church where I had last seen my family.

'Where are my family buried?' I asked Waldo, and he was able to show me a mound among others unmarked in the churchyard.

'Malgard promised to erect a monument,' said Waldo, 'but he never got to it.'

'I will get to him,' I said, the rage of vengeance rising within me. I had been so occupied with Harold's campaigns, and the need for anonymity given my outlawry, that I had not given as much thought to Malgard and revenge as I should have. It had always been something I would get to when the time was ripe – when I had grown enough to give strength and sinew to the silver-hilted dagger of vengeance.

'I must go to the house,' I muttered.

This had been the last thing to do and I dreaded it. The thought of Malgard living in my father's hall as thegn almost made me retch but I summoned Elric and, accompanied by Walt's team, we walked the half mile to my family home.

Waldo also accompanied us and described Malgard's misrule as we went.

'He did much to oppress the people since you went away,' said Waldo. 'Ever more fines and taxes he required of a land that could only give so much … and the abundance of Holgar's time soon dwindled into poverty and starvation. People were punished … even murdered if they tried to leave. He wanted men tied to the land as they have never been in this shire, and every little they made he took for himself.'

'I shall announce a tax amnesty for three years,' I said. 'That will bring industry back to the shire.'

'That would be just and wise,' agreed Waldo, 'and a fitting gesture from the son of Holgar … whose memory is still honoured, I assure you.'

My father's hall looked smaller than I remembered, but it was not abandoned. A handful of servants assembled in the yard as we approached and I recognised Everard, my father's chamberlain, and some of the wenches, a couple of whom nursed infants.

Everard's eyes filled with tears when he knew me and confirmed that Malgard had not been home for at least seven months.

'But his sergeant has been an occasional visitor,' said Everard. 'A right spawn of Satan that one ... and a slayer of many good men for no reason beyond his own amusement.'

I knew it could not be Angdred, as I had witnessed his death myself.

'Who is this sergeant?' I demanded.

'Gorik,' replied Everard, in a voice hushed as though Gorik might appear at any moment to punish him for speaking his name.

'So ... Gorik lives,' I sighed. 'Does he have a scar?'

'A terrible scar,' confirmed Everard, 'on the right side of his face.'

'Good,' I replied. 'I barely remember the bastard but the scar will help me know him when I see him.'

I quickly walked through the hall, remembering, but my place was back in the village and all of the servants joined us for the return. When we got back a celebration was in full swing. Salted meat from our wagon was stewed and augmented with fresh coneys and hares brought in by the foragers. Most of the villagers were able to contribute a little in the way of grains, herbs and pulses but I bid them save as much as possible for March planting and made my announcement about the tax amnesty, which was greeted with much rejoicing.

I spoke long with Waldo and Everard and learned something of Malgard's movements. All had heard rumours that he was with the Danes the night my family were killed. He had angrily denied that, at first, and threatened to execute anyone caught spreading the tale, but as the years went by and the village crushed into disrepair through his wasteful rule, he went more openly with Danish visitors and was even rumoured to be raiding his neighbours further up the coast.

'But, as I said,' said Everard, 'he's not returned for some time. Perhaps he is dead?'

'That would be convenient,' I replied, 'but my heart forebodes he lives yet and could still do some evil. It is his nature.'

The chief concern of the villagers was the fact of my imminent departure.

'It is one thing to return and deliver us from Malgard's rule,' said Everard, 'but if you depart for an unknown period, he might return with soldiers and how can we stop him taking over again? Can you not leave some men to protect us?'

It was a reasonable request and I discussed the matter with Elric and Aethelstan, the leader of my twelve swordsmen.

'The trick is to leave enough to defend the village ... but not so many as to overburden the local food resources as the village gets back on its feet,' said Elric.

In the end, I put Aethelstan in charge of Stybbor with three of his soldiers and a dozen archers who would stay behind after we left. They were instructed to hunt and otherwise assist in the rebuilding, as well as the defence of Stybbor should Malgard return.

Two weeks later, much had been achieved. We had restored some order to the village and rebuilt all of the houses as well as we might, given the materials available. Fields were readied for planting and a good supply of seed stock had been purchased from neighbouring shires. Monuments had been raised on the mounds in the churchyard and I spent some time in tearful remembrance at the mound where my family was buried – reading and rereading the names of my father, mother, brother and sisters and trying to recall every little moment of the life I had shared with them.

With the restoration of the village I had the feeling that much in my life had been put right. Only two problems remained – my unaccomplished revenge on Malgard was a source of bitterness, but there was something else that gnawed at my heart and caused me greater grief with every passing day.

On the morning we were due to return to Lundene, I went alone across the Arwan and entered the woods where I had escaped from Angdred. Quite quickly I found the clearing in which I had first encountered Valla, dressed in skins and carrying the wounded dog. I had been naked, I recalled, but so immediately smitten by Valla I had not noticed my disadvantage for several moments.

I had loved her immediately, and despite her many insults and threats to geld me over the next week or so, she had claimed, before we were separated in Wales, that she had also loved me at first meeting and had treated me ill solely through self-protection. 'The more I loved you the more I had to scorn you,' she had explained, and I found myself smiling fondly. It had been more than a year since the Wales campaign. More than a year since the love of my life had gone to pursue her great task, and all I had left was the recurring dream in which she fulfilled all my wishes but bade me lie with no other woman.

This then was the source of my torment. If the words 'lie with no other woman' meant not to fuck in the normal sense, then I had remained true. If, however, the words were capable of broader meaning, then my carnal adventures with Emma in Normandy must mean I had broken my word. It was a gut-wrenching regret that I felt for my behaviour, even though it had been ordered by Harold, but if it meant Valla would not return then I knew I would never be happy and complete in the rest of my life.

∞ ∞ ∞

Gorik could not believe his luck.

He had been dismayed, upon returning to Stybbor, to find it a hive of happy activity and filled with soldiers, but fortunately he had not been foolish enough to show himself. He had watched from a distance until he perceived that Brand had indeed returned and retaken Stybbor.

Malgard would not be pleased, but they had anticipated this possibility with the death of King Edward and the rise of Harold. That was the main reason that Malgard had gone off with Tostig – to further Tostig's interests, and thereby his own – and at the same time avoid Brand and his royal-supported vengeance.

Now Gorik peered along the shaft of the arrow that was aimed at Brand's back only fifteen paces away. It was such a simple matter – loose the shaft and Brand would be dead – but after a few more seconds, he lowered the arrow and touched the puckered scar that ran across his cheek and into the hair above his right ear, remembering with a rising fury the pain it had caused him. He wanted Brand to feel pain before he died and know it was Gorik that caused that pain. Just shooting him in the back was not enough to square the balance.

Gorik's eyes swept the forest and he listened intently for the presence of others. If he could get close enough he might fetch Brand a blow to the back of the head and spirit him away to a place where he could deal out pain and death at his leisure, but Brand was a big man and a warrior of some prowess, by all accounts. Approaching him would be dangerous and carrying him away would be difficult.

Gorik raised the arrow again. Better to get the deed done. He pulled back on the bowstring and aimed an inch to the left of centre so the arrow would take Brand in the heart and kill him instantly. He didn't want him crying out in pain or anger to bring hunters. Gorik would need as much time as possible to get away as there was only one road in and out of Stybbor, save the river.

Again he lowered the arrow.

At the very most he would have an hour after Brand was shot and it would take most of that to cross the river, skirt the village and get back on the road west. There were many soldiers and they would find him quickly. His only option was to go deeper into the woods and get full value from his hour head start, but Gorik hated the woods. It would be uncomfortable and he would have to hunt and forage for food, which was peasants' work.

Suddenly he smiled, and crept cautiously from the clearing in which Brand sat with his head in his hands. Gorik had had a better idea.

∞ ∞ ∞

I realised that the woods had gone silent which I'd always taken as a warning in the past, so I stood and glanced about, but no-one was to be seen, so perhaps the silence was on account of my own presence?

It was time to go but I sat again. I felt close to Valla in this place and wondered where she was. Still in Wales perhaps? I resolved that after Harold's kingdom was secure, I would go to Wales and find her.

Suddenly feeling light of heart with a decision made, I leapt to my feet and strode back towards the village. It was time to go back to Lundene.

Chapter 33

A Perfect Vessel

Valla stared into the blue – her hand on Malgard's head.

'Where are we?'

Myrrthn didn't answer for a while but gazed down from the cliff top at the ocean where lines of waves disappeared south into blue haze.

'It has no name,' said Myrrthn. 'And why should it? It is a high place above the sea ... facing the rest of the world. The blue mist is our protection ... keeps the killer god's magic at bay, but it has worn thin. Our task is to rebuild the haze so this isle will never again be found. The killer god will never catch us.'

'Rebuild the haze?'

'It can be done. Oh yes ... we shall achieve it. This is where we shall make the spell.'

'Yes.'

'All the ingredients are at hand. We simply need to blend them and do honour to the spirits of brook, forest, stone and field. It will take time ... several months at least ... but we shall achieve it.'

'Not much time,' said Valla, staring into the haze.

Myrrthn was quiet as he also peered in the direction of the continent.

'You are correct ... but there is enough, I deem, because of you.'

Valla turned to him.

'Because of me?'

'Because of you,' repeated Myrrthn and cackled with glee at the surprise on her face. 'All spells require a vessel. That vessel must be you ... and a perfect vessel you are. That is why you have been chosen.'

' … I see.'

'Your spirit is pure,' said Myrrthn. 'Purer even than mine … not least in that you kept yourself intact while living in an army of men for several years. This is evidence of the purest spirit.'

'Yes,' said Valla, even as she felt a pang of sorrow for her separation from Brand.

'That pure spirit is the strongest ingredient of all,' said Myrrthn. 'All others can be found anywhere … talismans of brook, forest, stone and field. But the key ingredient is given from your soul … something pure and permanent.'

'I know what it must be,' said Valla, her heart suddenly lightening.

'You have always known,' agreed Myrrthn. 'Oh yes. One other is necessary for the achievement of the spell … let us hope he is worthy of your trust.'

'He is worthy,' smiled Valla, suddenly overcome with inexpressible joy. 'I know it with all my heart.'

'That is well,' said Myrrthn, 'but men are weak and it troubles me that so much depends on him. Nevertheless we shall make a start, and let us look to the skies for a sign that the spell is working. We shall know soon enough.'

'The spell will work,' said Valla, her fingers twisted into Malgard's fur. 'His heart and promise are true … and afterwards I shall be his wife.'

'Perhaps,' said Myrrthn.

∞ ∞ ∞

William was in a red fury.

He had received the pope's blessing for the enterprise of Inglalond, even as Bishop John had foretold. He had received the papal banner from the pope's own hand and promises of absolution for any who fought beneath it in aid of that enterprise.

He had received pledges of support from counts and princes all over the continent and mercenaries poured into his camps around the Normandy coast. Everything was in place except for one thing – the most important thing of all.

His own magnates.

Vassals they were, and obliged to give him service and obedience. But they liked not the risk of invading Inglalond. William liked it not either but he had made such a clamour regarding Harold's perfidious usurping of the throne that he would look a fool if he did not attempt it.

And William hated looking a fool.

'By God, I will break any man who will not follow me!' he shouted at his inner council, chief of whom were his brother Odo, Bishop John of Fecamp and William fitzOsbern.

'I will threaten them with excommunication,' suggested Odo and there was a silence as William paced, considering.

'If I may,' said Bishop John, 'the threat of excommunication is a stick to beat them ... but wouldn't we do better with enticements to attract them?'

'Of course,' snapped William, 'but I have already offered enticements. There are counties and fiefdoms innumerable in Inglalond. All that fight with me shall receive land!'

'If we win,' said fitzOsbern.

William glanced at him as if to say something sharp, but thought better of it and continued his pacing.

'Let me talk to them Lord,' said fitzOsbern. 'I shall learn their minds and discover if there is some lever that might remind them of their duty.'

William waved fitzOsbern away, and eight hours later he had achieved through subtlety what his master could not through threat and bombast. He had spoken individually to all of the greatest magnates and reminded them of their martial duty – which, to a man, they reminded him was for forty days a year only and limited to Normandy. They owed William no service beyond its borders.

But fitzOsbern managed to give many the impression that they were the only ones out of step – that all others had agreed privately to support the invasion. They agreed to let him speak on their behalf and when William asked in public court the mood of the magnates, fitzOsbern said aloud that all supported the invasion and would pledge double their duty in terms both of men and ships.

There was a shocked silence, but none dared to speak out against fitzOsbern's declaration. William shook all of them by the hand, looked them in the eye and thanked them from the bottom of his heart, assured them that God was on their side and victory inevitable. He then issued orders for preparation – ships and barges enough for twelve thousand men and six thousand horses must be prepared.

'We must be ready by the end of summer,' insisted William. 'If we do not come this year then Harold will have at least eighteen months to secure his kingdom and prepare. His advantage will be too great, so we must attack before he is entirely ready for us.'

∞ ∞ ∞

Malgard watched with a sinking heart as the torchlight faded on the docks of Roskilde and flickered reflected in the dark waters of Zeeland.

Tostig had been rejected again – rejected by the king of the Danes, just as he had been rejected by his sworn brother, Malcolm of Scotland, and even his brother in law, the Count of Flanders.

'It doesn't matter,' insisted Tostig. 'We still have William for an ally … we need an army not so much to defeat Harold as to improve our bargaining position after William's victory.'

Malgard acknowledged the truth of that, but with every rejection his confidence in Tostig waned. Harold was an able king and had the home advantage. Malgard rather doubted that William could defeat him on his own account and suspected he was destined for a life in exile unless Tostig could muster a sizeable army to offer battle on a second front. All his wanderings had achieved so far was fifteen ships of vagabond raiders – enough to cause a nuisance, as they had done at Wight, but not enough to mount any serious challenge. And certainly not enough to be taken seriously by William, should he beat the odds and prevail over Harold.

'We will do better in Norway,' said Tostig and there was some reason for confidence. In Roskilde they had been approached by a man who claimed to be an emissary of Hardrada – greatest Viking ever to wield an axe under the Landwaster Flag. That man, Skeppi, sailed with them now to Norway but Malgard, better than most, knew a rogue when he met one.

'I do not trust Skeppi,' he muttered, with an eye on the man sitting in the bow.

'Neither do I,' boomed Tostig, in a surprisingly good mood, given the circumstances, 'but what does it matter? He may be an emissary of Hardrada or he may simply be angling for free passage to Norway … I care not because I mean to see this monstrous Dane with my own eyes.'

Harald Hardrada – reputed to be eight feet tall and as strong as a bull – was the king of Norway and acclaimed to be the greatest Viking of all time. Fearsome in battle, men flocked to his banner and he had never been defeated. He had travelled the world and had even, it was said, been captain of the emperor's guard in Mikkelgard – fabled city of gold, far to the east – and brought back untold riches.

Skeppi claimed to be an agent of Hardrada who himself claimed a blood interest to the throne of Inglalond and had heard about the falling out between the brothers Godwinson.

'My Lord Hardrada may be able to help you,' whispered Skeppi, upon approaching Tostig at the Danish court. 'These southern Danes are timid … soft and comfortable and forgetting the ways of their fathers. But we Norse have not forgotten. Hardrada is not a man to leave a ripe fruit hanging on the bough. He will take Inglalond and you shall be well rewarded if you bring men to the fight.'

Tostig was aware that agreeing to help Hardrada be king, when he had already agreed to help William be king, was a dangerous game. But who gives a fuck? He threw his head back and laughed as his ship turned north into darkness.

The main objective was the defeat of Harold. Let the bargaining commence after Harold was dead. Hardrada and William could fight over Inglalond while Tostig built up his own alliances and would decide at the critical moment which of them to support. And if he played the game as well as he thought he could, it might just mean, when the dust settled, that Tostig would be the last man standing, bringing not just the blood but also the spirit of Godwin to the throne of Inglalond.

Chapter 34

The Hairy Star

'There will be a sign. You will know it when you see it. Know that I am coming. It will not be as long as you think.'

∞ ∞ ∞

Lundene was a happy place when I returned in the middle of April at the head of my archery troop. Everywhere I went it seemed that people were building. Merchants prospered and there was a hum of activity and excitement such as I had never seen anywhere.

'It is the new king,' men said. 'He brings peace and certainty after years of doubt. Now we can have confidence to build and grow in his blessed kingdom.'

Harold himself never stopped working. In the mornings he would hear petitioners and give his judgments, and in the afternoons and evenings he was ever in council, issuing laws and giving orders for the preparation of the realm. For, despite the confidence, the claim of William the Bastard to the throne of Inglalond was a shadow felt by many – even if it was a fading shadow as Harold's sun rose high in the sky. And it was the sky from whence the troubles started.

Towards the end of April there appeared a new star in the south. Each night it seemed brighter and grew a long tail which flowed behind like the hair of a woman – and so it came to be known: the Hairy Star.

It was clearly a portent of doom, but what sort of doom? Some said it revealed the anger of God for Harold's usurping of the aetheling's throne and portending the end of his reign. Others claimed it was the approval of God, but certainly the impact was a dulling of the confidence I had witnessed only days before.

For myself, I knew only delight. In my occasional dream, Valla always told me there would be a sign to herald her return, and that I would know it when I saw it. With mounting excitement I remembered that the last time we had lain together I had cupped my hand over her womanhood and called it her hairy star. Clearly Valla's power was somehow responsible for this heavenly apparition. Or perhaps God was testing me yet again. Either way, I knew that I would surely see Valla soon and was filled with joy – not least as it seemed that my dalliance with Emma had not spoiled my promise.

Harold claimed not to care about the Hairy Star. If anything he worked even harder to prepare the realm against the possibility of invasion – more ships and weapons were commanded and teams of clerics in Lundene and at Waltham Abbey relayed orders and made lists of lords and their promises to provide housecarls and men for the fyrd. He even established small standing armies in all the locations most ripe for a landing – to maintain vigilance and organise quickly the local fyrd should it be required.

Information he gathered also about the movements of his enemies. William had sent a message via a couple of monks (not the Bishop of Fecamp, whom Harold had banished). The message demanded that Harold abide by his oath and recognise William as the rightful king appointed by Edward. When Harold refused, the monks had said, 'In the event of your refusal, Lord William bade us say: look to your coasts for I am coming … but if you do not see me within the year, you will never see me in this life again.'

'Not much of a threat, is it,' laughed Harold, but he redoubled his efforts and Inglalond bristled with sword, axe and spear.

One night, he summoned me to his hall and we walked out into the moonlight on a high balcony overlooking the west minster. It was a cool, clear night with the stars blazing and the Hairy Star looming above us, indeed like the head of a woman running with her hair streaming behind.

'What do you think it means?' he asked me.

'It is a good sign,' I replied.

'Really? I feared it might be a guiding light to the ships that haunt my dreams.'

'Nay Lord. Valla told me to watch out for a sign that would herald her return to me. I believe this to be that sign.'

Harold gazed upwards, considering.

'A heavenly sign can have more than one purpose,' he said, 'but I had forgotten your wife *more danico*. I sincerely hope you find her again ... but that reminds me of why I wanted to see you.'

I turned to face him and he gave me an odd smile.

'I too have a wife *more danico* ... living in my house at Bosham.'

I was keenly embarrassed by the turn of conversation, remembering my slightly drunken questioning of Harold's marital motives at the feast before we left for Normandy, two years prior.

'I know you are friendly with my lady Ealdgifu Swanneshals ... mother of my children and wife of my heart.'

I said nothing, as any answer it seemed, in my confusion, would be insufficient.

'My new bride is a political wife,' said Harold, looking up at the Hairy Star once again. 'I like her well enough, but she is not the Lady Swanneshals. She symbolises my wedding with Inglalond herself. It is a duty.'

I just nodded, and Harold placed an arm around my shoulders.

'I need you to do me a favour, Brand. An important favour that only my most reliable captain could achieve.'

'Name it, Lord.'

'Take your archers to Bosham and garrison the port. If William comes, he will most likely land in one of the ports along the south coast. Bosham is vulnerable so I need to know the Lady Swanneshals, and my children, can be taken swiftly to safety, should the need arise.'

This time he gave me a large supply of the new coins minted with his image and the word 'Pax' stamped to remind all merchants that these were times of peace and so to be confident in their dealings. We set off for the southern coast two days later and once again I was at the head of a column of soldiers marching and singing through the lanes of Sussex in the pleasant spring sunshine.

Elric was in his element – picking spring flowers and winding them into sweet smelling chains which he wore about his neck – and otherwise acting like a boy on his first outing, rather than second in command of a fell troop of slayers.

Elric also found it difficult to take seriously the threat of William.

'We have thirty thousand,' he said, 'and that's just the fyrd. With all the lords and housecarls as well we might put forty thousand in the field. There aren't enough trees in Normandy to build ships enough to carry men enough to challenge us.'

It was a strong point, but dangerously complacent to my mind.

'We have a very large coast and cannot defend all of it,' I reminded. 'William might gain a toehold at some fortress and use the same ships to ferry men back and forth ... and so build up a host beneath our noses.'

'It is a large coast,' agreed Elric, ' ... but with many eyes. The greater threat is Tostig. He might spend years building an army ... perhaps in Scotland to raid his own former Earldom. That would be his style.'

'Then why aren't you in Northumbria where you might get the opportunity to avenge your brother?'

'And miss out on the southern spring? Nay, I am happy enough here ... fixing all your mistakes and training your archers for you.'

We were in no hurry and so took the best part of a week to get to Bosham, by which time the Hairy Star had faded from the sky and no longer troubled the councils of the wise.

We arrived in the late afternoon and I left the main body of men at the inn where we had lunched on the day we left for Normandy.

'I can't house that many!' complained the innkeeper, but when I showed him a handful of Harold's coins he was happy enough to find space.

'We may be here some time,' I told him, 'so make sure there is meat and ale enough for a hundred and twenty men.'

'Yes Lord!' he thanked me and bustled away shouting instructions while Elric and I, and a couple of swordsmen, continued up the hill towards the Lady Swanneshals' house.

She was very pleased to see me and pressed me with questions about the court.

'I am, of course, invited,' she said, 'but I know Harold would prefer me to stay away while he beds down his political wife.'

I knew not how to respond to such a loaded statement, but answered willingly enough most of her other questions, to the best of my knowledge. Then she asked, 'So tell me Brand ... what news of your own Lady?'

'She is yet lost to me,' I replied, 'but she did tell me there would be a sign that I would know when I saw ... that would portend the occasion of her great task, whatever that might be, and her return.'

The Lady Swanneshals asked for my cup to be filled, then bade the servants leave the room so only she and I remained.

'I cannot be certain,' she said, lowering her voice, 'but I may have seen her.'

It is difficult to describe how I felt in that moment, but my heart was so overfilled with love and hope that words failed me and I must have gaped like a fool at an Easter fair.

'Where? When?' I eventually managed.

'In the woods to the west of the town,' said Swanneshals. 'I go there occasionally to walk the cliff tops and gather herbs in a secret glade.'

'Did you speak with her?'

'Nay ... and I cannot swear it was her ... but she was dressed in skins, as she was when you first came to our house in Theodford.'

'There are many in the woods who dress that way,' I said, hope fading.

'Perhaps,' agreed Swanneshals, and again she lowered her voice. 'But I recognised her in another way ... I felt her power.'

I just stared at her, and a cool shiver ran across my shoulder blades.

'Her power has grown,' continued Swanneshals. 'I wanted to call out to her but ... for some reason I could not. It was like a dream.'

'Maybe it *was* a dream?'

'Nay ... unless I dream still, for there was no waking.'

We sat in silence for a few moments as I attempted to understand what it could possibly mean.

'When did you see her?'

'Two days ago.'

'Can you take me to the place?'

'Of course.'

I had a ridiculous desire to run off at once, in the dark, to find the glade Swanneshals described but I forced myself to wait until the morning. Then at breakfast I was bombarded with further questions from young Godwin and Edmund about their father the king and obliged to watch their sword play.

They had both grown and were reasonably proficient, but my soldier's eye told me they were not ready for a real battle, despite all their boasting and assurance that they were ready to take their places in the shield wall.

When I told them so they attacked me at once and I was obliged to defend myself with the only weapon available – a farrier's rake, which I thrust in their faces still moist with dung. The pair of them leapt back and registered their disgust while Elric laughed from the barn door where he had been watching perched on a bale.

'You're disgusting!' cried Godwin, aghast at the turd stain on his tunic.

'Horse turd is better than blood,' said Elric. 'Which is what you would have if you truly took on the Lord Brand.'

'But we are princes!' seethed Edmund. 'You dare put turd on princes?'

'There's no such thing as princes on a battlefield,' said Elric, 'but plenty of turd … it pours out of men when they get scared.'

'And when they die,' I added. 'The battlefield stinks … of turd, piss and blood. Mainly turd.'

It was clear our words had had an impact. The twins' faces had gone white and they soon found an excuse to go indoors. Presently the Lady Swanneshals appeared, carrying a basket, and bade me follow her.

It was about noon when we took the path that led west of the town towards cliff tops and then woods. It was a pleasant enough day and the path was fragrant with hyacinth, bluebells and wild rosemary. Then stocks and butterbur bloomed abundantly in the forest with a strong sweet smell that was almost overpowering. Valla would love such a place.

'The fragrance is like a spell,' said Swanneshals, as the path meandered in and out of the forest near the edge of the cliff. We sat for a while on another of the carved stone benches that some forgotten mason had made and ate cold meat and bread from the basket, which we washed down with a skin of wine.

'Is he happy?' she asked.

I had been anticipating such a question but that didn't make it any easier to answer.

'He is too busy running the kingdom to have any thought for his own happiness,' I said.

Swanneshals smiled sadly and told me that I had certainly kept my word as far as staying his friend was concerned.

'My Lady … my answer was not evasive. He is so busy he never sees his new wife … whom he refers to as his political wife. If he has tender thought at all for anyone it is for you … the wife of his heart as he calls you. That is why I was sent to protect you.'

Again the sad smile, but also a fond one.

'Perhaps,' she said, refilling my cup, 'but he knows we are friends, you and I. Perhaps he wants you out of Lundene so you do not see the joy he has of his new wife?'

'Now I deem you are looking for sadness when there is no reason for it,' I said, as she turned away to stare into the blue haze that obscured the horizon.

'No reason?' she mused. 'Wives can always find reasons for sadness. It is for his sons though that I am mostly sad. They do not yet understand that he has taken a new wife mainly to make new sons … to supplant them as princes.'

'My understanding is that the main reason was to tie the sons of Aelfgar to him in any future conflict,' I said. 'The north has ever been unreliable. They prefer their separateness.'

'My sons will still be replaced though … whatever the reason.'

I had no answer to that so turned to stare myself into the blue haze and the lines of waves that approached the cliffs so unrelentingly.

'Will William come?' asked Swanneshals.

'I don't think so,' I said, after a pause. 'Harold believes he will attempt it, but even if he does, he cannot have any hope of defeating us.'

'Unless we are divided,' said Swanneshals.

'We have never been so united,' I countered. 'Harold has prepared well, and all rivers and beaches are watched.'

'And Tostig?'

'Tostig harries the south and east with his little fleet, but he cannot raise any serious challenge.'

'I have heard he is in league with Hardrada.'

' … Really?'

I turned to face her but she continued to stare south towards Normandy.

'I too have friends at Waltham Abbey,' she said, 'and receive some of the same messages that Harold receives. Tostig has spoken with Hardrada.'

This was news to me, and I felt the merest tremor of unease.

'Tostig has also spoken with William,' said Swanneshals, ' ... if they were to be in league and co-ordinate their attacks ... '

'We would still defeat them,' I said with certainty. 'It would be a hard fight, but we are too strong ... too numerous ... too well organised. And we would then be safer than ever once all those threats were destroyed.'

Suddenly the sun came out from behind a cloud and the place we sat was bathed in warmth and light.

'But come,' said Swanneshals, 'I did not bring you here to speak of our doom. Let us find the glade.'

We left the basket on the stone seat to collect on our return and I followed the Lady Swanneshals along the western path that now turned deeper into the forest.

It was a warm day for early May but cool under the trees as the canopy was thick and allowed only here and there a stray beam in which butterflies danced. Presently the track headed downwards into a hollow and I felt an odd sensation – as if we were being watched – and would frequently turn my head quickly as though to catch spies.

'Yes, we are being watched,' said Swanneshals, quietly, 'but have no fear. There are no enemies here.'

I didn't much care for the idea of hidden watchers, but if Swanneshals believed there to be no danger, I was content. The feeling of being watched, or rather the sense of a presence grew as we went deeper into the dell. Then the light grew as we came to a large pond into which a spring trickled down a wet wall of sparkling rock. Sunlight glittered on the pond which was dazzling after the darkness of the forest.

'This is the place,' said Swanneshals. 'There are herbs growing wild here and I come to cull basil and parsley ... and rosemary, of course, but that grows everywhere.'

'Where did you see her?'

Swanneshals sat on a rock which might have been carved, so perfectly commodious did it seem by the edge of the pool. She patted the rock beside her in invitation and we both removed our shoes and allowed our feet to bathe in the cool water.

'I was sitting here ... three days ago now, when I saw her on the far side of the pond.'

I stared into the trees across the pool and saw no-one, but the sense of being watched grew until I could barely control the urge to shout a challenge.

'It is a lovely place,' I said, 'but the air of vigilance catches my breath. Surely we are not alone here.'

'We are not alone,' agreed Swanneshals, 'but hush. Sometimes the watchers show themselves. We must be quiet enough that they forget our presence.'

'Who are they?'

'Hush ... be patient, and we shall see what we may.'

I tried to quell the sense of hidden watchers by focussing on that which could be seen. Small wrens flashed over the water chasing midges, and frogs sang all around us. Butterflies flickered and spun in the sunlight – in dazzling blue and shimmering green that reminded me of Valla's eyes. A heavy drone of bees arose from the many flowering herbs about the pool and it felt like an incantation. We had of course been drinking wine so were already a little affected, but the warmth, scents and music of the hollow combined to put us both in a trance. I don't know that we slept but the visions I recall were more like a dream than memory.

It seemed to me that two otters appeared in the pond – gambolling and frolicking in that silken sinuous way. They came closer and seemed to be watching me as I lay on my side and watched through half closed eyes, knowing somehow that if I sat up they would bolt. There was something very odd about their behaviour. It was almost a dance, and then just as it dimly occurred to me that otters would normally prefer a river to a spring pool, they vanished – two dark streaks under the water and they were gone.

Eventually I sat up, thick headed and uncertain as to whether I had slept, although the Lady Swanneshals lay beside me with her eyes closed and a smile on her lips. The light was beginning to fade in the hollow so it was time to start heading back. I put my hand on her shoulder and her eyes opened instantly.

'Did you see her?' she asked me.

'Nay,' I replied, 'although I seemed to feel her presence. I feel it still.'

It was a strange thing to say, and yet I truly felt close to her – as though she had only just left and might at any moment re-emerge from the surrounding trees.

'You will see her again,' smiled Swanneshals, 'I am sure of it.'

I was less sure, and again I had to wonder whether my dalliance with Emma was somehow holding Valla at bay. I was half tempted to ask for Swanneshals' judgment as to whether my actions had jeopardised Valla's return, but it was hardly a fit subject for the wife of a king.

She must have seen the question in my eyes however as she bade me say what was troubling me. I managed to convert my doubt into concern for the hour, so we stood and stretched and left the hollow to head back to the cliff tops. It was much darker than before under the trees and we needed the occasional slanting beams to show us the path, but we were soon back at the stone seat where we had left the basket.

I went to pick it up but just stared, then glanced quickly about the forest eaves, half expecting to see Valla emerge laughing.

For in the top of the basket was a freshly picked posey of bluebells.

Chapter 35

Cunning and Cruel

Three hundred ships!

Malgard exulted as he gazed at the fleet assembling in Orkney haven – only a hundred or so at the end of June but more were coming. Many more, according to the Jarl Thorfinn who had received regular messengers from Hardrada – including a direction to provide facilities for three hundred ships, some of them carrying as many as seventy warriors.

And such warriors!

This would be the greatest Viking army ever assembled, under the greatest Viking of all time – Hardrada the man mountain, cunning and cruel. They had stayed a month with him in his capital of Trondheim and Malgard's pessimism had been blown away by the reception received by Tostig. Hardrada knew of his reputation as a ruthless and successful fighter and welcomed him as a spiritual brother.

'You should have been a Dane,' laughed Hardrada many times as he and Tostig fought to drink each other under the table – with neither ever claiming the victory.

'I will a Dane be … in your new kingdom … of Inglalond,' Tostig would respond in the halting Danish that he and Malgard had been learning, and Hardrada would pound the table with delight.

He was a colossal man. Tostig was large enough by normal standards but Hardrada was the best part of a foot taller and far greater in muscled bulk. And he delighted in showing off his strength – frequently wrestling with the hugest members of his guard and never once being thrown.

The part Malgard found most difficult was his cunning. For at times he seemed like a halfwit – grunting orders in monosyllables and losing his patience in violent fury at the first sign of any failure to obey. He was like a spoiled child – with the power of life and death over every man and woman in his kingdom – and yet the tales of his exploits could only mean he must be a man of perception and wiliness when the need arose.

That need would never be greater than now, taking on the might of Harold, secure in his kingdom and building up defences as fast as he could go. And yet, as Malgard looked over the dragon boats and the hundreds – nay thousands of men already assembled, he realised it was impossible that Hardrada could not have at least some success. They would win Northumbria, and probably Mercia also. Harold might hang onto the south but the Danelaw was still strong in the north. Tostig had promised Hardrada that more than half the thegns of Northumbria would side with him when battle came – effectively doubling Hardrada's army and halving that of Edwin and Morcar. Then they would march on Mercia – with Malcolm of Scotland watching their back – and at last they would sweep up the south.

Malgard had been promised an earldom – a part of Mercia if they did not take the south immediately, but all of East Anglia if they did.

We must at least take the north, thought Malgard again, as yet another new longboat pulled into the haven with two score shields slung over the sides. The only question in his mind was William.

They had promised to recognise William's claim to the throne and to act on his part. That is why he had given Tostig several boats and allowed him to recruit more in the Norman ports. He would be furious if he knew Tostig had also made an agreement with Hardrada – and, knowing the extent of William's spy network, he probably knew already.

William lacked the men and ships to make any sort of realistic attempt on Inglalond but, with his papal banner and promises of land, Malgard had no doubt that he might acquire them eventually. Malgard could foresee a time, in a year or so, when Harold was all but defeated, and the Viking army successful but much depleted, when the Bastard might make an opportunistic grab for power.

'We shall have to fight more than one battle to hold our prize,' he said to Tostig.

'Good!' laughed Tostig. 'I like fighting battles … and if we defeat the Bastard, what's to stop us taking over his country as well as Inglalond?'

It was an incredible thought, but as soon as the thought was in Malgard's mind he couldn't stop it growing. Normandy was a rich and beautiful land and even a minor nobleman there would live a fine life indeed. Malgard was only one of several men close to Tostig in his exile and resolved for the hundredth time to make himself the most indispensible of councillors in order to receive the best rewards.

But no matter how promising the future looked, Malgard's mind would ever return to his greatest fear. It had been an unnerving sight that time at the gate of Harold's Lundene house – Malgard's nephew looking large and capable, and clearly on intimate terms with the new king. It was a disastrous outcome, and Malgard knew instantly that he could not return to Stybbor – not that that was any great loss. He had already screwed every last penny out of its thin fields and thinner peasants. Fuck Stybbor.

But Brand he could not ignore. While Brand lived he had the potential to destroy everything Malgard had worked for, and that could not be borne.

Still. He had made some provision. Gorik had been given plenty of money to hire more slayers and clear instructions regarding Malgard's nephew. He had had time enough. Perhaps the job was done already?

'Where is Gorik?' muttered Malgard.

∞ ∞ ∞

'I hear you're looking for archers.'

'Really?' said Elric. 'Who told you that?'

'Everyone was saying so … in Lundene … so I came after you to join up.'

Elric didn't much like the look of the man who had turned up looking for work, but then again he didn't much like the look of any of the poachers, thieves and murderers that made up their archery troop.

'We only recruit from the gaols,' said Elric. 'Service for freedom … plus food and ale. There's no pay.'

'Food and ale's enough,' said the man, who certainly looked capable.

Elric shrugged and bade Walt set up the butt for the usual test. The newcomer had his own bow and quiver and effortlessly shot three arrows into the gold from thirty paces.

'Good enough,' said Elric. He had an oddly negative feeling about the man as no-one else had volunteered for the archery troop. All the others shared a bond by virtue of their liberation from punishment. The new fellow would be different and difference was not a good thing when a man's life was dependent on the trust of his comrades. Still, good archers were valuable, and Elric was a practical man.

'What's your name?' he asked.

'Cedric.'

'Welcome to Brand Holgarsson's archers, Cedric. You can have him Walt.'

Walt grinned and took the fellow away to meet his new comrades, and Elric immediately forgot about him.

'That was easy,' thought Gorik as he forced a smile onto his face while Walt prattled happily about life in the archers.

Gorik knew he was taking a massive risk but was reasonably confident Brand would not recognise him. In the six years since the incident in the dark cellar, Gorik's appearance had changed. His newly white beard covered a good deal of the scar on the right side of his face, but mostly it was his hair that was different. Previously dark brown and cut very short, it had greyed and then whitened quickly, and he now wore it long – also helping to conceal the scar. But while his hair had whitened there was nothing wrong with his body. Gorik still had the hard muscles of a warrior at the peak of his strength and knew he was a match for just about any man.

Especially when the other man did not know the attack was coming.

∞ ∞ ∞

'It is beautiful,' exclaimed William. 'Utterly beautiful.'

He was staring at a ship berthed at one of the piers along the River Dives. It was the largest ship he had ever seen and brand new. Best of all, it was a present from his beloved Mathilda.

'I have named her Mora,' said Mathilda, delighted at the joyous wonder on her husband's face.

'How did you do this without my knowing?'

'I am not reliant on my husband for all things,' she smiled fondly. 'I do have money of my own.'

'You must have spent all of it to build such a ship,' he replied, as he marched up the plank connecting the ship with the pier. The ship was a marvel. At least twice as long as the next biggest in the fleet, it featured a deep hold under a full deck with rowing seats for sixty men and a tall mast for the sail. There was even a raised platform at the stern for the steersman with a cabin beneath for William and his councillors.

William breathed deeply the smells of fresh cut timber and tar.

'That's the scent of victory,' he exclaimed. 'How can I possibly fail when I ride to Inglalond in such a vessel.

It was only one of hundreds that now swayed at anchor or were tied to the docks in every river and haven in Normandy. His magnates, unwilling at first, had finally found their courage, and their purses. All of them had built, and were still building, ships for William's invasion. Mostly they were barges, big enough to carry men, horses, weapons and supplies across the channel to a landing somewhere in the south. Bishop John of Fecamp, furious at having been banished by Harold, had provided excellent maps of the south of Inglalond, over which William had pored for hours with his advisors – to find the best landing with the easiest march on Lundene.

'All places have their benefits and problems,' said Bishop John. 'It would be best to spend as little time as possible at sea ... no more than a day if that can be managed.'

'It can be managed with a southerly wind,' said William fitzOsbern, who had made the trip to Inglalond several times.

'That is so,' agreed the Bishop. 'We should aim for Hastings. It has a long beach in a sheltered bay where many ships can land at once.'

'Why not Bosham?' asked William, pointing at the map. 'I understand Harold's own house is at Bosham ... and his children.'

'That would be appropriate,' growled Odo, wearing, as ever, his polished black armour despite there being no prospect of a fight that day.

'Perhaps,' agreed Bishop John, 'but the harbour at Bosham is certain to be garrisoned ... and worse, it is a poor harbour for landing. We would never get the horses through the mud.'

William grunted in disappointment, but immediately deleted Bosham from the list of possibilities.

'So ... we land at Hastings,' he agreed.

'How are the roads between there and Lundene?' asked fitzOsbern.

'If we land unopposed it will be simple enough,' said Bishop John. 'There is a good northern road but it cannot be reached directly from the beaches.'

'And if we are opposed?' asked William.

'Then we will have to fight our way to the Northern Road ... through marsh and fen.'

'We will need to fight in any case,' said William. 'That's why we're going, is it not? It's just a matter of where.'

'Is there a defensive position at Hastings?' asked Odo.

Bishop John considered, and said, 'There is a hill to the north that might be defended ... although it could just as easily be defended against us if Harold gets there first.'

'Which he almost certainly will,' said fitzOsbern. 'You can guarantee that any beach in the south with a good landing will be watched ... and Harold's fyrd will be quickly in place. They're probably there already.'

'Good,' said William. 'Let them eat their stores and lose their patience while we bide our time in preparation.'

'And wait for a southerly wind,' added Odo.

They all leaned back in their chairs and looked to the north, from whence the prevailing wind continued. Even worse – it looked like a storm was brewing.

'What news of Tostig?' asked fitzOsbern.

William glanced at Bishop John and the two of them shared a rare smile.

'He is playing exactly the part I set for him,' said William, '... harrying the ports of Inglalond and firing the dreams of Hardrada.'

'The part you set for him?' queried fitzOsbern.

William just smiled but nodded at Bishop John to explain.

'Inglalond is strong and Harold has the great advantage of having his warriors already in place. Even if he disbands the fyrd it will not take him long to assemble a great enough army to cause us a problem ... and time is on his side. He can stall tactically until he assembles enough men to make victory inevitable.'

'Then why on earth are we even thinking about this mad enterprise?' demanded Count Eustace of Boulogne – one of those who had been most reluctant to indulge William's crusade. 'If we know Harold to be invincible?'

'We know nothing of the sort,' said William. 'We treated Tostig with less than the honour he felt he deserved and filled his head with the idea that Hardrada has the largest army in Christendom and might be interested in Inglalond now that he has given up on his war with the southern Danes.'

'He was a most attentive pupil,' laughed Bishop John. 'One of my agents is known to Hardrada and he approached Tostig in Roskilde to offer an introduction. I am told that Tostig accepted the invitation with alacrity ... notwithstanding his oath to see our Duke William on the throne of Inglalond.'

'The Anglais have ever been free with their oaths,' sneered William, 'but it would be a strong blow on our behalf if Hardrada attacks the north in strength. Harold cannot be everywhere at once. He will have to deal with the Vikings while we land at our leisure in the south.'

'And if Hardrada prevails?' asked Count Eustace.

'I rather doubt he will,' said William, 'but it is a calculated gamble. Whoever wins between those two will be sorely depleted ... giving us our best chance of prevailing through superior numbers. How many now?' he asked, turning to Bishop John who consulted his lists.

'Thirteen thousand men ... six thousand horses ... three per knight ... and seven hundred ships.'

'Is it enough?' asked fitzOsbern, doubtfully.

'Enough to offer battle,' growled Odo.

There was another silence, as the implications of merely offering battle were considered by each of them.

'It is enough to achieve the main plan,' insisted William. 'I don't care how many they have or where they stand. My sole objective is to kill Harold and his brothers ... and if, with God's help, I do that, then

Inglalond will be mine.'

Again they all looked north to where the storm clouds darkened and if anything the northerly wind was getting stronger.

Chapter 36

Death From Distance

The message came in the middle of the night.

I was woken from my usual dream of Valla and swore in anger at the servant who disturbed me, but then I apologised as he was only doing the duty I had given him.

'Lord Brand, there is a rider from Harold.'

I pulled a cloak about my shoulders and went out into the hall where a rider was being fed after his long journey from Lundene. When he saw me he leapt to his feet but I waved him back down again and bade him finish his meal.

'You can talk and eat at the same time, I trust?'

He grinned but remained standing.

'Lord Brand ... the king desires that you come to Lundene with most of your archers. He says you should leave enough men to protect the Lady Ealdgifu, but come at once.'

'The Bastard has landed?' I asked.

'Nay lord ... the threat is in the north.'

'Tostig?'

'Aye ... but he travels in the van of Hardrada. Three hundred ships we are told.'

'They have landed?'

'They have burned and pillaged several northern ports. We believe they are headed for Yorvik ... Tostig's former capital.'

'Makes sense,' I nodded, as Elric walked into the room already alert despite being himself wrenched from sleep – or more likely the arms of a kitchen wench, knowing Elric's taste.

'We leave at dawn for Lundene,' I told him. 'One troop we shall leave to escort the Lady Swanneshals to safety should the need arise.

Whose do you think? Walt's?'

'He is steady enough to be trusted with the task,' said Elric, 'but he will resent it. He's itching for a scrap, our Walt.'

'You're right,' I grinned. 'The man who is least eager for the fray will be the most efficient at getting Swannehals out of danger. Whom do you suggest?'

'Orald.'

It was a good choice. Orald was old, fat and slow, but quick-witted and defensively cautious. He would never have run from a fight (at least, one he had a good chance of winning) but was wise enough to prefer peace to the prospect of violent death.

'Very well, Orald shall guard the Lady and her children. Wake the rest before dawn. We're going to war.'

Four hours later I was marching at the head of a column of just under a hundred men, counting servants and my few remaining swordsmen. It was a cool, blustery morning with the north wind continuing and a thick cover of black cloud out to sea, but we turned our backs on the sea and headed north through fields and hamlets where red light twinkled through shutters as morning fires were lit and another day in Harold's Inglalond commenced.

The lads were soon singing in their eagerness for battle and folk would come to their doors to watch us pass, knowing that the fourteen years of comparative peace that had lasted since the return of Godwin from exile was about to end.

'God protect the king!' they would cry as we passed, and it occurred to me that these people were the ones who would truly suffer if the Bastard came. They had no-one to protect them and no weapons, save a handful of bows and bills. And as growers of cattle and grain they would be targeted by William needing to feed his army. Mind you, he was unlikely to come while the wind continued from the north, but my heart told me the wind would change while we were in the north dealing with Hardrada and Tostig. Accordingly, I had given strict instructions to Orald in the event that ships appeared from the south – increasingly unlikely as that seemed given the lateness of the season.

But for all my concern and preparation, my mind returned ever to the bunch of bluebells which had appeared so mysteriously in

Swanneshals' basket. That they were from Valla I had no doubt, but why had she not appeared herself? I kept one of them under my tunic, and felt sad that I was leaving the area in which she must surely be.

'And so it begins,' said Elric.

I was glad to have him at my side. Everything about Elric spoke of competence and certainty. We had fought many battles for Harold, on the edges of his realm, and had developed our own style of fighting – which mainly involved me wielding *Pighammer* and Elric darting left and right to protect my exposed flanks with his sword. We'd cut holes in defences from the Temes estuary to Wales but now I was required to lead – co-ordinating the efforts of others rather than ploughing furrows through the enemy myself. As to that, I was a little disturbed about the way the Normans would fight if they did cross the Channel.

'The Danes we understand,' I said. 'They will make the shield wall and the two armies will seek mastery through numbers and sword skill. That's why our archers may make a difference because the Danes are not accustomed to concentrated flights of arrows which can weaken a spot in the wall before the swordsmen engage. But the Normans are different.'

'Aye,' agreed Elric. 'The Normans fight on horses and have their own archery troops and foot soldiers that they use in waves. If William does come, we will have to adjust our tactics for each set of fighters.'

Elric and I had had this conversation several times already but we went over it obsessively – testing the tactics we wanted to drill into the troop.

'We will deploy in front of the shield wall to get closer to the enemy.' I said. 'We will take long spears to fix in place and thwart horsemen should they get past our arrows. We will defeat other archers through superior skill ... and we will retire behind the shield wall if we are confronted with too many foot soldiers.'

'The men will need to know the rhythms of such a battle so they can deploy quickly,' said Elric.

'That discipline is the task of the troop commanders. They will also need to be vigilant for both opportunities and threats, as always occur in battle.'

My own role would be to stand where I could see everything

and call the archery teams into action as suited the wider battle. Elric would convey my orders and both of us would fight with the swordsmen to press an advantage or cover any retreats.

'I'm looking forward to testing our system,' said Elric. 'This is a new way of doing warfare … it is almost a pity that Danes fight only with the shield wall.'

'They are very good at it,' I reminded. 'Why change your system when it always works?'

'There is that,' agreed Elric.

'And don't forget they have Hardrada. The greatest warrior in Christendom … if the stories are true.'

'He's only great if he gets close to you,' sneered Elric. 'Our archers will stick him with a hundred pins before he can lift his sword.'

'Let us hope so.'

On the evening of the second day we marched into Lundene – footsore and tired – only to learn that Harold had already left for the north and we were to follow immediately. Harold had set up a series of camps along the northern road to ease the passage of warriors and we had to hurry if we were going to be of any use to him.

I gave the men three hours to rest their feet and have a meal, but resolved we would follow the king in the dark. Fortunately, Harold had foreseen the need for us to catch him and provided guides with torches who knew the northern road and could lead us to the camps, even at night.

Indeed, so great was the sense of urgency among the guides that after two hours rest I decided that we must follow at once and the night was filled with groans as the news was conveyed to my archers.

'Come on lads,' shouted Elric. 'We are the archery troop … death from distance and first into battle. Those are our mottos and we must be with the king to prove ourselves.'

There was still some grumbling but within ten minutes they were more or less ready and we jogged off into the night. More than half a day behind Harold.

∞ ∞ ∞

Malgard could hardly believe how easy it had been to this point.

They had sacked ports in the north of the country – burning, killing, raping and thieving – but there had been almost no resistance. The first sign of organised defence had been at Scarthaborg, but that too had burned and now the ships were headed up the River Ouse towards Tostig's old capital.

'We will find resistance there,' insisted Tostig, 'but not much. I'll have Morcar's balls for my breakfast.'

The fleet stretched down the river behind them and Malgard laughed for the sheer pleasure of being invincible.

'What's funny?' asked Tostig.

'I am simply enjoying the prospect of our victory,' said Malgard. 'And what it will mean for the future.'

'You shall have an earldom,' said Tostig, 'and I a kingdom. What a fine day to become king!'

At a place called Riccall they left the boats drawn up on the eastern bank of the river and marched north to the Yorvik Road which crossed a bridge near the tiny village of Stamford. They moved quickly, hoping to maintain the element of surprise, and just as Malgard began to wonder whether they might find even Yorvik undefended, they finally encountered Morcar and Edwin's army at Fulford Gate, just south of the city.

Neither side bothered to parley. There was too much hate involved for that so two long shield walls quickly formed and quickly engaged. Morcar's men fought bravely, with the desperation of knowing there would be little mercy if they were forced to surrender. And for a long time they held out, but the superior strength and fighting experience of the Vikings meant that pressure built on the Saxon wall until it finally crumbled on the left wing closest to a marsh and Hardrada swept up their flank. Hundreds were slain by the rampaging Danes until Edwin and Morcar escaped the field and retreated to Yorvik – pursued by Hardrada and Tostig.

They had little choice. With the armies of both Northumbria and Mercia destroyed or scattered, the earls Edwin and Morcar had the options solely of death or humiliation. They chose the latter and agreed that Tostig would resume the earldom of Northumbria subject to the king of the Northern Danes who would henceforth hold the sovereignty.

'Harold will shit his pants!' laughed Tostig at the feast that evening. He had wanted to retake his city but Hardrada was a surprisingly cautious tactician and insisted on a withdrawal towards the boats.

'We don't know where Harold is,' muttered the giant warrior. 'I do not want to be surprised.'

'Harold is watching the sea to the south,' sneered Tostig. 'He is obsessed with the Bastard, and so has left the back door open.'

An exchange of hostages had been arranged for the following day to ensure the new political settlement would be fully observed. But for the moment, most of the men celebrated their victory and the riches that would follow. All would acquire land in Northumbria, and it was a green and bounteous land – so different from the thin rocky soil from which they scraped a living in Norway.

Tostig was unhappy with the hostage arrangement as he would have preferred simply to slay all those northerners who had defied him, but he knew there would have to be at least one more battle – possibly two – before he was confirmed as earl of Northumbria. The hostages meant that the remnant armies of Northumbria and Mercia would fight with the Vikings when finally assailed by either or both of Harold and William.

'We can deal with the hostages when they are no longer needed,' reminded Malgard, who as usual was staying sober as all around him tore into ale and wine in celebration of the victory.

'Deal with the hostages,' echoed Tostig drunkenly. 'I'll deal with the fucking hostages. I'll see Morcar swing from a gibbet inside the month.'

Not for the first time, Malgard regarded his patron with concern. Malice and bombast had their uses but, in the end, it was the calm and the cunning who prevailed and Malgard believed Tostig allowed his emotions too much sway. Even worse, he suspected Harold was being underestimated.

'What provision are we making for our defence?' he enquired. 'Harold will certainly send an army … if he does not come himself.'

'Fuck Harold!' snarled Tostig, but eventually his anger cooled and he seemed less puzzled by ale.

'Aye … he will come. Or else send the brats Gyrth and Leofwine … but our losses at Fulford were not many and even those will be replaced by Northumbrians. We can worry about Harold later.'

'Why not now?'

'Now?' exclaimed Tostig. 'Now is a time for feasting … so why aren't you drinking Malgard? I hate seeing men sober after victory!'

Malgard took a conciliatory sip of wine, but continued to be plagued with doubt. All of his eggs were in Tostig's basket and he liked that situation less with every passing moment.

'Where is Gorik?' he wondered for the hundredth time.

∞ ∞ ∞

Gorik muttered as he marched, but only because others did.

In truth he was perfectly content – travelling north in Brand Holgarsson's archery troop to where he expected to be reunited with Malgard.

But Gorik had been thinking.

He had been extremely impressed with Harold's organisation. Further, there was no mistaking the genuine affection with which Harold was held by the troops, even the former criminals who made up the archery troop. These men would certainly give their all in defence of Harold's realm and there were plenty of them. Gorik would be wise to wait until the outcome of battle was effectively determined before doing anything rash.

Like killing Brand, for example.

Oh, there was no doubt Brand would die, preferably in terrible agony over several hours – even days. But Gorik was not so stupid as to fail to perceive the possibilities.

Whoever won the coming battles would be unassailed in Inglalond for the foreseeable future and Gorik was in a unique position to side himself with any eventual victor – even William if Malgard played the game well enough. There would be any number of opportunities in the country that emerged from the imminent carnage, and if Gorik was a betting man – which he was – his money was currently on Harold.

Once again he cursed aloud the miles and the mud, but underneath he was laughing for no matter what happened, Gorik would come out on top in the end.

'You are an odd fellow, Cedric.'

Gorik took several seconds to remember that he was Cedric, then turned swiftly to look at Elric, Brand's red-headed sergeant, who regarded him strangely.

'Odd? How so?'

'You march along complaining with the rest ... with a huge grin splitting your face as though complaining is a kind of joke.'

'It is a soldier's lot to complain,' shrugged Gorik. 'I can moan about the hardship while remembering a funny story at the same time.'

'Really?' said Elric, 'Well if you have a funny story you should share it.'

Some of the men marching nearby agreed and Gorik felt himself suddenly at a loss and uncomfortably cornered.

'It wasn't that funny,' he mumbled, as Elric stared piercingly for a moment and then paused to banter with another group.

Gorik marched on with a face like thunder and one or two of his comrades raised an eyebrow at each other.

∞ ∞ ∞

On the fourth day of our march we caught up with Harold.

In the early evening we found ourselves on the outskirts of a small town which looked like a sea of twinkling torch light as we emerged from the woods and looked down into the flat Ouse valley.

'Harold's army must be enormous,' said Elric, 'unless, of course, we've missed him in the dark and this lot are the Danes.'

'Don't joke about such things,' I replied, and was relieved when the outlying pickets proved to be Saxon.

Harold was very pleased to see me and introduced me to two brothers who had come from Yorvik bearing news of defeat at Fulford.

'But no disaster,' insisted one of them, Oswald.

'The Lords Edwin and Morcar still live,' said Harold, 'but are supposed to exchange hostages with Hardrada and Tostig in the morning.'

Harold was clearly amused, as were his brothers Gyrth and Leofwine.

'Poor Tostig,' laughed Gyrth. 'He has regained his earldom but will keep it only a day.'

'Perhaps,' said Harold.

We all turned to him, as there was something clearly being left unsaid, but instead of explaining himself he asked me about the archery troop.

'The lads have done well,' I said and explained the configuration and battle tactics we had devised.

Harold was delighted with the basic approach and bade me use the archers as seemed best to me on the following day. 'For I am fairly certain there will be a battle,' he said. 'We may parley a little but if we catch them by surprise ... as I hope to do ... then we might do such damage as to render the Danes toothless for ever.'

'And Tostig?' asked Leofwine.

'Tostig will never be toothless,' said Gyrth. 'If you let him live he will never thank you.'

'Why do you think I might let him live?' asked Harold.

'Because you have never once said you mean to see him dead,' answered Gyrth, ' ... despite all his violence and treachery.'

Harold laughed grimly.

'He has done much damage to us when he could have been a mighty captain on our behalf. Nevertheless, he is our brother and I cannot deny I love him still and would prefer him alive. I would feel better facing William with Tostig at my side.'

'Surely it is too late for that,' said Leofwine. 'He has fought with the Danes at Fulford ... that can never be forgiven.'

'Kings forgive many things,' shrugged Harold. 'It is the business of kingship to forgive those convenient to forgive and punish those it is convenient to punish. Occasionally there may be justice in that, but ... in truth, justice is incidental to the practicalities of running a kingdom.'

He trailed off in silent thought for a few moments, then sent Gyrth and Leofwine with orders for the marshalling of the fyrd. We were to march two hours before dawn with the idea of catching the Vikings unawares somewhere east of Yorvik as they marched back to exchange hostages.

'I am looking forward to seeing how the Norman battle tactics work against the Danish shield wall,' Harold said to me. 'As well as your archers we shall also use some housecarls mounted on horses. It may be that their mobility can be useful … and I like your idea of using archers to weaken a point in the wall and then sending the fyrd against those points. We should have thought of it years ago.'

'There is much honour in the shield wall,' I ventured. 'Men are wary to change the ways in which their fathers found honour.'

'Honour is important to a warrior,' mused Harold, 'but to a king, honour is less important than victory. If winning means changing, then change we will.'

With that he slapped me over the shoulder and strode away chuckling. I didn't know whether to be cheered or embarrassed by his last statement, but had to admit that I did at least feel confident.

Of course, confidence is easy to have when you are yet to see the opposing army.

Chapter 37

The Destiny of Gods

'It is going well,' said Myrrthn, adding more dried moss and mistletoe to the bonfire on the headland. Smoke poured from the fire and drove south with the wind, adding its murk to the misty haze that turned the sea and sky into a seamless blue wall without horizon.

Valla sat before the fire, pouring her concentration into the maintenance of the spell and the confusion of their enemies.

'How long must we keep this up?' she enquired.

'Until it is done,' answered Myrrthn. 'The killer god is thwarted for now, but he has much patience. We will need to be strong and vigilant to keep him out … and you must be fully vindicated in the choice of your own contribution. It must be pure.'

'My contribution is pure,' replied Valla. 'The spell is working.'

Myrrthn closed his eyes and resumed the low, tuneless chanting he sang from time to time as the fire waxed and waned. Every now and then a stray gust turned the smoke towards them and they breathed deeply. Valla could feel the power rising in herself and felt a wild joy that they could use the power to shape the destiny of so many thousands of people.

And even shape the destiny of gods.

∞ ∞ ∞

'Curse this wind!' railed William from the deck of his mighty flagship, still anchored in the river. 'It is as though God himself defies me!'

William's fleet had been ready for over a month and despite a couple of false starts was yet to leave the river Dives. The last time they had moved the fleet a violent storm had flashed down from the north and sent them all scurrying back to the havens with the loss of several ships and two hundred men.

'The wind must change,' said fitzOsbern. 'No northern wind can last forever.'

'This one does,' raged William. 'When is the last time you knew the wind to stay constant in one direction on this coast. It is unnatural … and the men fear it. Perhaps they are right to do so?'

'My Lord fitzOsbern is correct,' said Bishop John of Fecamp. 'We have the pope's banner and blessing so the justice of our position cannot be doubted. The wind must change.'

'Tell that to the doubters,' muttered William.

There had been a flow of deserters from the army – mainly due to the dwindling supplies that obliged soldiers to forage further and further afield to feed the army. fitzOsbern and the other magnates begged William to open up the stores already loaded on the boats but he refused.

'Those stores must maintain us in Inglalond. We have no idea how well we will be able to forage over there and I will not take an army over water just to see it defeated for want of supplies.'

'We will have no army to take if we cannot feed it,' muttered fitzOsbern, and it was true. Desertions and sickness had sorely depleted them but they were still strong.

'The wind is not entirely against us,' said Bishop John. 'Do not forget that the Danes need a northerly wind to come from Norway. Perhaps this is God's hand sending the Vikings in to do the hardest work while keeping you safe, Lord. He will turn the winds around when He is ready for you to come to Inglalond.'

'That must be the message we give to the army,' growled Odo. 'I will tell the priests to preach it in their daily sermons.'

William nodded but continued to stare north as though trying to turn the winds by his will.

'Of course … there is another explanation for the wind,' he said. 'The pope may have given his blessing for the enterprise of Inglalond … but maybe God sees the matter differently?'

'You will know the answer to that when the wind turns,' said Bishop John.

∞ ∞ ∞

Malgard suspected he was the only man in the Viking army who was not going mad.

All around him the army straggled westward – muttering and groaning as they coped with the after-effects of drinking all night. Constantly men would pause mid-stride to double over and vomit beer as their comrades laughed. Others would suddenly drop their breeches and squirt the contents of their turbulent guts in the line of march while others cursed them, but at the same time laughed. It was a marching madhouse of turd and vomit but even Hardrada seemed to find it humorous.

'I shat for a week when we thrashed the Chudes in Mikkelgard,' he laughed, and Tostig laughed with him, his own beard stained and knotted with bile.

There is no discipline lamented Malgard to himself. We are overconfident and do not fear the Saxons enough in their own country.

There was little he could do about it. He had already been laughed at for his attempted warnings and knew that to try again would have him labelled a nithing or coward – which he could not afford if he was to take a senior place in the reordering of Northumbria. Or even of Inglalond if Harold himself might be later defeated.

Malgard was also worried about the fact that the normally cautious Hardrada had left most of his army with the boats, and was going to the hostage exchange with only a third of his men. Even worse, he had allowed the sick and drunken soldiers to travel light – without their mail and helmets. If the Saxons had sent another army in the night …

He forced himself to abandon that gloomy line of thinking as he crossed the bridge at Stamford in the van. The river Derwent was narrow but deep and fast flowing. Malgard paused to stare down into the dirty brown water and wondered whether it was fordable. The bridge was wide enough to allow a cart to cross but only three men abreast could manage it. If for any reason they needed to get back across the bridge quickly it would prove a bottleneck and men left on the wrong side would be vulnerable. He actually opened his mouth to call a warning to Tostig, but then decided against it and strode to catch up with the leading group.

On the western side of the narrow bridge, Malgard felt suddenly in peril – as though Brand himself might appear at any moment to make his nightmares real. He shook his head violently as if to clear it and at the same time punish himself for his nervousness. No new army could have come up from the south so quickly.

'Saxons ahead,' came the warning call from in front.

'That's just the exchange party,' said Tostig, but there was a hint of doubt in his voice.

'Then they are over eager to exchange,' muttered Malgard, his fears flooding back. 'They are some miles east of the appointed place.'

He was yet to spy the Saxons himself but there was confusion ahead of him and Hardrada shouted for Tostig.

'Who are they?' he demanded, and as Malgard came forward with Tostig he saw lines of men and horses emerging from the trees less than half a mile ahead.

Malgard heard Tostig swear, as two banners were suddenly visible – *The Red Dragon* of Wessex and *The Fighting Man* – either side of a man dressed in mail and riding a horse with a naked sword in his hand.

Desperately quelling the urge to flee, Malgard turned and saw Vikings still marching over the bridge. There was no escape back that way as he fought his choking panic.

Hardrada started bellowing orders and the sick and bleary Danes began to shuffle themselves into the vague semblance of a shield wall.

'They are only Saxons!' called Hardrada. 'We don't need mail or helms to evade their pissweak swords! Stand hard! Stand together! And we'll beat them as we did yesterday.'

At the same time he sent two runners back to the ships to bring up the rest of the army as soon as they could get there, but Malgard knew it would take at least four hours before they would see reinforcements – probably five. He would have gone with the runners if he could have slipped away unnoticed but, as one of Tostig's senior retinue, his place was near the front of the shield wall.

'Who is that?' demanded Hardrada as the mailed man rode forward, flanked by his two banner bearers.

Harold had done it.

A superb feat of organisation, leadership and unrelenting toil had seen him deliver an army to the north of Inglalond just in time to give the Danes a serious headache. We had watched them come for a while before showing ourselves because Harold wanted them on our side of the river, but as we emerged from the woods to the west of the bridge, the Danes went into a panic and started scrambling into defensive shape.

'Fools,' sneered Elric. 'They should have run back and defended the bridge.'

Harold rode forward with just Aethelnoth and Eadnoth holding his banners, while the rest of us watched and jeered the Danes who, clearly, were not expecting us.

'Fuck this,' I said to Elric, 'I want a closer look. Bring the archers forward.'

We began moving to the left of the field in our four troops and I was proud of our order as we moved quickly forward in tight formation – shadowing Harold to our right.

But about a hundred paces from the Danes, he stopped and held his hand up in token of parley.

∞ ∞ ∞

'Who is that?' repeated Hardrada as the mailed man paused in front of his army with his hand raised.

'I will talk to him,' said Tostig and beckoned Malgard to accompany him. Malgard felt as though his bowels were turning to water but before the eyes of the Viking army had no choice other than to accompany Tostig, who strode forward to meet his brother.

Ten paces from the three men on horses, Tostig paused, with Malgard a pace further back.

'Greetings brother,' said Harold. 'I trust you are well?'

'If you cared for my health,' replied Tostig, 'you would not have supplanted me in Northumbria to further your royal ambitions.'

'You are correct,' said Harold.

' … I beg your pardon?'

'I was wrong to take your earldom … and now I offer it back to you. And Mercia also.'

Tostig was shocked into silence, and Malgard's mind raced with the possibilities. If Tostig accepted, there would be no battle, or at least if there was they would now be on the side with greater numbers and better position. He began to feel the stirrings of relief, but then Tostig said, 'What of Edwin and Morcar … are they dead?'

'They are defeated and in hiding,' said Harold. 'Probably they do not know I am here … but if they live I shall find something more to their measure. Part of Wessex perhaps … but the north I return to you.'

Tostig stared at his brother, axe in one hand and stroking his beard in thought.

'Hardrada is my friend,' said Tostig at last. 'He has supported me when all others would not … what will you offer him?'

∞ ∞ ∞

'That's fucking Tostig!' said Elric. 'What'd I tell you? The brothers Godwinson will come to blows ere the end … and here they are, facing each other before armies … with drawn weapons.'

We had stolen to within a hundred paces of where Harold and Tostig spoke together, and a further hundred paces from the Viking host. Already I had started picking targets in the shield wall, but turned my attention back to the parley in mid-field. There was something oddly familiar about the man standing slightly behind Tostig.

'Who's that with him?' I wondered aloud, a weird shiver of destiny tingling across my shoulders.

∞ ∞ ∞

'Hardrada is your friend?' echoed Harold. 'Well in that case I shall give him his life if he returns to Norway at once. If he does not I shall give him nothing more than six feet of ground … or slightly more if he needs it. He looks a large man.'

Tostig was silent and Malgard could have screamed with frustration. 'Accept!' he was thinking. 'All your ambitions granted at one stroke. Take it!'

But Tostig shook his head and laughed.

'Did I not say that if you split our family you will lose Inglalond? You have done me too much insult brother ... I cannot accept your terms.'

'You will fight with the Danes?'

'Aye ... to the death.'

'You are outnumbered and ill-equipped ... unless you are hiding your helms and armour,' said Harold. 'Be sensible ... or must I take news of your needless death back to our mother?'

'You brought that news to her when you split our family,' said Tostig. 'You are the lightning bolt of Edward's dream. You have cloven Inglalond apart and God will not suffer her to be repaired until the tree grows green again. Much blood will flow before that time, including mine ... and yours.'

Malgard took a pace forward as though to shake some sense into Tostig and for the first time Harold noticed him.

'I do not know you, sir,' he said. 'Tell me your name so that I may beg you to restore my brother's wits and judgment.'

But Tostig laughed, and Malgard's blood ran cold at the sound, guessing what was to come.

'My dear brother,' said Tostig, 'allow me to introduce Malgard son of Rathgar ... thegn of Stybbor and appointed by Edward himself. I believe you have heard of him?'

Harold stared at Malgard, but said no more. Instead, he turned his horse and trotted back towards his army.

'Why did you do that?' asked Malgard, his throat constricted with anger and fear.

'What does it matter?' laughed Tostig. 'If we lose we are all dead ... Harold knowing your name changes nothing.'

But it did change something, thought Malgard bitterly as he followed Tostig back to the Viking army. It changed something really important.

∞ ∞ ∞

'That was Harold?' shouted Hardrada. 'That little man on the horse was Harold?'

Tostig shrugged, but Hardrada was furious.

'Why didn't you tell me you went to speak with the king? I should have been present!'

'He tried to turn me against you by offering me terms,' said Tostig. 'He offers you only death and I suspect that's the best offer you will get.'

Hardrada's eyes blazed, but before he could respond a shouted warning sounded from several men close by.

'Riders are coming!'

Tostig looked up and saw perhaps a hundred riders bearing down on them in two ranks, all holding spears.

'Shield wall!' shouted Hardrada, but Malgard said, 'Lord ... we should get back across the bridge. We can hold them there.'

There was no time. The horsemen had approached surreptitiously during the parley and now had only a short gallop to reach the Vikings, who formed up shield to shield, braced for the charge – but instead of hitting the wall the riders came within twenty paces and hurled their spears. Then they wheeled away and the second rank closed and hurled their spears. Not many found a mark but there were cries of pain amid the outrage as the Vikings jeered at the cowardly tactics.

'Come and fight us man to man!' roared Hardrada. 'Cowards and nithings that throw their weapons away ... shitting themselves at the thought of facing Danes!'

The man next to Malgard was shrieking with pain after protecting himself with his shield and a needle pointed spear had gone straight through shield and arm. His friend pulled the spear free and a great surge of blood poured from his arm as he sank to the ground in a faint.

'Here they come!' men were shouting and Malgard saw a running horde of Saxons screaming and brandishing axes and swords, and yet another group off to the right in an oddly tight formation that was somehow terrifying in its discipline.

∞ ∞ ∞

'Close to fifty paces!' I shouted. 'Keep your order!'

The Danish shield wall was about two hundred yards long and several men deep, bristling with weapons and shouting their violence. And yet I knew that we were about to destroy them. Their old way of fighting would be their downfall.

'Let's open a couple of holes, boys,' I yelled as our own foot soldiers bore down on the Danes. 'Now!'

Eighty arrows were loosed at two different spots in the shield wall and the effect was devastating. It was as though their own god Thor hammered them so instant was the impact of concentrated archery. We only got off three arrows per man by the time our soldiers raced whooping into the fray – driving into the gaps our arrows had made.

∞ ∞ ∞

'Back to the bridge!' shouted Hardrada, disgusted but dismayed by the cowardly, and yet deadly tactics of the Saxons. The Vikings turned and ran for the bridge but many of the mounted housecarls, having thrown their spears were now between the Vikings and the bridge and fighting with swords.

'Kill the horses!' yelled Tostig, and after a couple had been cut down and their riders hewn with axes, the rest got out of the way and let the Vikings win the bridge.

'Hold them here!'

Vikings poured over the bridge but too slowly. Arrows thumped into unprotected flesh from the northern side of the battle and the rear guard was a semicircular shield wall that shrank towards the bridge while holding the Saxon foot soldiers at bay. Dozens of Danes were already dead or dying in the field before the bridge and many more were in the fast flowing Derwent and stuck with arrows.

In his terror, Malgard ceased caring what others might think of him. He fought like a wild cat to stay in the thick of the men and didn't even notice the turd that poured down the back of his legs. Wildly he looked for a place to run, but was unwilling to leave the protection of the greater body of men that collected east of the bridge.

Then a great warrior, Snorri Olafsson, as big as Hardrada and one of the few who had come wearing mail, roared, 'Fuck this! We are

Vikings!' And he forced his way back through the press of men on the bridge and started laying about with his huge axe, enabling many more Vikings to get back across behind him.

∞ ∞ ∞

'Kill them!' I shouted. Arrows flew, and another layer of Danes was peeled away from the shield wall, which was now shrinking rapidly – partly from the damage we caused but mainly because the Danes behind were pouring across the bridge to safety.

'That arseling there!' shouted Elric pointing at a giant of a man with a huge axe. 'Kill him!'

Arrows flew but he seemed charmed as the arrows missed him or bounced off his mail coat. He was stuck with one or two but they only served to enrage him. Soon the entire Danish army was behind him and he stood in the middle of the bridge – a demon dripping blood – beckoning challengers and we could no longer shoot arrows for fear of hitting our own. In ones and twos Saxons went forward to face him with axe and sword and the bridge was quickly red with the blood of the foolish and the brave.

Gazing down at the fast flowing water, Elric shouted and ran to the right of the bridge and pointed down on the bank where a small coracle was drawn up and tied to a tree. He snatched up one of the spears thrown by a housecarl and said, 'Let the rope out and the current will take me under the bridge.'

Immediately I understood what he was attempting and with one of our swordsmen to aid me, freed the coracle and braced the rope around the tree as Elric clambered aboard. Then we played the rope out until Elric was directly under the middle of the slatted bridge with his spear poised.

Suddenly the huge Viking bellowed with pain and stumbled forward, and several Saxons leapt at him with axes. Moments later his body was flung off the bridge and Saxons poured across to chase the Danes.

∞ ∞ ∞

'Shield wall!' shouted Hardrada and men who had been in the midst of panic and ready to race back to the boats, paused, looked around and saw they were still a formidable host. Hardrada had the great Landwaster flag unfurled and on a small rise east of the bridge he stood rallying Vikings and they flew back to his banner.

They formed up in a great horseshoe shape about the hill and clashed axe and sword against shield – calling the Saxon nithings to come and prove their courage by fighting face to face instead of throwing spears and shooting arrows like the cowardly turds they were.

But the Saxons didn't care or didn't understand the insults. They regrouped on the Viking side of the bridge and resumed pouring arrows into the shield wall. Always concentrated in just one or two places Malgard noticed – despite his terror – and in those places the foot soldiers would run screaming through the gaps to attack the wall from the sides. It was a novel way of fighting and extremely effective against a foe that expected the traditional manner of warfare. Then Malgard was drenched with blood as the man next to him took an arrow in the throat, and without a second thought Malgard flung himself to the ground, managing to burrow beneath the dying man as he fell.

∞ ∞ ∞

'Look at that standard!' yelled Elric in his excitement as we stood watching our archers decimate the Viking shield wall. The troop leaders had the method down to a nicety – opening a gap with their concentrated shooting, then choosing another as the Saxon foot soldiers filled the holes.

The standard was a great yellow triangular flag with a black raven, red eyes gleaming and talons out, in the centre.

'The raven is their god Odin,' laughed Elric. 'Not much fucking use, is he!'

The battle seemed to pause for a moment as another giant Dane stepped out in front of the shield wall, with the great standard in one hand and an axe in the other.

'Hardrada!' men were shouting. 'Hardrada!'

The most famous and fearsome warrior of the age stood in front of his host bellowing for Harold to come and face him, but it was the last thing he ever did. A hail of arrows from Walt's troop picked him out and he fell to his knees – pulling at an arrow in his throat.

Then Tostig jumped from the ranks and raised once more the great standard of Odin, and before I could stop him, Elric was gone, racing for Tostig with his sword drawn. I chased after him, knowing what he intended, but knowing also that Harold would prefer his brother alive.

'Elric!' I shouted. 'Leave him!'

But I may as well have shouted at a charging bull. With the fall of Hardrada, the shield wall was collapsing. Some fled and some continued to fight a hopeless cause, but Tostig didn't fight. He simply waved the great banner in defiance of Harold and I swear he was laughing as Elric dodged the swords of two defenders and leapt at Tostig to avenge his brother. I chased after him to try and prevent Tostig's death and felt an arrow brush past me in my closeness to the Danes.

'Stop shooting!' I yelled, bursting through the press about the flag, which fell for the final time as I arrived. Elric was standing wild-eyed over the body of Tostig whose head had been hacked away, and I seized him by the arm.

'Get back to the men and tell no-one of this deed!' I shouted.

Elric stared at me for a moment as though I was an enemy, but then he grinned his usual cheeky grin and slipped away. The fighting just faded like mist in a warm breeze. The Danes were all flying in twos and threes, back to their boats, and hundreds of Saxons pursued them. But for me the fighting was over. Harold appeared with Gyrth, Skalpi and Aethelnoth and gazed down at his brother's body. They all looked at my sword, which was unblooded, and then Harold asked, 'Who did this?'

'I did not see him fall, Lord,' I said, which was no lie.

Harold stared piercingly at me, then sighed, his eyes glistening with tears.

'It is for the best I suppose. He could not have borne the defeat and would forever have been a source of trouble ... but it will be hard telling our mother of his death.'

Harold fell to his knees beside Tostig's body and his eyes squeezed shut for a few moments. Gyrth also knelt and the rest of us stepped back a few paces to give them a moment with their fallen brother.

'Where is Lef?' asked Harold as he stood, his eyes red with grief.

'He leads the pursuit, Lord,' said Aethelnoth, and Harold nodded. It had been a great victory with comparatively small losses, except for the terrible personal loss felt so keenly by the king.

'Divide our family and you will never rule Inglalond, he said,' mused Harold. 'And yet I do rule Inglalond ... and no longer is our family divided.'

The sun was falling towards the west so it was decided to erect the king's pavilion over the field of battle. Tostig's body was reunited with his head and wrapped in a shroud for burial back in his capital of Yorvik but Hardrada was buried on top of the hill he'd defended. Our own casualties would also be buried the following day but the Danes would be left where they lay, unless the local peasants wanted to bury them.

∞ ∞ ∞

'I see you Malgard.'

Malgard had not moved a muscle for at least two hours, lying half beneath the corpse of a cold and stinking Dane, but the voice filled him with hope.

Gorik sat down beside him and glanced about in the semi-darkness.

'We are unobserved. Move your hand if you still live.'

Malgard moved his hand, amazed to hear Gorik's voice but half fearing some treachery. He heard Gorik chuckle.

'Yes, I thought so. I had my eye on you the whole battle and saw you fall ... hit by no missile, it seemed to me.'

Malgard eased himself from under the dead Dane and rolled onto his back, rubbing the blood slime from his eyes.

'Harold is victorious?'

'Aye ... a great victory. Won in large part by the archery tactics devised by your nephew ... who is very high in the king's favour.'

Malgard said nothing for a few moments. The joy of surviving the battle swiftly evaporated in the realisation that Harold was now undisputed master of Inglalond.

'And Tostig?'

'Dead.'

'Fuck.'

Malgard was now totally without friends and facing life as an outlaw vagabond.

'How came you here?' he asked, sitting up and surveying the field in the last of the dying light.

Gorik briefly told his tale and Malgard was incensed that he had had so many opportunities to murder Brand but had taken none of them.

'There was always a complication,' sniggered Gorik. 'Even in the midst of battle I only had one chance to shoot at him without making it too obvious. He ducked to avoid a blade or I would have taken him in the neck. He certainly leads a charmed life.'

'Not anymore,' growled Malgard.

∞ ∞ ∞

Four days after the battle, when Tostig had been buried in the Minster and all other loose ends of the northern campaign were squared away, there was a victory feast in Tostig's former hall and Harold insisted on me sitting at his side.

'The archery tactics you devised were like something out of ancient tales of Rome,' he exclaimed. 'It was murder ... sheer murder ... and made our victory certain.'

'And kept no small number of our own alive,' added Gyrth. 'I've no doubt we would have won the battle of the shield walls, had it come to that ... but Brand's archers gave us a massive advantage and there are more alive to celebrate our victory than might have been otherwise.'

'And more alive to face the Bastard if he ever floats his army across the Channel,' added Leofwine, who had returned from the carnage about the Viking boats as the last of them were killed or chased out to sea – leaving most of their boats and weapons behind. A good part of Hardrada's fabled hoard also was now under guard.

'That was well done Lef,' said Harold. 'We have a lot to repair

378

after the raids. It is fitting that Hardrada's gold will pay for his own damage.'

But ever and again Harold turned back to me, shaking his head and laughing.

'Brand the Reliable!' he shouted, toasting me for the seventh time in an hour. 'Is there no task beyond you? Every problem I have turns to dust when you tackle it, whether it be Danish soldiers or subtle matters of the heart.'

As for that, his words reminded me of Emma, which naturally set me off pondering Valla again. I still had one of the bluebells, which I was certain she had spirited into the Lady Swanneshals' basket, twined into the thong which held *The Fighting Man* device I wore under my tunic. It was my most precious possession and I started to relax and hope that possibly the campaigns were over and that I might now go off and find my Valla so that we would never be parted again. But Harold was still speaking.

'I have promised this before and privately ... but now I state openly that the Lord Brand shall be an Earl.'

There was a silence, but then a tremendous volley of shouting and cheering as men acclaimed me and thumped me over the shoulders. Harold held up his hands for silence, which he only partly achieved – such was the ebullient spirit of victory.

'Yea, Earl Brand has passed every test and exceeded my hopes at every turn. All kings have need for such men, who should be the best rewarded in the kingdom.'

'Where shall be his Earldom?' asked Gyrth.

'I am yet to determine that ... there is much to reconsider after the events up here in the north, but a suitable place shall be found for him. I am richly in his debt. Hail Earl Brand!'

'Hail!'

Again the shouting, cheering and thumping and my perception seemed to fracture in a mist of gratitude and ale. It was possibly the happiest moment of my life, save the first time Valla told me she loved me, and I felt completely overwhelmed by joy and relief that the battles were over, for now at least, as it was well into the harvest season and way too late for any further campaigning. Harold and William would send their armies home and, with the best part of a year to consolidate his realm, I had no doubt that Harold would soon have Inglalond prepared as one great island fortress and the Bastard would have no choice other than to give up his claim.

'Good God!' laughed Harold, as the celebrations rolled around us. 'I nearly forgot to tell you Brand … At my parley with Tostig, who do you think was present?'

I waited for him to continue but, at that moment, a mud stained traveller forced his way to the king's ear and my heart sank as I saw him speaking urgently and the expression changing on Harold's face. I think I knew what he was going to say before he said it, but Harold sat staring at the floor for a few moments, then collected himself and stood.

'Friends!' he cried, once more raising his arms and this time, something about his mood got him the silence he'd not managed only minutes before.

'It seems we have one more fight to win. William, Duke of Normandy, has landed with his army at Pevensey.'

PART FIVE

Chapter 38

Driven By Greed and Pride

'Something has gone wrong?' asked Valla.

Myrrthn didn't answer, but sat naked – staring into the embers of the great bonfire and occasionally adding a small piece of dried moss or mistletoe.

'I think not,' he said, after a while. 'I think that the winds of the world can only be checked for so long ere they build like water behind a dam and must eventually have their way. We can rebuild the spell.'

Valla had been deeply upset when the wind had suddenly swung around to the south, despite all their effort, and the following day they had seen the ships. Hundreds of ships to the south-east with the largest of them bearing a sail blazoned with the red cross of the killer god.

'I do know this,' cackled Myrrthn, 'we have done him much damage. Oh yes, he would have been stronger ... much stronger ... if not for our spell. And now he limps onto our island ... driven by greed and pride ... with far fewer ships than he might have had. Greed and pride will be his undoing.'

He was silent for a while, rebuilding the fire, and as it burst back into flame Myrrthn capered about the cliff top as a westerly wind drove the smoke towards the invading ships.

'You see?' he said. 'The spell is more subtle than I perceived. Instead of just preventing the killer god from coming ... the spell allows him to come, in a weakened state. His forces can now be defeated which will mean a final end to foreign ambition. We will be safe from the killer god for a thousand years!'

'Safe,' repeated Valla, and immediately started pining once again for the man who would be her husband.

'How long before we can bring an end to this?' she asked.

'You wish to be with him?' asked Myrrthn, and Valla nodded – her heart almost breaking it was so full of love.

'Not long,' said Myrrthn. 'Indeed, I would suggest that even now your husband will be making his way toward us.'

∞ ∞ ∞

'What place is this?' demanded William.

'It is Bosham, sire,' answered one of the monks of Fecamp who attended him as guides. 'Our abbey owns land at Rye as well as lands in Normandy … I know this place well.'

'Bosham,' repeated William. 'And where is Harold's house?'

'Not far,' replied the monk. Above the point at the western end of the bay.'

William was still astonished by the absence of any resistance. They had been several days in Ingalond and, while scouts had been seen from time to time, no soldiers had made any attempt on William's army.

It had been a wholly successful operation thus far. They had left the haven at St Valery on the night of 27th September, and woken on the 28th in a silvery mist that shrouded the Mora – bobbing on the ocean without escort. Twice William bade men climb the mast to look for the rest of the fleet but they were truly alone with nothing but water and mist for miles. Some men panicked but William understood that the Mora was bigger and faster than any other vessel in the fleet. The rest of the seven hundred ships – mostly single sailed barges – were yet to catch him.

Finally, on the third climb, 'I see a mast sire! Nay … two masts!'

'Which direction?'

'To the south and west … nay scores of masts! I see the fleet!'

Signals were exchanged and the rest of the fleet rapidly fell into line and commenced the pull towards shore with the tide. As the last of the mist cleared, about the second hour, they could see a green land to the north with low white cliffs. They pulled into Pevensey Bay (according to the monks) and landed on the banks of a river, but William had immediately disliked the place – not least as their landing was observed by mounted men on a hill to the north and there were foul smelling marshes just beyond the beach through which he did not care to take so many horses.

On the next tide they left Pevensey and moved the fleet a few miles east to a long sandy beach at Hastings, where there were still marshes, but also a defensible peninsula. William, feeling a surge of destiny coursing through his heart, strode up the beach – only to fall face-first in the sand.

The army held its breath, wondering what the famously irascible Duke would make of such an inauspicious portent, but fitzOsbern laughed and said, 'Sire! You already hold Inglalond in your grasp!'

William had been delighted with the quip and rose to his feet with a handful of sand.

'Yea, I like this country and have already taken seisin,' he declaimed, getting shouts of laughter from those closest.

The landing otherwise went without incident and within hours they were putting together temporary fortresses and sending out foraging parties with instructions to kill every person they encountered, save only the clergy. Take all food and weapons, steer all cattle back to the camp for slaughter, burn all houses.

And now, just a few days later, William sat outside Harold's own house at Bosham – a few miles west of the camp. No-one was home and William continued to be dumbfounded by the absence of any resistance – only the very old were ever encountered, unable to move far from their hovels.

Harold's house looked a rustic but comfortable place and William was tempted to keep it for himself, but hardened his heart against the idea.

'Burn it!' he shouted. 'Burn everything.'

Could the strategy really have worked so well he wondered? Could Harold really be in the north of the country dealing with Hardrada while William did as he pleased in the south?

Torches were thrust under the eaves of Harold's house and it was quickly aflame. The barns also and the air was rent by the screams of terrified animals locked in their stalls, unneeded for the kitchens.

William stared into the fire and put himself in Harold's position. It was a strong position – despite the fact he had fought a major battle and disbanded the fyrd. He could still put a huge army in the field. William had more than twelve thousand knights and professional soldiers – the cream of Europe – but Harold had the home advantage and could put several times that number against William and gradually grind him down. It was what William would do in his place.

'We must make Harold hate us,' explained William to those about him – fitzOsbern, Odo, Eustace and other noble knights of Normandy and France. 'We must make him hate so he loses his judgment and cannot wait to fight us. If he keeps his head and has us hemmed in one place, we must eventually be defeated ... or go home.'

∞ ∞ ∞

We arrived in Lundene only four days after hearing the news of William's landing. All along the southern road Harold had collected his army – ordered to ignore the harvest in the emergency – and sent messages across the kingdom begging men to come to Sussex with all possible speed.

The news continued to be bad.

'They are killing and burning as they go Lord,' explained Cuthred, whom Harold had allowed to stay on as a lesser minister – putting aside personal dislike for practicality. Cuthred knew the workings of the kingdom and was not without his uses now that his allegiance was solely to Harold.

'These are my people!' fumed Harold in his council. 'William will rue the day he coveted Inglalond. I will destroy his army and make such an example of their leader as will never be forgotten.'

Harold was chafing to be at William but only slowly did the fyrd trickle into Lundene and the reports suggested William had landed with as many as fifteen thousand. Thegn Theobald of Wessex had seen them and suggested there might even be more than that, 'although it is difficult to tell with these Normans whether they are warriors or priests. They are all tonsured.'

'They are warriors and priests,' I said, remembering Odo. I would not care to face him and his mace and doubted not he had come.

We all urged Harold to wait until we had the entire army ready to crush William, but the fact that William was destroying Wessex and had even burned Harold's own house at Bosham was too much for Harold.

'Nay, I will go at once ... if only to prevent him doing further damage to my own people. There is a place called Caldbec Hill ... do you know it Theobald?'

'I do sire.'

'There is an apple tree there,' continued Harold, ' ... of great antiquity, and I am told it was cloven in two by lightning but now grows green again. I will raise *The Red Dragon* and *The Fighting Man* in that spot and let all my army meet me there in three days ... for I will make an end to this royal dispute and let God decide between us.'

The Lady Swanneshals had come to Lundene with Orald, who now rejoined my archers so that we were back to our full complement of five troops.

Swanneshals sought me out after the council.

'I have seen her again.'

'Valla?'

'I believe so.

'You aren't certain?'

We walked in a small green space near the new minster, where King Edward had been buried and Harold crowned.

'Are you certain Valla left the bluebells?' she asked.

'I am,' I replied, even though in truth, I could not be sure. But no other explanation made sense.

'In that case, I am as certain as you that I saw her. It was in the glade by the pool again ... or close by.'

'Did you dream ... or were you awake?' I asked.

'It is hard to tell the difference in that place,' said Swanneshals. 'It seems enchanted, but it is beautiful and I have no fear of the spell.'

'Did she say anything?'

Swanneshals pondered, her chin on her chest, and said, 'We had no speech. She was in a shadow of trees ... perhaps fifteen paces away ... but I seemed to hear a message.'

' ... A message?'

'A message for Brand ... the time approaches when our tasks are all done and our life together can resume. Stay true Brand ... lie with no other and remember your promise. It is only a little while now.'

I stared at the Lady Swanneshals, and her face fell.

'This message does not please you?'

'It pleases me greatly,' I replied, in a profound torment.

'You do not look pleased.'

I could not explain to her the reason for my distress, but perceived that perhaps my promise was still unbroken. If Valla was still sending messages then she must believe me to have stayed true, and perhaps that was all that mattered.

I managed a smile, suddenly confident I was going to see her shortly – not least as we were headed south again on the morrow. The Lady Swanneshals also was smiling. Edith had stayed in the north with her brothers who had both been badly injured in the fight at Fulford Gate – so injured that Harold had left Yorvik in the safekeeping of Maerleswein, Reeve of Lincoln. All of which meant that Swanneshals had no rival in the south for Harold's attention and was quickly back in his favour.

'I look forward to the time when we can look back on all of this,' she sighed. 'I also look forward to seeing Valla again. I have always liked her and it is pleasing to see two people so deeply in love. Perhaps your tale can be sung in your own hall when you are an ancient earl with many sons?'

'There will have to be another fight before that can happen,' I sighed.

∞ ∞ ∞

Malgard was feeling a lot better. Gorik had slipped away from the archery troop – presumed dead, no doubt – and the two of them had followed the army back south, more or less at their leisure. They still had the money provided by Tostig, and could afford to take their time.

They had heard the news of William's landing – the whole country was abuzz – and small groups of housecarls and fyrdmen all over Inglalond were making their way to Sussex.

Snug by a fire again, in the old inn at Breahinga, Malgard and Gorik weighed up their numerous options.

'It is all but certain that Harold will have the victory,' said Malgard, 'which means your job is to get close to Brand in the fighting and finish him. I will be working my way towards Harold and trying to get involved in the fighting when victory is all but complete.'

'He won't know you from Stamford Bridge?'

'I believe not ... my helm has a nose guard and my face would have been largely obscured. I shall change my name to Rathgar, cousin of Holgar, and claim Stybbor ... and who will care? Brand will be dead, and Harold will have too much to put right after the battle to be concerned with such a small matter. And if my sword is well and truly blooded in his presence I may even win some of the favour he now looks to bestow on Brand. How I shall wail when his body is discovered after the battle ... rent with many wounds.'

'And his cock cut off,' laughed Gorik, unconsciously touching his scar.

They sipped their ale and glanced about the room, heaving with the excitement of other warriors headed south.

'But what if William wins?' asked Gorik, lowering his voice.

'I don't see how he can,' said Malgard, 'but we must be alert to the possibility. Indeed, a victory for William is the better result for us. He knows me from my visit with Tostig and the last we spoke I was sworn to help him win the crown. The rewards would be far better than anything we might cadge from Harold.'

'Tricky ... changing sides in the middle of a fight,' said Gorik.

'Yes ... we would have better standing with William if he saw us in his ranks prior to battle.'

Malgard stared into the fire for a few moments, then snapped his fingers and grinned.

'I have it! I know exactly what we will do.'

Chapter 39

Friday the Thirteenth

Several days later, as the sun rose in the east, Harold Godwinson – King of Inglalond – raised his banners on Caldbec Hill. *The Red Dragon* of Wessex – a long fiery pennant in the manner of a wyvern; and *The Fighting Man* – a large triangular standard that showed a warrior with shield and sword in an oddly angular pose, picked out with jewels red, green and blue on a pale field, bordered in red and gold.

Caldbec Hill was in Sussex, only a couple of miles from Duke William's camp. All around the king were his closest companions – his brothers, Gyrth and Leofwine; the stallers Eadnoth, Aethelnoth and Skalpi, and thegns innumerable. Beyond those were the first to arrive of the fyrd – several thousands at least but many more were on their way. In three more days we would have as many as thirty thousand to put against William – which meant Harold's victory was certain. All he had to do was prevent William from escaping the Hastings peninsula and his sheer weight of numbers must prevail.

For so many men, it was strangely quiet, but then Harold began to speak.

'My countrymen and loyal subjects ... our island, Inglalond that we love, is coveted by others. Fell men from foreign lands will ever be jealous of our bounty, and so we must protect ourselves and our property ... perhaps until the end of time.'

He paused to look around his army – looking into the very soul of each of us, as though to test our resolve and hardiness.

'Some of you will have heard,' continued Harold, 'that Duke William charges me with perfidy ... says I took by stealth the throne that was promised to him by King Edward. He even says I swore an oath to be his man and take his part in Inglalond when the time came. Well part of that is true! I did swear an oath to William ... to be his man in Normandy.

'But this is not Normandy!' he cried, and for the first time there came a cheer from the ranks assembled. 'This is Inglalond ... and I swear before you all that Edward chose me to be king. With his dying breath he said, into your hands I commend my kingdom ... before witnesses ecclesiastic and lay ... and this choice was confirmed by all the magnates and bishops of Inglalond!'

Another cheer, and some words of support were shouted, but Harold held up his hands again for quiet.

'William can claim all he likes that Edward promised him the throne. I have never heard that from Edward's lips ... but even if he did, Edward changed his mind. In his dying hour he determined that Harold Godwinson should be king after him and I plan to honour his wish by fighting to make it true ... and if William disputes it, then let God decide who is fitter to be king!'

Again Harold had to hold up his hands for silence, so loud and raucous was the acclamation as thegns and housecarls and even fyrdmen clashed swords and spears against shields and shouted their love for their king.

'But I will not lead any man to battle,' said Harold, 'who does not believe ... with all his heart ... that I was Edward's true choice. If any man here has the slightest doubt, then I beg you to leave this field and go anywhere else ... even to William. For I will have only those beside me who are entirely free of doubt that my claim is the true claim. To fight against the true claim is treason and we would all be jointly complicit if William's claim were better. Does anyone doubt?'

'No!' came the roar in response.

'Am I the true king of Inglalond?'

'Yea!' from ten thousand throats.

'Will you stand at my side to help me rid our country of those who would lie and perjure their way onto the throne?'

'Yea!' came the cry again in terrifying unison.

Once again Harold waited for silence, or close enough. Then he gestured to the hoary apple tree behind him – scorched and cloven.

'Many of you will have heard,' said Harold, lowering his voice again, 'of the late king's dream. Two monks told him that God despaired of Inglalond. Faithless and riven with discord … Inglalond would never be at peace or know God's mercy until a tree, cloven in two by lightning, might grow green again.'

All turned to examine the blackened tree, split in twain by lightning, and all of us perceived that green shoots were emerging from its boughs.

'This is the tree,' said Harold, his voice thick with emotion. 'This is the sign that God is ready to forgive … ready to side with Inglalond against foreign invaders.'

Again the raucous cheer.

'God is with us!' cried Harold. 'And if God is with us, do we need anyone else?'

'No!'

'Then let us attack them!' shouted Harold. 'Let us drive William and his curs from our soil or drench it with their blood!'

It was Friday the Thirteenth of October and unless William were to renounce his claim and depart, then the following days would see the greatest battle ever to be staged in Inglalond.

∞ ∞ ∞

Men continued to pour into Harold's camp, although conspicuously absent were the housecarls of Edwin and Morcar, who should have been with us days before. There was a rumour that the brothers had quarrelled with Harold over their actions at Fulford Gate and were furious that he had buried his brother as the Earl Tostig restored. Even more furious were they to hear that I had been made an earl. Well, injured they may have been, but they would rue their pride if they were not represented on the battlefield at Hastings.

There was quite a lot of coming and going between Harold's camp and William's that day. Scouts, of course, from both sides tested each other's disposition and resolve, and monks of Fecamp did intermediary work between the rivals seeking a last minute resolution – but it was all a show for the sake of future lawyers and historians. Neither had the slightest intention of abandoning their claim so battle was inevitable. It was solely a matter of where and when.

From our lofty place on Caldbec Hill we could see down onto the next ridge – known to the locals as Senlac – and beyond to where William was encamped. I had gone with Elric down to Senlac to look upon William's army and it seemed to me they were very numerous and with good discipline. There was almost none of the drinking and fighting you would see in a comparable number of Saxons – or Vikings for that matter – which was a little disturbing.

'They take this argument very seriously,' whispered Elric, as we watched from the eaves of the wood. 'Look at all the horses!'

'There aren't enough of them,' I replied. 'I estimate twelve to thirteen thousand warriors. We have nearly that many already and by Sunday could have three times their number. Harold cannot lose ... as long as he bides his time.'

'What's to stop William running away in his ships ... perhaps to fight another day?'

'He will not come back,' I replied. 'If he waits long enough to see the size of our army he will know he can never win.'

'Then why does he wait?' wondered Elric. 'Surely William's only chance is to attack while Harold is unreinforced by the other fyrds.'

'I know not the answer to that,' I replied. 'But you are right ... if William attacked today it would be a hard fight.'

We were not the only ones scouting. There were quite a number of Harold's army moving about in the forest, and even as we watched another delegation of monks from William, escorted by a small troop of soldiers came up Senlac Hill on horses.

'William won't enjoy attacking up that hill,' laughed Elric. 'If we form up on top of the ridge it'll be like waves trying to run up a beach. They can only get so far before they run out of force and must fall back whence they came.'

'William should try to win the ridge now,' I said, ' ... while it is undefended. What has he been doing since arriving here but killing and burning? He could have gained a much stronger toehold in the fortnight he has had so far.'

'He is loath to move too far from his ships,' said Elric. 'I believe he has made a giant gambit ... perhaps expecting Hardrada to win in the north ... and now he is here and finds to his dismay that he must face a victorious Harold with all Inglalond in support.'

'I believe you have guessed it,' I said, with a grim smile. 'Can you imagine William's rage upon hearing of Harold's victory?'

'Aye, and his fear,' responded Elric. 'He must have thought that at the very least Harold and Hardrada would have been mired in the north … possibly for months, with their armies reduced. Instead, Harold won a decisive victory … not least through our archery … and William finds himself trapped. It is as though God were truly on our side and moved the pieces about the board to suit His design.'

Immediately I felt the old quiver across my shoulders at the thought of God's designs and how He might once again be testing me. I had a strong feeling that Valla was not far away and that I would see her if I could perform some great deed or solve a riddle that yet refused to make its propositions clear.

'Let us steal a little closer to William's camp,' I said. 'I'd like to see whether we can discern aught of their morale. Do the soldiers know they are trapped? Or is that ill news known only to the lords?'

∞ ∞ ∞

Malgard and Gorik sat outside William's tent, their weapons taken and surrounded by four swordsmen.

Malgard was nervous but affected nonchalance. His only concern was that they had been announced nearly two hours ago and were yet to be seen. Was William simply overburdened by the cares of his office, or was he refusing to see them?

Finally, a monk of Fecamp emerged from the large tent and Malgard recognised him.

'Bishop John?'

The Bishop glanced at him, then paused.

'Malgard … companion of Tostig?'

'It is I,' said Malgard.

'How come you here … and why are you a prisoner?' asked the bishop, his eyes narrowing.

'I bring news to William of Stamford Bridge,' said Malgard. 'I swore my loyalty to William in Normandy and that loyalty remains, though Tostig be dead. Perhaps I can be of further service?'

The Bishop considered Malgard, not quite liking what he saw, but knowing William would be eager for a first hand account of Stamford Bridge.

'You were there? When the Danes were destroyed?'

'We both were Lord,' said Malgard, indicating Gorik at his side.

The bishop pulled at his beard thoughtfully, and then returned to the tent. A couple of minutes later he beckoned to them, but also their armed escort and ushered them inside.

Malgard felt confident when they were summoned, but that confidence was rocked when he entered William's tent and felt the tension in the room. William's magnates stared at Malgard with white-faced enmity and were frankly suspicious.

William himself seemed as though he could barely restrain himself from attack and directed his first question to the captain of the guards.

'How were they caught?'

'We found them in the wood, sire ... just north-east of our camp.'

'Spying?'

'So it looked, sire.'

'What say you to that?' demanded William, turning to Malgard.

'We were not spying Lord,' said Malgard, 'although I forgive the captain for his error. Before a battle, all men outside a camp are spies until proven otherwise.'

'Indeed,' said William, 'so how can you prove otherwise?'

'Did we hide from you?' enquired Malgard of the captain. 'Did we resist your challenge?'

'Nay,' replied the guard, 'but you were outnumbered and would have fared poorly if you had. And now I deem you twist words to save yourselves.'

'Lord William,' said Malgard, ignoring the guard's accusation, 'I swore loyalty to you in Normandy and remain true to that oath. I believe you to be the rightful king of Inglalond and would serve you if I can.'

William stared long at Malgard as though he might see straight into his soul and discern a falsehood. Then he said, 'The bishop tells me you were at Stamford Bridge.'

'Aye, sire. We fought with Tostig and the Danes.'

'But Tostig swore to take my part,' growled William. 'Why would he be fighting with Danes?'

'You bade him bring a large army to the north sire ... to split Harold's attention and weaken him. I believe Tostig regarded his alliance with the Danes as temporary. It certainly achieved what you asked of him.'

'And yet Harold is here,' said William in disgust, 'with more men than I have and more coming every hour.'

'The Danes proved less adept as warriors than anyone might have expected,' said Malgard, 'but no blame attaches to Tostig for that. He fought bravely sire ... and fell. Even though Harold offered him his earldom back ... and Mercia as well.'

'He did?' asked William, for the first time showing interest in Malgard's tale.

'I was there, sire, when Harold and Tostig spoke before the battle. The earls Morcar and Edwin had been defeated and shown themselves unfit. They are not with Harold now.'

'And what of the armies of the north?' enquired Bishop John.

'Sire ... I think they will not come. Harold is not as popular as he believes.'

Immediately William was on his feet and pacing, rubbing at his chin.

'If only I could believe this report,' he said, then turning to the Bishop demanded, 'What was the last count?'

'We have two thousand knights ... a thousand archers and crossbows ... and more than ten thousand heavy infantry. Harold has more, but they are all foot soldiers and two thirds are little more than farm lads.'

'They have the numbers, we have the skill,' said Odo, dressed as ever in his black mail and plate despite battle being unlikely that day.

'We also have the horses,' mused William. 'Why the Saxons don't use horses is beyond me. They still use the shield wall which makes them easy to defeat with cavalry and archers.'

'They do have some archers,' said Malgard, 'and a small number of horses. Indeed, Harold used archers to great effect against the Danes.'

'Did he indeed?' said William, 'He must have been paying attention in Brittany.'

William summoned a servant and directed him to pour wine for Malgard and Gorik. Then he said, 'So ... tell us everything about the battle in the north, and spare no detail of Harold's tactics and better fighters.'

Malgard spoke for over an hour as the light perceptibly waned outside. His tale was interrupted by numerous questions from William and his captains, and also by the many messages conveyed to William from scouts and others, but at last the tale was told.

'We escaped the battlefield when all was lost, and made our way south when we heard you had landed,' said Malgard. 'And now you know all that happened up to the time we were captured by your guard.'

There was a silence as all digested the story told by Malgard. Then fitzOsbern said to William, 'If I may sire ... why should a Saxon fight with the Danes ... or us ... against his own people? I like not this man and his convenient answers.'

'Well?' demanded William.

'I was Tostig's friend,' replied Malgard. 'Harold did him great insult and even the return of his earldom was not enough to cure it. As Tostig's sworn man, his fight was my fight, and now it continues despite his death. I would help you if I can to destroy Tostig's enemy.'

'But my men don't like you,' said William. 'And I don't believe I like you either. Still, you are here ... and I cannot fathom any reason for you coming so openly unless it be to aid us.'

William pondered for a moment, then he said, 'Does anyone know you are here ... besides us in this tent?'

'Nay Lord.'

'Would it be possible for you to get into the Saxon camp?'

'Aye Lord.'

'And would it be possible for you to get close to Harold?'

Malgard paused, keenly conscious of the high stakes he was about to play for.

'I believe so Lord ... although I am not loved by Harold Godwinson. He knows me to be a close friend of Tostig.'

'I see,' said William, ' ... and now I think I understand your presence here a little better.'

Malgard feared that the conversation was about to turn ill, but

William waved his hand as though to brush away a fly.

'It matters not why you choose my side, as long as you do so choose. In fact, now that I know you are not trusted by Harold, I trust you more myself. I have a job for you Malgard.'

∞ ∞ ∞

The light was fading as we peered from the woods to the west of William's camp. As far as we could tell the Normans seemed in good enough spirit and began to cluster about the various cooking fires for the nightly meal.

'Their morale is strong,' whispered Elric. 'They don't seem to realise their lords have led them to their deaths.'

'Their discipline is very good,' I agreed. 'It was the first thing I noticed in Normandy and indeed I would like our archers to behave in the same manner.'

'Good luck,' laughed Elric.

It was time to leave and head back up Senlac to Harold's camp, but something about the darkened forest to the west of us intrigued me.

'Is that voices I can hear?' I wondered aloud, staring into the dark.

'It is nothing,' whispered Elric. 'We should get back.'

I turned to go with him, but again I seemed to hear something – like a tune being hummed on the other side of a thick wall.

'There it is again. Surely you hear it.'

Elric paused, motionless, listening, in the very last of the light.

∞ ∞ ∞

Malgard and Gorik crept through the wood to the west of William's camp.

Malgard was delighted with the way the audience had gone with William – not least as William had asked him to do the very thing he would have offered, if necessary: to get close to Harold in the fighting and murder him.

Malgard had absolutely no intention of doing that but every intention of trying to get close to Harold, and if the fight went against Harold he could reasonably claim he'd been trying to do what

William asked. On the other hand, if the fight went against William, as Malgard expected it to, it would be well to be seen fighting with Harold's housecarls. At the appropriate time, of course. Malgard would not be joining the fray until Harold's victory was certain and Gorik had murdered Brand in the thick of battle.

Smiling grimly to himself, Malgard was startled out of his reverie by Gorik suddenly throwing up a hand to halt their stealthy progress, and then utterly amazed when he saw two figures not thirty paces away, staring into the darker woods to the west.

Gorik raised a finger to his lips and very quietly strung his bow.

'Good God!' breathed Malgard. Even from behind, in the semi-darkness, he knew instantly that the two men were Brand and his red-headed friend, pointed out by Gorik only a week or so prior, in the wake of Harold's army hurrying south.

Gorik finished stringing his bow, nocked an arrow, then stuck a second in the ground for fast loading. He raised an enquiring eyebrow at Malgard, who weighed their chances of dealing with the red-headed fellow after Brand was dead, and then nodded. He drew his own sword and prepared to charge.

Gorik pulled back on the drawstring and sighted along the arrow at the centre of Brand's back, then half exhaled in preparation of shooting.

'Malgard!' shouted Brand, and darted forward in the very moment Gorik loosed the arrow, which flickered into darkness. Gorik was so surprised he leapt behind a tree – second arrow unshot. Malgard also hid himself and they heard running, but when Gorik drew his sword and jumped out again he saw Brand and Elric disappearing into the forest to the west.

'How on earth did he see me?' complained Malgard, as though Brand had broken some fundamental rule of fair play. 'He had his back to us!'

Gorik was cursing under his breath as he knew the job of killing Brand, now that Brand knew they were after him, had just become ten times harder.

∞ ∞ ∞

I had never been so happy to see a dog.

Staring into the darkling murk of the woods at dusk, I thought I'd heard voices, and then to my disbelief, astonishment and unutterable joy, Malgard trotted out of the darkness, took one look at me, then turned and bolted.

I shouted after him and ran, heedless of my closeness to the enemy camp. If Malgard was at hand then Valla must be close also.

'Brand!' shout-whispered Elric, running just behind me.

'It's Malgard,' I replied, ' … the dog. Valla must be close.'

The deeper we ran into the forest, the darker it got, but I still caught glimpses of Malgard and could hear him running through bracken and leaf mould.

We must have run the best part of a mile when I realised I could no longer see or hear him and we stopped, in a small clearing under the early moon. The sun was gone and it was cool as our breath steamed and sweat beaded.

'Brand,' panted Elric, 'someone shot at us … just as we started to run.'

'Really?'

'An arrow missed you by inches. If you hadn't run when you did, I fear you might have been slain. Me also probably … patrols tend to be in strong numbers.'

'Could they have followed us?'

We both slipped out of the moonlight and stared back the way we'd come, listening for stealthy movement. After a minute or so there was nothing but the night sounds of trees and crickets, and we relaxed.

'Valla must be close,' I repeated. 'I swear the dog was Malgard … I'd recognise that red-brown mongrel anywhere.'

Some clouds must have passed beyond the moon because it was suddenly much brighter in the clearing.

'That is no way to speak of he who has now saved your life on two occasions,' breathed a voice in my ear.

It is difficult for me to convey how I felt when I heard that sweet voice – missed and lamented for three long years.

'Valla!'

'My darling.'

Immediately I swept her into my arms, squeezing her and

breathing her essence, consuming her with all my senses.

After – I don't know how long – I partly released her, enough to see her beautiful face in the moonlight.

'Where have you been? And how come you here?'

She just laughed, her eyes shining, and said, 'You know where I have been Brand … the Place of Dreams.'

'And your great task?'

'Is all but complete.'

There was so much I wanted to tell her. So much I needed to ask. I didn't know where to begin and turned to Elric, who shrugged, grinning at the two of us while rubbing Malgard and telling him what a good dog he was.

'But why are you here?' I asked again. 'There is going to be a battle in the next days … the greatest battle ever in Inglalond. It is not safe here.'

'I know all that,' said Valla. 'Indeed, I have played my own part, to ensure your victory … as long as … '

She went oddly silent and seemed almost embarrassed, if such was possible.

'As long as what?'

She released me entirely from her embrace and turned away.

'What is the matter?'

I took her by the shoulders and drew her back to me.

'Come Valla … I have ached for this moment for three desperate years … do not be coy with me now.'

'I also have ached, Brand,' she whispered, 'but now I can hardly bear to ask you … your promise.'

I had known, or should have known, that she would ask me that, so I was glad of the semi-darkness that must have masked my expression – for I know I hesitated.

'I have kept my promise, Valla.'

Her eyes searched mine in the moonlight, and then she was back in my arms.

'It is more important than you could possibly guess,' she said, 'and not unrelated to your own affairs.'

'Really? How could that be?'

I realised her hands were exploring my body – squeezing my arms and tracing the muscles and scars in my back and shoulders.

'You have grown,' she said, changing the subject.

'Of course I've grown,' I laughed, running my hands along her sides and hips. 'And so have you. You were little more than a child when we met.'

'*My* child,' interrupted Elric, 'so I'll thank you to stop molesting her in my presence.'

The three of us laughed, and Elric said, 'Why don't we continue this family reunion back at the camp. There are still patrols in this wood I fear.'

∞ ∞ ∞

King Harold gazed down at the lights of William's camp and knew he should have felt more confident.

'You see,' he said, to Aethelnoth, Eadnoth and his brothers Gyrth and Leofwine. 'William's army is large ... and yet not so large as ours.'

'But ours grows, Lord,' reminded Aethelnoth. 'There are hosts still marching that will treble your army in a matter of days. We need only wait and our victory is assured.'

'Might they not slip away if we wait?' wondered Leofwine. 'It would be good to do some damage to William's army ... to give him pause for thought ere he covet Inglalond again.'

'We should have ships off-shore,' said Gyrth, 'to bottle him up and make a final chapter to the farce of his ambition.'

Aethelnoth and Leofwine laughed but Harold bade them be silent.

'Speak not these words of complacency,' he said. 'You seem to assume our battle already won but I remind you that William is a formidable foe who has never been beaten. Even leading men as a fifteen year old he had victories when outnumbered, and now he has a huge army of mounted knights and professional soldiers ... the best of Europe. This fight is far from finished.'

'That is why I urge you to wait, Lord,' said Aethelnoth. 'We have the position and probably already the larger army ... but give us two more days and our growing numbers must prevail.'

There was muttered agreement and then silence as the five men continued to watch the fires below.

'Where is Earl Brand?' asked Harold. 'I would have his counsel in the disposition of our forces … how to make best use of our archers. This will be a different fight to the one we had in the north.'

A runner was sent to find Earl Brand but at that moment further torches appeared on Senlac Ridge.

'Another deputation,' said Gyrth, and sure enough the torches made their way directly to the king and another of the monks of Fecamp bowed insolently before him.

'My Lord … I bring the final command from King William.'

'I know of no king by that name,' said Harold. 'There is a Norman Duke William but no king … unless he is king of some small country far to the east.'

'You know of whom I speak,' replied the monk. 'Your own King William commands that you give up this folly and recognise his right … promised by King Edward and confirmed by you in Normandy only two years ago.'

'By God, I will not!' replied Harold. 'Edward promised me the succession in his dying hour and I am willing to risk my life to honour his choice.'

'He who would invoke the Lord's name,' replied the monk, 'would be wise not to do so in support of a false claim.'

Harold was incredulous.

'You dare speak to a king like that?' he asked. 'You dare stand before me and accuse me of falsehood … even to my face?'

'I speak as King William bade me speak,' said the monk. 'Your claim is false, so in his mercy he gives you a final chance to renounce it.'

'William stood not at Edward's bedside when the succession was passed,' said Harold, 'so his claims of my alleged perfidy are made only to suit his ambition. I never heard Edward say William was his anointed. Indeed, Edward's choice was the aetheling his whole life … until he changed his mind in the shadows of death.'

'A convenient tale,' answered the monk, 'which suits your own ambition. William knows only the promise he received from Edward … to be king after him … and confirmed by your own oath in Normandy just two summers ago.'

Harold had to restrain himself from physically attacking the man

– a monk, after all, but so political and arrogant was his bearing that it was hard to remember his estate.

'I swore no such oath,' seethed Harold. 'William knows it. I swore only to be his man in Normandy … and even that was mere politeness on my part.'

'Politeness?' queried the monk. 'The world will not remember it that way. Oaths cannot be partial … nor conditional. All Inglalond and all of Christendom know that you swore to be William's man and must now do his bidding. He commands you to surrender the crown, and if you do not you will be damned for all eternity as an oath breaker.'

With that, the monk turned and strode away with his escort, leaving Harold in a passion of rage.

'By God, I will destroy that abbey of Norman monks at Rye,' he snarled. 'By what madness did we allow our enemies to take root in our own soil under the cloak of the church?'

'Brother,' said Gyrth, ' … let me lead the attack on William.'

The request was so unexpected that Harold forgot his fury and turned to his brother for an explanation.

'Regardless of the truth,' continued Gyrth, 'it will suit parts of Christendom to believe William's charge of perfidy if you fight him. But I swore no oath … let me fight on your behalf and no-one can accuse you of oath-breaking.'

Harold smiled at his brother, then clasped him to his breast.

'Nay brother … but I thank you with all my heart.'

Harold released Gyrth, and then embraced Leofwine.

'You also Lef … and all my friends. I am grateful.'

He released Leofwine and embraced Aethelnoth and Eadnoth, then turned back to gaze at the lights of William's camp.

'I am even grateful for the haughty words of the monk,' said Harold. 'For my purpose is now clear.'

The others all turned to Harold.

'Clear?' queried Eadnoth. 'Was it not already clear? To rid Inglalond of William and his usurpers?'

'Yes,' laughed Harold, 'but now I mean to do it quickly. I liked not the waiting, for it seemed disingenuous … to allow William to remain one second longer when honour demands that I scour him from the land of his crimes as soon as the chance allows. I have the chance already.'

The others stared at Harold in confusion for a few moments, then Aethelnoth asked, 'You mean to attack in the morn?'

'I do.'

This time the silence was profound – if brief.

'But Sire,' protested Gyrth and Leofwine in unison. Then Leofwine continued, 'We must await the rest of the fyrd. To attack before we have the full army at hand is to risk … '

'To risk losing?' asked Harold. 'I have no fear of losing. Mine is the just claim so let God choose between us. I do not fear His choice.'

There was no answer to such a statement but the four companions were troubled.

'Lord,' said Aethelnoth, 'has it not occurred to you that the monk was sent here to antagonise you into a precipitate battle? William must know your army is growing and that if he does not fight you soon he has no chance of victory.'

'Then let him attack,' said Harold. 'We've been here two days … he could have attacked by now.'

'He fears to lose contact with his ships and supplies,' said Gyrth. 'Unless you stand and fight him close to his base, he knows you will cut him off when he is overstretched. He needs you to fight him near Hastings or he cannot win.'

'He cannot win anyway,' said Harold, 'and if we truly believe so then honour decrees that we destroy William sooner rather than later. I am resolved to fight … but who approaches now?'

Some figures approached without torches from Senlac Ridge below them. Gyrth and Leofwine drew their swords and stepped closer to Harold.

'Put up your swords,' called a familiar voice, and all relaxed as they recognised Elric.

'Elric,' called Harold, 'do you have the Earl Brand with you?'

'I am here,' replied Brand, 'and I have brought someone to see you.'

∞ ∞ ∞

An hour later, Valla and I sat in Harold's tent with just the king and his Lady Swanneshals. Valla had removed her coat of skins and was wearing another green dress similar to the one she had received from Harold's Lady upon first meeting. Swanneshals had been as delighted as I at Valla's return and embraced her as she might her own daughter.

She questioned Valla at length about her absent activities and I tried to listen, while also talking to Harold about how we might deploy the archers against William's diverse forces. I explained the tactics I had devised against horses, archers and foot and he nodded in agreement.

'I mean to form up on top of Senlac Hill,' said Harold. 'There is a knoll ... just below the ridge on the right wing.'

'I know it.'

'That seems a good and defensible place for your archery.'

'I agree, Sire. The knoll is steep sided to the south and will be hard to attack. We should be able to do considerable damage to the left wing of William's army ... if he comes.'

'He will certainly come if we occupy the ridge,' said Harold. 'With every passing day his chance of victory fades. He will attack the ridge, even if it means he must attack up hill.'

'Why does he not just leave?' I wondered. 'He has his boats ... he could get back to Normandy.'

'The weather is already changed since he landed,' replied Harold. 'The sea is not friendly to such barges and he would lose many in the crossing ... but that is not what keeps him here.'

The two women laughed suddenly and we turned to listen for a moment, then Harold, smiling at their animated conversation, said, 'It is honour that keeps him here. He has been to the pope in Rome shouting about his righteous cause and my alleged perfidy. He will look the biggest fool in Christendom if he returns to Normandy unfought.'

Harold lifted his cup and drained it, then refilled it, having dismissed all servants from his presence. He refilled my own cup and tossed a couple of faggots into the brazier burning in the middle of the room. Then he said, 'Do you remember our Welsh campaign ... three summers ago?'

'I do, sire.'

'There was one particular battle ... a short siege ... and we burned the fortress of Daffyd Ap Rhiwallon.'

'I remember it.'

Harold paused again, staring into the brazier as though a scene was being played out in the glowing coals.

'Do you remember his wife, Ygrene?'

'How could I forget her?' I replied, with a small shudder.

'She burned,' said Harold, 'with a babe in her arms. And with her final words she cursed me.'

I said nothing. That scene was still etched in my own memory – too vivid to forget.

'I see your doom invader,' quoted Harold. '... when a new star lights the sky then all that is yours will be taken away. Your house will be burned as mine burns, and all your deeds forgotten. Only your death will be remembered.'

I winced at the memory, and said, 'The Hairy Star is gone ... months ago. Surely the power of the curse has faded and if anything ill were fated to happen, that time is passed.'

We were aware that the two women were now staring at us – had joined our conversation.

'Your house was burned,' said Swanneshals. 'I was lucky not to be in it when it happened ... but if that is all the words portend then I think you may ignore them.'

'I don't believe she referred to my house at Bosham,' said Harold. 'I believe she meant my dynasty ... which now hangs in the balance of God's own scales.'

'Then wait,' I said. 'Wait for the rest of the fyrd and let William gnaw himself to nothing. He has no further supplies and must—'

'Nay,' laughed Harold, 'I have already said I will fight him tomorrow ... on my birthday.'

'Is not Sunday your birthday?' asked Swanneshals.

'I've never been certain, to tell the truth. The fourteenth or the fifteenth ... but surely I cannot die on my birthday.'

'You truly fear death Lord?' I asked him. 'You ... the greatest warrior in Inglalond?'

'All men are equal on a battlefield,' said Harold, ' ... with the same right to be struck down by aimed or random blows. Hardrada was killed by an arrow and he was a greater warrior than I.'

'You will not die on your birthday,' said Valla, and we all turned to her, staring into the glowing embers of the brazier, and I felt the air cool on the back of my neck as though some ethereal presence had entered the room.

'Then surely that is further reason to wait,' said Swanneshals. 'If Sunday is your birthday you are safe ... but if Saturday is your birthday and you wait to Sunday, you will at least command many more thousands.'

'And where will they stand?' laughed Harold. 'There is only so much room on the ridge.'

He sipped his wine and said, 'There is something else that has been troubling me ... my oath to William.'

'What of it?' I asked.

'It is true I deceived him,' said Harold, and then raised a hand to quell my protest.

'Yea, I made an oath which I knew he would hear differently from what I intended. A small deceit perhaps ... but my conscience is troubled by it. Giving William something closer to an even chance is the least I can do to make reparations with God ... to truly let Him decide between us on the field of battle.'

I opened my mouth to counsel a wiser and more ruthless course, but the look on Harold's face was resolute, and you argue with kings only so far.

∞ ∞ ∞

'So, you are an earl?'

We were alone in my tent at last, illuminated by two candles. Valla was still wearing her green dress and I was determined to take it off her.

'Yes. I have been made an earl ... which makes you a countess.'

She smiled but then turned away sadly.

'What's wrong?'

Valla lifted the green dress and pulled it over her head, perfectly naked beneath, and it was all I could do not to fling myself upon her.

But she lay down beside me on the blanket covering our dried bracken bed and I just gazed at her – filling my soul and senses with her presence.

'I feared I would never see you again.'

'Did you not receive my messages?'

I sat up to remove my leather jerkin, and opened my shirt, and she smiled when she saw the fading bluebell twined into the thong around my neck.

'Why did you not speak with me that day?'

'The time was not ready,' she replied. 'I was still working with Myrrthn … to accomplish the great thing we have done.'

'And am I allowed to know about this great thing?' I asked, running my hand along her side and marvelling at her beauty. She had grown fully into womanhood and was quite the most perfect creature I had ever seen.

'You will know tomorrow,' she said, pulling at my shirt and staring at my own body which was also somewhat different from when she had last seen me. 'So many scars Brand … it's a wonder you survive them all.'

'I didn't get the wounds all at once,' I laughed. 'There are tokens of many battles on my skin … but none of them cost me too much blood.'

Having removed my shirt she then attacked my hose and presently the two of us lay naked together in the flickering candlelight and I felt an imminent need to be wholly one with her. I said no word but Valla knew what I was thinking.

'Just one more night Brand,' she said, lowering her eyes.

'Really?'

'The great thing we have done must culminate with the battle,' she whispered. 'I dare not affect the work with the premature loss of my maidenhood.'

I didn't understand, but just hugged her against me, so hard it hurt us both.

'Just one more night my darling,' she whispered, 'and the fruit of our long wait will at last be ripe.'

With my nose against her neck I made no answer – just revelled in her scent – transported by her presence.

'You didn't realise did you,' smiled Valla, 'that while you were keeping your promise to me, you were also helping keep Harold's enemies at bay.'

'Was I?' I murmured, on the edge of sleep.

'It was the most important part of the spell ... the purity of your promise and the faith with which you kept it. I am so full of love and pride for you, and that love was the final ingredient of our great spell. It is why Harold will have the victory tomorrow.'

Chapter 40

A Flicker of Light in His Mind's Eye

I didn't sleep, much, and was woken by Elric just as I finally fell into an exhausted doze.

In my stupor, it took me a few moments to make sense of his urgency, but then I kissed Valla on the forehead as she continued sleeping and dragged myself into my fighting gear – thick woollen breeches reinforced with hard leather; linen shirt and leather jerkin; sheepskin boots wrapped with thongs and studded with iron cleats for sound footing in ground slippery with blood. My archers were similarly attired but also wore a leather sleeve over their left arms to aid their art and protect their flesh from whipping bowstrings. I also had my shirt of rings which I would don before battle, but that was too heavy to wear for who-knew-how-many hours beforehand.

My weapons were still *Revanche* and *Pighammer*, and the silver-hilted dagger in my boot, although I didn't expect to have much need of them. I mainly fought these days by watching the battle and directing the blows of others – but I was reassured by their heft and grip as I followed Elric in a thick mist given a silvery tinge by the wolf light before dawn. Stumbling and slipping on the wet ground we eventually saw emerging from the fog a pair of orange balls which turned into flaming torches at the entrance to Harold's pavilion.

Inside, the old debates continued. Gyrth and Leofwine were again urging Harold either to wait, or let them lead the battle. I don't know why they wasted their breath. Harold had decided that his best chance of victory was to offer William an even fight, and as for the idea of Gyrth and Leofwine leading the battle on his behalf …

'Kings do not leave their fighting to other men,' said Harold, with a tired smile. ' … no king worthy of the name.'

Harold was wearing the gilt hauberk given him in Normandy by William, and he must have seen me staring for he smiled.

'You think my choice of gear in poor taste, Earl Brand?'

'Nay Lord … just curious.'

'Well … it is an excellent hauberk and marvellously light,' said Harold, 'but most importantly it was a gift from William. By wearing it openly I am saying that there is no bond precluding me from opposing his will … not in Inglalond.'

'It is sure to make him angry,' I laughed. 'Was that your intention also?'

'Decisions in battle are best made by men with clear heads,' said Harold. 'The more William has to think about, the less he will be focussed on making wise choices in the fury of fighting. Besides … I see I'm not the only one dressed in William's gear.'

I followed his eye to where Elric stood grinning, also wearing the hauberk he'd received in Normandy.

'I prefer the heavy shirt I took from my uncle's retainer,' I said. 'It would be bad luck to change now.'

'That Norman hauberk sits well on you Elric,' laughed Harold, ' … and may it bring you safely through the battle.'

'If I am to be an Earl, Lord,' I said, 'then Elric will be one of my thegns. One of your thegns, I mean.'

'Then let him be a thegn now,' said Harold, and there were immediate murmurs of approval from other thegns and housecarls nearby. 'He has proven himself in battle a hundred times. Let him fight now as a thegn … although I warn you Elric, fighting as a thegn is very different to fighting as a man with nothing to lose.'

'Life is precious enough to lose,' said Elric. 'A title will make no difference to my sword arm.'

'You say that now,' laughed Harold. 'Wait until your foemen learn of your title … the arrows around you will be slightly thicker. Is it truly worth it?'

Everyone laughed. Elric was beaming with pride and happiness, and it struck me how far he had come from the day at Theodford when Harold had branded him and bonded him to me. Strange are the fates of men, although my own was even stranger I supposed and my thoughts turned again to Valla. The Countess Valla she would be, and I ached to be with her.

Spiced wine, warm and fragrant, was poured by servants as we discussed the ordering of the army. Gyrth would lead the right wing and Leofwine the left, with Harold in the centre. Some of Harold's best and bravest had already fallen or been badly injured at Stamford Bridge, but there were still many housecarls and thegns to stiffen the front ranks of the shield wall to give heart and experience to the greater press of fyrd men.

My own troop of archers would be arrayed as Harold and I had discussed, on a small rise to the right of the approach William must make to offer battle. From that position we would be reasonably safe from cavalry and foot soldiers. Only other archers could threaten us and I liked our chances against those – for while my men weren't professional soldiers, they were expert at archery as only poachers and murderers are. I'd trust them to beat most other archery troops – especially with the advantage of higher ground.

At the end of the council we took some sacks of bread from the victuallers and went in search of our men. The mist was still thick but brighter now and we were constantly on guard as strange shapes emerged from the swirling grey to become lines of men marching down to the ridge – which had been scouted throughout the night in case of surprise attack.

Just before the top of Senlac Hill was a copse that stretched the length of the ridge and marshals met us there.

'Do not pass beyond the trees,' we were told. 'King Harold does not want us to be seen until he is ready.'

We took the opportunity to hand out the loaves and warned men not to eat them all at once.

'It may be a long fight,' I heard Elric say many times. 'You must keep aught for your strength later in the day.'

I wasn't remotely hungry myself – not least as I was aware of the impact bread can have on nervous guts – especially guts tender from too much ale and wine the night before. And sure enough, within minutes of handing out the loaves the first of the men were ripping their breeches down and shitting noisily as others laughed, but then moments later were tearing down their own breeches to relieve the fear-driven pressure.

'They weren't like this against the Danes,' I muttered disgustedly as the stench of turd wafted about the small wood.

'They've seen the size of William's army,' said Elric, ' ... and the horses.'

The horses were the worst of it. I had never seen so many (and so large) and the thought of hundreds of the beasts attacking all at once was an alarming prospect.

'We should aim for the horses when they attack,' said Elric, which was an excellent idea and the word was quickly passed.

'It is the one thing I hate about battle,' I sighed as the sound of shitting and nervous laughter intensified around me. 'Why is there always so much turd?'

∞ ∞ ∞

Duke William of Normandy had been on his knees for nearly two hours – waiting for the feeling of immanence that would normally come over him to reassure him that God was on his side.

He tried to free his mind of doubt but the feeling would not come. 'Lord,' he whispered. 'Let me do your work and scour from these lands those who follow an oath breaker who received my crown from an excommunicate priest.'

Still the feeling would not come, and William in his mind travelled back to previous times on the brink of battle when God's grace had descended over him – murmuring support and promising victory. Never had the feeling let him down, but what was he doing wrongly? Could it be that God would not take his part?

Unthinkable. The papal banner was proof enough of that – and it was the papal banner that held his army together now – that, and terror of the Saxons. A few dozen had tried to slip away from the camp as confidence waned but their bodies had been found – not far away – grievously tortured and despoiled. And always with their genitals removed.

William shuddered and forced himself back into the moment. Only God mattered. A victory for God and the crown of Inglalond would be William's reward for his part in it – and in that moment William felt the merest tremor of grace, like a flicker of light in his mind's eye.

It was enough. God's glance in his direction filled his heart with hope and gave strength to his bones and sinews. He rose to his feet – knees throbbing with pain from his vigil – and roared for his page to complete his dressing. More servants brought drink and morsels for his breakfast as the last of the brass and iron plates were attached to his hauberk.

Then he went out into the open air where a thick fog swirled greasily and dampened the spirits of his tired army, many of whom had been awake and armed throughout the night in case of sudden onset. Now they were drawn up to hear a mass said by Odo, who once again was wearing his plated armour and holding a huge black mace in place of his crozier.

Odo nodded at his brother and began chanting the familiar Latin as all fell to their knees. In his sermon, Odo reminded them of the justness of their cause but said, 'Nevertheless … God's work cannot be done without cost, and today that cost will be many lives.'

He paused, his eyes sweeping over those nearest to gauge the effect of his words.

'Many lives,' he repeated, 'but we shall have the victory. Those who wish to survive this Saturday battle must swear to God that never again will they eat meat on this day. Do you swear?'

There was an unconvincing response, and Odo smashed his mace onto an earthenware jug which flew into a thousand fragments – as did the small table on which it had rested.

'Do you swear?' he roared again, and this time the response was more to his liking. There was an oddly receding reprise of the response as Odo's required oath was repeated to those further out, but at last he was satisfied and concluded the mass with communion – helped in this task by dozens of priests who went among the army to bring them closer to God in case they be required to meet Him in the next hours.

After conferring with fitzOsbern, and de Fereis, his Chief of Cavalry, William summoned his knights and they went to the large corrals where already their horses were caparisoned and saddled and ready for war. With the aid of mounting blocks they clambered onto their horses – every man having another two in reserve – and William led them to the dyke at the bottom of Senlac Hill, as the Saxons called it, where already the rest of his army was arrayed, peering up through the thinning mist and wondering whether any stared back down at them.

∞ ∞ ∞

Malgard was enjoying himself.

He and Gorik had made themselves anonymous towards the back of Harold's vast encampment. They hid their hauberks under the garb of common fyrd men, although their weapons were better than most and they knew well how to use them.

Malgard's plan was for the two of them to linger at the back of the war hedge and wait for one or other army to prevail. Either way, Gorik would get close to Brand and take his chance when it came – as it must in such a battle. Malgard himself would have to make a choice ere the end, but he expected Harold to win. The position, the numbers, the reinforcements that were yet to arrive – William was doomed, but Malgard was delighted to have arranged his salvation (and possibly his reward) should The Bastard somehow defy the odds. He had done it before, after all.

But not against this many and so far from home. There were thousands of men in the wood above the hill, and thousands more still coming down the road from Caldbec beyond. And yet thousands more expected to arrive in the next day or so. In all likelihood the two armies would halve each other today but then Harold's would be doubled again tomorrow and William would be defeated. Harold would stay king, so the most important death of the day was Brand's.

It was chaos in the still swirling mist but Malgard never took his eyes off *The Fighting Man* – Harold's standard which told his position. He would be ever to the fore and Malgard shuddered at the thought of really trying to kill such a warrior – even in stealth from behind. It would be no simple feat, but Malgard found himself laughing.

Gorik turned with a raised eyebrow, but Malgard ignored him. He had decided that should William have the victory, however unlikely that might be, he would try to blood his sword on Harold's corpse and the idea struck him as so funny he found himself keening with half-repressed laughter like a sot at a fair.

There was a bit of a commotion down towards the edge of the wood in which they hid, and they realised the army was moving forward. Malgard and Gorik were in the main press of men towards the right of Harold's centre – an excellent vantage from which to watch the battle and make their choices.

'This will be a famous day,' thought Malgard, still amused at the thought of a king's blood on his sword. 'The death either of a Duke or a King ... and the death also of that inconvenient nephew of mine.'

In fact, so many would die that, whoever won, there would need to be a massive redistribution of land. With just a bit more cunning and luck, Malgard would be thegn of a territory much larger than Stybbor by the end of the day.

He moved forward with Gorik – wearing the hugest grin in the army.

∞ ∞ ∞

'There they are my Lord!'

William heard the shout from Eustace of Boulogne and looked up the ridge to where he pointed – and sure enough there were banners and men emerging from the woods on the brow of the hill.

Immediately William's trumpeters began their raucous din to herald the fight that would surely happen that day and they were answered by another blast of brass from above. William felt once again the touch of God's grace, like a pair of firm hands resting on his shoulders, and his confidence soared. He called to his page and received a velvet purse which he placed around his neck and tucked under his hauberk. The purse contained the relics of St Peter upon which Harold had sworn his oath in Normandy – and the feeling that God was on his side grew even stronger.

William sat his horse beneath the great papal banner – a long white pennant with the red cross of Christ – held by Vital, one of Odo's men, and addressed his army one final time. And again he emphasised: '... these men are not soldiers. They are peasants ...

stiffened with a handful of Harold's men ... but mostly peasants. Will you ... the cream of Normandy, Brittany and France ... allow yourselves to be beaten by coopers, smiths and farmers? And after you have won ... the land they farmed will be yours. Every man that fights with me today will win a share of Inglalond according to his measure.

'Finally ... what we do today, we do for God. It is God's kingdom for which we fight ... that is why He will fight with us ... to ensure His victory despite the Saxons having the advantage of position and numbers. They cannot fight God so victory must be ours.'

As he finished, the first beams of the dawn broke through the mist to the east and William's silvered hauberk shone with a radiance that could only come from God.

'Never has such a knight been seen under heaven!' cried Eustace and the army acclaimed him – the true king of Inglalond from whom they would receive rich reward if they fought hard and won his victory.

'There is the Oath Breaker,' said Vital, pointing up the hill at a large triangular banner with an odd device whose gems picked up the first rays of the sun to cut through the mist.

'We will wait all day for them to attack us,' said fitzOsbern. 'They will not surrender the high ground.'

'Well enough,' replied William, loud enough that many around him might hear. 'In any case of theft it is the prosecuting counsel who must open proceedings. In God's own court, shall we make our opening charge?'

A blare of trumpets announced the intention of William's forces and an answering blare sounded from Harold's above.

'Send the archers,' cried William.

∞ ∞ ∞

On a promontory, some miles west of Hastings, Valla and Myrrthn sat, once again naked, before the fire they had rebuilt as a stiff breeze from the west sent the smoke to the east.

'The killer god is strong,' breathed Myrrthn, 'but our gods are stronger. See how they attack him ... carry our spell to him?'

Valla had woken as Brand left the tent in the darkness, then immediately felt a great urgency and had returned to Myrrthn as he rebuilt the fire on the morning of the battle of men that would coincide with the battle of gods. She was worried about the outcome – something about Brand's mood had unsettled her – had somehow shaken her absolute faith in their inevitable victory.

But now as she felt the strengthening breeze her faith was restored. The vigour of the wind and the richness of the smoke could only mean the spell had been truly built from the purest ingredients. Her heart was glad and she began to sing with Myrrthn – strange words that had never before been sung – created specially for the purpose of slaying a god.

∞ ∞ ∞

As the mists thinned and the trumpets rang out to make our challenge, I led my archers down to the small hillock to the right and to the fore of Harold's army. The ground had been well prepared to even out William's advantage of horses. Besides the fact that he must attack up a steep slope, there were also many ditches, tree trunks and other obstacles to prevent him riding over the top of us.

Looking back up the hill I felt my confidence grow with the numbers and disposition of the fyrd. The fierce Kentishmen as ever were in the front and centre with vast numbers from Cornwall, Wiltshire and other parts of Wessex. There were so many I could still see half the army on the road between Caldbec and the top of the ridge. It was a sight to gladden the heart and so strong were we, and so well defended our position, that I found myself feeling sorry for the doomed soldiers of William who had been brought here under a false claim and must die for their fealty, unless Harold showed mercy and allowed them to escape.

Once again, there was a blast of trumpets from below and I caught just a small whiff of smoke on the breeze – a fragrant tang as though carrying incense and I felt my heart sing with the joy of battle.

'Out! Out! Out!' cried Harold's army to the invaders below but, as we watched, the first wave of foot soldiers began moving up the hill, accompanied by a small number of knights on horseback.

One such knight galloped ahead of the rest and then slowed to a walk, and as he got closer we perceived he was singing – a tune I remembered from my time in Normandy. Despite his allegiance to William, I couldn't help but admire his bravery. He was a fair looking young man and was even smiling as he confronted our army single-handed.

Walt called for his team of archers to take aim at the young knight and immediately I countermanded his order. Such bravery should be respected, but alas – he drew his sword and foolishly charged at Harold's position in the very centre as William's army below cheered him on. The front ranks opened to let him through, but then immediately closed and I saw him dragged from his horse. Then his fate was obscured as several axes rose and fell and the cheers below turned to anger and dismay.

'What was the point of that?' asked Elric at my side.

'We must all make an end somehow,' I shrugged. 'His was one of the finest I have seen ... and see how it has stirred his fellows.'

The foot soldiers were now running up Senlac Hill towards us – shouting and shrieking –and many carried bows and crossbows. Our own army was a wall of shields, bristling with spears and stretching a quarter mile from wing to wing and as much as ten ranks deep in places. As William's archers approached the Saxons took up javelins, small axes and even rocks to throw at the men below, whose arrows and bolts made little impression on the long shields of the defenders.

'Kill them!' I roared, and a volley of shafts flew from our raised position and mowed down the Normans nearest like a scythe through long grass. After two more volleys, not one was left standing within a hundred paces of our hillock as the music of battle commenced – the shrieking of dying and wounded and the deeper notes of defenders who continued shouting, 'Out! Out!'

The Norman archers withdrew – well away from our position – and were immediately replaced by a wave of cavalry. None of whom tried to get too close to the shield wall but threw their javelins and wheeled away from the pits and barriers thrown up to defy them. Some of the javelins found a mark and I saw several men fall and be replaced in the front rank – but men were still flowing down the road from Caldbec so every man that fell was replaced by two others.

Suddenly, there was a squadron of knights making straight for our position. 'Aim for the horses!' yelled Elric, and a second later the screaming of men and beasts was like a hymn of Hell. None of them set so much as a single hoof on our hill and I found myself laughing. 'They can fight like that all day, if they wish,' I shouted. 'Kill them lads!'

As the cavalry departed, leaving many of their fellows dead and dying, some of my Saxons ran down past the obstacles to finish the knights with long knives and collect arrows and anything else of value. But they had to be quick for a very large body of foot soldiers were making their way up Senlac carrying spears, halberds and swords.

The real battle was about to commence.

Chapter 41

The Thrusting, Hacking Madness of War

King Harold stood on a small mound beneath his twin standards – *The Red Dragon* of Wessex and *The Fighting Man* – and watched William's army running towards him like a tide over the flats at Bosham.

He knew the first attackers had been but a feint – no serious test at all – but done to get close-hand knowledge of the defence so William might better devise his tactics. And now the first real attack crashed into the Saxon shield wall with sword and spear and the thrusting, hacking madness of war commenced.

To Harold's right, Gyrth fought like a demon – wielding his sword two-handed as two of his housecarls protected his flanks with shields. To his left, Leofwine paced behind the struggling line of men, shouting encouragement and occasionally reaching through a gap with his sword to find a target. The screams of damaged and dying men rent the air and the smell of blood was thick and sweet.

'There is not enough room for our army,' shouted Aethelnoth. 'Ten ranks deep and we still fill the road down from Caldbec with men unfought.'

'Then let us kill some Normans to make room for them,' laughed Harold. 'I cannot have too many friends on this hilltop.'

With that he launched himself into the battle, despite the protests of his stallers and housecarls, but none could withstand him and many were hewn down by his furious blade.

'Please Lord,' panted Eadnoth, during a lull in the fighting as they leaned on their swords and watched the Normans draw back for a few moments. 'Do not risk yourself needlessly … we need you to lead rather than fight.'

'Nay Eadnoth,' laughed Harold, the battle joy singing in his blood. 'I must enjoy it, for this will certainly be my final battle. If we win there are none left in Christendom to challenge me. But if we lose … I rather doubt I will get the opportunity to hold a sword again.'

'You will not lose,' shouted Eadnoth. 'You cannot lose … but you could be injured by any stray blow. I beg you to be more cautious.'

'We shall discuss it later,' shouted Harold, watching the Normans reforming, 'But for now we must fight again!'

∞ ∞ ∞

William watched his army flow up the hill, negotiate the hurdles and break against the Saxon shield wall. Having received his information regarding the disposition of Harold's forces he had made his plan. Leofwine was the youngest and least experienced in battle – he should therefore be the focus of William's strategy.

But not too quickly, nor too obviously. William attacked all parts of the shield wall at once, for now, keenly aware that Harold was reinforcing even as the battle progressed – while every Norman who fell cost William dearly.

And many were falling – especially those who assailed the numerous warriors wielding the huge battle-axes which could cleave man and horse in a single, double-handed blow.

'Send archers to kill the axemen,' he ordered fitzOsbern, 'and prepare for a mounted charge.'

fitzOsbern pulled a great horn from a baldric and blew a double blast in the direction of the surging foot. William pulled his long sword from its scabbard and, with his brother Odo at his side, began walking his horse toward Senlac as squadrons of cavalry formed around them.

'I submit to your judgment, Lord,' said William, spurring his horse to a canter. 'Will you have me or Harold on the seat of Inglalond?'

∞ ∞ ∞

Leofwine was enjoying himself.

It was his first major battle and he had been consumed with doubt beforehand. Would the men follow him? Would he fight well himself in the terrifying chaos of the shield wall?

The answers were yes and yes, and Leofwine knew the joy of victory and felt his confidence surge. Twice he had seen off cavalry and twice more archers and foot soldiers, and no impression had been made on his position. He had blooded his sword and laughed for the sheer fun of fighting and killing.

'Here they come again Lord,' shouted Hedwig, his housecarl, as a fresh wave of foot soldiers ran shrieking up the hill towards them, but by the time they reached Leofwine's shield wall their momentum had entirely stopped and it seemed some could barely lift their swords. 'Kill them!' shouted Leofwine, knowing that the battle was already won and when the Normans quickly broke the imminence of victory was sensed by all in his section of Harold's army.

'Kill them!' was the cry repeated by many voices, and without any order given, Leofwine's entire host suddenly left their safe positions and chased after the fleeing Norman foot soldiers, hacking at legs and backs and whooping with murderous joy. The Norman's couldn't defend themselves in their desperate flight and scores were cut down as horns sounded both above and below.

'Get them back!' shouted Leofwine who, despite the rout, sensed it was too early to leave the security of their ranks behind the logs and ditches. Hedwig blew the retreat again and again but the noise of battle was deafening and confused by horns from below and to the sides.

'Stay here!' shouted Leofwine to those that remained, ' … except Hedwig and your kinsmen. Come with me to form a rear guard! Quickly!'

∞ ∞ ∞

'What the fuck is he doing?' shouted Elric as the whole eastern third of Harold's shield wall fell upon the Normans like the bursting of a dam. 'They'll be trapped!'

Even as we watched, the Saxons chased the Normans down the

left side of Senlac Hill, drunk on victory. But it was too soon. A huge troop of cavalry charged across the field, led by William himself who checked the flight of his own troops then encircled the pursuers and set about the business of revenge.

'Walt, Orald,' I shouted. 'Your troops only ... follow me!'

Without waiting to check that they followed, I flew down the hill and cut across the face of Harold's army – bolting for the carnage two thirds of the way down Senlac. But it was too far. By the time we got close enough to start shooting at the cavalry, many had been cut down or simply ridden over by the huge beasts trained for killing. Nevertheless, our arrows, concentrated in one place, opened up a gap and some three score managed to escape back up the hill – but hundreds lay dead and dying in a great circle, as the cavalry retreated.

'I thank you indeed!' shouted a voice as a hand clapped me over the shoulder.

'Leofwine,' I said, turning, then gestured helplessly at the pile of dead.

'I couldn't hold them,' he said, his face white with grief. 'They thought the battle won and ... '

'Let us get back to the top,' I said, as another wave of Norman foot soldiers commenced the march up Senlac.

'I need to see whether any of my men can be saved,' he shouted and would have gone despite the danger, but I seized him by the arm and said, 'You must not risk capture! Would you have William ransom you to Harold?'

Poor Leofwine was in an agony of choice – turning from his brother above to the piles of broken men below, and tears welled in his eyes.

'All choices are ill,' he cried, but he headed back up the hill with me as more men flowed down from Caldbec to take up the spaces left by Leofwine's over-eager soldiers.

I left him back in position – crestfallen and ashamed of the damage he had done to Harold's army.

'We are still in charge of this field,' I told him. 'Avenge your men on the Normans.'

Then I led the two troops of archers across the very front of the main host where we were cheered by those who had seen our fast action. Harold himself nodded at me, from the front of the centre, his eyes like steel – his sword blooded – and I made my way back to the hillock on the right more certain than ever that we could not lose while we held our defensive position.

But in the midst of my strategic musings, a sudden rumbling in my guts told me that I, also, had eaten my bread too quickly.

∞ ∞ ∞

Gorik sneered in contempt as Earl Brand bowed before the king while the whole army cheered him. Blessed he seemed. Or charmed. Nothing ever seemed to go wrong for Brand but Gorik was determined that his luck would change. Then, even as he watched with narrowed eyes, Brand spoke briefly to his red-headed sergeant and ran for the woods to the west and rear of the army.

And Gorik slipped away from the rear of Harold's position.

∞ ∞ ∞

I had to go quite deep into the stinking copse to find a place that hadn't already been used for a mass latrine, but at last I found a tree against which I could set my back and ripped my breeches down.

The battle was going well I deemed. It was simply a matter of holding our position which, despite the madness of Leofwine's men, was growing stronger by the minute while William's army weakened with every assault. By tomorrow, when another host as large again as the one that held the top of Senlac Ridge would arrive, William would have no choice but to surrender, if he yet lived. Then Harold's position would be inviolable. William would be executed or imprisoned for ransom, but either way his claim to the crown of Inglalond would be finished. Before all of Christendom, God's choice would be made clear and never again would any army assail us.

I suddenly had a sense of peace, such as I had never known before – had never had time to even contemplate. With Harold's crown assured I could finally settle down with Valla and enjoy my earldom. I smiled to myself at the thought of Valla living as a great Lady – a Countess – in a fine house, which I would build near my capital. I expected Harold to give me East Anglia – the county of my birth – so I would undertake a processional to determine a site most suitable for my own hall. Stybbor, of course, I would give to Elric – and he would remarry if he could not find his own Valla, and already I was entertaining visions of us all growing old together, surrounded by our children in happiness and peace.

'Shitting yourself eh? And so you should be.'

A blade was against my throat and pressed harder as I went for my sword – which my attacker was standing on.

'If you make a sound, I will slay you instantly,' he said, reaching down for my sword then flinging it into the bracken some twenty feet away.

The man was vaguely familiar, with long silver hair.

'Who are you, and what do you want with me?' I demanded, trying to pull up my breeches but was not permitted to do so. I remained squatting against the tree with my breeches around my knees – weighed down by the shirt of rings.

'What do I want?' he echoed. 'Only your death ... although I would make you suffer if I could, to repay the suffering you caused me.'

'That I caused you?' I queried. 'I don't know you, so how have I caused you to suffer?'

In response, the man pulled back the hair to the right side of his face and I beheld a long, pink scar – puckered and twisted from a terrible burn.

'Gorik,' I breathed, my body rigid.

'So you do remember,' he laughed. 'That pleases me ... not least as you surely understand now the certainty of your death. I would prefer to flay the skin from your body over several days but I don't have time for that. So, you will get the quick death you don't deserve and I will return to the battle to win favour with either Harold or William ... as will your uncle.'

'Malgard is here?'

'Of course ... as he was at Stamford Bridge, fighting with the Danes. We are survivors, Malgard and I ... and as we grow old our most cherished memory will be your death. I must carefully remember every detail as Malgard will ask me to describe it often over the course of our future lives.'

Desperately my eyes swept the immediate vicinity for weapons and possibilities for escape. The silver-hilted dagger was concealed in the top of my boot but my breeches were in the way and I wouldn't be allowed to untangle myself. My only hope was to keep him talking – to give me time for an intervention. But from whom? Valla? Elric? I had left him in charge of the archers and, even as I considered him, the sound of battle swelled again behind us. Elric was busy, so time. Time was all.

'How will a victory for William help you and Malgard?' I asked, sinking a little lower against the tree.

'We are well known to William,' grinned Gorik. 'He believes us to be on a secret mission to murder Harold … but none of that matters for you. I seem to remember you once referred to my cock as a mouse cock. Well, now that I can see your own shrivelled up scrap of a cock I feel far less insulted. In fact maybe I'll start by cutting yours off. You won't be needing it anymore.'

I slid lower down the tree trunk, almost to the ground to evade him and he laughed again as he moved his sword away from my throat to threaten my manhood. But in that second I was able to reach the only weapon at hand. I snatched up a handful of my own warm turd and flung it at Gorik's face, simultaneously throwing myself to the side as his blade slashed into the ground where I had been a heartbeat before.

If he'd slashed again immediately I would have been helpless, but he paused to wipe the turd from his eyes and mouth then came roaring at me as I struggled to my feet, pulling my breeches up as I went. His sword came down at me again, but I was still off-balance and there was no time to avoid it. All I could do was turn my back and trust in the shirt of rings to take most of the force, but it was still like being hit with a blacksmith's hammer and I sprawled onto my face.

The shirt of rings had saved my life but it was a hindrance – weighing me down and preventing me getting up quickly. Expecting the sword to take my head off at any moment I again flung myself over, just in time to see the sword thump into the ground an inch from my shoulder. Then, as he raised it again, standing right above me, I whipped the dagger from my boot and thrust it deep into his groin.

Gorik shrieked and I was splashed with hot blood, but the sword came down. Ill timed, poorly aimed and with little of his natural strength, it still took me in the side of the head and the pain was searing as he collapsed to the ground next to me, screaming.

I dragged myself to my feet and picked up Gorik's sword, but there was little need for it. The blood was pouring out of his wound and his screaming died away. Nevertheless, I raised the sword above my head – remembered the time he had been on the point of raping Valla in the basement by the Temes – and brought it down on his throat with all the fury and violence in me. An explosion of blood and Gorik's head was all but severed from his corpse, which twitched and then was still.

I dropped the sword, then blinked through blood – my chest heaving with the effort. I spat at what remained of him and wiped my face, but the blood kept coming, pouring through my fingers as I probed the injury to the upper left side of my head. It badly needed binding.

Feeling very sick, I managed to pull my dagger from Gorik's body and wiped it clean on his shirt – my hands also. I found my own sword – *Revanche* – where he had thrown it, then headed back towards the clamour and din of the battle – now sounding curiously distant.

In my pain and confusion, I vaguely regretted that I had broken my oath and used my father's knife on a man other than Malgard, but any other course of action would have seen me lying headless in Gorik's place, so I managed to forgive myself.

∞ ∞ ∞

'I thank you,' said William, and fitzOsbern bowed from his saddle.

It was an excellent ruse,' continued William, 'but still I rue the exchange. They can afford to lose a thousand men better than we can afford a hundred.'

'They did lose a thousand,' said fitzOsbern, 'or nearly so. Our cavalry are fell handed and few escaped the trap.'

'They have learnt to use mobile archery, I see,' mused William. 'We need to take out their archers.'

'They occupy a mound to the left of the field, Lord, and shoot very well. We could destroy them but the exchange would not be in our favour … and meanwhile Harold's army grows.'

There was a hint of defeat in fitzOsbern's voice, with also the implied suggestion of surrender.

'Nay, my friend,' smiled William. 'There is still hope of victory if we can but slay Harold.'

'He fights bravely, and to the fore of his troops,' said fitzOsbern, heartened again by his Lord's reminder of the main strategy.

'Yes … he does not lack for courage, as we saw in Brittany.'

'He lacks only the honour to respect his oath,' said fitzOsbern.

'As you have always done,' smiled William, 'but come … we can talk of rewards at the end of the day when Harold is slain and his army scattered. Let us attack the centre again … and have the archers fire over the main press to dismay those of lesser courage at the rear of Harold's position.'

∞ ∞ ∞

'What the fuck happened to you?' demanded Elric as I slumped to the ground, back on the hillock we occupied on Harold's right.

He examined my head wound with rough fingers and called for a binding.

'What happened?' he asked again, the concern in his voice disturbing.

'Gorik,' I muttered, ' … but he is dead.'

Elric swore softly and wrapped my head in linen. Then he bade me drink some water and produced a short strip of salted pork which he thrust into my hand.

'I was saving that for later,' he said, 'but clearly you need it now.'

'I'm not hungry,' I complained, struggling to my feet, but he pushed me down again.

'Sit … or lie down if you will. The Normans have retreated again so there is no need for your leadership right now.'

I allowed myself to be ordered by Elric and took a bite of the pork – discovering myself to be hungrier than I'd realised.

'Here they come,' cried a voice, and I felt the discipline of the men as they snapped from casual observers to tightly formed ranks of archers. I wanted to be one of them and pushed myself to my feet – swaying slightly as the Norman cavalry, followed by lines of infantry, once again charged up Senlac.

∞ ∞ ∞

'Here they come, Lord,' shouted Aethelnoth and laid a hand on Harold's shoulder, in gentle restraint.

'William himself comes this time,' remarked Harold, acknowledging the large papal banner – red cross on a white field – at the centre of the cavalry charge.

As with all previous sorties, this new charge came almost to a halt by the time it reached the top of the steep Senlac slope and navigated the defensive obstacles, but the might and prowess of the Norman knights – fighting from the vantage of giant horses bred for war – made them still a formidable force. The shield wall, bristling with long spears set against the chests of the horses, was desperately pressed and the shouts and screams of raging men and terrified horses was like a song of Satan.

Harold himself was in the thick of the fighting but such was his prowess, and that of the stallers and housecarls about him, that he was still unscathed and a wall of Norman bodies rose before and below him.

But axemen fell. Those who wielded the two-handed axe were like towers of assault that none could come near and Harold knew they would become targets. Sure enough the Norman archers and crossbowmen hunted them and poured shafts and darts at them until, one by one, they were taken out of the fight.

Harold glanced over to the hillock where his own archers were stationed and noted with satisfaction that they had seen the danger and were pouring off the hill to attack the Norman archers.

∞ ∞ ∞

'Walt … Orald,' shouted Elric. 'Take your men and kill their archers!

Stay together and keep moving!'

I felt firmer on my feet after eating and drinking, and nodded in appreciation of Elric's orders.

'Harold's prowess will be his undoing,' I said, pointing at the pile of bodies at the centre of the battle – over a hundred yards away. 'He opens a field of fire for their archers. He must not stay at the front.'

'Go and tell him,' laughed Elric.

The battle was still going well despite the fact that the flow of soldiers from Caldbec had all but stopped. Our army was still as large or larger than it had been at the start while William's had already shrunk by many hundreds. Gyrth's men, closest to us, had seen little of the action, being most protected by our archery, but I noticed he was sending men behind the shield wall to reinforce Leofwine who was facing the brunt of the attack.

'We make no difference now,' I said to Elric. 'Take the rest of the archers around to support Leofwine. We will leave our hill.'

'And what will you do?' demanded Elric.

I pulled the silver-hilted dragon blade from its secret sheath and grinned.

'I go to hunt my uncle.'

∞ ∞ ∞

The sun reached noon and continued into the west. The wind driving the smoke from Myrrthn and Valla's fire continued east but it was dropping, and by mid-afternoon there was no wind at all. The world was curiously quiet with not a note of birdsong or chirrup of insect.

'Is the spell ended?' asked Valla. 'Could the battle be over?'

Myrrthn didn't respond – just kept singing in his low voice, eyes closed as though concentrating on a scene inside his head, while Valla stood and stared to the east where the fate of Inglalond was being determined.

'What is happening?' she wondered aloud, and was suddenly consumed with the need to be with Brand.

Without another word, she picked up the long green dress she had dropped onto the ground when she'd arrived at dawn.

'Goodbye Myrrthn.'

'Goodbye,' he muttered without opening his eyes. And as though she answered some dreadful summons, Valla ran into the forest, knowing – somehow – that reaching Brand was a matter of urgency.

Chapter 42

The Fighting Man

In the great seething press of men behind the king, Malgard felt terribly alone.

Gorik had not returned, but he had seen Brand emerge from the woods – covered in blood and staggering. Clearly he had been in a fight and had emerged victorious, if somewhat worse for wear, and Malgard doubted not that Gorik was slain.

In its own way, that was welcome news – Gorik's knowledge of Malgard's activities was something that would have become inconvenient so, once Malgard was fully established under whichever king prevailed, Gorik would have met with an accident. Apparently, that was no longer necessary, but Malgard felt vulnerable without his slayer and was forced to review his plans.

He was realistic enough to appreciate that he could never beat Brand in an even fight, so had to make it uneven. The man next to him moaned and Malgard was splashed with blood. He turned to see the man slumping to the ground clutching an arrow in his throat and instinctively ducked. One or two others around him were also struck by arrows and several more ran for the trees before being turned back by the snarling marshals whose job was to order the fyrd.

Then there was a cheer as the archers under Brand left their hill and went after the Normans who had started shooting over the heads of the shield wall to dismay those of lesser experience behind. A good tactic, acknowledged Malgard, his eyes never leaving Brand.

His archers gone, Brand was alone and walking towards the back of the shield wall – directly towards Malgard, who pushed deeper into the press to avoid him.

∞ ∞ ∞

William's archers, assailed from the sides by Saxon archers, were forced to retreat and gradually the Saxon shield wall began to assert its superiority. Many were falling and William knew that if nothing changed the battle was surely lost.

He pulled back from the fighting and shouted at his brother Odo, Eustace and fitzOsbern.

'Take your cavalry to the bottom of the hill and then sound the retreat.'

fitzOsbern and Eustace stared.

'You mean to argue terms, Lord?' asked Eustace.

'I mean nothing of the sort,' replied William. 'We have seen how the Saxons respond to a retreat … perhaps they will do it again.'

'They couldn't possibly be so stupid,' said fitzOsbern, but Odo laughed.

'Yes they could … especially if they think William is slain.'

William grinned at his brother and pulled his visor down.

'Spread the word. Let the army know I am dead, just before we sound the retreat. The Saxons may find the resulting panic irresistible.'

With that he turned his horse and rode away followed by dozens and then scores of horsemen as fitzOsbern and Eustace rode behind the army on the Norman left wing, shouting that William had fallen. There were shocked looks on the faces of the men who had believed William invincible and looked to him for their reward. With William fallen, victory was impossible and the only reward likely was death.

At that moment the general retreat sounded from the bottom of the hill and several thousand men immediately broke on the Norman left – bolting down the hill to safety, many shouting that William was dead.

∞ ∞ ∞

'Did you hear that?' said Eadnoth to Harold as they watched half of William's army break and fly down Senlac Hill. 'William is dead!'

Harold frowned.

'I have not seen him in the fighting … how could he have fallen?'

'The archers perhaps?' guessed Eadnoth. 'But look at them fly! Victory is yours Lord!'

Despite his cautious instinct, Harold could not suppress the exultation that filled his soul, and clasped Eadnoth close – pounding him on the back with relief and joy.

Soon everyone was shouting that William was slain and the celebrations on top of the ridge began. Men embraced and shouted joyous insults at the flying Normans.

'The Bastard is dead!' was shouted again and again. Then someone yelled, 'Kill all the other bastards! Kill the scum!'

There was no order to advance, but first a trickle, then a torrent of men on the right wing of the Saxon army went chasing after the Normans, Gyrth and his housecarls among them.

'No!' shouted Harold in the midst of his celebrations. 'Not yet!'

He seized a horn from Eadnoth and blew himself the retreat, but none seemed to hear it in the ecstasy of victory.

'Get them back!' cried Harold to his stallers. 'Have they learned nothing?'

∞ ∞ ∞

William stood in his stirrups, his visor raised, as Odo blew blast after blast on his horn.

'Why do you flee?' shouted Count Eustace, pointing at William. 'Your Duke yet lives!'

The army were amazed to see William still alive and desperation turned to relief.

'Why do you flee?' repeated William in a voice like doom and thunder. 'There is nowhere to run. We cannot return over the sea so we must fight to the end. And look! The Saxons are once again in disarray. Watch as our cavalry destroy them!'

The result was even better than the first time. Once again the Norman cavalry turned from retreat to attack and encircled the hundreds – the thousands who had thought the Normans routed and finished. And once again they became the hunted as the far more mobile horseman circled back up the hill and cut them off from retreat – caught in a gully between the cavalry above and the vast army of foot soldiers below.

'At last we make an impression Lord,' laughed fitzOsbern. 'Harold's army is now almost even with yours.'

'Yes,' agreed William. 'They have now only the advantages of higher ground, home soil and better supplies.'

'We have God on our side,' growled Odo, watching the last of the slaughter in the gully. 'He makes his presence felt through the decimation of Harold's army. Your victory is at hand, brother.'

'Perhaps,' said William, 'but there is much yet to accomplish up that hill. If we are to do God's work, let us finish it today.'

∞ ∞ ∞

King Harold watched stricken as the Norman trap was sprung.

'But why do they continue to fight?' wondered Eadnoth. 'With William dead, their cause is lost.'

'William is not dead,' sighed Harold, thrusting down the feeling that God had made His choice. 'Sound again the recall for those that can yet be saved … and let all know that no-one is to leave the shield wall without my express order.'

'We still outnumber them Lord,' said Aethelnoth. 'We still have the higher ground. All we need to do is hold them until nightfall. Hereward and others are leading hosts to this place and by the morn your army will double or treble. The battle will be over.'

Harold glanced down at his shield and was surprised to see it stuck with three arrows. He hadn't noticed any of them striking. Eadnoth and Aethelnoth followed his eye and Eadnoth said, 'Lord, I beg you to stay away from the front rank of the fighting.'

But Harold laughed and said, 'God has spared me thus far when I might have made an easy target … but where is Brand? Has he seen off their archers?'

'Lord!'

Harold turned to where Skalpi stood, his arms covered in blood but his eyes full of tears.

'Skalpi,' said Harold, his throat tightening with fear. 'You have news?'

'Grim news Lord … your brother Gyrth.'

Harold hung his head as Eadnoth groaned.

'Say no more, for now,' sighed Harold, his own eyes brimming.

'The Normans are coming again so let us avenge the fallen ere their spirits leave the field.'

∞ ∞ ∞

I had seen the rout. Hundreds of men corralled and murdered by the Norman cavalry, and as I looked now along the ridge top there were gaps in Harold's army, with no more trickling down from Caldbec.

We were still a formidable host but William's successes were a drain on morale. It was clear that Harold – presuming he still lived – must fight a defensive action until further reinforcements arrived.

But none of that mattered for the moment.

Gorik had said Malgard was present so I went hunting him, my heart filling with wrath and vengeance for all the hurt he had done my family. And me. If it were possible I would prefer to capture him – to have him accused and tried before the king so all might hear of his evil crimes and bear witness to the king's justice. But on a battlefield I was unlikely to effect an arrest. Death was his inevitable reward so, as long as I got to look him in the eye before killing him, I would be satisfied.

But what did he look like these days?

It was six years since I'd seen him in that dark, stinking cellar by the Temes and I barely remembered him. Tall and slim he'd been, when I was a lad, but I was taller than most men now so, in all likelihood, I'd be looking down at him.

I remembered he had a white scar running under his beard, which he wore neatly trimmed. And his hair was black. But his beard and hair may have greyed and grown. How then would I know him?

His eyes would give him away – and my father's ring if he still wore it.

I remembered his eyes, even though it had been dark in that cellar. Cold, grey eyes revelling in the evil he intended to me and Valla. I would never forget those, and felt another moment of triumph as I remembered the look on Gorik's face as he realised I had slain him in the very instant he thought to take my head off.

Mind you, he had very nearly succeeded. I was still having moments of swoon and weakness as I staggered about the ridge top, leaning on my sword and feeling weighed down by my shirt of rings and *Pighammer*, still strapped to my back.

Every now and then I caught a glimpse of Elric and my archers as they moved about the battlefield in their troops – already an excellent fighting unit, making the approach more difficult for the Normans and helping to shepherd them towards the ditches and obstacles in front of our army – but those ditches were already filled with the fallen and horses could ride straight over if they wished. Even as I watched they did exactly that – showing no respect for their own dead in their wild eagerness to reach the king.

William must kill Harold, I realised. His entire strategy must be about killing Harold. Nothing else will work for him.

In that moment I perceived that the battle, which I'd thought all but won, truly rested on the knife's edge of Harold remaining alive and I found myself running for *The Red Dragon* and *The Fighting Man* – the banners that showed where the king fought tooth and nail for his kingdom.

∞ ∞ ∞

Once again Harold felt that he was God's choice. Every warrior who stood before him was swiftly hewn down and he was obliged to keep moving to the right to evade the mountains of bodies that hindered further killing. His limbs felt light and the joy of battle had never run so hotly in his blood. Both his brothers had fallen but that was a sorrow for later – for now, he would thrust and hack and swing until the land was purged of the Norman menace and the battle of this day went down in history as the greatest victory by a Saxon king, with William forgotten – excepting only that a victor must have a vanquished. William the Bastard would forever be known as the man who led so many thousands to their needless deaths on the shore of Inglalond. And Harold would go on to become the greatest of kings – rivalling Alfred, and even Arthur in justice, wisdom and kindness to his people. Even as he fought his mind was filled with visions of the court and kingdom he would produce – fair and flourishing – and every Norman soldier that stood in his way was a threat to that Elyseum, that paradise.

'Lord!'

To Harold's dismay, his sword broke as he smashed it into the helm of yet another Norman warrior, but Earl Brand was at his side and shouting.

'Lord … I beg you! Pull back! Let others take up the fight.'

Harold reached for Brand and pulled him closer, to shout a response over the ringing of swords and the screams of men and horses.

'Nay Brand. I have made a pact with God, and he will only keep His bargain while I stay in the front line.'

With that he seized the Earl Brand's mighty battle axe from his back, grinned and said, 'Take my standard Brand and fight with me!'

∞ ∞ ∞

What choice did I have?

I took *The Fighting Man* from the hand of a white-faced housecarl who had been badly hurt and needed to retire from the field. I nodded him towards the copse and he staggered away, while I turned back to the fighting. Harold was already swinging *Pighammer* through swirling figure eights and forcing back even horsemen from the fray. I leapt to Harold's side, where Eadnoth and Aethelnoth yet fought. Skalpi also was with us and it seemed none could withstand us. Every now and then I heard men shout that William was at hand but, if he was, he stayed out of the front line.

Then Aethelnoth fell. A man who had been my friend since the Welsh campaign and a fell handed warrior, he slipped on the blood-drenched ground and was pinned by a spear. I hacked at the spear and Harold swept the man who held it from his horse, but Aethelnoth was screaming until a sudden surge of Norman cavalry rode over him. We pushed them back with a furious surge of our own – Harold shouting for Aethelnoth to hold on – but the heavy war horses had finished him. For the next few minutes we took our revenge – clearing the ground before us as none could face our rage and skill.

Then the cowering Norman infantry seemed to part like the fabled Red Sea of Moses and a fresh troop of riders poured through.

'William!' someone shouted. 'William is at hand!'

A shower of arrows fell all about us, as though shot in a high arc from deep behind the shield wall, but I cared not for arrows. I raised *The Fighting Man* and waved it in the setting sun – defying William to come close enough to taste the wrath of Harold and his stallers.

Then Eadnoth fell with an arrow in his heart and it seemed that all went quiet on the field. William and three others rode towards us as time itself seemed to slow – as it always did in battle. I could make out every detail on William's horse as it charged ponderously towards us – eyes red and rolling under an armoured head dress – mud shining on its hooves – caparison clinging wetly to its sides. I set the pike-headed standard before the king to deflect William's charge but Harold fell against me, and as I turned his body staggered forward.

'No!' shouted Skalpi from behind, but I failed to comprehend his grief.

William was still charging directly at Harold who was now down on his knees, *Pighammer*'s head resting in the mud. In desperation I threw myself at William's horse to protect the king.

∞ ∞ ∞

Malgard could scarce believe the turn of the battle.

Harold outnumbered William and had the stronger position, but the Normans fought like they knew there was no tomorrow and their fury made the difference. They still died – two for every Saxon – but the numbers about Harold were whittled away and Harold was exposed to archers and cavalry when he should have been directing a defensive operation from a position of safety.

Of course, Malgard's detestable nephew was with the king – fighting at his right hand and even holding one of his standards. How like Holgar he had become – a large warrior of great prowess – flicking away Norman infantry with contemptuous ease while protecting the king's flank.

Malgard knew that his only chance now lay in a Norman victory. If the Saxons won, Brand was too close to the king for murder.

Then everything changed. Harold slumped forward and great shouts of dismay sounded from those about him. Fyrdmen rushing back obscured Malgard's vision but when he could see again, four

Norman knights were off their horses and hacking at a body while all around them Harold's housecarls lay on the ground.

An unbelievable panic seized the Saxon host, despite their still overwhelming numbers. Men were shouting, screaming, flying from the field in their hundreds as more Norman knights came forward to surround the spot where Harold had fallen.

Malgard's moment had arrived. He flung off the peasant's cloak he had worn in the fyrd to reveal his knightly armour and strode down into the group about William. On the ground he saw the body of King Harold rent apart and, to Malgard's great joy, Brand also lay face down in the mud, bloodied and unmoving.

'Pursue them!' shouted William to the knights around him. 'Harold is dead but there are still too many for our army. We must kill them while they are in disarray and rout.'

Most of the knights rode off at once and William turned to Malgard, who knelt before him.

'So Malgard,' said William, 'you have survived the battle. What have you done on my behalf?'

'I did not slay Harold, Lord,' said Malgard, 'although, as you see, I managed to get close enough and might have slain him given the chance.'

'How do I know you weren't fighting at his side?' demanded William, who had decided he didn't much like Malgard – although there were many in his service he didn't like, so that did not count against him. 'Show me your sword.'

Malgard drew his sword and offered it hilt-first to William, who did not touch it.

'Unblooded,' he said, ' … so at the least, you have not been killing my soldiers.'

'I swore to support your claim Lord,' said Malgard, full of pride, 'and played the part in the battle you bade me.'

'I suppose that is true,' said William, exulting as his infantry streamed northwards after the knights pursuing the last of Harold's army. 'We shall discuss your reward later. For now I ask that you stay and guard the place where Harold fell. My place is with my men.'

William climbed back onto his war horse, leaving Malgard in charge of the dead. He turned back to examine the fallen. Harold's body was barely recognisable, hacked apart with several mortal wounds and crushed under the hooves of horses. Others of his household were also clearly finished but Brand was still in one piece, though covered with blood.

It has been a glorious day, thought Malgard. All his dreams had come true and he would be the unquestioned ruler of a large part of Ingalond. He would claim not just Stybbor but all of East Anglia and had no doubt that William would confirm him as Earl. He peered more closely at Brand to see whether he was still breathing and decided to take no chances.

Malgard touched his sword against Brand's throat, the point drawing a trickle of blood that suggested his nephew lived. Only just though, judging by his inert body and half-closed eyes that moved not a flicker. Malgard could easily have driven the point through windpipe and veins but the occasion deserved a more dramatic flourish.

'Six years,' he mused aloud, as the rest of William's army streamed past him. 'Six years I have hated and hunted you ... needing you to join your father and brother so I might enjoy Stybbor in peace.

'But you would not die,' he sneered. 'Oh no ... despite all the dangers and perils your Lord Harold could devise. Instead of dying you prospered and grew mighty in his service, jeopardising the position I risked so much to gain.'

Malgard felt the wild laughter rising but thrust it down to retain his dignity at this most solemn of moments.

'You would not die,' he repeated, calm again. 'And for that I should be grateful for it means that I, Malgard, Rathgar's son, get to achieve the task that was beyond so many others ... the slaying of Earl Brand Holgarsson. It would sit well among my deeds in my latter days but I suppose I must remain discreet. There are some who would not perceive the honour ... the magnificence of my actions.'

He looked about the field but he was all alone. No man as much as glanced in his direction, so he raised again his sword, eyeing the blood on Brand's throat as his target.

'Give my greetings to Holgar and Gram,' he sneered and swung the sword down.

∞ ∞ ∞

It was like a dream.

I heard Malgard talking with William, calmly discussing the darkest treachery against my Lord and king.

Then William left and I heard my uncle's confession and hatred – wanting desperately to rise up and slay him for his hideous crimes – but my limbs were like lead and I found I truly didn't care whether I lived or died. I even felt a moment's joy as he bade me give greetings to my father and brother, but then the dream changed.

A heavenly scent of bluebells seemed to rouse me from my stupor, and I opened my eyes to see Malgard's snarling face – just for an instant – before my world turned red and I felt hot blood. At first I assumed it was my own, but then pain seared through my head and at last I could move. Blinking in the fading light I tried to sit up and found Malgard lying across me, staring at the sky with his left eye only. From his right eye protruded an arrow.

I rolled him away and glimpsed Valla standing at the edge of the copse, holding her bow.

Malgard was still moving and the dream changed again. I found the dagger – the silver hilted dragon blade – in my hand and saw a rent in his hauberk directly above his heart. It was as though the hands of my father and brother guided my own hand, giving me strength, and I know my uncle still lived when I plunged the dagger into his chest. His back arched for just a moment and then he slumped – banished into the blackest of hells, and even that was better than he deserved.

Then I saw Harold's body, hewn and trampled, and felt like a dagger of ice had cloven my own heart. A cry of terrible grief sounded from somewhere – perhaps from me – as I dragged myself from Malgard and crawled to Harold, cradling his beloved head despite it being so damaged by the swords and spears of the enemy.

That's how Elric and Skalpi found me, rocking back and forth in the deepest despair, my eyes filled with tears for Inglalond's tragedy.

'Save your grief for later,' said Elric with a hand on my head. 'We have urgent work to do.'

There were still lagging members of William's army pushing past us but none seemed to take any notice as Elric found a flask and washed my face, and forced me to drink.

'Where is Valla?' I asked, wondering why the Norman warriors who ran past us seemed to take no interest – as though we were ghosts. 'She was here a moment ago.'

'I haven't seen her,' said Elric, 'but if we are to fight again we need to get you off this field before William returns.'

He and Skalpi dragged me to my feet where I could see the completeness of Harold's defeat. So many of his friends and household lay dead around him – the flower of Inglalond's nobility trampled in the bloody field of Senlac Ridge. Tears filled my eyes again and I cried unashamed.

'Never a nobler man drew breath on these shores,' I said. 'Inglalond's loss will be keenly felt until the end of time.'

'But before then,' said Elric, 'we must take Harold's body before William puts his head on a spike to go before his conquerors into Lundene.'

Elric dragged *The Fighting Man* from the mud and pulled Harold's ruined corpse onto it.

'I may only have been thegn for a day,' he said, 'but that is enough to know I must not leave my king for William's sport. Help me Skalpi.'

'They will know the body is missing and come hunting it,' said Skalpi.

'No they won't,' said Elric.

As he spoke he peeled off his own Norman hauberk, identical to Harold's, then tore away the hauberk from Malgard's corpse. We guessed his purpose and helped him dress Malgard in Elric's hauberk. Then Skalpi smashed Malgard's face with the staff of *The Fighting Man* until it could no longer be recognised, while Elric hacked his leg off with *Pighammer* and drove his sword into the body until it was impossible to tell him from Harold.

'Just to be certain,' I said, undoing the clasp at the back of my neck to remove the small figure in bronze and silver in the same shape as *The Fighting Man* device on Harold's standard – wound about also with the faded bluebell.

'It is the most precious thing I own,' I said. ' … but more precious still is the thought of Harold's body in a hallow of our choosing rather than mocked by the Normans.'

I removed the bluebell and arrayed *The Fighting Man* token around the neck of my hated uncle.

'He stole the place of my father and brother. Let him now take the place of Harold in this Norman victory.'

In that moment I remembered my father's ring and exclaimed in triumph as I saw it on Malgard's hand.

'This I reclaim!' I said, twisting it from his finger and exulting in its return. 'The dagger he can keep.'

With that we left the field, Elric and Skalpi carrying Harold's body rolled in his standard as the last of the light faded beyond the western hills.

'Where is Valla?' I asked again, a shadow growing in my heart as I remembered the last words she had spoken the night before: 'It was the most important part of the spell ... the purity of your promise and the faith with which you kept it. I am so full of love and pride for you, and that love was the final ingredient of our great spell. It is why Harold will have the victory tomorrow.'

'You will find her again,' said Elric, struggling with his burden. 'I am sure of it.'

'As you found your own Valla?' I demanded, my eyes filling with tears again.

'Do not torture yourself,' said Skalpi. 'If you are meant to find her, then you will. Until then ... Harold may have fallen but he still has sons, and I regard them now as the rightful heirs of Inglalond. We have work to do.'

They were surprisingly comforting words and, rediscovering my resolve, I took up a corner of *The Fighting Man* and helped bear Harold from the field.

Epilogue

Three nights later, in consecrated ground adjoining Waltham Abbey, we laid Harold to rest – shrouded in his standard of *The Fighting Man* – in a place the Abbot swore would be quickly concealed by new building works.

'If Harold's line is restored,' said Abbot Osgod, 'the works can be removed and a more fitting tomb established. Until then, his resting place must remain secret.'

Our ruse concerning Harold's body had worked perfectly. William, apparently, had not recalled an arrow in Harold's eye so had sent for the Lady Swanneshals. That Lady, pre-warned by Elric, had examined Malgard's battered corpse and confirmed it as Harold's.

'He was also confused by a dagger in Harold's heart, but under his hauberk,' smiled Swanneshals through her tears. 'That was well done, and I can never thank you three enough for delivering Harold to a sacred place. Malgard's head now sits on a spike outside William's pavilion and William himself wears Brand's token.'

I regretted the loss of *The Fighting Man* badge. The return of my father's ring was inadequate compensation – not least as the thegnship it signified was entirely lost, unless William might be defeated in the weeks and months ahead. But nothing could compensate for the loss of Valla, who I had not seen since that one glimpse on regaining my senses at the end of the battle.

The sad chanting of the monks faded and they all filed away with their torches until only Elric, Skalpi, Carl and I remained in purple twilight with the Lady Swanneshals.

'What will you do?' I asked her.

'I will look after my sons,' she replied, 'and prepare them for kingship. Perhaps you might help me Earl Brand? And you also,' she said, turning to Elric and Skalpi. Carl also had survived the battle and accompanied us by secret ways to Waltham Abbey.

We all nodded our assent and I felt the resolve harden within me.

'William is already terrorising the land,' said Swanneshals, '... raping, burning and killing as he goes. We still massively outnumber him but no-one can rally against him. My sons, Godwin and Edmund, must become the rallying point so we can organise to retake the kingdom. It is what Harold would expect of us.'

Skalpi went down on one knee, and said, 'My Lady Swanneshals ... I will swear fealty to your sons and hold them as my rightful liege lords until one of them takes the kingship again. Anything I can do ... even laying down my life ... I will do in honour of you and the memory of my Lord Harold.'

Immediately, Elric and I followed his example and I kissed her hand, my whole being flooding with purpose once again after the disaster of our defeat.

'I thank you all,' said Swanneshals, 'but for now I ask you Carl, Elric and Skalpi to leave me alone with the Earl Brand. There is a matter of the heart to discuss.'

Elric and Skalpi rose and departed with Carl, murmuring words of respect to Harold and to the Lady Swanneshals. She just gazed at me a while, then took my hand and raised me to my feet.

'Do you remember the night we met ... in Theodford?'

'Yes, my Lady.'

'That was the night I met Valla, and she explained to me the reality of your marital arrangement.'

I nodded, remembering.

'What you didn't know at the time was that she loved you from the moment she met you, but was frightened by her love and kept up her antagonism to protect her maidenhood.'

'I know all that. She has since explained it.'

'Perhaps ... but I suspect you have never fully understood Valla's purpose. The mortal struggles of men are but a shadow of the true struggle ... the battle of the gods for mastery of these isles. That is more important to Valla than her own happiness, and with William's victory she must go on fighting. You let her down, didn't you?'

'Yes,' I nodded numbly, 'but ... '

'I do not want to know the details,' said Swanneshals. 'I am sure the transgression was marginal ... and yet it was enough. She has returned to the Place of Dreams.'

'How do you know all this?' I asked her. 'Have you spoken with Valla since the battle?'

'No ... well, not face to face as we are speaking now. But I know her heart, and ... I also know something of her great task.'

I looked up at her – wise and majestic – keeper of many secrets, and understanding dawned.

'Yes Brand' she said, seeming to perceive my very thought. 'I too have borne the power in my time but it has passed. Others must take up the struggle, but I have some hope for you.'

'That Valla will return?'

The Lady Swanneshals glanced up at the stars and considered.

'All I will say is that she loves you very deeply ... and a time will come when she can no longer conceive. This happens to all women so I believe she may seek you out before it is too late to pass on the power ... but she is still young and that time may be years away. Before then you must atone for your error. Help Valla in her great task by fighting William and lie with no other woman as she bade you. If you do that, then I deem you may have another chance with her.'

Hot tears coursed down my cheeks and I blinked up at the stars – blurring wetly silver and black.

'Whatever it takes, I will do it,' I said, touching the faded bluebell wound into a new thong around my neck – riven with grief for the loss both of Harold and Valla in the same hour.

'In the meantime,' said Swanneshals, 'we must continue telling Harold's story ere the Normans lessen his fame.'

I glanced down into the freshly dug grave, where the greatest of all kings of Inglalond lay in a box of stone, shrouded in his banner.

'If that story is to survive,' I said, 'we'll have to be careful what we say ... and how we say it.'

'It would be best to praise William,' said Swanneshals. 'And in so doing, praise Harold also ... for were they not worthy adversaries? The more we praise Harold, the greater thereby was William's victory.'

'You are wise Lady Swanneshals,' I said, 'but however great was the glory ... memories fade and men pass on.'

'A more permanent record of Harold's deeds must be devised,' said Swanneshals. 'Let us think on it.'

Historical Note

The Fighting Man was first conceived when I was looking at pictures of *The Bayeux Tapestry* and saw a man in a green tunic walking down stairs with Harold Godwinson prior to getting into ships for Harold's mysterious trip to Normandy in 1064. (Scene IV)

'Who are you?' I wondered of the green man – clearly one of Harold's closest friends – and before I knew it I was inventing (or reinventing) his story for him, winding a fictional tale among the known historical facts.

The thing is, so much is unknown of that period. Very few records remain and they were mostly written by the victors – people wanting to prove the justness of William's claim to the crown. There are no sources at all written by Saxons taking Harold's part and explaining his motives. Even the *Tapestry* is a mystery. No-one knows who commissioned it and the story it tells is itself full of holes. This may be a problem for an historian, but for an historical novelist it is perfect. I was able to fill the many holes with my own interpretations including the fiction.

For example, Turold (Scene X) is one of the few named characters in the *Tapestry* – clearly he was well known at the time, but no written record remains of him or his deeds. A further mystery is Scene XV where a woman is being slapped by a churchman. No-one knows who either of the characters are or why the woman is being slapped, but there is a tantalising possibility in the border below where a naked man with a large phallus is portrayed. I had fun putting these together in my tale and who can say that my guess is wrong?

For the rest of it, I have used the history as more-or-less agreed between the few bits of the Anglo-Saxon Chronicle, Orderic Vitalis, William of Poitiers and The Chronicle of Florence of Worcester that I've flicked through. *The Bayeux Tapestry* by Lucien Musset was useful and Peter Rex's books *The Last English King* and *1066* were also very valuable.

What was less useful was some of my own on-the-ground research. I wanted to visit some of the physical locations in the story and most of these were very informative – Battle Abbey at Hastings, where I walked the battlefield, was excellent. Stamford Bridge was disappointing (in that no-one knows the exact location of the battle) but still gave me important information regarding the river. Seeing *The Bayeux Tapestry* in the flesh is something I highly recommend but I also wanted to see the castle where William the Conqueror (nee Bastard) had grown up in Falaise.

It's a long way from Avoca Beach, Australia, to Falaise in Normandy and so it was with some excitement that I walked up the ramp to enter the ruins of Falaise Castle, preparing to immerse myself in the shreds of William's ambience that might subtly inform my story. As I entered, my wife (Karen) drew my attention to a sign: Falaise Castle, built 1147.

Blast!

Readers will note that the end of *The Fighting Man* leaves open the prospect of a sequel. It is well known that William the Bastard became William the Conqueror and ruled England for 21 years. It is probably less well known that his coronation was not universally accepted and that the Saxon majority continued the fight on behalf of the aetheling and Harold's sons for many years – Brand, Elric and Skalpi among them. Their continuing story will be told.

If you enjoyed *The Fighting Man* please take a moment
to give the book a rating on www.goodreads.com

Also by Adrian Deans

Mr Cleansheets

Eric Judd is 39 and his girlfriend wants him to give up playing football. Eric (aka Mr Cleansheets) is a goalkeeping legend at his amateur Sydney club because in his youth he received a letter inviting him to trial with Manchester United. The letter said to 'come when you're ready' — and six days before his 40th birthday, Eric is finally ready.

Inspired by the dying wish of his Uncle Jimmy, Eric travels to England, but does not quite receive the welcome he had hoped for. Instead, he encounters all manner of villains: murderous football hooligans, Irish mafia, dodgy agents, beautiful pop stars, international terrorists and a range of supporting players with any number of overt and hidden agendas.

But he does get to play football.

The ultimate holiday read – a non-stop rollicking yarn that keeps the pages turning, and if you're anything like me, you'll be starting to panic as the pages disappear in your right hand.
Lawrie McKinna, Central Coast Mariners

If you put Lock, Stock & Two Smoking Barrels, the News of the World and Four Four Two into a blender, the result might well be Mr Cleansheets.
Simon Hill, Fox Sports

Adrian Deans is at his best when writing about football.
Dan Silkstone, The Age

www.adriandeans.com

Also by Adrian Deans

Straight Jacket

Morgen Tanjenz is a lawyer with an overactive sense of justice. His mission in life is to reward the virtuous, punish the ignorant and avenge those who won't avenge themselves. He dispenses justice via his favourite pastime ('life sculpture'), in which he takes an anonymous interest in strangers – pulling strings in the background to change their lives as he thinks they deserve.

But Morgen isn't the only one changing lives in the city. There is a serial killer on the prowl who taunts police in letters to the local rag but, as the body count rises, Detective Sergeant Blacksnake Fowler can hardly focus on the job with so many distractions. His boss hates him, his deputy is trying to undermine him, and the woman he loves is having an affair.

Deans has expertly crafted the novel so that Tanjenz's life sculptures seamlessly segue into the crime mystery, contributing high-stake clues to the watertight plot. Straight Jacket is not only a well-thought-out and exciting crime thriller, but also hilarious entertainment.
Newtown Review of Books

Deans has a great feel for the relaxed narcissism that oozes from Sydney's professional classes, and the middleclass banality of Sydney's northern suburbs provides a surprisingly good setting for a book about psychopaths and serial killers.
Law Society Journal

The first person narrator is unconventional, hard to sympathise with, and generally unlikeable for most of the book. However, there is something about Deans' writing that makes you want to read more. The novel doesn't let up, going deeper and deeper into the psyche of the narrator, and into the origins of his warped sense of justice.
Crime Fiction Lover

www.adriandeans.com

Also by Adrian Deans

THEM

Rob Lasseter is the great grandson of a legendary explorer. His prized possession is an old parchment, which is thought to be a map showing the location of the fabulous reef of gold. Unfortunately, there are no points of external reference on the map. The only words are 'You are here', next to an X, but Lasseter doesn't know where X is – he doesn't know where to start looking.

Inspired by the strange disappearance of the White Haired girl, and the receipt of a letter addressed in his own handwriting from a place he had never been, Lasseter (with his friend Miles, who claims to be dead) embarks upon an odyssey into the centre of Australia and has some very strange adventures. Lasseter thinks he is looking for gold, but instead he finds something far more interesting.

The ultimate solipsist journey ... an Australian story of pan-cosmic enormity.

www.reallybluebooks.com

www.adriandeans.com

Also by Adrian Deans

Political Football: Lawrie Mckinna's Dangerous Truth

Growing up in darkest Scotland as the son of the local poacher and then rampaging across Europe with a pack of Rangers hooligans is not the best preparation for high office in Australia.

Father at 18, professional footballer at 20, Lawrie McKinna was living the dream until he uprooted for Australia at 25 to play in the NSL. Then he became a successful coach (NSL, A-League and China) and ultimately was elected to political office as an independent after being courted by both mainstream parties due to his massive popularity. These pages chronicle his journey, telling his dangerous truth with fearless candour, infectious enthusiasm and a wicked sense of humour.

Very readable, but not for the PC at heart.
Andy Harper

I read it in five hours flat and could not put it down.
Roy Hay

Compelling and mesmerising.
Con Stamocostas

An amazing journey.
Ashley Morrison

www.adriandeans.com

www.ingramcontent.com/pod-product-compliance
Lightning Source LLC
Chambersburg PA
CBHW051940020726
47501CB00001B/207